To Griff

with Best Wishes.

Francis Ken Young

The engineer inserted a cigarette between his quivering lips, his right wrist trying to steady the shimmering flame licking the tipped end of his cigarette. Inhaling deeply he keeled over in a spasmodic fit of coughing, the cigarette spat to the deck. He drooped over the coffin momentarily in an effort to catch his breath. His ear touched the copper dome on the lid.

"Oooooo!" repeated the demonic moan from within.

This was too much for the young man. Like one demented he dived from the room and barrelled up the ladder four steps at a time. He reached the working alleyway heaving until his breathing eased. Fear seemed to be playing havoc with a certain set of sphincter muscles. "Why did I ever join the navy?" he gasped and ran in search of the senior second engineer.

Also by Francis Kerr Young

Children's Stories
The Paperweight
Wing-Ding!

Poetry
The Legend of the Mary Celeste and Other Poems

Short Stories
Round About Christmas and Other Roundabout Stories

TSTS *Queen of Dalriada*

Engineroom Log

HANG ON A SECOND!

FRANCIS KERR YOUNG

HANG ON A SECOND!
was originally published in paperback
by www.lulu.com in 2006

ISBN: 1-4116-5726-8

HANG ON A SECOND! Hard Cover

ISBN: 978-0-9813447-2-0

Jacket design by author
Port Maneuvering Wheels
in After Engineroom of
RMS *Queen Mary*
March 1962

Pict Line Badge on jacket by:
S.M. Bass & Co Manchester Ltd
Manchester, England

Contents

This book is dedicated to
the Engineer and Electrical Officers
of RMS *Queen Mary* with whom
I had the pleasure to serve with
during the years 1962 to 1967

FOREWORD

Nowadays cruising has become the norm. A short ocean voyage can be the ideal way to break up the winter blahs, an economical vacation when one compares prices to yesteryear. Holidaymakers may laze in canvas chairs on sun-drenched decks and ponder the absolute serenity of a calm blue sea. A glance up to the ship's bridge implies security when an officer in sharp tropical whites scans the horizon with binoculars, the liner's speed and direction at his fingertips.

Passengers savour the peace and beauty of sky and sea with never a thought for the heart of the vessel. Below in the engine spaces, encapsulated in a transparent air-conditioned box, a ship's engineer is besieged by computers that control and monitor the pulse of the engines. Changed days from fifty years ago, when shipping companies were beginning to feel the pinch from airlines inveigling their passengers and cargo because crossing the Atlantic by air was faster and cheaper.

As the sizzling sixties played hotfoot to the fabulous fifties, the British Government terminated compulsory National Service. Before that era, many engineering apprentices joined the Mercantile Marine to escape being drafted. A few years later they returned to shore to settle down. During work break these old shellbacks span embellished deep-sea yarns to the current bunch of apprentices, which in turn helped to swell the engineering complements of this great establishment.

Ex-members of Her Majesty's armed forces also told exotic stories of their travels and conquests in foreign lands, but it was the Merchant Marine that captured the majority of would-be globetrotters. It was common knowledge that food was better, wages were higher and discipline was much more relaxed in the Mercantile Navy than in the armed forces. Officer rank was automatic and last but not least, one was allowed to quit at any time (within reason).

Now this new breed of engineer officers were not running away to sea to escape but to find something, mainly themselves, as they quickly matured in their brand new environment. Finding employment was not a problem, for although the sun had set on the British Empire, it still shone on that country's merchant ships sailing on the many seas of our vast globe.

Up to this period in time only the very wealthy could afford to travel on ocean cruises. Shipping companies were slow to adopt the latest business practices of hotel management, cruise directors, modern entertainment and myriad other ploys devised to cater to the whims of the prudent tourist. There were no scanners at sea to pick up television signals because satellites were still looked upon as novelties. Technology was yet to progress enough to enable satellites to haul sumptuous gargantuan liners with their frivolous cargoes around from port to port on microwave towlines.

This book tells of one of those young intrepid engineer officers on his very first ocean voyage. Engineroom descriptions for this novel have been drawn from this author's experience aboard the old RMS *Queen Mary*. The fictitious characters in this novel may be found aboard almost any ocean-going vessel.

Some of the events of 1961 would affect our present. Yuri Gagarin and Alan Sheppard flew into space, the Cold War heated up, the Bay of Pigs debacle, war in Vietnam began and South Africa left the British Commonwealth. Rock 'n' Roll was less than a decade old. Homosexuality was still a criminal offence although society was slowly becoming more tolerant. The United Kingdom still used the old avoirdupois and Imperial measures. Since then, with the exception of the United States of America, the world has adopted the metric system.

Francis Kerr Young

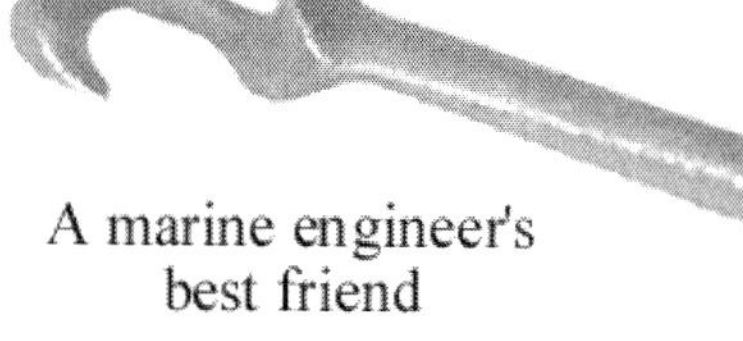

A marine engineer's best friend

Pict Line

The First Step

Monday morning, October 30th, 1961

The waiting room of the doctor's office was empty. A young Scot stood by a window peering out at a hodden-grey sky. His eyes looked down on a typical waterfront scene of Glasgow; warehouses, tenements, limestone, sandstone, and redbrick office buildings, all caked with the same morbid feature: filth. Generations of coal-burning ships and smoky industries had left a legacy of soot and grime on roofs, walls, and windows. Even the building that he was in, the Seamen's Pool, had gradually accumulated its own special brand of residual dirt.

Turning away from the dismal landscape the youth sighed and nervously slid onto a hard wooden chair. He reached forward to extract a tattered *Reader's Digest* from a pile of thumb-worn literature on a nearby table. Lounging back he flipped randomly through the thumb-worn magazine to stop at *Humour in Uniform* and stared blankly at the print to reflect on his interview earlier that morning at the Board of Trade. Happily his credentials were adequate for eligibility for membership to that unique profession: marine engineers.

And why not, after a tough five-year apprenticeship in the steel industry? Hopefully the forthcoming medical would assure him of the coveted Seaman's Card. Was it tedium, bureaucracy, or both that tried his patience? He bolted upright startled by the sudden opening of a door. A nurse peered down at him. "Mister King?" The youth nodded. "Come in please," she pleasantly invited. "Strip to the waist. The doctor will be here in a moment."

He was left alone in the ether-tainted room. Baring his chest he perched on the edge of a hard chair in front of a writing desk and began to show interest in the room's decor. Sterile walls of white held framed certificates, old prints of dreadnoughts, cruisers and other warships with photographs of various crews grouped under the inevitable fifteen-inch guns. Twin glass-door cabinets arrayed surgical tools and instruments. A sandalwood box lined with black velvet contained a brass microscope and lenses.

Leather wallets lay agape displaying gleaming scalpels and lancets of various sizes. Stainless steel implements such as tweezers, pincers, scissors and oddly formed hooks lay in regimental lines along the glass shelves. Hypodermic syringes ranked with needles. They progressed by size and occupied a complete shelf. They ranged from teeny-weeny to *Oh my Goodness*! The Spanish Inquisitor General Tomás de Torquemada would have been enraptured with these exquisite exhibits of pain.

An aged white-coated physician toddled into the room. He had long white hair and a grey moustache. The passing years had bent his body into a permanent stoop. King guessed that he was about seventy years old.

"Good morning! Mister King, is it?"

"Guid mornin' Doctor," reciprocated King.

Wheezing loudly the doctor flopped into the chair behind his desk. He stretched for the bulky briefcase on his desktop and extracted a sheaf of papers. Riffling through the documents he was soon rewarded in his search, and donning a pair of wire-rimmed glasses, the old gentleman confirmed his find. "Aye," he lilted. "This is 'em."

Highlander or Islander the youth speculated.

"Now let's see, King - aye. A sept o' the Clan Colquhoun, are ye?"

"Ah dinnae ken - maybe."

A glower was the response to this inconclusive answer. His attention reverted to the foolscap in his hand. "Okay," he drawled, a grudge creeping into his tone. "We'll just ratify my nurse's information. Your given name is Angus?"

"Aye Doctor."

"You live at 63 Douglas Street, Carluke?"

A nod.

"Red hair -" a quick glance at the youth followed every entry. "Aye. Fair complexion - aye. Grey eyes - aye. No scars. We'll find out about that soon enough. Height - five foot eight."

He peeked over his glasses at him for affirmation.

"Weight?"

"Nine stone eleven."

The physician mentally tabulated to see if it corresponded with his nurse's answer. "That's right, one hundred and thirty-seven pounds. What age are you, laddie?"

"Twenty."

The old man fumbled around his desk until he found an indelible pencil stub. He licked the point and cautiously printed this vital information on the appropriate line.

The age and general health of his patient's family history came next. "Is there any insanity in your family?"

"No."

"Any hereditary diseases?"

"No."

"Have you ever had the measles?"

"No."

"Chicken pox?"

"Aye."

"Smallpox?"

"Scarlet fever?"

"Aye."

"TB?"

"No."

"Heart problems?"

"No."

"Diabetes?"

"No."

"Ok. Moving right along here," said the physician, placing that page aside and moving onto the next sheet. He glanced absently at the document.

"Anthrax?"

"No-o!"

"Myxomatosis?"

"No-o!"

"Foot and mou - Oh! I seem to have my papers mixed up with my son's. He's a veterinarian, y'ken."

"Is that a fact? Ah was beginnin' tae wonder!"

The doctor explored the briefcase again until the apt questionnaire was flushed out. He mused on the theme of the next question momentarily before continuing.

"So laddie, plan to join the Merchant Navy, do you?"

"Aye Doctor."

The old man hunched forward beaming lasciviously and placing both forearms on the desk he brought his face closer to his patient's and asked, "Dae ye like the lassies sonny?"

"Aye Doctor," he grinned.

"Right then - have you ever had VD?"

The youth was shocked and vehemently denied the suggestion. “Christ, no-o!”

“I’ll brook no blasphemy, my lad!” warned the doctor. Sucking on his pencil tip he laboriously printed *Not yet* on the form, ending that phase of the examination.

The old man slowly eased up from the chair and edged his way round the desk. “Breathe in.” The ice-cold diaphragm of his stethoscope planed goose bumps on his chest. “Exhale.”

His commands were repeated with every systematic sounding. “Good,” he said. “Stand up, please.”

He stood up and the old gentleman wearily occupied the now-vacant chair. “Face me and drop your trousers - shorts too.”

Angus complied. The doctor held the exposed scrotum in his right hand and said, “Turn your head and cough.”

Angus coughed.

“Turn around, please.”

The victim executed an about-face.

“Bend over and spread your cheeks.”

He bent over, hooking a forefinger in either side of his mouth. Pulling the corners of his lips apart, his face likened a tragicomedy mask. Seconds later a slap on the rump startled him.

“These cheeks, laddie!” admonished the physician. “I meant these cheeks!”

The snap of a latex glove heralded the rude intrusion of his middle finger up King’s rectum.

“Aah! Ooh! Aaah!”

There was a rap on the door and the nurse poked her head in.

“Doctor, don’t forget that meeting in ten minutes,” she reminded him.

"Eh? Oh, aye - thanks Molly. I'd better get my finger out. Heh, heh, heh!"

A sly chuckle associated the old man's remark with the situation as the irritating digit withdrew. "Now that's what's known as a bum rub, laddie! I've always wanted to shove it to a Colquhoun!"

The disgruntled victim pondered on this comment and wondered why he had been the unfortunate recipient of a rear action assault. There was probably some obscure grudge between the Colquhouns and the doctor's clan. But as far as he knew there were no Colquhouns in the King family. Maybe he should ask his dad when he got back home.

"Pull up your breeks, laddie! You might as well get dressed anyway because I have to leave right away," the old man said. "What shipping company do ye plan to sail with?"

"The Pict Line!" he proudly replied.

"Aye - a fine Scottish firm," agreed the doctor. "They'll give you a thorough physical anyway. They demand a high standard of fitness in their employees. You're A1. You'll likely get your Seaman's Card in the post next week. Good-bye and good luck." With a parting smile the doctor trudged wearily from the room.

Ten days later he received his Seaman's Card and Discharge Book in the mail. This new development was relayed to the Pict Line's personnel office. Some days passed until a letter arrived to inform him that an appointment had been arranged for him at the company's head office in Glasgow for another medical followed by an interview.

On Monday next he punctually showed up in the foyer of the Pict Line Shipping Company's head office. Upon identifying himself he was immediately ushered into the company physician's office. His experience from the previous week bore dire thoughts towards this next encounter.

The doctor did not introduce himself but merely handed the applicant a specimen bottle and directed him to fill it. This task was duly performed in an adjoining toilet. He submitted the flask containing his golden achievement to the doctor. A slip of paper dropped into the effluent was reluctant to change colour. This appeared to be a satisfactory result.

As he washed his hands the physician gestured at a seat across from an eye chart. "Sit over there," he said, drying his hands on a white coarse towel.

"Do you have any breathing problems?"

"No Doctor."

"Good. Start reading off the letters from the chart on that wall."

"E . . ."

"Good! Read out the numbers camouflaged on this card."

"Aye. Six - twenty-three -"

"Very good." The examiner shined a light in his ear. "Do you have trouble with your hearing?"

"Eh?"

"*Do you have trouble with your hearing*?"

"No Doctor."

"Hearing perfect," concluded the doctor, all the while scribbling on a scrap of paper. He handed the chit to him. "Go up to the third floor and show this to the Marine Super when you're called for your interview."

Angus knocked on the superintendent's door.

A deep voice hailed. "Come!"

He timidly entered the room. Seated behind a large paper-strewn mahogany desk was a middle-aged gentleman with a serious expression on his face. He stared blankly at the interloper and snapped, “Yes?”

“Eh, Ah’m King. Angus.”

“King Angus?” repeated the gentleman, humour softening his features. “Oh yes, I see! I’m Bob Fleming, the marine ‘super’. Please sit down.”

He handed over the chit. “Thank you,” said Fleming, tossing it aside unread. “Now, how soon can you start?”

“Weel,” Angus was hesitant, surprised by the sudden offer. ‘Ah’ll need tae give my present employers two weeks notice.”

“Fine,” smiled Fleming. “I expect you’ll want to have a little holiday when you finish working. How does December the eleventh suit you?”

“Eh - ok Ah guess.”

“Splendid! Report to Harry Ford, my assistant, at the Clyde Docks. Here’s the address,” Fleming told him while holding out a slip of paper to Pict Line’s latest employee. “Please be there for oh-nine-hundred. Welcome aboard Mister King!” He rose, shook his hand and escorted him to the door. The young man went home dazed yet excited. He was in the Merchant Navy at last!

Another week passed when a registered letter from the superintendent arrived. It contained a formidable list of articles that had to be acquired before sailing day. The inventory included four sets of uniforms; two peaked caps with company badges, white shirts, black shoes and socks, white shoes and socks, black ties, white coveralls for the engineroom, personal clothing and a few hand tools.

A form had to be completed by his family physician stating that the bearer had been recently vaccinated against smallpox. He had to open a chequing account so that his salary could be transferred into his bank monthly. The manila envelope also contained a pass for boarding company ships.

Sea duty came sooner than expected. A week before he was due to start work at the Clyde Docks a telegram arrived. It requested him to report to the chief engineer's office by noon on the following day aboard the TSTS *Queen of Dalriada.* The price of his train ticket would be reimbursed. The note went on to say that the ship was presently berthed at Ocean Terminal in Southampton.

A mad rush began as King speedily packed. That night after saying farewells to friends and family, he boarded the southbound express for London from Motherwell.

The lurching motion of the tandem steam engines arriving at Crewe roused him from a sound sleep. The train sighed to a smooth halt alongside one of the many platforms in the large station. Both engines were hissing huge clouds of water vapour as if trying to catch their breath for the next leg of the journey. A sudden movement inside a brightly-lit waiting room caught his eye and for a brief instant he witnessed a drama through soot smeared windows.

A tall burly man was grinding a younger man's bloodied face against a grimy windowpane. The youth's long, mousey hair swung from side to side across his face each time his aggressor punched him. An attractive middle-aged woman with reddish hair, too bright to be natural, was trying in vain to haul the fellow away from his victim. Then the scene was gone as if part of a dream devoured by darkness with the train accelerating into the night.

Fatigue hampered him when he hauled his suitcases through Euston Station. He started to perk up during the taxi ride to Waterloo Station. A leisurely breakfast saw the weary traveller boarding a connecting train. He arrived in Southampton two hours later.

Wednesday morning, December 6th, 1961

A cold light breeze swept up Southampton Water across the basin where the Rivers Test and Itchen meet: A prelude to winter. Beyond Town Quay and the Royal Pier Southampton dockyard teemed with shipping. The newcomer stood on the dockside at Ocean Terminal looking up in awe at the bows of a great ocean liner. He had never dreamt that anything could be so massive and still float. He was to discover that his new home was seven hundred and sixty-one feet long with a beam of eighty-six feet. Weighing in at fifty-one thousand, five hundred and seventy-three tons, the gigantic passenger liner was tethered to the dockside by a myriad of enormous hempen ropes.

Apparently helpless, she just bided her time like some steel Gulliver. Above the leviathan's hefty anchor, QUEEN OF DALRIADA was delineated in large ebon letters above her jet hull. The vessel's white super-structure gleamed and her twin fore-and-aft amber funnels were black topped. Superimposed on the both sides of the forward stack was a claret lion rampant ensnaring a Scottish thistle with its forepaw.

The hustle and bustle of loading the ship piqued his interest. With cantilevered jibs pointed to the sky slender cranes slewed their netted burdens above the vessel's well deck. Hand signals were given and loads descended into the forward cargo holds.

So it continued everything from packing cases to cars descended like huge spiders into the bowels of the behemoth.

Struggling with his luggage he lurched towards the gangway bearing the least amount of traffic. Here, at its base, two men were in dispute. One man dressed in street clothes had a battered suitcase and a bulky navy-blue grip at his feet. He held a bottle of gin in his right hand while gesticulating with his left. An officer in Her Majesty's Customs livery kept shaking his head.

When King approached, the civilian touched his arm and asked, "Hey buddy! D'you like gin?"

"Ah cannae stand the stuff," scowled the newcomer, his face screwed with revulsion.

"Me neither," the stranger concurred glumly.

"Whit's the problem?"

"I'm going on leave and my train is due soon. This cu . . ." the man hesitated before continuing. "Customs Officer says that, according to government regulations I have to break the seal and take the neck from the bottle. The duty-free gin is for my missus and I don't want to waste it by pouring it into the dock. I'd rather let somebody drink the shot.

He called to a passing dockhand. "Hey, buddy! D'you like gin?"

A wizened old docker vigorously nodded his head.

"Would you like to drink the neck from my bottle?"

The old man's face lit up, his head bobbing even faster than before. He seized the newly opened bottle in gnarled bony hands and upended it on his dry lips. The neck of the bottle was partially hidden by his puckered cheeks. With his Adam's apple pulsating in his scrawny throat, the level of the bottle diminished with amazing rapidity, and was gurgling at the halfway mark before being aggressively snatched away from the clutching digits.

The aged dipsomaniac's tongue licked his lips in a futile search for any droplet that he might have missed.

"A noice drop o' gin thaat sor," grunted the old docker, in a West Country accent. Knuckling a forefinger to his brow in salute, the fellow growled as he scurried away. "Thank 'ee, sor, thank 'ee."

"That fulfils the government liquor concession, sir," smirked the official.

The victim glowered at the ravaged bottle and shook his head sadly. "Just my luck, out of all the dockies, I have to stop a plonky!"

He stowed the gin bottle in his grip, slashed the zipper shut and stormed away. Angus laughed and boarded the ship.

He found himself in a long passageway of standard room height and perhaps twelve or fifteen feet wide. The walls and the ceiling were painted beige and the floor had a dull red sheen. He was soon to learn that walls, ceilings, and floors were called bulkheads, deckheads and decks, respectively. The long passageway was divided up into sections by open bulkheads, each with machined tracks on the deck. These tracks allowed the passage of a massive cast-steel watertight door that would effectively seal each space in an emergency.

The compartments varied from about fifty to eighty feet in length. People were scurrying to and fro, carrying or wheeling sacks, sides of meat, boxes of fish, crates of vegetables, and multiple sundries. A great ship was readying for a sea voyage.

He was completely lost. Passers-by continuously directed him upwards, deck after deck until he eventually discovered the engineers' living quarters, a labyrinth of corridors which were about thirty inches wide. His meanderings through these narrow alleyways ultimately brought him to his destination, the chief engineer's office. He stuck his head into the small open window and gave his name to the chief's writer.

"Mister King? Now let's see," mused the chief's writer, running a pen down a roster. "Ah! Here we are: cabin forty-three. Here's the key. Just climb up that companionway and turn to your left. Please come back as soon as you're settled."

He returned fifteen minutes later.

"Ah! Mister King again - everything hunky-dory?" asked the writer, referring to a schedule on his desk. "According to this, you are on the twelve-to-four watch. Please report to Mister Robert Christie on the engineroom platform at midnight tonight. Have you signed on yet?"

"No. Where dae Ah dae that?"

"The Port Garden Lounge," the writer informed him. "And since you missed Boat Drill this morning, your presence will be required at the special one held for the watchkeepers who were on duty during the main drill. It's at four-thirty this afternoon. And by the way, you have been assigned 'floater' for this trip."

"Ok thanks," he sighed wearily and drifted off in search of a Port Garden Lounge.

People that he met on his travels helpfully kept steering him in the right direction so that he duly found the lounge on the Promenade Deck. He wandered into the large room. A queue of men and women straggled loosely away from an ornate table serving as a desk for the bureaucratic gentleman seated behind it.

The youth joined the queue.

The botanical decor made him realise why the room was called a garden lounge. Pot plants abounded; hanging baskets cascaded fronds of ivy, grasses bowed gracefully, ferns curtsied, and small palm trees waited for customers to shade. These verdant arrangements were strategically placed around the room. Wicker woven chairs lay siege to glass topped tables with legs of scrolled wrought iron. The complete seaboard side of the room was immured with windowpanes giving the area a plush greenhouse atmosphere.

Time dragged past and the dwindling queue found him at its front. Now were about twenty or thirty potential crewmembers trailing behind him.

"Discharge book please," requested the wearied Board of Trade official. He leafed through the pages pausing briefly on some detail. The civil servant selected a page, stamped it and then deftly scribbled his undecipherable initials on the violet imprint. Snapping the book shut he placed it among a stack of blue companions.

"Your book will be returned when you sign off the vessel." He made a light cross on a specific line on the lengthy manifest. "Sign here."

King picked up a pen from the table and eyed the broadsheet headed, TSTS *Queen of Dalriada*. Below this legend a list of engineer officers with signatures, ranks and salaries had been neatly compiled. He could see his name typed at the bottom of the list. A blank space awaited his signature. His rank and salary was alongside, 6th Junior 6th Engineer Officer: £69-0s-6d/month. He scrawled in the space provided.

The BOT man winked at this latest crewmember. "You're not at the bottom of the heap, you know. Look at it this way, you're holding the rest up!"

Throwing him a lopsided grin King left the lounge.

His next port of call was the chief engineer's office to ask the writer, "Whit's the dress for Boat Drill?"

"Full uniform and a life jacket," replied the clerk leaning back in his swivel chair jabbing a pen at one of his clipboards.

"Your station is Number Seven Lifeboat, starboard side of the Boat Deck."

Back inside his cabin he unpacked his dunnage and stowed most it into drawers beneath his bunk. A battery of wooden coat hangers, each stencilled Pict Line, were pressed into service and reloaded into the wardrobe. Flopping into one of a pair of easy chairs, he kicked off his shoes. He opened a drawer beneath his wardrobe to store them away. This action revealed his lifejacket. He placed it on the coffeetable between the chairs.

A combination writing desk and chest of drawers was the only other piece of furniture in the cabin. A sink with a mirror was mounted on the after bulkhead near the door. Red and white chintz curtains draped the door and his bunk.

He changed into uniform and presently the mirror on the wardrobe door reflected a grinning brand-new Angus. He preened a little by straightening his tie and removing a mote of dust from his shiny brass-buttoned doeskin jacket. Light captured the strip of braided gold on each sleeve. An edging of purple velvet below the gold signified his profession. His peaked cap sported the company badge: gold laurels encompassing the lion and thistle. By the time he'd donned his life jacket it was time to go on deck.

He wasn't completely ignorant of navigating around a ship. He had gone 'doon the waater', a colloquialism for sailing on a Clyde steamer, many times on day excursions. He knew that forward meant in the direction of the bow (the pointy end), with the port side on the left side of the vessel while starboard was on the right and aft was at the stern (the blunt end).

Sunlight glinting through a round window on a wooden door led him to the open deck. He pushed the door ajar and stepped over the high coaming onto a landing. From this elevation he could see into the lifeboats that sat in their davits. He skipped down the ladder to Boat Deck and strode through a cross alleyway to the starboard side, pausing momentarily by the ship's rail to look down. Far below on the quayside folk scurried like ants. Daylight was fading and streetlights were flickering on. Soon the boat train would arrive and excited passengers would be embarking.

He made his way forward to where a small crowd of people loitered. Like him, they wore orange and blue carapaces stuffed with kapok. Some milled around impatiently while others stood chatting. Some of the officers, identified as engineers by their royal piping, remained quite apart from the rest of the boat's company.

He approached them.

A tall handsome fellow with black curly hair and a tanned complexion smiled at the newcomer, his hand extended in welcome.

"Hi! You must be the new guy," he said, before introducing himself. "I'm Will Keyes."

He noted the one-and-a-half bars on the friendly engineer's sleeve. "Ah'm glad tae meet ye - my name's Angus King. Are ye a Fourth?"

"Aye," was the reply in a strong Maryhill dialect. "Man, it's guid tae hear a fresh voice frae back hame. I'm frae Glesga."

He threw Keyes a curious look. "Ye didnae sound Scottish when ye introduced yersel'."

"Ye'll soon find out that Sassenachs hae trouble understandin' us," explained Keyes with a laugh. "Just dae whit Ah dae, particularly on the telephones doon below for it's gey noisy there. Try an' mimic the dialect o' the guy who's talkin' tae ye. Communication works much better that way."

His advisor continued. "Mind ye, it'll take you quite a while tae make sense o' the Scousers an' Geordies." He spoke aloud with a plummy tone. "Now hear this you English buggers! Another Scot has been sent south on a mission to educate some of you Sassenachs. A hopeless task, I must admit."

Upon overhearing this insult the English engineers went into a huddle and shunned them.

"Och, dinnae bother with them," Keyes advised his newfound companion. "They're a' bluidy Mushers anyway."

"Whit's a musher?"

"Somebody frae Mushland."

"Mushland?"

"Anybody born in Southampton are classified Mushers. Don't ask me why. Maybe their ancestors were huskies."

The Glaswegian ruminated briefly before adding laconically, "I know that from personal experience, a lot of the women who live around here can be real bitches!" Keyes kept up his humorous banter, his dialect slowly but noticeably reverting back what it was upon introduction.

Later in the voyage the first tripper was to learn that the fellow was a seasoned engineer having served on other company vessels, among them the SS *Albanach* and SS *Princess Eilidh.*

King's eyes casually scrutinized the rest of the boat's complement. Stationed beneath one of the davits two other officers were conversing in low tones. White, and light-green piping, both with gold braid denoted purser and wireless officer respectively. Four stewardesses and one nurse made up the feminine contingent of the boat. A dozen ten stewards were present as well as a motley bunch of greasers, firemen-trimmers from the engineroom black gang.

A one-and-a-half-ringer from the bridge came striding along the oaken deck officiously toting a clipboard. He came to an abrupt halt below the precise centre of number seven lifeboat's keel. The fourth mate executed a military right turn and stomped to attention facing the crowd. This bearded officer looked like he'd just stepped from the front of a Player's cigarette packet and received instant promotion.

"Oh - oh!" grunted Keyes from the side of his mouth. "We've got a right one here."

"All right you lot!" bawled the mate pointing to a specific plank on the deck. "Form a line right here and come to attention."

Instantly everyone, except the engineers, shuffled around to form a ragged line.

"I mean everybody!"

The engineers ignored him and just mumbled to each other. Given time maybe it would go away. It didn't. Solemnly they shook their heads in despair.

The mate reddened. "That order included engineers!"

King's newfound chum eyed him casually. "Say please."

The mate's face flushed even more. "I'm a ship's officer!"

Keyes moved to the side of the most senior engineer present and tapped the two-and-one-half rings on his sleeve. "What do you think this is? Spilled advocaat?"

The mate was just about to explode when an elderly gentleman dressed in street clothes, a bowler hat, and carrying a walking cane, emerged from an adjacent cross alleyway. His authority was strengthened by his manner. "What's going on here Hodgkin?"

"These engineers are insubordinate sir," seethed the fourth officer.

Captain Cowell stared straight into his junior's eyes for a moment. "Years ago engineers were made officers and gentlemen by an Act of Parliament. You will respect that. Mister Parr here," he beamed a smile at the engineer. "Is a Second Engineer Officer and outranks you. You should always be civil to fellow officers or anyone else for that matter. Civility costs you nothing but it may earn you some respect. Do you understand that Hodgkin?"

"Aye-aye Captain," replied a crestfallen mate.

"Very well then. Carry on!" breezed the master, and twirling his cane lightly he set himself on an easy course towards the bridge.

"Gentlemen, would you form a line please?" The request made a difficult passage through clenched teeth.

The engineers, feeling the chill of the late afternoon breeze, soon formed ranks. Swiftly names were called and ticked off the roster and the boat complement was dismissed.

As the engineers trooped along the deck towards their quarters Mister Parr stifled a laugh. He removed his cap to scratch his pate and realign the last few dozen snow-white hairs remaining there. "Y'know," he began on reflection. "The skipper's reference to that government act was not absolutely correct."

Keyes stopped abruptly to ask, "How do you mean, Mister Parr?"

"Well, he's partly right about an Act of Parliament making us officers but," the old man paused for effect, and with a twinkle in his blue rheumy eyes added: "It'll take an Act of God ever to make us gentlemen!"

A passing seagull mewed in agreement and the ensuing laughter faded into the darkening sky. Angus returned to his cabin and removed his clothes in tired abandon. He hauled his tired body into his bunk and fell asleep instantly.

0005 Thursday

"Mister King! Mister King! It's time to go on watch."

Bleary eyes focussed on the interloper who wore a blue denim shirt and jeans. "Who in the hell are ye?"

"I'm the storekeeper. I look after the engineroom tools and issue spare parts and material," explained the sallow faced rating. "I also call the relieving watchkeepers. Didn't the guy on the eight-to-twelve watch call you, sir?"

"Ah dinnae ken. Ah dinnae remember," mumbled the bewildered engineer. He rubbed his eyes before combing fingers through his dishevelled hair. "Weel, Ah'm wakened noo." He assured the storekeeper. "Thanks for callin' me. Eh, whit's your name?"

"Jeffries, sir."

"Jeffries, eh? Whit time is it?"

"Five minutes after midnight. You're late for watch sir!"

"Och shite!" exclaimed King, scrambling down from his bunk. He was frantically pulling a drawer open just as the rating was closing the door. "Here, hang oan a second! Wait until Ah get my bilersuit oan. Ye'll need tae show me where the engineroom is."

He dressed hurriedly into his working gear, took an adjustable spanner and torch from a drawer and shoved the tools into a back pocket. He donned his cap and nodded to the storekeeper to lead the way.

"Four white valves"

0010 Thursday

The ship's Second Junior Second Engineer Officer was sprawled across a high writing desk, a sentinel that stood near the top of the port ladder that accessed the engineroom manoeuvring platform. Carefully raising his head he pushed a soiled cap from his bushy eyebrows and reset it squarely on his throbbing pate. His lank dark hair was partially tangled in the legs of his horn rimmed glasses.

He squinted up at the clock mounted centrally above the engineroom's control board: ten minutes past midnight. The man shivered. The whole place felt like a refrigerator. The second engineer eased his fleshy frame away from the desk and coaxed his long legs into taking him across the checker steel plates to a bank of phones.

Lifting the singular receiver he flipped a switch connecting him to Number One Boiler Room. A light indicator flashed 1BR. He buzzed twice then waited. Presently a crackling of static was heard clearing instantly and a voice, heavily imitating an East Indian accent, said, "Number One Stokehold Sahib. What is your desire, oh wicked one?"

"Cut out the clowning Mister. Where in the hell's that bloody bilgediver?"

A snappy response came back in a Southampton accent. "He's just gone aft with the cocoa Sec."

"Ok. That's what I wanted him for." He shuffled back to his desk and lowered his head until his forehead touched the cool varnished lid. It felt ice-cold, an illusion of relief.

He was grateful that the engines were shut down. It was peaceful in there, almost like a cathedral, a steel cathedral. The platform's monitoring console might have been the high altar, its long vertical manoeuvring wheel spindles emulating organ pipes. Polished brass telegraphs were fat stubby sconces. In lieu of hymn numbers turbine nozzle positions were chalked on a small blackboard that hung by his desk.

On the same level of the port and starboard engines casing tops, a centre runway travelled aft from the platform. Each engine consisted of four sizable steam turbines, all of which were linked into a massive gear reducer. At sea these twin gearboxes transmitted power to the enormous propeller shafts.

Midway between the platform and the engineroom's after bulkhead was a wide ladder that rose from the centre aisle to a catwalk on D Deck level. Ladders connected this ironwork to a network of others that progressed upwards to the engineroom hatch, a bell-less belfry, some sixty feet above. The transepts or port and starboard platform wings led to the main condensers, evaporators, pumps, coolers and other units.

At sea this complete area would be reverberating with thousands of sounds but for now it was quiet, except for the occasional watery fart from a leaky steam trap. A buzzer sounded rudely and an indicator light flashed 3BR, the telephone connection to Number Three Boiler Room. It was an urgent plea for someone to answer.

"Engineroom."

A tinny voice said. "Can you spare a drop of water?"

"Will do."

He hung up and readjusted his cap, which made him wince: "God, even my hair hurts!" He moaned. "Work is the curse of the drinking class."

Hollow echoes of feet clambering up the platform ladder captured his interest. Anticipating the bilgediver with his fanny of cocoa he craned round to face the gleaming white apparition standing before him.

A young man stared nervously back at him. Of average height he was perhaps half a head shorter than the second engineer. He was slim with rosy cheeks still hinting of baby fat. Bright red hair spiked out at all angles from beneath a brand spanking-new peaked cap.

The second's bloodshot eyes shrivelled from the glare of the newcomer's searing white boilersuit. Eyes with veins verged on haemorrhaging closed their lids for almost half a minute before reopening them. It was still there. His whole body shuddered.

"Who and what are you?" the second roared, his neck cringing into a starboard list, a reminder to keep his voice lowered. His continued whisper was still marked by lethal undertones. "Why are you doing here?"

"Angus King sir. Ah was telt tae report tae Robert Christie oan the engineroom platform." proclaimed the youth and with an afterthought, said: "Ah'm your new floater!"

"Suffer the little children," quoted his new boss. "Why in the hell do I get the green ones all the time?" he asked himself aloud. "I'm Christie," he announced. "Mister Christie to you! Black Bob to my friends of whom I don't have. After working for a couple of watches with me you'll begin to think that I'm a bastard. But I'm not really . . . I'm an arch bastard! Now, piss off and close the harbour drains. We'll be warming through shortly."

The liner's newest engineer's cheeks blushed in unease and he remained in situ as if welded to the footplate.

"What the hell are you waiting for? A fanfare?"

"Please sir, where an' whit are the harbour drains?"

"Harbour drains," sighed Christie. "Are devices invented by a marine engineer who had a phobia about water in steam turbines. When the engines are shut down, steam condenses into water that gathers at the bottom of the turbines. If that condensate were allowed to remain there until start-up, the vanes spinning at high speed would throw it with great force and shatter against the turbine casings.

"Naturally the firm would take a dim view of this and leave us all standing in the dole queue. That is, those of us who were lucky enough to remain alive.

"To prevent such occurrences from taking place a colleague has kindly opened them for us when the engines were shut down. You can now reciprocate by closing them. They're down there," the second benevolently imparted with a thumb down gesture at a ladder that led into the dark murky depths of the bilge. "They're painted white," he added. "Don't come back here until you have closed - four - white - valves."

"Four - white - valves," the nervous neophyte repeated in awe.

"Do you have a flashlight?"

"Aye sir."

"You'll need this," assured Christie him, holding out a wheelkey. "Do you know how to use it?"

The peculiar device required some contemplation. It had greater resemblance to a weapon than a tool for manipulating valve hand wheels. It consisted of a steel round bar about ten inches long with a tee on the one end. On the right side of the tee was a perfectly formed hook with its point curving downwards. On the left hand side, a concave lug had been fashioned to nest against a hand wheel's rim. The tool had been drop-forged.

If applied properly a wheelkey is a boon to any marine engineer providing one is acquainted with the Fist Theorem which may be defined as: dexterity with any wheelkey is directly proportional to the area of skin abrasion divided by the amount of contusions.

"Ah'll soon find oot," he conjectured before vanishing into the dark mysterious depths of the bilge.

The bilgediver finally arrived toting a large fanny of cocoa. He was of medium build with strong hands and calloused fingers, the result of operating countless bilge valves in the Herculean task of keeping the ship pumped dry. The rating wore a short-sleeved shirt that had been light pink at one time but now was stained by rust, grime and splattered grease. His splotchy jeans marred by the same dirt bore a tear around his right knee and his feet were shod with oily sneakers. Where fashion was concerned Charlie Everton was forty years ahead of his time. "Smoko!"

Christie grunted morosely. "'Bout bloody time too!"

Charlie removed three mugs from inside the writing desk and filled them with thick hot kye. "When do we sail Mister Christie?"

"Seven-bloody-thirty!" he moaned. "I don't know why but this watch always seems to catch the manoeuvring standby."

The rating shrugged indifferently before leaving to have cocoa with his friend, Ronnie Livingstone, the engineroom greaser.

Christie sipped his kye just as the phone buzzed. It was 3BR again. "Engineroom."

"Wa-ter . . . Wa-ter . . ." gasped a seemingly parched throat.

"*Jesus Murphy*! I'm sor - I forgot!" From Christie, an apology was unusual but this would be as close to one as the stokehold engineer would ever get. "I'll push some through right now."

"Thanks Sec," came the breezy reply.

He scrambled down the starboard ladder to the auxiliary feed water pump to the boilers. He opened a valve to introduce steam but the pump refused to start. A large wheelkey lay within easy reach. A vicious smack jarred the pump's shuttle valve into movement. The pump jumped indignantly and with a shoo-ow of reluctance its piston whooshed slowly up and down grunting purified water forward to the boilers.

Minutes lapsed and three short buzzes on the phone signalled stop pumping. He killed the steam and climbed back on the platform to find his junior watchkeeper relaxing over his cocoa. His normal sallow complexion went dun.

"Get up off your arse, you lazy git! Nobody sits down while I'm in charge of this engineroom."

The junior jolted up from his stool. "Sorry Sec!"

"You'll be glad to know that we have a new floater with us. I sent him down to close the harbour drains. Get your bloody arse down there and make sure that he hasn't drowned in the bilges. And if he has, give the bilgediver shit. He's supposed to keep 'em dry!"

"No problem Sec!"

"It had better not be!"Christie bawled after him. "And check all those valves yourself. Make bloody sure that they have all been shut tight! I don't want any vacuum leaks!"

But the junior was long gone, disappearing beneath one of the port turbines.

The floater was beneath the after end of the same turbine in process of closing a valve. His flashlight had fallen into the bilge and had gone out. Warily he scanned the darkness mesmerized by small luminous creatures darting about in the gloom. They gave him an eerie feeling as he leaned over a pipe to retrieve his flashlight. The movement eased leg cramps that had developed from crawling around.

A hand touched his shoulder.

"Aaa-ah!" yelped a startled Angus, jerking his head up against the turbine casing. He shined a light into the fifth engineer's face.

"It's only me," the intruder assured him, squinting against the direct light. "I'm the platform junior of this watch. My name's Jacques White. You can call me 'Jake' - right?"

"Jake Wright?"

"No Jake White."

King stuck his pinkie in his ear and gave it a twist before saying, "Ah'm sure that ye said Jake Wright."

White pursed his lips in exasperation. "Look - uh - whatever your name is -?"

"Angus King."

"Uh - Angus, my name's - uh - Jake White - right?"

He was about to repeat Jake White Wright but thought better of it. "Weel anyway Jake, ye fairly gave me a fright." He tenderly touched the bump on his head and shook hands.

"You got all the drain valves - right?"

"Aye. Ah think so."

"Show me," pressed the fifth. A light beam flitted across the bilges illuminating each valve in sequence. "All right," he drawled with apparent satisfaction and a leap of faith. "Let's go up and get some cocoa."

On their return to the platform the juniors found Christie chatting to a tall heavyset engineer, his black hair greying around the temples. The fellow had nut-brown eyes and a weathered face. The new junior seemed to draw his interest. "Who's that?" he asked.

"Big John MacKay," replied White. "He is - uh - the Second Senior Second Engineer. But - uh - he's usually termed - uh - the Walking Second of the watch."

Christie beckoned the juniors over. Angus was introduced to Mister MacKay, pronounced Mac-Kye. The walking second, on hearing his accent, inquired: "What part of Scotland do you come from, lad?"

"Carluke sir," he responded, secretly relieved the senior engineer had a civil tongue in his head unlike the bad-tempered Christie.

"I'm from Cupar myself," said MacKay. "I hope that you'll enjoy your life on board. The *Dalriada* is a happy ship and we want her to bide that way. So keep your nose clean and everything will be hunky-dory."

Angus smiled. "Thanks Mister MacKay!"

Sensing the interview was finished White nudged him and led him to the juniors' writing deck on the other side of the platform. The walking second departed from the engineroom to begin his rounds.

Black Bob approached the juniors just as they were draining their mugs. The floater's grimy boilersuit brought a malicious grin to his face. It widened further when he noticed that King had barked his knuckles.

"I see that you're beginning to break in just fine," he said before directing his attention on White. "Go and start the lube-oil pumps. Take him with you and show him the ropes.

Divulge your hesitant knowledge of ships' engines. That should about five minutes!"

White jerked his head at the new guy indicating that he should follow. The juniors went aft in and stopped at the lubricating oil pumps for the main engines. After the pumps went into operation the neophyte was advised on the importance of maintaining proper trim in the lubricating oil tanks. The student endeavoured to ask the obvious question for he was curious about the consequences of an empty lube-oil tank at sea.

"Uh, a tank would not empty completely," his companion began. "When the oil drops to a certain level - uh - a float closes a switch that triggers an alarm. A sequence of - uh - weird and wonderful events happen. Klaxons go off and - uh - bells ring, and lots of coloured lights flash on and off.

Jake paused for a moment.

"And - uh - all the while, great clouds of steam are - uh - gushing from the turbine glands. In a very short time the manoeuvring platform suddenly becomes staffed by - uh - a multitude of bewildered engineers in all states of dress and undress - right?"

"If ye say so."

"These gentlemen in their prompt reaction to the emergency also eject steam, usually from their ears and assholes! And when - uh - the shit finally settles they seek out the culprit who allowed it to happen and take turns shoving the oil float up his backside! Right?"

"If ye say so," repeated Angus laughing. "Ah suppose anybody who did that would get fired."

"Uh - not necessarily," countered White, still on a roll. "It all depends on how far he could swim! Right?"

The tour advanced, the juniors becoming better acquainted. Angus honed in on his mentor's soft hesitant drawl. "Excuse me for askin' Jacques but Ah've got a wee problem wi' your accent."

"Huh! I would've thought that you had enough goddamn problems with your own!" retaliated White, then smiled. "I'm just kiddin' you, Angus. What's your problem, eh?"

"Well, your accent sometimes sounds a wee bit like an American's an' sometimes like an Englishman's. Are ye a Canadian by any chance?"

"Give that guy a Studebaker! Yeah," he affirmed. "Jacques Canuck, that's me!"

Exchanges of personal experiences were constantly interrupted as new tasks kept cropping up. The new sixth was bombarded with the rudiments of preparing the ship's engines for start-up. Valves had to be opened while others had to be shut. Many temperatures and pressures had to be set and maintained; tanks levels checked, filled, emptied or trimmed to specific levels. The varied terminology boggled the mind.

Halfway through the watch the bilgediver made an appearance. Upon their return to the platform the juniors found that their mugs had been replenished with tea sweetened by condensed milk. The platform second gave them little respite. "Get up there and open the bulkhead stops," he snarled. "And make bloody sure that the drain cocks are still open."

At deckhead level they heaved open the bulkhead stops, the main steam supply to the engineroom. He was shown the mechanism that automatically closed these valves to protect the main engines in the event of lubrication failure. Along with this explanation came another droll monologue.

"Uh - in preventing the engines from being - uh - turned into a molten mass of garbage, Isaac Newton's Third Law of Motion: for every action, there is an equal and opposite reaction becomes physically reality or unreal depending on one's point of view - right?"

"If ye say so."

"Now supposing - uh - we're making steam for - uh - twenty-five knots and suddenly - uh - somebody or something shuts off the tap. What do you - uh - suppose would happen?"

He received a shrug and a blank stare.

It was warm near the confines of the engineroom deckhead. Jake dabbed the sweat on his brow and ran a hand over his cropped black hair. "Now - uh - because the steam has to go somewhere it - uh - lifts the safety valves on all boilers - right? And d'you know what? It makes one helluva racket! The noise wakes up - uh - the watchkeepers who are usually half-dozing in their stokeholds and mobilizes them into - uh - one of three plans of action."

Feeling cramped from his hunkered position the floater asked open-mouthed. "An' whit might they be?"

The fifth used his fingers to tally. "Well, A; they can crap in their shorts! B; they can run around in ever decreasing circles or choose Plan C, which is; quickly extinguish all the fires in the boilers. The cool engineer will always choose Plan C but others with a nervous disposition tend to show a preference for plans A, B and C, in that order! It can be a nerve-wracking experience for all concerned."

The humorous anecdote brought a laugh. There was much more to this cynical gentleman than met the eye. Mulling over some of the newly acquired facts, the new engineer was still puzzled. Like many ambitious people Angus had discovered that the more one learned, the more a person wanted to know. He wondered what his own job description entailed and asked his new friend.

Jake thought for moment.

"Uh - a floater is the spare engineer or dogsbody of the watch. When at sea his job assignments usually come directly from the Walking Second. He'll assign you to the odd jobs that crop up during the voyage. You'll give shit relief to the fellah in a stokehold or jenny room. The first time you asked to do this you might wonder who's needin' the shit - you or him! Right?

"But - uh - mainly you'll be with the walking second for the first two or three watches. Make damned sure that you learn his routine!" White emphasized his face stern. "That way - you'll know where he's likely to be at any given time. Heaven help you if you're not around when he needs you. You literally have to -" he punned. "Hang on a Second!"

"Ok - noo anither thing - let's back up a wee bitty. When we were doon below the turbines, whit were yon luminous things runnin' aboot a' ower the place?"

"Uh - silverfish," Jake told him. "They're - uh - little bugs that thrive in warm damp areas. They are very shy creatures shun the light. Cockroaches on the other hand are - uh - more intelligent and sociable. They prefer our company and often drop into our cabins for a beer. Also, when the storekeeper switches on the engineers' cabin lights to call the new watch the roaches scurry across the deck, their carapaces clicking loud enough to wake each somnolent soul. In effect one could say that they call the watch."

"Anither thing," persisted Angus." Is Mister Christie mad at us just because he's got a hangover?"

This brought a chuckle at his companion's naivety. "We should be so lucky! Black Bob is always like that. He was ten years on tankers - right?" he said, as if it explained everything. He peered down through a maze of insulated pipes. "Speak of the devil it looks like - uh - our illustrious leader requires our services again. It seems to be quite vital from the way he's jumping up and down - right?"

It was noticeably warmer and noisier on their return to the platform. Plumes of steam floated above turbine glands and gauges showed higher readings.

"The stokeholds are screaming for water!" Christie ranted. "Go and start up the feed pumps!"

The juniors scampered below to the main feed water pumps for the boilers. Jake spun open some valves and disappeared like a genie in plumes of vapour. Steam whoo-shed and hissed everywhere and whining noises began. Sounds quickly built up, both in volume and in pitch, as a pair of rotors accelerated to ambient speed to quench the thirsty boilers.

For the green engineer it was an exciting yet frightening experience. Quite suddenly the air cleared and he could see his partner by the hotwell fine tuning a pump governor. When the juniors clambered back to the platform, their mugs had been replenished with fresh cocoa. Lighting up cigarettes they stole a short break at the writing desk to watch Christie striding back and forth checking various instrument readings. His observations seemed to be satisfactory because he didn't disturb the juniors at their repast.

The new junior had time to study his mentor. White was slightly taller than him and had a similar build. His white even teeth, consistently exposed by smiles, were a sharp contrast to his tanned complexion. His dark brown eyes darted back and forth along the console consuming information. They would rest briefly on some gauge before peeking at another. He speculated that he made quite a hit with the ladies.

"So you come from Carluke, right?"

"Aye. Dae ye ken it?"

"Not the one that you're thinking of," he was assured. "I live near a farm area called Carluke."

Angus reflected on what he knew about Canada. He'd done well in history and geography at school. The Plains of Abraham clicked in his mind to a battle or something where both commanders, Wolfe and Montcalm, were killed. He had reasoned that if both generals had been killed it should have been a draw. But the British said they had won and the French had cried, 'Foul!' And have been crying foul ever since.

Another memory of Canada stood even stronger in his mind but he wasn't sure of the exact year. At that time sweets among other things were still on the ration although the Second World War had ended some four or five years before. Fresh fruit had also been a rarity. He had seen and tasted his very first banana when he was about ten or eleven years old.

Living in the Clydesdale fruit belt helped for soft fruits such as strawberries, raspberries, gooseberries, red and black currents could be had in the summer season. In autumn tiny hard pears, Victoria plums, greengages, ultra sour bellyaching 'cookers' and tiny eating apples could be had if one was smart enough to avoid a farmer's dog or bull.

A large box stencilled *A Gift from the People of Canada* sat on the classroom floor in front of the desks. The lid of new pinewood slats had been split open and the teacher was handing out apples. Each child received an enormous red apple wrapped in tissue paper. He recalled getting his apple.

It seemed to be the size of his head and the skin was blood red. He had patiently smoothed out the tissue paper to read the logo: Red Delicious Apples from British Columbia. Although he had spent the rest of the day polishing it against his jersey Angus could never ever remember eating it.

A hand waved in front of his eyes interrupting his reverie. "Hello - anybody home?"

The Scot's mind leapt to the present. "Where dae ye stay?"

"The steel city of Hamilton, Ontario."

"That's funny, the steel town o' Scotland is Motherwell an' that's only two miles frae Hamilton," he was informed.

They were given further orders. Expansion readings had to be taken and the engines had to been turned over at twenty-minute intervals. "No rest for the wicked," said Jake, cramming a small slate and a tapered gauge in his back pocket. "C'mon Angus, school's reopened."

Initiating the newcomer to the complex field of marine engineering made the watch pass swiftly and his mind boggled with perplexing terminology; high and low pressure steam turbines, closed feed systems, condensate pumps, expansion readings, main wheels, turning gear, poker gauge readings and many, many other little technological gems.

Inside the propeller shaft tunnel a thought occurred to the fifth. Presently he glanced at his watch. "Oh-oh!"

"Whit's up?"

"Christie'll be madder than a bear with a burnt ass!" prophesied Jake. "It's nearly the end of the watch."

On their reappearance the juniors found three other engineers on the manoeuvring platform. Christie was propped against the seconds' desk chatting to his relief while the others were grouped near the starboard air ejector.

"Our reliefs are here," he was told. "C'mon and I'll introduce you."

The relieving juniors were in deep conversation as they approached close enough to overhear. "Then what?" the taller of the pair queried. "How did you make out?"

"I didn't even get a sniff at it!" complained his little rotund companion. "After we left *The Spa*, we walked for about fifty yards then I puked my ring up. Cor! She wasn't half disgusted! She buggered right off and left me right on the spot anchored to a lamppost. Ooh! That's the last time I'll drink Guinness!"

"Don't blame the Guinness, you greedy little man you. It serves you bloody well right! You'd been guzzling the stuff all bloody evening. If you'd just had a couple or four like any normal guy you would've been all right. But no-oo, you were trying for a place in their Book of Records!"

"You're right Bomber," agreed his pal. "When all's said and done there's supposed to be a baby in every bottle."

"If that were true why in the hell weren't you arrested for mass infanticide?"

"Uh - if you pair of clowns are quite finished," butted in Jake. "We would like to be - uh - relieved so we can get some grub. I'm starving."

"Well, if it isn't Mister Right White, our resident - no I mean - our hesitant Canadian." said Bomber.

Ignoring the jibe White motioned a thumb at the taller junior. "Angus, this is Maxie Harris. Bomber - Angus King."

"Pleased tae meet ye," said Angus with a firm handshake. "Eh, tell me somethin'. How did ye get the nickname, 'Bomber'?"

Maxie giggled.

"You'll find out soon enough," the little fat man assured him with a grin. "I'm Tony Ball, known as 'The Sphere' for obvious reasons!"

"Pleased tae meet ye."

"Frrresh oot o' the heathurrr!" purred The Sphere.

"Good job Bomber," Jake told his relief with a grin. "Everything is set up. All you have to do is remove the turning gear and take your log. Trial of engines is at five-thirty. See ya!"

The two juniors headed for the platform ladder.

"*Hoi*!"

They stopped in their tracks. Black Bob was glaring over his horned-rimmed glasses at them. With a wicked forced grin he crooked a forefinger and beckoned them. "What kind of a way is that to end a watch, Mister?"

"What d'you mean Sec?" asked White.

"What I mean Mister is," growled Christie, his dark eyes fixed on White's. "Where's the bloody slate? How d'you expect me to keep a log when you're carrying the flamin' information around in your pocket?"

"Sorry Sec," apologised White giving him the slate.

"Now put the poker gauge back so others can use it."

He ambled off. Christie shaking his head in despair, commiserated to his relief. "I don't know what kids are coming to these days, Jimmy. All they've got on their minds is pussy. It wasn't like that when I was a junior."

Jimmy Parr dryly retorted, "That's probably why you're so miserable now Bob! Introduce me to the new chappie."

"All right. Mister King, this is Mister Parr. He's the Platform Second Engineer on the four-to-eight watch."

"Pleased tae meet ye Mister Parr," smiled Angus.

"Welcome aboard Mister King."

" Uh - is it ok to leave now Sec?" asked White, returning.

"I'll tell you when you can leave!" snarled Christie. He directed some of his venom at the floater. "Mister King, this watch begins at twelve on the hour, not twenty minutes after! It will benefit both you and the engineer whom you relieve if you're here ten minutes before the watch commences so that the job is handed over properly. I will not tolerate bad relief!"

"The reason Ah was late was because Ah couldnae find my way doon here," protested King. "Ah've never been oan a boat as big as this afore!"

"This vessel is a ship," corrected Christie. "And I didn't ask for excuses," he continued, shielding the plea with the palm of his hand. "Now gentlemen and I'm using the term loosely, you may leave the engineroom. Piss off!"

Descending the platform ladder they ambled forward until they came to a lift near 3BR access door. The elevator raised them to the engineers' quarters on Sun Deck and deposited them into a vestibule panelled by large notice boards. Rosters predicting shipboard life for engineers were tacked up everywhere. Ranks, cabin numbers, emergency and lifeboat stations; fire inspections, the watch bill, a leave rota, fog standbys, wardroom games tournaments, swimming pool and banking hours were all listed.

"You'll have to memorise this lot by the weekend."

"Whit?"

"Just kiddin'. You'll soon learn the ropes - right?"

The short vestibule ended at a tee junction. A door on the left was the rear entrance to the engineers' mess. Turning right an alleyway led them through the maze of living quarters that Angus recalled from the previous day. Neatly typed cards alongside each cabin door named its occupant. He remained in tow with Jake who stopped to unlock a door and invite him in.

"I live here," said White. "D'you fancy a beer?""

"No thanks Jake. Ah'm knackered. Besides, Ah'm lost. Ah'll need tae search for my ain cabin."

"What number is it?"

"Forty-three."

White pointed his key back in the direction they had come. "Go to the end of this alleyway and hang a left, then take the companionway. Your cabin should be the third or fourth on the starboard side."

"Thanks."

"By the way," he said. "If you're hungry, the messroom is just round the corner here."

"No thanks," sighed King, beginning to walk away. "Ah need a shower an' some sleep."

"Hold it!" called Jake. "One more thing - uh - wear your patrol suit when you go into the mess for breakfast. I'll show you where the engineers' changeroom is and - uh - where you can do your dhobi - right?"

"If ye say so. Thanks again. Cheerio!

Full Away!

0717 Thursday

"Wake up, Mister King. Standby!"

He awoke with a start and gawked drowsily at the spectral figure beside his bunk. It had white hair, a pallid complexion, and decked out in a white jacket. The stranger had pale-blue eyes and could have passed for an albino. An irritated groan crept up from between the sheets. "Whit's happenin' noo?"

For the second time that night his sleep had been disturbed. A disturbing dream triggered an alarming thought in his sleepy head. "Are ye the Spirit o' the Christmas Present? Because if ye are, ye've got the wrang guy!"

"The storekeeper is calling Standby Mister King," urged the man. "I'm your steward, Barnes. We're sailing in about ten minutes."

A faint whistle blasting from afar validated this truth.

"Ok - eh - Barnes. Thanks - sorry aboot the comment. Ah dinnae seem tae be gettin' much sleep lately."

"That's all right sir," consoled Barnes watching his latest charge clamber from his bunk to hastily dress.

A haggard face glowered back from the mirror while the steward assisted him with his jacket. "Man, Ah look like somethin' the cat dragged in. Ah badly need a shave but Ah dinnae hae the time." He combed his fingers through a tousled mat of amber before heading for the engineroom.

The first thing he noticed upon his arrival was an increase in temperature. Wisps of steam drifted up from the turbine glands. His next observation was that the bridge telegraph indicators had changed position. They'd moved from *Finished with Engines* to *Standby*. Extra engineers were on duty.

He rightly deemed that the officer regaled in full dress uniform with four gold bars on each sleeve was Alan Lindsay, the chief engineer. He was stationed aft on the platform chatting with John MacKay. Jake White and another engineer waited by the starboard manoeuvring wheels. Bomber Harris was crouching by an access ladder while The Sphere's head could just be seen sticking up from behind the starboard HP (high-pressure) turbine. Mister Parr fiddled around with the alarm indicator reset buttons for the freshwater evaporators.

Christie, who had been hunched over a portable rostrum near the platform's centre to record telegraph movements, hastily drew erect when his new floater came in sight. Still disgruntled his arm made a slashing motion directing him towards the port controls. He hurried to this spot and smiled uneasily at the engineer beside him.

"First tripper?"

"Aye."

"Scotchman?"

He corrected the fellow.

"Scotsman."

"Tough luck!"

Angus stood stiffly in front of the enormous control wheels, raptly entranced by the glazed face of the telegraph. Adrenaline was coursing rampantly through his system.

A brass plate fastened to the supporting guide bracket for each manoeuvring wheel dictated the shaft rpm needed for each movement. His eyes remained glued to the face of the polished brass quadrant. Contrasting thoughts trickled into his mind implying a dilemma; when the order came what should he do first? Supply power to the engines then acknowledge the telegraph or vice versa? Perhaps he should ask somebody.

A loud clamour rang through his musings when the green telegraph indicator ordered the first movement, *Half Astern.*

He froze.

The ringing persisted until an arm festooned with gold braid materialised above his left shoulder and a hand at the end of it shoved the gleaming brass handle to align it with the green needle. The bell stopped and the chief jabbed a pudgy finger at the astern wheel. "Open that bloody valve! *Now*!"

He seized the valve wheel's rim and pulled frantically for all his worth. Nothing happened.

"The other bloody way!"

He heaved in the opposite direction. Nothing happened.

"*Jesus Christ Almighty*!" blasphemed Lindsay and gripping the wheel with his left hand, gave it a quick practised jerk. The wheel moved and rotated smoothly. "Keep opening it until that steam pressure gauge reads one hundred pounds per square-inch!" he bawled over the throaty whine of the astern turbines. The more he spun the valve open so the noise increased in volume and pitch.

"All right lad, keep her there," he said and stepped back.

Nervously the first tripper risked a hurried glance around the engineroom. Handrails, gauges, copper pipes, lights, and floorplates were quivering with the tremendous vibration. Great billows of steam surged from the astern turbines. White's engines remained at rest. He swivelled his head back just in time to catch the next engine movement.

Stop.

Presence of mind allowed him to answer the telegraph promptly and he quickly closed the astern valve. Glimpsing back at his superiors his smug grin demonstrated that he now had the hang of the situation.

"The ahead wheel!" called Lindsay.

He gaped at the wheel and back at the chief again, a perplexed frown on his face. The chief drew alongside him and eased the ahead manoeuvring wheel open. "Look," he said, pointing at the tachometer. "Momentum is still turning your turbines astern. You must brake them by using the opposite wheel."

"Ok Chief."

Full astern.

Immediately he introduced steam to the turbines.

"That's better!" yelled Lindsey.

Sound and vibration built up to a crescendo until the telegraph rang *Stop* two minutes later. He reacted to it smartly and spun the astern wheel shut. Lending his weight to the ahead wheel he gave it a great heave. The valve spun open with the sudden force. The uproar generated by the turbines ceased quite suddenly and instead of the accustomed sounds of deceleration there came a singular distinctive clunk!

Accompanying this unusual sound was a high-pitched moan that echoed eerily through the engineroom. He gulped. Cautiously he peered aft to find everyone staring at him. Christie eyed the chief engineer and they nodded in solemn agreement to MacKay's thumbs down gesture. The walking second clumped up to close the ahead wheel.

"Mister King," he admonished. "The Chief told you to brake the engine not," spelling the word out, "B-R-E-A-K it!"

The young man was almost in tears.

"Don't look so worried lad," he grinned, slapping his shoulder. "This engine always does that after yon movement.

It's done that since Year One. Don't get excited - just ease open the opposite wheel in future."

His face lit up in relief. "Thanks very much, Mister MacKay. For a wee while there, Ah had visions o' gaun back tae the steel works."

The walking second frowned when he noticed the steam pressure was low. He reacted to the situation by moving the boiler room telegraph to *Slow*. Port and starboard telegraphs rang simultaneously.

Angus delivered power for dead slow ahead and Jake sped up to half astern. Minutes later the indicator swept across the starboard telegraph.

Dead Slow Ahead.

No further movements rang down for the standby watch. The eight-to-twelve watch relieved the four-to-eight who took control from the twelve-to-four. The Sphere tapped King's shoulder. "Ok Angus, I've got it," he declared with authority. "When you go topside, nip up to the bridge and tell the skipper that The Sphere is driving. Set his mind at ease!"

"Righty-ho Sphere," he replied. "Ah'll dae that. Right after the Scottish Parliament sits in Edinburgh! Drive carefully!"

"Bugger off!"

Thirty minutes later the first tripper was sauntering across Boat Deck to the port railing. The ship was slowly moving into the basin formed by the Rivers Itchen and Test estuaries. The vessel stood off between Ocean Terminal and Hythe. Assisted by a pair of tugs the great bow of the liner was beginning to swing into Southampton Water.

Early morning mist and drizzle hampered visibility and made him shiver. He could sense his stomach sending gurgling messages for sustenance. The open deck was desolated. No passengers were waving farewells on this cold and wet autumn morn.

In the warmth of his cabin he was pleased to discover that his bunk had been made and his quarters tidied. He pressed the call button for the steward and had a wash and shave during the interim. He had donned his best blues by the time Barnes answered his summons. "Yes Mister King?"

"Could ye tell me if Ah can get some breakfast?" he inquired, patting his jacket for a comb.

"Yes sir," Barnes assured him with a smile. "The mess opens at 8:40 a.m. for the four-to-eight watch but you can get some food too. It closes at 9:30 and reopens again at 11:20 for the twelve-to-four's breakfast. High tea is available at the end of your watch or if you wish to wait, dinner is at seven."

"That sounds fair enough. Eh - now - where can Ah get some fags?"

"When the bar opens at noon I'll get some for you sir," offered the steward. "The evening bar hours are from six until nine." He continued. "I can lend you a pack of cigarettes for this watch. I'll leave a carton for you on the coffeetable. What brand do you prefer?"

"It disnae matter. Any filter-tipped kind will dae me."

"Yes sir."

"Eh - thanks, Barnes." A thought occurred to him. "Eh, Ye ken, a case o' beer widnae go wrang either. Put one oan the coffeetable wi' the fags."

"Very well sir. What kind of beer would you like?"

"Whit kind dae ye hae?"

"Barclay's, Whitbread, Watney's, Tennant's -"

"Stop right there! Tennant's lager sounds fine. How much is that?"

"Thirty-five shillings sir."

"Aw, that's grand! An' how much is it gaun tae cost me, includin' the fags?"

"That is including the price of the cigarettes, Mister King," emphasised Barnes.

"Is duty free no' bluidy marvellous?" He handed out two Scottish banknotes. "Keep the change."

"Thank you, sir."

"Ah'm gaun tae eat the noo. Ah'm starvin'."

He entered the engineers' mess. There were two rows of tables running fore and aft. Tables by the port bulkhead could each seat four people while inboard tables were set for six. About a dozen engineers were dispersed throughout the room.

Jake, seated inboard, drew his attention. He sauntered over to his shipmate and took a seat facing him. "Nearly break the engines did you?" he laughingly teased, giving him a menu.

His friend threw him a look before peering at the card. "Ah damned near shit mysel' when Ah heard that bluidy clunk!"

The Canuck chortled again and hacked into a thick slice of Virginia ham before pointing his fork at the Scot. "You should've seen your face. Boy, was that ever funny - right?"

"Not tae bluidy me!"

"Never mind old son! Every first tripper gets that one. It only happens on that manoeuvre. Nobody knows why," he chuckled again.

A steward came. "Can I take your order now, luv?"

He gaped up at a head of newly permed blonde hair. Light-green eye shadow and heavy mascara accented his large, baby blue eyes. A row of even, dazzling-white teeth was the highlight of his powdered and rouged face. "Eh, a glass o' orange juice an' some porridge."

The steward wiggled for'ard towards the pantry. Angus leaned over the table and whispered, "Here, how can that be allowed here?"

"Because Toni's the best damned steward we've ever had in this mess - right?" He jerked his fork back over his shoulder. "Did you notice them fangs of hers? They cost her a thousand bucks in the Big Apple. She got them done - uh - by some dentist who does teeth for movie stars."

"A thousand dollars?" the Scot gasped incredulously. "That's . . ." he hesitated briefly to calculate. "That's aboot five months wages!"

"You can say that again laddie," said White. "And that's why she's known as 'The Tooth Fairy' - right?"

Angus laughed. "Has everybody on this bluidy ship got a flamin' nickname?"

"You got that right!"

When Toni sashayed back to his side with his order, the penny dropped when the Scot suddenly understood why Bomber Harris had called his new friend Right White. At the same time it dawned on him what caused the mix-up when he was first introduced to Jake. The Canadian's habit of ending his sentences with the word, right, had earned him that nickname. He also suspected that Jake wasn't too happy about being saddled with that sobriquet.

Scooping some porridge into his mouth he began to chew the thick cereal. He scowled, laid down his spoon and gave the cereal a liberal dusting of salt. Mixing it like mortar he supplemented the concoction with cream then tasted his efforts. Apparently satisfied he began to shovel it into his mouth with great gusto.

"You Scotchmen sure like to lavish porridge with salt!"

"We're Scotsmen. Porridge is guid for ye an' so is salt," Angus patiently informed him. He slid back his empty plate a little and sighed mightily, "A-ah, that was grand!"

The steward glided back and retrieved the plate. "Would you like something else, sir?" he pouted.

Making up his mind on the steward's gender he said, "Aye lass, some hickory-smoked ham, a couple o' fried eggs, a wee bit bacon, fried spuds an' maybe a sliver o' liver. An' eh - some Scotch baps tae."

"A sliver of liver?" echoed White.

"Weel, they didnae hae kidney!" rhymed Angus.

"I give up!" said Jake, catching the steward's eye. "Toni, my love! I'll have - uh - some Scotch baps too."

The steward beamed, fluttered her false eyelashes and bounced away, her hips swaying provocatively. Angus ogled the diminishing stern and shook his head.

"Fancy her?" hinted Jake with an air of innocence.

"Of course not!" he retorted angrily, his eyes squinting, in response to the tease. "Ye're pullin' my pisser, aren't ye?"

"I wouldn't do a thing like that, right?" Jake denied with mock indignation then leering, "Why don't you ask Toni?"

"Bastard!" laughed Angus.

Will Keyes overheard the insult as he joined their company. "Two minutes on board and already he's been reading my mail!"

"Hi Wheelkey!" the Canadian greeted the newcomer, introducing Angus. "This is Gus King,"

"Hi Right," said Keyes acknowledging Angus. "We've already met on Boat Drill."

Touching his countryman's forearm he censured him lightly with a whisper. "By the way Gus, take it easy when you're drivin', that clunk fairly loosened up the superheat tubes in my boilers!"

"Christ, don't *you* start!"

"Who in the hell rattled your cage?" demanded Keyes.

"Och, Ah'm sorry lads. Ah'm no' mysel' this mornin'."

"You're not - uh - schizophrenic are you?" Jake ventured curiously.

"Ah can see that your style o' humour is gaun tae take a wee bit o' gettin' used tae," murmured Angus as the steward served him.

"That looks good," said Keyes, beaming up the steward, his eyes blinking provocatively. "I'll have ham and eggs dreamboat and a large grapefruit juice please."

"All right darling," cooed Toni.

"Where are we?" asked Jake.

"It's too bloody cold out on deck to be hanging around," remarked Keyes. "But for the ten or fifteen seconds I spent out on the starboard side, I thought that I could see flames. So we must be passing the oil refineries at Fawley."

"That brings up anither question," said Angus. "Noo that we ken where we are, can ye tell me where in the hell we are gaun?"

"You signed on without knowing where you were going?" Keyes cocked his head in surprise.

"Sure, whit difference does it make? Ah've got tae work no matter where the ship travels."

"That's true enough," conceded Keyes. "But don't ever do that in Tangier. Engineers are chained to a bench with a bloody great oar stuck in their hands and told to row like hell. They're the main engine!"

Angus chuckled at that one.

The boiler engineer continued on this vein. “If you think that’s funny, ratings have to get out and push!” Just then his order arrived. “Ta honey,” he simpered.

She flounced off to another table.

“Why dae ye patronize him like that?”

“Because,” Jake patiently began to explain. “If you do, she’ll give you excellent service. As a matter of fact, she’ll bend over backward for you - right?”

“Don’t bend over forward for her,” Keyes warned slyly.

“Anyway,” continued White when the ribaldry died down. “Uh - in answer to your first question, we’re - uh - bound for New York and uh - from there we have three cruises scheduled for the Bahamas - right?”

“If ye say so,” he replied absently. “It must be nice tae be rich enough tae go oan a cruise.”

“It’s something new that the company’s starting up Gus,” Jake informed him. “You see, normally this old girl just does a ferry run all year round from Southampton to New York. Sometimes she stops at Cherbourg, France.”

“Aye,” chimed in Keyes. “But the airlines are moving in on us and all the other shipping lines too. A Boeing 707 takes less than seven hours to cross the Atlantic. So very few want to take the slow route which is too expensive anyway.”

Jake cut in. “The head office in their infinite wisdom came up with the idea of short cruises that are affordable to the man in the street.”

“A sort of floating Butlin’s holiday camp,” said Keyes.

“Och, Ah see noo.”

Jake went on. “The company hopes that people who live in the northern States and Canada will want to get away from the ice and snow to spend some time in the subtropics. If it works out I hear that they may do the same for the Brits; Southampton to the Canaries or Madeira."

"Sounds guid tae me."

Other engineers filtered into the mess, among them was The Sphere and Bomber Harris, who sat beside the trio. When Toni had served the newcomers Jake wrinkled up his nose in disgust at Bomber's hasty and noisy consumption of French onion soup. He tossed a statement to the company. "I suppose Emergency Drill coming up in the near future."

The Sphere and Wheelkey nodded ominously. Everyone except the new engineer centred his attention on Harris. The liquid in Maxie's spoon bubbled merrily as he giggled.

"Whit's so special aboot Emergency Drill?"

"You'll find out," his shipmates chorused and Bomber giggled again.

In haste Harris and Ball consumed their breakfast and went back down below to relieve those engineers still on standby. Jake and Angus lit up and lolled back in their chairs in complete satisfaction to enjoy their coffee.

Jake yawned. "I'm off to my cart."

"Aye me tae," concurred Angus rising.

Lavishing butter on some toast Keyes leered, "Keep your hands above the sheets!"

1120

He was up and about and dressed in his patrol suit when the storekeeper knocked on his door and peeped in. "Nearly time for watch Mister King!"

"Thanks!"

He stepped out onto the open deck and propped himself against the ship's rail beside Lawrence Treen. Although the fog had gone, visibility was only about five or six miles. "Mornin'. You'll be the new guy?"

He nodded proffering his hand. "Angus King."

Treen gripped his hand firmly. "Larry Treen - pleased to meet you Gus. You can call me Larry." With a growl he added, "Some of the bastards on board call me 'La Treen' behind my back!"

His stature was similar to King's although he was, perhaps, a little stockier. His brown hair was combed straight back and darkened by the oil that held it in place. A grin lit up his lightly tanned face as he changed the subject. "Do you play darts by any chance?"

"Aye," he replied, his eyes scanning the greyish-green choppy surface beyond. "Whit's yon big steel-plated tower over there wi' the light oan top o' it?"

He pointed to a large black cylindrical structure with rust streaks down the side of it. The tower was about a league away on the starboard quarter. It rolled from side to side in the swell.

"That's Nab Tower." Treen informed him and gestured to a blurry coastline astern. "And that's the Isle of Wight. When we're abreast of the Nab, we'll drop the pilot and be full away." He touched Angus' sleeve and said, "If we nip over to the port side we'll probably see the pilot boat approaching."

Both engineers crossed to the port side. Treen drew his attention to a tender bumping slowly across the whitecaps. Vibration through the ship's rail could be felt from the engines going astern. Propellers churned up light-green and creamy-white froth beneath the liner's counter. The tender had to veer off a couple of times before stopping alongside by a shell door that had been opened for that purpose. Rope and tyre buffers protected the tender as it dipped and rose on the treacherous waves. It could be quite dodgy transferring from vessel to vessel.

"Ah thought ye said that the pilot was gettin' aff here," said Angus, staring at a stocky gentleman in a tweed coat and matching flat cap risking life and limb to board the liner.

An extension ladder leaning against the coaming of an open shell door bobbed up and down on the swell. The man was on the bottom rung when a gust of wind exposed his balding head by lifting his scone. The seaman who was steadying the ladder's base grabbed the cap in mid-flight and handed it back to its owner.

"He is," Treen assured him, watching a hand line snake to the tender. "Hey," he pointed. "It looks like they're going to haul suitcases aboard. That guy climbing the ladder must be a passenger who missed the ship at Southampton."

Two suitcases were swung aboard and the pilot dropped lightly to the tender's steel deck. He waved to a figure out on the wing of the bridge. When the tender was at a safe distance the ship got underway.

A rosy-cheeked half-ringer of a purser trying to act important by the way he brandished his clipboard shook Homer Davison's hand. A couple of seamen secured the shell door. "Just a formality sir, but could I please see your passport before I take you to your cabin?"

The bewhiskered newcomer opened his London Fog raincoat and withdrew the standard dark-blue British passport from the inside breast pocket of his blazer. The purser cursorily glanced at the mug shot that had obviously been taken from an earlier era. The smooth-faced subject bore a slight resemblance of the white-maned gentleman who was glaring back through brown serious eyes as if daring him to reprove him. The young man deigned to take up the challenge. The passport bearing the name, Richard H. Davidson, was handed back to the passenger.

"Welcome aboard Mister Davidson. Now if you'd kindly come with me I'll take you to your suite on Main Deck. I'll arrange for a steward to bring your luggage."

The passenger looked down at his suitcases before peering meaningfully into the youth's nervous countenance. "You look like a strapping young fella, sonny. How's about we save some time and you be the pack mule? Here, give me your clipboard laddie and lead the way."

Flustered the purser complied and regretfully toddled off with his unexpected burden to Cabin M24 while Davison trailed in his wake perusing the passenger list. The panting purser was only too glad when they reached their destination.

"Here's your key sir," he said. "I'll go and fetch your steward to unpack for you and make sure everything inside is shipshape."

"Fine thanks," replied Davison, reaching into his pocket to come up empty-handed. "Oh I guess it's against policy to tip ships' officers. Never mind about the steward I'll press the bell tit when I need him."

Holding the purser by the arm he gently but firmly escorted him out the door with a gruff thanks. Davison checked round the stateroom before he stowed away his gear. He threw a few banknotes on the dressing table before pressing the call button for the steward. He went into the bathroom and removed his brown-tinted contact lenses. He was halfway shaving off his beard when he heard a tap on the door. "Yeah?"

"Sir?"

"Yeah?" Davison repeated but much louder this time.

"My name is Cameron, sir. I'll be your steward on this voyage. I can see that you've already unpacked. How may I help you?"

The passenger yelled through the door, "Can you bring me some grub and a pot of coffee, please?"

"Certainly sir. I'll be back in fifteen minutes."

About ten minutes later he was trimming his moustache when the door was rapped again.

"Yeah?"

"Your food is here on the table sir. It's mostly cold cuts, bread and salad. I did however manage to scare up a bowl of hot chicken soup."

"Splendid," he shouted back through the panelling.

"Shall I pour coffee sir?"

"No thanks. I'm gonna finish my shower. Oh - er - Cameron?"

"Sir?"

"There are some bills for you on the dresser."

When Davison heard a distant 'thank you' he knew that the first stage of his plan had been successful. At the right time he'd revert to his birth name, Homer R. Davison. He recalled John Johnson and John Johnstone, two men with whom he'd served in prison. The confusion called all sorts of problems. He hoped that his ploy would bring similar results.

1155

Standby had rung off by the time King reported for duty on the engineroom platform. The telegraph indicators pointed at *Full Ahead.* The eight-to-twelve engineers were engrossed with working the engines up to speed. Glancing aft he noticed an engineer down beside the port LP (Low-Pressure) turbine trying to catch his attention. He concluded this might be the fellow that he was supposed to relieve. "Are ye the eight-tae-twelve floater?"

The engineer nodded and wiped grime and oil from his right hand and held it out. "Paul Harding, alias The Mekon."

His relief burst out laughing. The nickname fitted the fellow to a tee. The short skinny engineer's head appeared to be much too large for his frail body. He appeared to have a touch of anaemia, which gave his complexion the light-greenish pallor to associate him with the famous comic book villain. Taking his hand he introduced himself.

"Good job." The Mekon assured him. "The gland steam for the turbines is set. Bye!" And he quickly disappeared.

Jake double-checked and explained the valve settings. A shadow caused them look up. The smile that Christie beamed on the pair was reminiscent of a dog voiding razor blades onto a thistle. "Hey Bibbidi, Bobbidi, Boo!" he hollered, and swung his arm for emphasis. "Get back up here!"

They stared at each briefly then back at Christie who was stalking back to his desk. Puzzlement remained in their minds as they trailed in the second's wake.

"Bibbidi, Bobbidi, Boo?" repeated White. "I believe that he's finally snapped! Right?"

"Wait a minute!" Comprehension lit up King's face. "Cinderella - mind?"

"Sure," replied Jake. "Walt Disney's Cinderella. So what?"

" Dae ye mind o' the twa wee mice?"

"Yeah - what about them?"

"Whit were their names?"

"Who in the hell can remember them?"

"Me," said Angus. "An' obviously so does that bugger."

"So?'

"Gus and Jake!" he explained with a grin. "That's us!"

"Oh no! For fuck's sake, don't tell anybody or it will go through the ship like a dose of salts!"

Leaving him with that warning he began a routine consistent with the ship getting up to speed. Christie was recording revolution counter readings when the bridge phone buzzed angrily.

"Get that!" he snapped.

"Engineroom," said Angus.

"Ah-one-ah, seven-ah, fo-ah revolutions please."

"Eh?"

"One-seven-four-revolutions!"

"That's better! An' ye didnae need tae shout. Ah'm no' deaf ye ken!" He slammed down the receiver. "A hundred an' seventy-four revs Mister Christie."

"Ok," replied Christie. "Tell the stokeholds that we're going to open up a bit."

Jake arrived while the order was being called through.

"Ok," said the second. "Mister White, take the starboard wheel. Mister King, you take the port. Ease them open until I tell you to stop."

The juniors took up station by the controls and Christie monitored some key gauges. Minutes later he was satisfied with their efforts. The bilgediver's distribution of hot coffee brought a welcome break. A little later the stokeholds were warned that more steam would be needed. The engines were opened up again and the procedure was repeated at regular intervals.

At 1300 the bridge phone buzzed. Christie was in the process of calculating the average rpm for the past hour. "Oh shit!" he swore irritably. "I haven't finished working out the revs out yet." His pencil broke and he bellowed at the floater. "Tell the bastards to piss off!"

Angus lifted the receiver. "Engineroom."

"Could I have the revs and the sea temp please?"

"Piss aff!"

He hung up in time to see Jake splutter into his second cup of coffee. The bridge phone burped again. This time the Canadian grabbed it.

"Engineroom."

"May I talk to the Second Engineer-of-the-Watch please?"

"Speaking," lied Jake.

"Who was that on the phone just now?"

"I don't know," returned White. "I've just returned to the platform. I'm the only one here at the moment."

"This is the Officer-of-the-Watch speaking, somebody in your engineroom just told me to piss off!"

"What audacity!" commiserated the platform junior in a plummy tone? "I wonder who that could have been?"

"I want you to find the culprit and reprimand him."

"No problem," said Jake and promised: "I'll have him scouring the bilges for a month! Uh - what were you calling for anyway?"

"Oh! Mm, could I have the revs and the sea temp please?"

"One hundred and twenty-six point four rpm and forty-two degrees Fahrenheit."

"Thank you." The phone went dead.

He turned to his new buddy in laughter. "You Scotch twit! You shouldn't have repeated what Christie told you. You have to be diplomatic when you talk to these cocksuckers on the bridge."

With an indifferent shrug he replied, "How was Ah tae ken? Ah was just daein' whit Ah was telt."

"If he ordered you to jump over the wall - would you?"

King shook his head.

"He will," prophesied White. "And before this trip is over."

"Why did ye say that ye were the Second?"

"Because if he had answered that call," he replied, jerking a thumb in the general direction of Christie. "He would've had your balls for breakfast!"

The second showed a minor interest in the phone message. The Canadian blithely related a general lack of understanding of the Scottish accent. "Damned idiots! Tell 'em that the revs per minute are one hundred and twenty-six point four."

Jake walked off to the phone and pretended to comply.

"Tell me Jake," began Angus. "How did ye ken whit the revs were?"

"That bastard isn't the only guy who can count around here. You subtract the noon rev counter reading from the one o'clock reading and divide the remainder by sixty, the minutes running. And that's it - revs per minute. Simple!"

For the remainder of the watch boilers had their superheat dampers gradually adjusted until steam temperatures rose to 400°F and the bridge requirement of one hundred and seventy-four revolutions per minute was achieved. Although MacKay had shown his face briefly to make sure everything was ok he had not called on the floater for other duties.

The watch was relieved without incident and the engineers changed from their coveralls into their patrol suits after a brief wash. A smorgasbord of cold meats, salads, cakes, fresh fruit and sundries was laid out for them in the mess. It was a high tea that he would write home about in his next letter. When the meal ended Jake declined his invitation of liquid refreshment saying that he needed to nap for an hour or two.

After enjoying a hot shower and a beer, he decided that this would be an ideal time to explore the ship. He dressed into his Number Ones and set off with a spring in his step.

It's just one thing on top of another!

1705 Thursday

TSTS *Queen of Dalriada* nosed through a head sea. It had just turned five o'clock in the afternoon yet the sun had already set. The Promenade Deck was brightly lit. Winds buffeting against the plate glass windows smeared the raindrops so that they reflected and dazzled like chromium or mercury strips. The ship's yawing, pitching and rolling made walking a new experience for Angus and forced him to lurch as if in some kind of hesitation waltz.

King wondered if there were any passengers on board at all when he observed a steward fussing around a deckchair mounded with plaid rugs and shawls. An elderly gentleman arose from beneath the blankets like some wizened butterfly from a chrysalis. Treating the steward like an irritating fly he feebly swatted at the persistent administrations and hobbled into the Long Gallery.

He followed them inside.

Complimenting shades of panelling held large oil and watercolour paintings depicting Scottish scenery. On display were smaller etchings, woodcuts and statuettes. Upholstered armchairs and sofas allowed artefacts to be enjoyed from comfort. Here and there doorways led off to smaller rooms or corridors. Moving across the deep piled Axminster carpet kept sound to a minimum although the vessel's constant movements pried frequent creaks from panelling.

He perceived an impressive exhibit of arms mounted on the forward bulkhead. It consisted of a pair of matched claymores with their crossed blades inverted, their ornate hilts inlaid with semiprecious stones. Superimposed on the claymores was a targe made of highly polished hardened leather. Two Scottish dirks, their blades secured in opposition to the claymores were part of the same exhibit. Only their pommelled hilts were visible, their long slim blades hidden by the targe.

New sights and interests spurred the clock and he had still much to see of the ship. Passengers were few and far between; perhaps winter in the North Atlantic was not to their liking. He was intrigued by the many public rooms and shops. Glass showcases located in various public squares displayed flags, banners, antiques and artefacts. Some were valuable gifts donated by famous personages who had travelled at one time or another during the ship's odysseys.

Often, he referred to *You Are Here* layouts that could be found in most public areas. He entered a lift to take him up another deck. When the doors slid open on Sun Deck he was facing his new shipmate, Jake White.

"I'll say one thing for you buddy," said Jake, tapping his wristwatch. "You're punctual - right?"

"Whit dae ye mean?"

"It's opening time - right?"

"If ye say so."

They'd met forward of midships, port side. Gesturing impatiently Jake guided his friend directly aft along a short corridor and ushered him into the engineers' wardroom. In the British Merchant Navy the officers' lounge or recreation room is called a saloon. The first chief engineer of the *Queen of Dalriada* was ex-Royal Navy and out of habit had always called the saloon 'wardroom'. Over the years the name stuck.

"A couple of pints of Dow porter please, Charlie!"

The little Irish bartender shoved a tankard under the single spigot and flicked it on. As cold beer gurgled and foamed he laughed courteously. "Mister White, you know we don't sell Canadian beer."

"You got that right. Well, give us two pints of lager," ordered Jake, slapping half-a-crown on shiny teak counter top. "Keep the change - eh?"

"A whole sixpence!" Sarcasm chilled his tone. "Gee t'anks!"

Jake ignored him. He lurched drunkenly past a collapsible ping-pong table. "Bring the beer over here Gus, and I'll find us some darts - right?"

"If ye say so."

The wardroom's interior piqued his curiosity as he lolled against the bar. The room was about thirty-five feet long. Four portholes, their blue-velvet curtains still open, stared out at the blackness of ocean. The inboard bulkhead was panelled with mahogany and honoured the inevitable portrait of Her Majesty, The Queen. Fore and aft of this painting were two fairly large gilt framed photographs of the ship steaming at high speed, one in wartime grey, the other in company livery.

A small library appropriated a large portion of the after bulkhead. It appeared to be equally stocked with comic books, hardbacks and paperbacks. The dartboard was in the outboard corner. Wide easy chairs and a couple of card tables cluttered the room's perimeter. Under the after porthole stood a small writing table, which at that moment was having one of its drawers rummaged for playing darts. A loud hoot proclaimed the discovery of the elusive projectiles.

A brace of foaming tankards came sliding onto the polished bar countertop.

"Thanks Charlie," grinned Angus, grabbing one.

The bar's design was worthy of scrutiny. It had been solidly constructed in the corner diagonally opposite to the dartboard. The countertop was solid mahogany and the front and side was padded with red vinyl. The brass foot rail had seen plenty of use. A dozen stools girdled the bar behind which a few shelves were adorned with silver cups, plaques, mementoes and other trophies from inter-company ships' contests won by unknown engineers in a dim bygone era.

"Hey - are you going to hold up that bar all night?" hollered Jake. "Let's play darts."

"Ok, Ah'm comin'. Dinnae get your knickers in a twist!"

He grabbed the second tankard and fox-trotted towards the dartboard in cadence to the ocean's swells without broaching any liquid.

"Ah!" sighed Jake, after taking a sip with all the finesse and appreciation of the true beer connoisseur. "Now to thrash another Scotsman - right?"

"We'll see."

"Middle for diddle - right?"

Jake threw first, lodging his dart in the outer bull. His opponent's dart ricocheted off the knurled surface of the former onto the deck. "Hey!" he protested. "Robin Hood didn't wear a kilt! Throw again!"

The next throw was better. "Bulls-eye - nice dart!"

"Three-oh-one?"

"Ok. Go ahead. Play for a beer?"

"A' right," agreed King, accepting the challenge. His darts straddled double nineteen.

"Tough shit!" the fifth sang out with little sympathy. 'You need hair round it - eh?"

The game was short and sweet for the Canadian who slurped down his winnings with exaggerated relish.

During the second game Angus came into his own. The weather had veered a few degrees, inducing the liner's motion to become more erratic. Jake had played darts many times at sea but he had never quite developed the knack for timing throws with the ship's movements. On the other hand the Scot seemed to synchronise his missiles perfectly. Whether naturally or by chance White could not determine but he realised that the competition was going to be stiff.

The third game had just checked off when Larry Treen bowled in with a fat Welshman in tow. When he and Taffy Morgan espied the players Larry nudged his companion.

"Look who's here, Taff - the Bobbidi Twins!"

Taffy flagged Charlie for a couple of lagers and lilted, "I thought it was the Bibbidi Twins!"

Jake, who was throwing, said nothing but his neck reddened noticeably. He missed his target by a wide margin.

"Hey Right, do you fancy a foursome?" Larry called over.

"Yeah," responded the Canadian, hauling his darts out. "Bring over four beers - eh?"

"I meant darts Right," retorted Treen.

"I know what you meant," laughed White. "Bring the beers over anyway. It'll save you a trip when we beat you - right?"

The newcomers waltzed over toting a lager in each hand and watched Jake meet his Waterloo.

"Ok," said White, dialling the mechanical calculators to five-oh-one. "D'you guys want to diddle for partners?"

"Larry, how's about me 'n' you play the Bibbidi Twins?" proposed Taffy.

"I'm game," agreed Larry.

Halfway through the second game when was his turn to throw, Taffy carelessly left his tankard adrift from its fiddle. It slid on the next roll and upended on the parquet deck. Larry was disgusted. “Look at that! You can’t bring him anywhere!”

“Charlie!” White hollered. “Have you got a wiper handy?”

“I’ll clean it up Mister White,” volunteered Charlie.

The steward opened a panel nearby to reveal a broom, a mop, and a bucket, in which to clean up the spill. Morgan tried to save face with a bit of humour. The broom was commandeered as an imaginary guitar. ‘Bibbidi, Bobbidi, Boo’ was hushed in mid-boo when Jake’s fist hovered under the Welshman’s button nose.

Undaunted he tried another ploy. Inverting the broom, he tucked the bristled crosspiece under his left arm and leaned on the makeshift crutch. Raising his left foot he utilized a chair’s armrest behind him to keep the lower portion of his leg from sight. With somebody’s cap placed sideways on his head, he closed his left eye. Taffy seemed to have the ability to cause his other eye to bulge at will. This repertoire must have been practised on a regular basis because these contortions appeared to have come naturally.

“’Ere Jim lad!” he growled, mimicking Robert Newton’s caricature of Long John Silver. “Fetch me an apple from the bahr’l. Aarrr!” His chubby features flushed with his efforts and his shipmates, showing evident amusement, coaxed him deeper into character. “The name be Silver,” he said, quite unnecessarily. “Long John Silver. Ah-haarrr!” Suddenly his tone leapt almost three octaves into a falsetto cry, “Pieces-of-eight! Pieces-of-eight!” The deep, crushed granite voice returned instantaneously, “Furk orf, ye baarstard!” he shouted, swiping a phantom parrot from its flabby perch.

The wardroom resounded with hilarity. Charlie mopped up and the game resumed. The deteriorating weather appeared to give the darts a mind of their own. During one particular game Treen completely missed the dartboard twice out of three throws.

This was enough to incite Taffy to exclaim, "Flint's ghost! And Oi thort Oi was playin' with Jim Hawrkins and 'ere, boi thonder, it's Bloind blody Pew!"

Treen redeemed himself by winning the game with a bulls-eye. Taffy waddled over to confirm the shot. Gloating at the opposition he just couldn't resist another Long John imitation. "The black spot, boi thonder! Them those dies'll be the lucky uns! Ah-haarrr!"

The bartender reminded the group that it was time for dinner. The friends finished their beer, promising to resume their match later.

1911

The Tooth Fairy patiently waited while Angus perused the menu. He had never witnessed such a correlation of foods. It was obvious that ships' officers dined in the style of first class passengers. He ordered pineapple juice and consommé Mikado before passing the menu to Jake who passed it to Larry without even a glance, asking the steward, "Toni, what - uh - horses' doovres d'you recommend tonight?"

"Hors d'oeuvres, Mister White?" corrected Toni. "There are two kinds of herring available; herring in tomato, and Bismarck. Both are very nice. Then there's Bordeaux sardines and *Endive a la Grecque* that you like."

"You got that right. I'll have them with - uh - some of the herrings in tomato, none of that Hun crap sweetheart. Chuck in a couple of sardines and - uh - put some *saucisson d'Arles* at the side - right?"

"Very good luv. Mister Treen?"

"I'm going straight into the main course tonight, Toni. What's that *Scallopini Imbotti* like?" Larry inquired.

"The continental speciality, sir?" Toni rolled a hand back and forth with a Gallic gesture before replying, "*Comme Ce, comme ca.*"

"Ok then. I'll have the grill - minute steak, *Beurre Michael*, with baked Idaho potato and braised onion *au jus*."

"Thank you sir - and Mister Morgan?"

"Grapefruit juice please and I'll have a plateful of this *Potage Cultivateur*."

Service was swift and exact. Remarks were passed on the steward's memory and alertness as they dined. Toni was quick to remove empty plates or advise on the next course.

"You got that right! She deserves a pat on the back, eh?"

"Or the bum," grinned Larry.

At meal's end Taffy ordered some *Pont l'Eveque* cheese, crackers and coffee.

"Haven't you finished yet?" Larry asked.

"I just want the cheese," Morgan answered him, and beamed. "The crackers are for the parrot!"

2106

Cigarette smoke palled in the crowded wardroom. Two card games were in progress and a few engineers propped up the bar. The dartboard was not in use. Just clear of dart fallout range two adventurous souls were engrossed in a chess game. Angus fetched a round of lager while his three comrades warmed up. Engineers trickled in for a drop and others dropped out for a trickle. Around nine o'clock the dart players unanimously called it a day. White and King left first.

On Sun Deck Square Jake pressed the lift button.

"Where are ye gaun?"

"I'm going for writing paper," replied Jake.

"Ah've got some in my cabin that Ah can gie ye."

"No thanks buddy. Do you know what? You'll get more prestige if you - uh - use the ship's notepaper."

"Where dae ye get that?"

The elevator doors slid open.

"Come with me and I'll show you - right?"

"If ye say so."

A middle-aged lady and a young man, who may have been her son or gigolo, were the only passengers in the Long Gallery when the engineers ambled through. King was led to a tiny writing alcove inset from the main public room. A pristine blotting pad topped a veneered writing table. Loose sheets of pale-blue writing paper, each bearing an RMS *Queen of Dalriada* header, were stacked neatly on the table. Letter-postcards sporting a coloured print of the ship were available too.

"Whit does RMS mean?"

"Royal Mail Ship," replied Jake. "The British Government gives that honorific to a ship if it carries mail."

"So how come she's listed TSTS on the engineroom log?"

"That's how she's powered: Twin Screw Turbine Ship."

They purloined enough writing materials for their needs before heading towards the plate glass doors nearest the Scottish arms exhibit.

"That's a bit strange." Jake stopped short in his tracks.

"Whit is?"

"One of the dirks is missing," he replied. "One of the dockies must have nicked it while we were in port - right?" His shipmate shook his head, assuring him that it was there when he had passed through at earlier that evening. "Really? Maybe we should tell somebody."

A passing steward was delegated to relay this information to the proper authority: The chief steward? The chief master-at-arms? The bridge? Jake neither knew or cared, he just wanted to catch some zizz time before going on watch.

2115

The chief steward and the chief master-at-arms were already aware of the missing dirk. They also knew where it was, as did all of the ship's department heads. It was next door, in the bedroom of Cabin B17. They lingered quietly in the plush stateroom of that cabin eyeing the captain mull over the flimsy that had just been handed to him by a wireless officer.

Christina Hastings, the ship's comely photographer, was collapsing a studio light tripod. Her face was ashen. The chief steward responded to a rap on the door. The bosun stood on the threshold reluctant to enter.

"Come in Bosun and close the door," said Robert Cowell, the master. He waggled the radio signal at the group. "This is from our Marine Superintendent. The Criminal Investigation Division in London has relayed this wire through him. They don't want the American police involved in this case." He faced the chief medical officer and taking a deep breath asked, "Do you have an approximate time of death, Doctor?"

The diagnosis was confirmed. "Death probably occurred around seven or eight this evening," he surmised. "The bodies were still quite warm when I examined them."

"Very well that brings us to you Mister Brooke." The captain gazed across the room at his third officer. "I'd like you to ask the carpenter to knock up a box big enough to hold the pair of them."

The third mate nodded silently. The engineering department was next on the agenda. Forensics (CID) had directed a method to keep decomposition to a minimum by recommending that the coffin be sealed with copper sheeting.

The chief engineer was sure the plumber had a fair stock of sheet copper on board and was quite adept with his sheet metal brake. He could fabricate a sheath for the coffin in no time at all.

"I don't suppose you've used much fish since we sailed," guessed the captain. He watched the chief catering officer nod his head in glum agreement. "You'll have to make room for it in the fish refrigerator somehow. Use more of it on the menu or something."

"Captain, nobody wants to eat fish once they find out there's a stiff keeping them company," groaned the chief steward. He went on, "And it's pretty hard to keep it a secret. How long is the coffin going to be in the fridge anyway?"

"When the New York Health Authority have affixed their seal to the coffin, it'll be placed in bond by American customs ready to be loaded on board MV *Eithne* which sails for Glasgow shortly after we dock."

On land or at sea the old adage 'the person most concerned is always the last to know' in this case applied to the bosun. He was reflecting that he was the only Indian among all those chiefs when the captain turned to him.

"Well Bosun, it's Galbraith, isn't it?" He observed the reluctant assent. "Have you got a strong stomach?"

The bosun had seen quite a bit of life - and death - in his time but he had this ominous feeling that the next few minutes were going to be unpleasant. Cowell opened the bedroom door and gestured with his head for the bosun to accompany him inside. Galbraith's brown eyes panned the solemn faces around him and gulped. He went into the bedroom, the MA in his wake.

A luxurious king-sized bed held a naked man coupled in death with a slim woman whose damp streaky hair lay fanned in ropes across her pillow like some russet Medusa. The man was transfixed to the woman in the missionary position by the Scottish dirk from the Long Gallery instead of the customary appendage. Surprisingly there was little blood, just a few drops that had welled in the small of the dead man's back. Twin crimson smears caused by the last futile grasping of the woman's right hand had congealed above her lover's left kidney.

It must have taken great strength to plunge the weapon through both bodies at once. Perhaps the killer just leaned his full weight against the pommel after stabbing the man and let the woman squirm underneath. Triple mirrors on an adjacent dressing table reflected the macabre vision over and over again into infinity.

Cowell hailed through. "What are their names again?"

The chief purser nervously referred to his clipboard but remained where he was. He had absolutely no intention of getting any nearer to the tragedy than he had to. "Mi - Mi - " he stuttered. "Mrs. Katherine Davis and George Brown QC. Mrs. Davis has - eh - had Cabin A34."

The skipper's observation was somewhat sardonic. "They weren't married to each other in life but they're certainly cleaved to each other now." He cupped the bosun's elbow and applied gentle pressure to coax the man nearer to the bed. "Well Galbraith, this is what needs to be done. CID doesn't want 'em separated and they certainly won't want any clues disturbed. God, talk about having their cake! Anyway let's cover them up."

The three men drew the sheets over the corpses. "Get a bit of sail cloth under them. Tilbury here was a copper before he became an MA. He'll help you to make sure none of the clues are lost. And for God's sake, don't touch the hilt of that dagger. You can sew 'em up after that," he resumed. "You don't have to put the last stitch through their noses like the old days."

The bosun threw him a startled glance.

"But you'll get your tot of rum anyway, or maybe it should be two?"

The bosun was not going to argue with his boss although he did hint that a little Dutch courage might make his task easier. The department heads were dismissed and the chief steward was bid to lock the cabin and hand over the key to the chief officer for safekeeping after the bodies had been moved.

2345

It was quite peculiar, he thought, checking his watch for the third time. The watch was due to commence in fifteen minutes yet he had not seen any of the watchkeepers, not in the changeroom nor in the elevator. He had even seen the usual black gang on their way to the engine spaces.

Strange.

Not being hungry King had bypassed the mess. He shook his watch and listened carefully. It was still going. Late again!

Climbing into his boilersuit he philosophically resigned himself to another rollicking bollicking from the crabbit Christie.

The platform second showed evident surprise observing his descent into the engineroom and glanced meaningfully at the control board clock with his approach. "You are very early tonight. I wish my relief was as good, Mister - ah?"

"King sir. Ah'm just reportin' ten minutes early as per Mister Christie's instructions."

"My name is Ken Wood, the Platform Second of this Watch, and you are precisely one half hour early."

Puzzled King asked, "How dae ye figure that oot?"

"Didn't anyone tell you about the ship's clocks being stopped at midnight for one hour?"

"That's news tae me!"

"For every fifteen degrees longitude travelled west the clock goes back or rather stops for one hour," intoned Woods. "That means, my Scottish friend, that every evening watch is twenty minutes longer. Understand?"

The boiler room telephone buzzed.

"Would you answer that please?" he requested.

"Engineroom."

"Finished blowing tubes."

"Ok."

He relayed the message then asked what it meant.

"About time too!" grunted the second. A pleasant smile suddenly enveloped his face. "Now then - er - Mister King, in answer to your question: soot collects around every boiler's watertubes, insulating them, which lowers their efficiency. This soot is blown off every night by jets of steam and sent up the funnel. We always do this when the passengers are asleep.

That way nobody gets annoyed when great gobs of black shit falls on them." From the console came a faint ringing sound. "Damn!" he grimaced. "We still haven't got rid of it!"

"Whit's wrong?"

"A mild case of condenseritis! It's an ailment common to steam engines," joked the second. "We'll continue treatment with another injection of the marine engineers' wonder serum: sawdust!"

He leaned over the handrail on the starboard wing of and bellowed at his two juniors below. "Do it again!"

Angus eyed The Mekon squatting below near the condenser's base brushing sawdust from his hair and body, a burlap bag at his side. The other junior unscrewed a big plug from a pipe connected to the condenser. They poured sawdust into the opening and Wood explained their intent.

"Inside each condenser are thousands and thousands of copper tubes through which seawater is pumped. As exhaust steam from the LP turbine passes between these tubes, it condenses and the resulting water is reclaimed for the boiler feed system.

"At this very moment there's a tiny leak in one of those tubes. The vacuum created within the condenser is sucking in minute quantities of seawater that contaminated the distilled water. That gauge there on the console monitors the purity of the system. If the salt level registers more than zero point two grains per gallon it activates that bell that you just heard.

"What we're doing now is mixing sawdust with the seawater supply to the condenser in the hope that the vacuum sucks a chip of sawdust into the hole and plugs the leak." Woods acknowledged his juniors' completion signal. "Ok? Open the cocks!"

"Whit happens if ye cannae plug the leak?"

"We'll have to shut down the engine, climb inside the condenser, and search for the tube that created the problem. Then we'll plug it."

The engineers' efforts achieved success that time and the warning bell remained silent, which satisfied Woods. King, always seeking answers to aid him in his new career asked, "How many tries did it take ye?"

"Five," replied Woods. "Sometimes, if you're lucky, it seals first time. I remember . . ." he broke off, a spark of mischief in his eye. "We had a really bad case of condenseritis on this one trip. We shoved in tons and tons until we ran out of sawdust and all to no avail."

The greenhorn rose to the bait. "Whit did ye dae?"

"Well, the Chief was a Scot like yourself and with typical Scottish ingenuity he commandeered five bags of oatmeal from the cook. He had a theory that when injected it would expand like sawdust and plug the leak.'

"Did it work?" the junior pressed.

"Yes. It took all of the oatmeal but it worked. It was an absolutely brilliant idea," Woods solemnly assured him. Then a curious expression came over his face. "But the very next day shortly after sunrise, the skipper got him on the blower and gave him shit!"

"Whit for?" queried Angus, before guessing: "Because he wasted food?"

"No," answered Wood keeping his face straight. "That night after we had blown tubes, the whole Boat Deck was covered in black gooey porridge!"

That is hilarious, thought Angus. He was still chuckling when The Mekon came to hand over the watch. With a nod he acknowledged James Johns, a lanky sandy-haired junior. The Mekon introduced him. Johns was in his late thirties and was of average height, a sallow complexion with blue eyes and greying sandy hair at the temples.

Since he was listed below another engineer called James Johns on the engineers' roster, this chap was distinguished as Jas. Johns. With a ready smile the fellow surprised him by performing a brief tap dancing routine before extending a hand in a finale. Delighted by King's gaped expression he beamed, "You can call me 'Jazz'."

He motioned his head at the mute alarm. "It looks like we got it that time Mister Woods."

Woods agreed and told the Mekon that it was now ok for him to hand over the watch to his relief.

Ten minutes later Christie materialized at the top of the engineroom ladder attired in a clean boilersuit and flaunting snow-white work gloves. Supporting his full body weight on the ladder handrails he held his legs balanced horizontally in front of him then slowly slid down to platform level. Jake White showed up a couple of minutes later and the watch changed over. A quick check ensured all was running normal. The regular watchkeeping duties would take effect right after a welcome cup of tea.

The walking second climbed wearily up the platform's access ladder. He discussed the condenser problem with Christie then charged the floater to accompany him on his rounds.

By the time they had gone through the rest of the machinery spaces to be introduced to the rest of the watch engineers it was time for smoko. They adjourned to his office for the usual cup of cocoa.

Over the brim of his cup MacKay thoughtfully gazed at his junior. By and by he made up his mind and broke the silence to ask him, “Tell me, do you know how to solder, lad?”

“Och aye, nae bother.”

“Are you squeamish?”

“No - Ah dinnae think so,” the floater replied slowly, and at the same time wondering where this was leading.

Persistent MacKay edged forward in his chair. “What I mean lad is - are you afraid of the dead?” His sepulchral tone stirred the young man’s imagination.

Warlocks, beasties and ghosts birled and danced through the fertile mind. A long drawn-out no-o came hesitantly. “Ah dinnae think so.”

“That’s just grand then,” beamed MacKay. “I’ve got a fine wee job for you. It’s quite unusual and by rights the plumber should be handling it because he’s got all the brazing gear. But he’s a nervous soul and that’s why I’d like you to do it.”

‘Whit have Ah got mysel’ in for?’ Angus ruminated with foreboding.

“Come along then Mister King,” encouraged MacKay, suddenly vacating his chair. “I’ll explain on the way.” They left the office and made their way aft along the working alleyway. “Two passengers were murdered last night.”

The impact of this statement would have brought him to a sudden halt except for the fact that a massive hand encompassed the youth’s upper arm. Without breaking stride the second steered him along the alleyway quite oblivious to his junior’s sudden reluctance. He either had to resume the pace or lose his arm.

“It’s been decided to place them together in a sealed coffin. That’s where you come in. I want you to it.”

They descended to D Deck.

"Is that no' the carpenter's job? A' he has tae dae is screw the lid doon."

They halted by a large door. MacKay hauled on its thick wrought-iron handle. The heavy door creaked open with a nerve tingling screech. They entered to find a long copper clad box perched across two sawhorses. Curiously the pommel of a dagger protruded from a hole in the copper lid. The second bent down, picked up a fire bar from the deck and let it drop on the lid of the box. A hollow thump resounded throughout the dimly lit storage space.

He showed the junior a portion of the wooden lid by lifting a corner of the copper sheeting.

"You can see why Chippy couldn't fit a lid on top," he said. "Use this broken piece of fire bar as a clamp. It'll help to prevent the copper sheathing from warping. The soldering gear and some other tools are over in the corner there. All right lad?"

No answer.

"I said, 'All right lad?'" repeated the second with a nudge.

"Eh - eh - oh - aye - right!"

"If you need me, I'll be in my office," said MacKay. "Oh - I almost forgot, you'll find one half of a copper float from a lavatory cistern with the tool kit. Use it to cap yon dagger hilt and then solder it to the lid."

The door closed behind him moaning that same awful squeak. He methodically set up the plumber's gear. There were three heavy soldering irons, a Primus stove with a cradle to support them, some flat files, soldering wire, flux, some steel wool, a flask of methylated spirits and a can of paraffin, or kerosene as his Canadian buddy would've called it. He figured that the most convenient place for the stove would be on the deck beneath the coffin.

While he waited for the stove to heat up, the heads of the soldering irons were filed clean ready for coating with flux. He hand pumped the stove to pressurise the reservoir and used the cradle to position the irons in the flames. Steel wool burnished the sealing surfaces until they too were ready to be smeared with a liberal coating of flux. He aligned the copper sheet and started to tack the corners.

Angus had only been working for a couple of minutes when he became aware of the strange creaks and groans that are typical of a ship at sea. A wisp of smoke billowed up from the melting flux. Uneasily his eyes panned the gloomy room. Flickering flames from the stove cast shadows of dancing wraiths on the dank bulkhead. His knees trembled.

The vessel's stern dipped and shuddered in a following sea and he was forced to maintain his balance by clinging to the coffin. It was at this particular moment that he heard a noise from inside the casket. He stared at it in terror.

Thump!

There it was again and definitely from within! That was enough to send him bounding for the door. With a sob he grasped the handle with both hands and heaved for all his worth. This powerful effort was just too much for the screw nails in the tired wood. He gaped at the handle dangling limply in his hand before throwing it at the coffin. Leaning weakly against the door the engineer let out a little yelp when he found himself falling backwards. In his panic he'd forgotten that the door opened from the opposite direction. He leapt to his feet, darted up the ladder and ran like hell for the second's office. He babbled his tale to the astonished gentleman who phoned the doctor. They arranged to meet by the coffin as soon as possible.

0305 Friday

The ship's second medical officer used surgical scissors to cut the sailcloth stitching. The two engineers stared at the horrific embrace as the doctor casually peeled back the fabric to search for signs of life. Angus recognised the dirk that pinned the lovers together. What a terrible sight! It didn't take long for the doctor to reconfirm his diagnosis.

"It's just as I told you Mister MacKay," said the doctor, stuffing a stethoscope into his jacket pocket. "Both of them are as dead as doornails."

"But Mister King heard something. What was it?"

The MO eyed the cadavers. "It's possible that the motion of the ship caused an arm to slip. Rigor mortis is still in progress. I can't think of any other reason."

"Thank you Doctor," said MacKay. "Carry on Mister King, and you were right to call me."

He was alone again. There was something about the pair inside the coffin - something over and above the horrific coupling that he had just witnessed. Concentration on the task at hand pushed this feeling back down into the deep dark morass of his subconscious. He had only been soldering for about ten minutes when his taut nerves were plucked by a muffled moan.

Shakily, he downed his tools. "Take it easy," he whispered to himself. "Dinnae panic again."

The engineer inserted a cigarette between his quivering lips, his right wrist trying to steady the shimmering flame licking the tipped end of his cigarette. Inhaling deeply he keeled over in a spasmodic fit of coughing, the cigarette spat to the deck. He drooped over the coffin momentarily in an effort to catch his breath. His ear touched the copper dome on the lid.

"Oooooo!" repeated the demonic moan from within.

This was too much for the young man. Like one demented he dived from the room and barrelled up the ladder four steps at a time. He reached the working alleyway heaving until his breathing eased. Fear seemed to be playing havoc with a certain sphincter muscle. "Why did Ah ever join the navy?" he gasped, and ran in search of the senior second engineer.

"Let me guess Mister King," the second calmly ventured. "You've heard another noise."

With hands on his knees and chest heaving the floater acknowledged between gasps. His senior shook his head and reached for the phone.

The trio rendezvoused by the coffin again. The doctor puffed at his pipe while the junior broke open the partial seal. The young engineer gave an involuntary yelp when he slid off the cover. All his attention was riveted on the woman's face. Her eyes were open! The couple was pronounced dead for the third time that night.

"But there were twa moans!" he insisted. "An' look, her eyes are open!"

The physician tapped his pipe against one of the sawhorses and jabbed the stem at the oil stove below. "The heat from that thing probably expanded the gas in her stomach or maybe his stomach. It would make a noise passing through the glottis. The muscles that open her eyes probably contracted by the heat. There is nothing to worry about Mister King."

His reassurance did little for the youth's sense of well being.

"Carry on, lad!" ordered MacKay and escorted the doctor to the door.

"Haud up ther!" protested Angus, his burr becoming much, much broader. "Ah dinnae waant tae be disrespectfu', bit wid youse baith bide oan here this time until Ah feenish the joab?"

The physician glanced at the senior engineer. "Roughly translated - does that mean that he wants us to stay until he finishes the job?"

The second nodded.

With a shrug the tired medical officer sighed. "I suppose I must. I was only going to grab some sleep anyway." And winking at MacKay said, "That's the trouble with this profession - it's just one thing on top of another!"

Angus had trouble getting to sleep when that watch had finished but fatigue soon subdued his active mind. However his imagination ceased to be curbed for nightmares made him toss and turn until sunrise.

Penguin Patrol

1045

The combined efforts of the storekeeper and a clamouring bell managed to rouse him from a deep slumber. He shied from the light, his eyes blinking furiously before glaring their bloodshot rancour at the rating.

"Dinnae tell me it's time for watch already!" moaned a tired Angus.

"No Mister King," the storekeeper replied brightly. "Can't you hear the emergency bells ringing? It's quarter-to-eleven. Emergency Drill is in fifteen minutes."

"Ok thanks."

With supreme effort he hauled his weary body from the soft warm bunk. Stepping into his trousers he groped his way to the sink. The mirror reflected a drawn face, its chin coated with russet stubble. A yawn followed a shudder that tried to suppress an ice-cold spine-tingling sensation triggered by recollections from the previous watch.

He vigorously shook his head in a hopeless attempt to physically expunge that train of thought. Cold water sloshed on his face flushed the sleep from his eyes. The completion of his ablutions made him feel much better. He dressed into his doeskin uniform and enveloped himself in his lifejacket then donned his cap.

Engineers of all ages, shapes and sizes loitered in the vestibule waiting for the elevator. He blended with the milling herd. The lift doors clattered open and he was caught in the sudden surge to fill the void. Harris squeezed in just as the doors were sliding shut and someone yelled, "For Christ's sake, throw that bastard out!"

The engineer nearest to Harris shouldered him back out before slamming the doors in his face. Why Bomber warranted such treatment still remained an enigma to Angus. Prior to the doors closing, he had caught a glimpse of the Canadian's head bobbing about in the throng awaiting the next shuttle.

The elevator jerked to a halt on C Deck and vomited a river of white-capped turtles with blue and orange carapaces. King anchored himself to a handrail and let the mob gush past. Anticipating another rabble from the returning elevator he was surprised to see the solitary figure of Bomber Harris. Maxie, forlorn and unwanted, trailing in the spoor of the first load of engineers. Jake was part of the lift's subsequent cargo that disgorged with the same boisterous abandon.

Angus hooked onto his friend's lifejacket to become another piece of flotsam until the Pig Deck came into view. The Emergency Generator Room was on the port side of B Deck at the top of the companionway directly aft of the 'Pig and Whistle', the crew's bar and recreation area.

They melded into the human amphitheatre that had formed around a huge engine and generating motor assembly. Engineers chatted and joked until the full complement was present. Emergency bells, which were strategically placed at points throughout the ship, suddenly became silent to everyone's relief. Claus Milton, the Hotel Service Engineer, was a tall lanky fellow, balding in early middle age.

As his job title implied he was responsible for all machinery units affecting the welfare of the passengers and crew. There were myriad units that consisted of such things as air conditioning, galley equipment and other little gems of comfort that are always taken for granted aboard ship. The HSE's other responsibilities included the maintenance and operation of the emergency generator engines, all deck machinery; lifeboats, watertight doors, and steering gear.

But the emergency generator's driving engine was his pride and joy because he looked after it as a benevolent uncle might treat a favourite nephew. Gleaming proof of this ardour reflected in highly polished brass and copper fittings.

Making some final adjustments, and satisfied that the ancient engine was ready to go through its paces, the HSE recited a timeworn procedure for starting this mechanical wonder to bored and interested alike. King and White squeezed through the tightly knit throng. Closer observation revealed that the Perkins engine had sixteen cylinders in line and would be started on gasoline before being switched over to kerosene.

"It was probably old - uh - when Henry Ford was an apprentice - right?"

"Aye," replied Angus. "An' maybe it lit Edison's electric bulbs!"

The HSE completed his repertoire and was gearing up for the grand finale. "Gentlemen, could I have your full attention please? I will now demonstrate how one should start this engineering marvel." He pointed to a brass spigot in the carburettor feed line. "Open that brass cock somebody."

A hand reached up and complied.

"Right - watch this!"

"Are you watching Right?" asked somebody.

With great effort the HSE cranked the starting handle. Gradually the speed built up until sweat on his brow and farts from his backside inspired him to believe that he had sufficient momentum. "Now!" he gasped.

A bystander firmly pushed a rod, which closed the decompression cocks on all sixteen cylinders simultaneously. A loud bang preceded a puff of blue smoke from a hole in the exhaust manifold. The HSE grimaced in pain, favouring his starboard wrist. The engineer next to Angus held out his hand palm upward to receive a ten-shilling note from his neighbour.

MacKay who had been chatting away to the chief engineer and the nearly somnolent Slack Jack Williamson, the Third Senior Second Engineer and walking second of the four-to-eight watch, became aware of what had happened. He bulldozed his way to the front of the crowd and edged the stricken HSE unceremoniously to one side. He reset the linkage rod, pressed the ignition button before reapplying total compression.

The enclosed space of the emergency generator room magnified the engine's roar of triumph, inducing part of the audience to step back in awe. He nodded to the electrician by the switchboard. Some copper knife switches were thrown in. Lights dimmed into orange rosettes which were unwilling to flicker back to half their original brilliance. The electrician reversed the procedure and normal power was resumed. MacKay killed the engine before reverting his attention to the suffering HSE.

"I've warned you before. The batteries quite are sufficient for the job," he berated him. "If you have 'em checked on a regular basis we'll have no problem in a real emergency. I could've bloody well walked ashore by the time you've taken to get this thing going manually!"

From behind came a whisper. "Now Big John thinks he's the bloke from Galilee!"

"Aye," was the reply? "Somebody should tell Uncle Miltie to touch big John's gold braid. It'll save him the trouble of going to Sick Bay!"

"Don't be daft man," a wag objected. "That only works for syph!"

The sea of engineers parted, allowing passage for a muttering HSE and his sympathetic helpers. The generator room evacuated and everyone went to his emergency station so that his name could be ticked off the mate's roster. The whole drill only lasted for about twenty minutes or so. Alarm bells rang again briefly to signify its completion.

Again they were milling around near the elevator doors awaiting transportation back to their quarters. Angus was last to enter the cage. Harris shoved into the lift at the last instant, forcefully cramming him against the throng. The doors slammed shut and the UP button pushed before retaliation could take place.

"God!" wailed a voice. "What idiot let him in?"

Harris giggled before initiating a countdown: "Five, four, three, two, one . . . Bomb gone!"

A ghastly stench permeated the restricted space. Someone gagged. King poked his nose into the soft lining of Bomber's life jacket and inhaled sparingly. His peripheral vision picked up a diverse range of facial hues that only could've been envied by a chameleon.

Harris smacked the stop button to drop another disgusting audible outrage.

"Oh no!" whimpered a voice.

"Start up this bloody lift!" snarled someone else.

Reaching around Bomber's waist Angus restarted the lift. The doors crashed open at Sun Deck level and grown men staggered out with tear-filled eyes.

"Boy, that was close!" wheezed Jake. "I was nearly looking for Hughie there."

"Who's Hughie?"

"D'you know what? It's a term for seasickness - right?"

"How can it be right when Ah dinnae understand?"

"You will when you see a guy hanging over a rail shouting 'Hew-aaay!' Right?"

The penny dropped, bringing a chuckle from him. Jake considered it odd that his new shipmate was unaffected by the barnyard stench. "So - uh - how come you're not barfing? You were right in the line of fire."

"Simple. Ah just stuck my nose intae Bomber's life jacket an' used it as a filter."

"Really? Hey, I wish I hadda thought of that!"

"Ye will Jake," he predicted. "Ye will!"

Reverting back to the subject at hand, he said. "Ah've smelled some wicked farts in my time but nuthin' like Bomber's!"

"Tell me about it. They're absolutely fucking putrid!" Jake assured his companion. "It's not just a hobby with him. It's a way of life! Not only must that guy have something wrong with his guts he - uh - capitalizes on his affliction by eating all the wind food available; cabbage, peas, beans, and stuff like that. And then - uh - adds onion and garlic for flavour!

"And you know what? He'll - uh - stalk some unsuspecting group and then let one go for maximum effect. Shitting in the elevator is just one of his favourite jokes." The Canadian screwed up his face as if he could taste it. "Huh - joke? One of these days somebody's gonna paint that bastard black with - uh - a white streak down his spine! That guy gives a whole new meaning to the word: Gag! Right?"

"Man! If he could dae that with perfumes," envisaged King. "He could dae a' the scent companies out o' business!"

"You got that right!"

Distant screams coming from the bottom of the elevator shaft interrupted their strange conversation. Bomber's ear was pressed hard against the door listening, his suppressed giggles making his frame quiver. He glanced at the pair watching him and tee-heed.

"Just sent one down by itself. Delayed action!"

1815

His first afternoon at sea was being spent sprawled out on an easy chair totally absorbed in the Ian Fleming novel, *Thunderball*. The main character was honing in on Blofeld, the boss of SPECTRE when the curtain screening his open doorway rippled catching his eye. He blinked up at Jake's grinning face.

"Whit's up?"

"While you were - uh - wasting your time with your nose stuck in a book I was down at the - uh - cabin class swimming pool arranging a date for us with a couple of chicks. You are interested - right?"

The paperback was tossed aside. "Sounds guid tae me." He frowned. "Is it no' against regulations tae entertain passengers in our cabins?"

"You know what? Rules are made to broken fella!" Jake declared airily. "Do we trim in these girls or not?"

"Right oan!"

"Ok. Here's - uh - the setup," proposed Jake. "When the stewards have knocked off for the night, I'll - uh - trim the broads into my cabin. You're the lookout. Warn me with a whistle if any brass appears - right?"

Angus gloated and rubbed his hands. "Grand stuff!"

The mystic hour passed, and by nine thirty, the lechers had managed to get their charges into White's cabin undetected. Both girls were American and came attractively wrapped in low-cut dresses. Sylvia, a tall and buxom blonde, had been described by Jake as 'a forced draught job', a lewd expression which convinced the Scot that she could fan any mediocre ember into burning desire with minor effort. The tanned brunette, whose violet eyes sparkled with excitement, was shorter than her companion but was just as desirable.

Yvonne's gait sort of bounced and swivelled the most curvaceous parts of her body when she moved. Both girls had been warned about amorous seafarers.

Offers of drink sped through introductions. Sylvia requested a Bloody Mary and Yvonne showed preference for a screwdriver. This turned out to be quite fortuitous since the engineers' pooled resources were vodka and beer. Light banter broke the ice and the hosts presently discovered that the girls were winding down from a long vacation, which encompassed the French Riviera, London, and Scotland.

The mention of his homeland stirred King's attention but he was disappointed to learn that they had only been to Edinburgh. Late autumn was *gey dreich*, as he put it, to be touring the Highlands. The ladies admitted that they had sampled haggis and pooh-poohed his techniques for catching the legendary beast. A loud rap on the door threw a hush into the conversation.

Jake moved against the door and murmured through the ventilator. "What's the password?"

An indelicate bellow pierced the door slats. "A big Wheelkey! Now open this fuckin' door!"

"It's Will Keyes!" groaned Jake. Flustered, he unlocked the door and opened it just enough to peep out. He staggered back under the full impetus of the Glaswegian's weight heaving the door fully ajar.

"What in the fuck is going on?" he demanded.

"Sshh - there are ladies present!" warned White, a finger to his lips,

If Jake expected him to heed this warning and depart he couldn't have been more wrong. In fact it was an incentive to barge in. Ignoring his reluctant host he just elbowed past him into the cabin. "I apologise for my profound language ladies!" he said, pouring on the charm while deftly closing the door behind him.

White corrected him. "Profane, you idiot!"

"Profanity is in the ear of the beholder," he replied, accepting an unasked-for beer. With a grin he canted the bottle against the edge of the coffeetable and its cap was smote away by the heel of his hand.

"So piss in yours!"

Froth oozed over his knuckles onto the carpet. The interloper sat down next to Sylvia, gave her a lecherous wink and chug-a-lugged on the filched beer. A long mournful blast from the ship's whistle filtered into the cabin to pry the bottleneck from his lips.

"Hell's bells, shit, and damnation - a foggie! And my name's next on the bloody schedule! Shit and damnation!" he repeated vehemently.

"What's the matter?" asked Sylvia, anxiously.

Jake placed a reassuring hand on her bare shoulder. "He must go back down on duty - right? There's no problem," he added hurriedly. "Mister Keyes here can handle any trouble that may arise. This marine engineer has no peer - right?"

"Piss off, Right!" snorted Wheelkey, irked by the flattery and reached for the door.

"Where's the powder room?" asked Yvonne.

"Wheelkey - uh - check the bog when you go by, will you? Give us - uh - a whistle if all the traps are clear - right?"

"Ok Right."

A low whistle scudded up the passageway and the engineers escorted the giggling girls to the toilet.

"Ah guess yon Yankee lassies are smarter than Ah thought," King admitted to his fellow sentinel.

"No damned way," grunted White, craning his head round a corner in response to a noise in the passageway. It was an engineer returning to his cabin from the opposite direction. "I'll prove it to you when these two dames have finished draining their beavers - right?"

Sylvia had lived in Niagara Falls, New York, since she was fourteen. This information gave her and Jake common ground to discuss the Golden Horseshoe and the surrounding area. Periodical blasts from the foghorn would punctuate the conversation every three minutes. During one of these lulls White dolefully said, "I hope this fog clears up before the end of our watch. I'm next - uh - on the rota."

"Why are you required to do extra duties during fog?" asked Sylvia curiously.

"And what do you two do in the engineroom?" added Yvonne, her soft voice sparked with interest.

Casually Jake gave his shipmate a slow wink as he topped up their guests' drinks. Solemnly he laid it on with a trowel. "Well - uh - you know what? There are always two of us on standby at the same time - right? One engineer operates the brake in case we have to stop in a hurry. The other guy is on penguin patrol."

"Penguin patrol?" chorused both girls.

In spite of Jake's forewarning this off-the-cuff disclosure had Angus surprised as well but nevertheless he managed to maintain a straight face. He wondered if this unheard-of migration from Antarctica should be documented and forwarded to *National Geographic*. Either that Wheelkey could be out on deck right now scrounging for foil-wrapped chocolate biscuits.

The yarn continued. "It all stems from - uh - the sinking of the *Titanic*. It struck an iceberg back in 1912 - right? After that tragedy the American, Canadian and British coastguard - uh - established an ice patrol in the North Atlantic to destroy icebergs. Unfortunately - uh - penguins live on these icebergs. When their homes are obliterated, they - uh - become prey to polar bears and killer whales which chase them on board any ships that might be in their vicinity - right?"

"But penguins can't fly," protested Yvonne. "How can board an enormous ship like this?"

"You got that right," agreed Jake. "They can't fly but - uh - they can achieve such tremendous speeds in the water that when they break the surface - uh - the penguins actually glide through the air much - uh - in the same way flying fish do - right?"

"What happens to them when they land on deck?" insisted Sylvia, swallowing all this guff.

"The guy who's on penguin patrol clubs 'em to death and chucks 'em back in the sea," was the callous reply.

"Oh, that's cruel!" exclaimed Yvonne.

"But whit can we dae? Bird droppin's rot a' the planks."

"Right on!" asserted White. "We once to kept them for zoos but - uh - now they're overpopulated with penguins."

"Surely something can be done," persisted Yvonne.

"I'm afraid there's no solution," replied Jake, shaking his head. "Of course we could - uh - just toss 'em over the wall without killing them but they would probably come back on board again - that is - the ones that aren't dragged into the propellers and - uh - minced up - right?"

He sought to embellish this already bizarre tale with further thought. "Now - uh - roundabout at this time last year a deckhand forgot to coil a rope up properly and an end fell into the drink during some rough weather. Nobody noticed it hanging over the wall and during a foggy night, a night just like this." He paused to listen at the foghorn bleat its desired effect. "A polar bear climbed up the rope and ravaged the Boat Deck. And what a terrible scene it was! Y'know, merchant officers aren't armed so we had to fight it with clubs and marline spikes - right?"

"What happened?" panted Sylvia, totally enthralled.

The Canuck flexed his left shoulder and winced as if recollecting the injury that he had received during the chimerical battle. "The bear tore through our ranks and galloped up the bridge ladder. It - uh - smashed into the wheelhouse and went for the helmsman, but - uh - luckily for him the Skipper was in the chartroom at the time and he killed it with a harpoon that he'd kept as a souvenir from his whaling days."

"All this talk of violence is making me sick," complained Yvonne. She took a scented handkerchief from her handbag and gently dabbed her nose. "It's beginning to give me a headache."

"Really?" uttered Jake. "I'm sorry if our story upset you."

"I'm going back to my cabin - coming Sylvia?"

She shook her head. The carnage had excited her.

"Never mind Yvonne," said Angus in the masquerade of a gentleman. "Ah'll take ye back tae your cabin."

The lookout system was adopted again and the young lady was escorted to her cabin on A Deck forward. She felt better after the walk and some smooching developed outside her cabin door. He thought his luck had changed but the approach of a master-at-arms dashed his hopes. The MA was still a fair distance away but his quickening pace signified that he had been spotted. With hurried apologies to the girl, he casually sauntered away in the opposite direction.

At the end of the passageway and out of the MA's sight he scurried away piling on the knots. Bounding up a series of companionways he could hear the warrant officer challenging him to stop. This incensed greater speed. The after funnel was only yards away yet it was just a shadow in the swirling fog when he burst out onto Sports Deck. He bumped into a ventilator and felt his way around it. The indoor lighting faintly silhouetted the MA. A light beam sliced through the mist towards him.

'Jings, he's got a bluidy great big torch,' he breathed. Panic induced him to vault a rail that separated Sports Deck from the lifeboat access catwalk. The quarry kept moving aft, stumbling over wire ropes and pulleys until he was abreast of the engineers' quarters.

Minutes later he was in his cabin gasping with relief. In spite of the cold night air he was soaked in sweat. He stripped off and girded himself in a bath towel in order to take a shower before watch. Still trembling he snapped the cap off a bottle of beer and drank thirstily. A sudden thump on his door startled him into gagging and spluttering. Surely that master-at-arms had not tailed him all the way back to his cabin?

His door swung open revealing an ecstatic Jake. “Tell Jazz Johns I’ll be a bit - uh - late tonight,” he said, grinning like a Chihuahua chewing chili. “I’ll make it up to him when we hit port. So how did you make out?” After Angus related his escapade. He commiserated with a certain lack of sincerity. “Tough tittie! I’m going to trap me some beaver!”

A shout pursued him down the alleyway. “Lucky bastard!”

0015 Saturday

Harding was jubilant at being relieved eight minutes early. “The fog standby rang off twenty minutes ago,” he said. “Good job Gus,” he beamed and was gone.

“He disnae believe in hangin’ aroond, does he?”

“I don’t blame him,” grumbled Jazz, rapping a impatient tattoo on the desktop. “I’m gasping for an ice-cold one myself.”

“Weel, ye’ll need tae gasp for a wee while longer,” said Angus. “Jake’s trimmed in a dolly. He wants ye tae stick aroond for a wee while. He promised tae make it up tae ye in New York.”

“Dirty bastard!” Jazz sighed. “I wish it was me!”

Christie had relieved his ‘oppo’. He charged across the platform and roared at Angus. “Well, where in the bloody hell is he?”

Angus was about to explain but thought better of it.

"He'll be down in a few minutes Sec," volunteered Jazz. "I don't mind if he's a little bit late."

"Well, I bloody do!" bawled Christie. "There's no excuse for being late on watch. Mister King, watch the fort. I'm going up to get that bugger!"

The juniors watched him scoot off.

"Noo he's for it," predicted Angus.

Presently the engineroom ladder's polished rails conveyed the second's weight to platform level as normal. The only difference seemed to be when he glided down was his ecstatic grin. Jake arrived looking severely chastened.

"Whit happened Jake?"

"I don't want to talk about it," snarled Jake.

MacKay came partway up the ladder to platform level. A crooked finger motioned to Angus. "Come with me lad," said the walking second. "It's time you learned a bit about boilers."

Off they went to 3BR the walking second the chase, his long purposeful strides prompting the floater to lope at his heels like a well-trained beagle. The stokehold's increased air pressure compelled him to swallow once or twice to clear his ears. Gigantic force draught fans copiously supplied the greedy oil burners that fired six boilers which were listed alphabetically. Ear discomfort was a typical effect of the sudden change of air pressure one felt when passing through the double doors that interconnected the various sections.

The floater was on his knees peering through green-tinted goggles into the hellfire of D3 Boiler with MacKay crouched at his back when Larry Treen, 3BR's watchkeeper, drew near. "Good morning Mister Treen," boomed Big John, glancing up. "I'm just showing Mister King this damaged furnace wall. Everything else is copasetic I trust?"

"No, Mister MacKay, the bilge pump has seized up."

The walking second did not react to this vital update. Instead he pointed up through a grating above him. "See that valve up there, lad? That's the feed water supply for this boiler. Isn't that right Mister Treen?"

"Yes Mister MacKay. The bilge pump's seized up!"

"And that big valve up there is the steam outlet. Right Mister Treen?"

"Right Mister MacKay," established Treenie. "The bilge pump's seized up!"

Eventually it dawned on Big John that this engineer might be trying to tell him something of importance. "Eh?" He grunted, cupping his ear. "What's that you're saying?"

"*The bilge pump has seized up*!"

"There's no need to shout Mister Treen," MacKay gently admonished him. "Nothing was ever achieved by getting excited, y'know. Let's all take a walk round and take a wee gander at it."

The junior engineers were led behind D3 Boiler to the Drysdale pump where Treen was ordered to lift off its cast-iron cover. A wisp of blue smoke drifted out from the exposed casing. MacKay peered in, his head bowed as if in prayer. What was originally a brass crown wheel was now a heated clump of metallic faeces. The bearings carried beautiful prismatic streaks along the outer races. The rollers had disintegrated.

"*Jesus Bloody Murphy*! *Sabotage*!" roared Big John.

The juniors stole a glance at each other.

"The Viet Cong!"

"I beg your pardon Mister MacKay?" squeaked an astonished Treen.

"The Viet Cong," repeated the distraught second. "They must be on board the *Queen of Dalriada*!" He glared at them. Eye contact oscillated from junior to junior as if he expected one of them to drop on his knees and confess.

"Fix it!" he rumbled finally before storming from the stokehold.

When Scar Davis, the fuel-oil engineer, came by to swap over settling tanks Larry asked him to work on the pump with the floater while tubes were being blown. King didn't know what to make of this chap. His long mousy hair drooped down from beneath his 'steaming bonnet' covering his gaunt face each time he bent over. Every now and then he'd smooth it back under his cap.

His new workmate appeared to be a few years older than he was. His soubriquet Scar did not come from the two-inch lesion on his right cheek but was a diminutive of Oscar. He was still under a cloud for being late returning from leave.

The two men worked together with minimum communication - just the odd gesture or monosyllabic grunt. Davis acted reservedly, disdain showing on his face whenever a greasy tool or pump unit marred his whiter-than-white cotton gloves. Still, reflected Angus, the job was going well and was interesting to boot.

Four hours later both engineers were liberally covered in filth and sweat. Scar was tightening the last nut on the repaired pump when Larry was relieved.

Keyes crouched down beside Angus who was preventing a bolt head from spinning. "Did Black Bob give Jake a hard time, Gus?"

"Ah dinnae ken. Ah've been in here a' watch," he responded. "Onyway, how in the hell dae ye ken whit happened?"

"I was passing Jake's cabin - about midnight it was - when I heard a shout. So I looked in . . ." He had difficulty containing his laughter. "It was the funniest thing I've ever seen!" he gasped, clutching onto the bilge pump for support.

"What's happened? What's going on?" asked Larry.

Angus told him about how Christie had dashed Jake's romantic designs at the beginning of the watch. Keyes burst out laughing again.

"Well, tell us for God's sake!" urged Treen. "Don't keep us in suspense!"

"When I shoved open the cabin door," tittered Keyes. "Christie had lifted poor old Right off the chick. You know how strong that four-eyed bastard is. Jake had on a clean boilersuit so he could make a quick getaway to the engineroom, I guess.

"Anyway, there was Black Bob gripping him by the seat of his pants and the scruff of his neck. Right squealed like a pig. 'I'm nearly there!' He's pleadin'. 'I'm nearly there!'"

He broke up again. "So I presumed he was on the short strokes. His arse was going up and down in midair like a Weir's shuttle and she's trying to pull him back down on top of her. I guess she was on the vinegar strokes too!"

The morose Davis didn't laugh but fretted on the condition of his once clean gloves and mumbled about finding his relief.

"What's the matter with him?" asked Keyes when he'd left. "Has he gone queer or something?"

"Dunno," shrugged Treen. "Something's been bothering him since the day before yesterday."

"Have you heard the rumour that he might be going into hospital for an operation soon?" inquired Keyes.

"No. What's the matter with him?" asked Larry.

"I've heard that his gloves can only come off under anaesthetic," sneered Keyes sarcastically.

The trio laughed, and when Davis was forgotten, they went back to discussing the Canadian's misfortune.

"Wait until we get to the Bahamas," predicted Wheelkey. "Jake will find himself some Obeah woman to make him a four-eyed voodoo doll to stick pins into for the rest of the trip."

"Yes, he'll get back at Christie somehow," agreed Larry. "He's a pretty vindictive bastard."

"Ah'm heidin' back tae the engineroom tae get relieved."

Back on the platform he broached White just after the watch had been handed over. "Will Keyes telt me whit Black Bob did tae ye," he grinned. "Ah'm sorry it happened but it must've been gey funny tae see!"

"Re-eally," grimaced Jake. "I'll get even with that bastard. Just you wait and see."

"Och - forget it. C'mon up tae my cabin for a beer."

"You can stuff your beer up your ass!" was Jake's retort and brightening visibly, said: "I've got better things to do. Sylvia is still in my cabin, y'know. And I'm back on beaver patrol - right? YAHoooo!" he cheered and streaked right up the engineroom ladder.

"Ye're still a lucky bastard!" Angus called after him before plodding in his wake.

Lost and Found

0420 Sunday, December 10th, 1961

His letter for home lay unfinished because he couldn't concentrate. King presently arrived at this oxymoron: he would go out on deck for a breath of fresh air and a smoke. He lingered momentarily on the landing outside the engineers' quarters. Although it was snowing lightly, blustery conditions made it difficult to determine the wind's true direction. At times it would gust from aft to cause a temporary balance with the ship's slipstream so that snowflakes drifted straight down.

Wee whirlwinds unwound themselves from cross-alleyways to scour some yardage of pathway from snow banks before collapsing. Viewed from above he could see that snow had deposited on lifeboat covers on the inboard sides but outboard, it was whisked off to the blackness beyond. He descended the ladder and stepped over fresh mounds of snow that the wind sculpted from older drifts on the Boat Deck.

In the shelter of a davit he slouched against the ship's rail gazing out over the Atlantic Ocean. Thoughts of home and recent experiences jostled and danced through his mind like the flecks of snowflakes zipping across the crescent of starlight created by the horizon and the clouds above.

"Excuse me, but could you give me a light please?"

The voice came from the huddled confines of a tweed jacket, its collar turned up against the weather. His heart skipped a beat at the intrusion and he let out a startled cry, "Where in the bluidy hell did ye come frae?" Noting that he was addressing a passenger he excused himself with "Oops! Sorry sir!"

The person who had surprised him ignored the apology and hunched closer if to peck his nose with his cigarette. He couldn't see his face too well because the nearest light standard was behind the passenger. The Varaflame provided brief illumination, enough for him to observe the man's greying moustache and ice blue eyes. Even although the middle-aged gentleman's cap covered most of his scalp, his high forehead hinted at his probable or partial baldness.

No, definitely bald, he guessed but for the life of him could not fathom how he knew. A pair of white silk gloves, clutched in the man's left fist, almost got singed when he cupped his massive hands to shelter the flicking flame from the gusting wind.

"Thanks," he said, his melancholy countenance shadowed again. "Is this your first trip?" There was a hint of a nasal twang in his voice.

'American,' surmised Angus, the timbre of his voice reminiscent of the film actor Ray Milland. The man faced the ocean, his elbows pushing the odd snowflake from the ship's rail. He was over six feet tall and stocky with broad shoulders.

"Aye," he replied, assuming the same posture after lighting his own cigarette. "Is it that obvious?"

"The braid on your epaulettes has not yet tarnished," was the explanation. "Besides, I was sailing these waters long before you were a twinkle in your father's eye." Smiling he held out a massive hand and introduced himself. "My name's Richard Davidson. My friends call me, Om - short for my middle name: Homer." His smile was lost in the gloom. "Much nicer than Dick I think."

Flinching in the grip Angus responded with his name whereupon Davison gave him a synopsis of his war experiences. He reflected on how he had set sail on one ship only to arrive at his destination on another. "It was beginning to become a habit after my third ship was sunk so I chucked it in that Christmas before the war ended."

He went on.

"I did learn one thing though, every time I boarded a different vessel, I made darned sure of where the escape routes were from any compartment that could be sealed by watertight doors. I also found out where the bilge valves could be opened from outside flooded compartments by finding their extended spindle locations, something I bet that you don't know, young Angus."

The youth did not reply, well aware of the value of silence and remembered the day that his grandfather admonished him. 'Ye'll no' learn bugger all if your bluidy tongue's daein' a' the waggin'!'

"Darn!"

The vee in his fingers brushed tiny sparks from the end of Davison's cigarette when it stuck to his lip. He swore in pain and annoyance and because he had let go of his gloves which were greedily stolen by the wind. "Oh well, I wasn't planning to use them for much longer anyway," he stated philosophically.

"I've got a son at sea," resumed the war vet. "Don't know where though. He joined the MN a while back when I first started having problems with my wife, That's all over and done with - now. You don't want to listen to this crap anyway, young man." He gave him a friendly nudge. "You're probably single and ready to grab the world by the balls!"

The engineer smiled in the gloom, shivered and decided to leave on that note. “Goodnight tae ye Mister Davidson, Ah’m turnin’ in. Ah hope ye hae a guid trip.”

“Goodnight,” replied Davison, his eyes on the sea.

He climbed to the landing outside the engineers’ quarters where the door opened to reveal Larry Treen. “Aye-aye Angus,” he greeted good-humouredly. “Been sunbathing on deck have we?”

He sparked his Zippo lighter and lit up a cigarette. A puff of smoke dissipated in the cold crisp air. He shivered and buttoned the neck of his tunic jacket.

“Naw,” replied King and jerked a thumb over his shoulder. “Ah was just chattin’ wi’ yon passenger doon there.”

“Where?”

“Down th - ” he pointed. “ Och - he’s awa’!”

Treen’s smile froze, his keen eyes absorbing details from the snow-covered deck below. Noting his shipmate’s apprehension Angus queried, “Whit’s wrang?”

“Look Gus! There are your footprints going to and from the ship’s rail and there’s the passenger’s going to the same spot and not returning. I think he’s jumped over the wall!” “Och, ye’re haverin’ man!” Angus retorted. “He’s likely walked aft alang yon clear bit there.”

“We’d better check to make sure,” urged Treen, hurriedly skipping down the ladder with King in tow. The engineers scampered along the clear section of deck. A few paces later the virgin snow revealed the answer. “I’d better phone the wheelhouse!” announced Treen before sprinting back towards the engineers’ accommodation. Angus turned to follow when something in the scupper caught his eye. It was a silk glove. He stuffed it in his pocket then raced inside after Larry.

Not long afterwards the vessel heeled to starboard as she came about. At her present speed the diameter of the liner's turning circle was about sixteen times her length and took quite a few minutes. She steamed on this reciprocal course for a time before heeling over to starboard again to plough back along her own wake at reduced speed.

Searchlights mounted on both wings of the bridge, and at the stem, raked their beams across the ebon sea to no avail. Off watch engineers sensing the ship's change of direction peered out into the night. While all this was going on crewmembers were detailed to discreetly search the ship to ascertain if anyone was missing. And if there was then whom?

His feelings were in turmoil. On one hand there was anxiety for the man whom he had just met and on the other, horror and puzzlement: What could trouble someone so much that suicide was the only solution? Excitement generated by prospects of a rescue and bolstered by adrenalin churned through his veins. He returned to his cabin to get something warmer. He tossed the damp glove onto his coffeetable.

He was putting on his overcoat and decided that perhaps a woollen sweater wouldn't go wrong either. Removing a jersey from a bottom drawer his eye fell on the glove. What he had first determined to be a rust streak from the scupper now resembled dried blood. A reddish-black mess was congealed to the inner lining. He hung the glove up on his marline washing line in case Barnes tossed it out as garbage. He left his cabin deciding that someone had better be informed about the glove in the morning.

Outside on deck Hodgkin, the supposed rep. from Players, was grilling Larry and scrupulously recording each statement in a black notebook. King's facts were added to the agenda.

Seemingly satisfied with the particulars the fourth mate dismissed the pair and advised that the captain may require further information later on, probably that morning.

The probing lights dimmed, proclaiming the futility of a further search, and gradually the ship worked back up to speed. Hodgkin delegated a couple of able-bodied seamen to hose the snow off the Boat Deck.

When the mate had left the scene Angus accepted Treen's proffered cigarette. He patted his clothing for his Ronson but couldn't find it. Larry supplied the light and the engineers went back inside.

On Sports Deck, above the halo of light cast by the illuminations below, Davison watched the proceedings from among the shadows. 'That cheating bitch and her boyfriend won't trouble me anymore,' he thought.

A whiff of funnel smoke reminded him of better days, cleaner days, the days of sail. Large flakes of snow swirled gently around him quite unlike the driving ice pellets of the Horn. On some occasions his fingers had near frozen to the ratlines as he had scampered up the shrouds to make or reduce sail. Tying or loosening gaskets demanded near impossible dexterity from purplish-blue digits. Clambering up that lifeboat davit had been a piece of cake, even for a man of his late years.

He smiled to himself, recalling his very first trip on *Seaswift*, a steel-hulled Cape Horner destined for Valparaiso. There, tons of fossilized bird droppings called guano were loaded and shipped to Germany. The stuff was rich in phosphorus and used to manufacture munitions. How ironic that only a few months later they would return to the windjammer's hull as exploding shells, his very first shipwreck.

He had lost everything to the sea; his savings, though they weren't much - boys were only paid pittance - and all his dunnage. After that he sailed schooner-rigged, just the minimum amount of seagoing gear. Every time he signed off his money went into a bank that earned the most dividends. This led to the accumulation of stocks and shares.

Twenty years after the big war ended had found him in Capetown, South Africa. He was a third mate by then and his ship had just been sold from under him. The gold fields held his interest but it didn't take him long to realize that prospecting or mining was not for him. He was, however, offered a good deal on some gold rand, which he purchased using most of his investments.

He set out for Australia as mate on a schooner. From there he ventured into the South Seas inveigling copra, mother-of-pearl, and a few good pearls from the natives. News of the Wall Street crash reached him as he was celebrating the New Year of 1930. The entrepreneur realized just how lucky he was by investing in gold whenever possible.

Eventually Davison moved back to the States and got his first mate's ticket in steam. He shipped in tramps from New England and Canada to Europe. It was in Marseilles that he first got involved with smuggling and other sordid escapades. For five years he had made mad dashes all over the Mediterranean carrying guns, gems, tobacco, gold, brandy, anything that could turn a profit. This continued until he got mixed up in Franco's war.

It was in Morocco that he somehow found himself in a cellar with Cathy Davis, an English girl, who'd taken the wrong time and place for a holiday. Franco had just taken over command of the Spanish Army with his sights on Spain. But he managed to get her out of the country and back to England before the balloon really went up.

From such propinquity romance blossomed and they were married the following summer. Their son was born eight months later. Oscar was a quiet lad who sort of kept to him most of the time. He grew up to be a good student, taking his brains from his mother. Shortly after he was born Cathy resumed her studies in electrical engineering while her mother babysat Oscar. She studied to earn a diploma in electrical engineering at Liverpool University.

She'd designed a diode that increased the efficiency in aircraft radar and caused a stir in among her colleagues in electronics. She patented it and went into business. He had supplied the funds to buy a small manufacturing workshop in Everton.

Post-war interest in commercial aircraft nourished the business and her clever mind generated other patents. Since he'd given up the sea his new job was financial director in that lucrative business. The company branched out and built plants in small towns where real estate could be bought for a song. One of them was Rhyll in North Wales. Cathy loved the surrounding countryside and purchased a home there.

He never even saw it coming. At a third quarter meeting when a two million-pound discrepancy was discovered he was charged with embezzlement. Cathy brought in George Brown, a young King's Councillor, to defend him. Some defence. Before he knew it he was sent down for twelve years. Around the time of the Suez Canal crisis Brown had obtained a divorce for Cathy.

Just two months ago he was released for good behaviour. He headed straight for Rhyll only to find that his house was up for sale. In a pub outside the factory he plied some beers onto some of the workers at quitting time. The gossip revealed that his son had changed his name and supposedly joined the navy. His mother, the company's CEO, was about to secure a big contract in the United States and it was supposed that she would be sailing to New York in the near future.

He had dual citizenship passports. Contacting an old lag he had the photos switched over on his up-to-date British passport and US passport that was now skilfully made current. Davison became Davidson on the UK passport. All during this period he had feelers out with various travel agencies hoping to discover his wife's mode of transport. It was back in that same pub in Rhyll that he hit it lucky. It seemed that she had boarded the Royal Scot that previous evening in order to catch the boat train for Ocean Terminal, Southampton. Davison followed a day later, catching the regular train for Southampton Central at Waterloo Station.

That young purser was unlikely to recognise him now that he'd ditched his brown contact lenses, the mane of hair and had trimmed his moustache. His steward had never seen him. Only that young engineer who was directly below him at that moment had a vague idea of what he looked like and he had practically witnessed his 'suicide' just as Davison had planned. His Davidson passport lay in his cabin along with other regalia. The stuff that he still needed was in a carryall behind a fan room thermotank on A Deck.

Meanwhile below him on Boat Deck the cold had driven the two seamen inboard. He considered his next move.

Captain Cowell sat at his desk reviewing the evidence that had accumulated since the discovery of the murders. An update had just come in over the radio. Two police officers from The Yard would be boarding with the pilot at Sandy Hook. Obviously they were hoping to catch the murderer before the passengers disembarked. Now it looked as if the leading suspect had already left the ship the hard way during the night.

This new engineer, King, seemed to be popping up quite a lot in the case. It was he and another engineer who had noticed that weapon was missing from the display in the Long Gallery. The second medical officer had mentioned him in his night log too. Coincidence probably but it occurred to the captain that maybe he should have a word with the fellow. He phoned the chief engineer's office to find out on which watch he was standing. The skipper considered summoning the engineer but recalled that he had to lead the Sunday morning sermon. Tilbury could catch him in the mess and request his presence later at the end of the engineer's watch.

1130

At breakfast, over the hubbub of the busy mess, they were relating the 'man overboard' event to Jake but the Canadian's interest was being drawn elsewhere. He sat upright and craned to one side to see past Angus. "Whit's up?"

"Tilbury, the Chief MA just came into our mess," he replied. "It looks like Toni's putting the finger on you."

Treen chimed in with, "Oh - oh! Here comes Policeman Plod now, hot on the scent of a Jock!"

Tilbury approached their table and acknowledged the company with a stern nod before addressing the Scot. "Ahem - Mister King?" Angus looked up. "I believe that you're the last person to speak to Mister Davidson?" There was a quizzical look. "The man that went overboard early this morning," supplemented the MA, moving to one side to allow another watchkeeper to be seated.

"Och aye," replied King. "Aye, that might've been the name he gied me. Whit aboot him?"

A small black notebook materialized in Tilbury's hand. "Could you tell me what you talked about? I think the mishap may be linked to the murders."

Toni wiggled past the MA with a simpering 'excuse me please' and served Treen a platter of ham and eggs. While scribbling down the gist of the engineer's recollections Tilbury was forced to move every couple of minutes or so due to the continual traffic of engineers and stewards. The MA's interest was piqued when he heard about the bloodied glove.

When Scar Davis and Beresford (Beery) Sudbury, the Main Generator Room engineer, simultaneously arose from their table they effectively pinned Tilbury against a chair's back near White. The Canadian gestured to the vacant chair, which the policeman was clutching and advised: "Mister Tilbury - uh - why don't you sit down there before you get trampled into the deck?"

He caught the steward's eye.

"Toni, fetch some coffee for this gentleman please."

"I'd rather go to Mister King's cabin for that glove," growled Tilbury.

"An' Ah would like tae finish my breakfast in peace" interjected Angus. "Just sit doon. Yon glove's no' gaun anywhere."

Fifteen minutes later he led Tilbury along the alleyway to his cabin. A pile of crumpled bed sheets on the deck lay in his open doorway. The glove was no longer on the line. The men watched Barnes draw near with an armful of clean linen.

"What seems to be the problem?"

"Barnes, did ye happen tae see a glove hangin' oan my clothesline?"

"Yes I did, Mister King. Did you hurt your hand in the engineroom?" He glanced at the dangling laundry. "Where is it? I was going to give you a hint on how to get the bloodstain out."

Tilbury jarred Barnes. "How long's this door been lying wide open?"

Distrust flickered in the steward's eyes. "About five or ten minutes."

"What took you so long? The linen locker's just at the end of the passageway," countered the MA.

"I stopped for smoko," retorted an irritated Barnes. "What is this - 1984? Take it up with my boss, Mister Bloody Constable!"

"Take it easy Barnes," soothed Angus. "Ah dinnae suppose that ye've seen anybody suspicious hangin' aboot here in the last wee while?"

"No Mister King," he replied. "The only people I saw were the watchkeepers preparing to go on duty."

The engineer gave Tilbury an apologetic shrug. "Ah'm awfy sorry Mister Tilbury, Ah just dinnae ken whit tae say. Ah'm due tae go oan watch. Ah'll get a haud o' ye if anythin' else comes up."

"Very well, Mister King," replied the disgruntled MA. "I'm going to report this to the Captain. I'm thinking that he'll be wanting to ask you a few questions before long." He clumped off.

While Barnes made up the bunk Angus pocketed a fresh pack of cigarettes to go on watch. He patted his patrol suit for his lighter and then recollected that it had last been used to give that passenger a light. Maybe it had slipped out of the breast pocket of his tunic into the snow when he'd bent over to pick up that glove.

Nearing its ascendancy the bright sun, accompanied by a couple of fluffy white clouds, cheerily lit a sea of deep blue where hundreds and hundreds of white caps were jostling each other. The straight broad wake of lime-ripple could be seen all the way to the horizon. It was a perfect day with a light breeze sweeping over the port quarter. Perfect that is, unless one wanted to sunbathe. The air temperature was 30° F.

The Boat Deck was clear of snow and it shone bone-white in the brilliant sunlight. Of passengers there were a few brave souls warmly wrapped in winter clothing striding briskly along the deck on their morning constitutional.

He eyed his wristwatch and reckoned a couple of minutes could be spared to search. He scooted down the ladder and dashed across to the section of ship's rail where the glove had been found. A careful search brought sight of a scupper rose plugged by debris. He knelt down to reach between the bars of the ship's rail.

A soggy brown-paper bag covered some candy wrappers and a multitude of sins from the tobacco industry including plain, cork and filter-tipped cigarette ends, cellophane, tinfoil and cardboard packaging with the inevitable collection of used matches. Pushing this junk aside uncovered his lighter that was nestled in the mate to the missing glove. He put the Varaflame in his pocket. The act of retrieving the glove revealed another sin, a used condom. Lovemaking on the open deck in Winter North Atlantic, he reflected, must give heated sex a whole new meaning.

A brief examination revealed that this glove's palm had been sliced and that the material had soaked up an even greater amount of blood than its mate had although the stains were fainter. The fury of the deck hoses probably wouldn't have helped either. He took it below with him to dry in the engineroom. At the end of the watch he placed it in a brown paper bag, which was put in a drawer below his bunk.

Banjoed!

1145 Sunday

The felon had slept uncomfortably in an A Deck fan room behind a thermotank, a heating unit that served a block of cabins. Nearby a huge fan motor droned steadily, its impeller sucking fresh air from a vent somewhere above on the open deck. The machinery space was dim because many light bulbs were dud, a negligence that suited his hidey-hole admirably. But now camouflage was needed and he was famished.

A bridge electrician has the run of the ship. He is responsible for the various electric and electronic equipment applicable to the bridge, radar, emergency and navigation lights, watertight door and fire control indicators, deck winches, batteries for lifeboat radios, telephones and other equipment.

Shop electricians also have the run of the ship. They look after circuits that affect the welfare of the passengers and crew. In most cases these fellows have a lot of ground to cover. Some legwork was done by ratings that changed light bulbs or topped up batteries for the ship's telephone system and other mundane chores according to the demand.

Just as someone seeing a person clad in a white lab coat and carrying a stethoscope in hand might assume that the individual was a doctor or a nurse Davison knew that a similar ploy had to be used. Cabin stewards don't miss much. When a strange face enters their jurisdiction they might report their observation to the chief steward. That thought was in his mind as he riffled through a duffle bag that he'd stashed previously behind some ductwork.

He put on a clean set of engineers' white overalls and donned a peaked cap. With the leads of an electrical circuit tester dangling from an electrician's tool pouch from which the inevitable flashlight protruded, or torch, as these Brits insisted in calling them, he was ready to blend in as one of the ship's electrical officers.

2145

A hazy sullen sun finally dipped below the horizon. Winds were rising in short blustery gusts with the first star. Other stars, twinkling feebly in the darkening sky, jostled their way through the brief gloaming. Their chorus of light gradually diminished when scudding clouds brought along their own orchestra. Angus stood hunched over a railing with elbows splayed on the smooth teak surface, cradling his chin in his hands. He revelled in the brisk fresh air. White caps whipping past on the choppy sea below lulled his thoughts into semi-mesmerism as they dwelled on the experience of the past couple of days.

The wind, piqued by an indifferent audience, angrily previewed a hint of the coming attraction. It pouted under the skip of the engineer's cap giving it lift. His headgear skimmed gaily across the open deck revelling in its freedom. It slammed into a ventilator and was quickly recaptured. Above him he could hear muffled shouts escaping from an unclosed porthole.

Curiosity prompted him to investigate the commotion in White's cabin. He cocked an ear against his friend's louvred door. There was definitely something happening within. A minor riot seemed to be in progress. Strongly aware of the friendship and camaraderie between ships' engineers he became concerned. The voluble explicit language prompted him to knock on the door. Nobody answered. He threw open the cabin door at the sound of breaking glass.

A fantastic sight beheld him. He blinked, his eyes focussing the scene. Scattered around the cabin were half-a-dozen engineers in all states of dress, or rather, the lack of it. Two just wore shorts, another one's only attire was a singlet, the other three were stark naked. In one corner a couple of engineers were at each other's throats. In the opposite corner an engineer was masturbating with much enthusiasm.

Another pair was jostling one another in front of Jake's bunk. Then finally there was the instigator himself, White, in his bunk on top of a naked girl who was ardently returning his advances. He was dumbfounded. The sluggish rhythmic movements of the Canadian's bare stern signified an epilogue to climax. He dismounted, checked his unloaded weapon and sauntered over to him. Surveying the uninhibited and rowdy scene he threw back his head in laughter when Angus asked, "Whit in the hell is gaun oan?"

"We trimmed in this horny bitch earlier, right?" replied Jake. "Four drinks later - uh - she was bragging how she could satisfy everyone in the cabin. She's either a nymph or else on a diet of Spanish fly! Naturally we obliged her or at least, I did. Look at those fools, they can't settle on who's next!"

The obviously natural-blonde stewardess whimpered about lack of attention, her hand reaching for the closest engineer. She pulled him into an embrace, nibbling on his ear while he responded by fondling her starboard breast. The two engineers wrestling in the corner also responded. They called a truce.

One of them seized the new paramour by the testicles while the other grabbed an arm and a leg. Together they drew the unfortunate officer from the bunk and heaved him aside. A corresponding shriek accompanied this spirited action but ended abruptly when he hit a bulkhead. Even before the unfortunate had crumpled to an untidy heap his assailants were once more in mortal combat for the fair lady's hand, or more to the point, specific parts of her anatomy.

White was disgusted with his colleagues. "There's only one way to settle this, right?" It was a rhetorical question. "D'you fancy a bit of the beaver yourself?"

The idea of sloppy seconds didn't appeal to Angus. Besides he preferred to work without an audience and so respectfully declined.

"Ok. I've already decided on who goes next, right?"

"Who?"

White beamed, "Me!" He hopped onto his coffee table and yelling, *Geronimo*! bounded into the waiting arms of his horny companion.

The floater vacated the cabin in disbelief and laughter.

2350

The Mekon's relief had just reiterated a flamboyant description of the orgy as he took over the watch. "Boy, I wish I hadda seen that! I can just imagine old Baz choking the chicken!" He was still cackling when the bridge phone light flashed, catching his eye. He jerked the receiver from its hook shortening the buzz.

"Engineroom."

"Officer-of-the-Watch here. A radio warning from the mainland has just reported a tropical storm heading our way. Our new course may take us close to the storm's perimeter. Stand by for a possible speed reduction."

"Ok." He hung up and lurched across to Christie, who stood with Woods near the centre of the manoeuvring platform, both swaying in time to the ship's increasing rolls like a pair of hula-hula girls. The Mekon waited until the watch changed.

Christie peeked over his slate at the junior. "Well?"

The message was relayed. The second's eyes rolled upwards, allowing his vision to hurdle his spectacle rims to focus on the highly polished inclinometer. The brass pointer indicated that the ship was leaning seventeen degrees to starboard. His dark eyes whipped back and glared venomously into his junior's nervous orbs.

"Approaching the perimeter of a storm, are we? We're in a bloody storm right now! That's just typical of the bridge wallahs. They huddle round the radio listening to weather reports. Why in the bloody hell don't they look outside once in a while?"

Woods left to go topside. His relief shook his head resignedly and ordered White to warn the stokehold engineers of an imminent slowdown. He complied and fox-trotted back to Angus. "Bad news Gus, you'll have to start earning your porridge and kippers. Taffy needs your services in 2BR. He's got a busted gauge glass on D2 boiler."

"Aye - aye, Ah ken," he said to The Mekon laconically. "Guid watch."

When the floater stepped over the airlock coaming he found Morgan by the door groaning. He was hunched over in pain clutching his lower abdomen. "Where in the hell have you been? Guard the fort for ten minutes. I'm dying for a shit!" He vanished into the airlock and a muffled *Christ, that beer just runs right through me*! could be heard just after the door slammed shut.

With hands clasped behind his back he casually explored the stokehold. Each boiler was inspected in turn by the simple tapping of a knuckle against an occasional instrument dial. This air of confidence was for the firemen's benefit though they viewed him with disinterest. Any car salesmen would have recognized the tyre-kicking mannerisms of the novice. He hadn't the faintest idea of his responsibilities.

The ship's motion made boiler water levels disappear from their sight glasses with alarming regularity. Starboard boilers would overfill while the port units would empty. Rolling the other way reversed this pulse-racing phenomenon. Disaster loomed at his shoulder, but that was of no consequence, all he had to do was appear cool, calm, and kind of intelligent for when all is said and done: Ignorance is still bliss.

Scar Davis, the fuel-oil engineer, entered the stokehold. "I'll be changing over settling tanks!" he yelled over the constant gush of forced draught fans and vanished behind C2 Boiler.

"Ok Scar, go aheid!" hailed back Angus.

Davis could've told him that he was going to hook the fou-fou valve into a reciprocating flange and the floater would have blithely swallowed this guff. He stationed himself by the console watching the oil burner sights on the boilers. Seven flickering lights on every furnace indicated that all was well.

One by one the glasses went dark, fires fizzling out like candle wishes on a birthday cake. The same thing was happening on the other five boilers. Pressure gauge needles dipped alarmingly and the engineroom phone buzzed with irate interrogatory tones. Scar reappeared near C2 boiler and said *Oops*! before seemingly dematerializing again.

From inside the furnaces dull pops signalled the resume of normalcy as burner jets rekindled against the bricks, which were still white-hot. The stokehold resumed ambience. Angus hadn't moved an inch. He seemed to be glued to the control console when the fuel-oil engineer came by to apologise.

An explanation followed: Seawater tends to seep into oil tanks. To remedy this fuel-oil is pumped into a pair of matching tanks located opposite each other on the port and starboard sides of the stokehold. The oil is allowed to settle. Gravity separates the heavier water which is drained off. The tanks are then ready for use.

One tank is always in operation while the other is settling. When Davis changed over the water in the full tank hadn't been drained off properly and gone into the system to kill the fires.

"We're back on the original tank," announced Davis. "I'll drain off some more water after I've had a coffee then I'll try switching over again."

He clambered up a nearby ladder heading for the upper airlock doors on D Deck level. The fuel-oil engineers' office was just aft, next to the fan room supplying that stokehold.

Feeling queasy King was still trembling from the fright when Morgan came back. "Everything ok?"

"Aye - noo Ah've got tae leave."

"Here, what about the broken gauge glass then boyo?" Morgan reminded him.

"Bugger the gauge glass!" shot back Angus. "Ah've just had a sudden urge tae hae a crap. Ah'll fix it later!"

Soon he was back with the damaged instrument removed and stripped on the workbench. He worked with some difficulty because the ship was riding heavy in the storm. When the unit was rebuilt the floater scaled up the outer structure of D2 until he'd reached the steam drum.

He began hauling the heavy gauge up by rope. The weight swung back and forth like some demented pendulum instead of hanging plumb. The pitch and roll of the vessel was growing more erratic by the minute. Later Jake White informed him that instead of bypassing the storm, the ship had steamed directly into its centre.

Homer Davison watched the young engineer replace the light behind the gauge glass. Having gradually wound this way down through the decks, he'd found a set of airlock doors in a fan room on D Deck. He moved slowly across the catwalk on the upper reaches of 2BR to another set of doors on the port side and entered the pressurizing compartment.

The fuel-oil engineer finished his coffee and left his office, heading for those same airlock doors. Davison, peering through the dirty spyglass on the outer door, caught a glimpse of another engineer coming towards him. He flattened his body against the bulkhead, his flashlight poised to strike the man. Davis had almost reached the door when he recalled that his gloves were still in his office. He retraced his steps.

The floater hallooed down to Taffy that the job was done and moved aside while the stokehold engineer bled some steam into the glass to bring it to ambient temperature. Using fly-catching hand signals Angus indicated to the Welshman that he was going topside for tea by way of the upper airlock.

Air gushed noisily through the equalizing ports into the compartment and the inside light died when he jerked back the steel door handle. He stepped over the coaming and turned around, drawing the door shut. Davison hit him with his flashlight. Seeing that the other engineer had disappeared he sealed the inner door intending to escape by the other route. He opened the other door to be confronted by the fuel-oil engineer. He raised his flashlight again but stopped when Davis called out, “Dad!”

Ten minutes later Taffy figured the gauge glass would be warm enough to put back into service. A drop of blood splattered the cuff of his white boilersuit as he untied the marline twine that held the controls in place. Directly above him his shipmate lay prone on the highest catwalk. Yelling urgent instructions to his firemen, he called the engineroom.

The senior second received the message only to find the floater partially recovered and lolling against a steel column when he came through. He was dabbing the back of his head with a blood-impregnated rag. MacKay asked him if he could walk. There was searing pain when he nodded the affirmative. The firemen half-carried him to the ship’s hospital on C Deck.

The night nurse instructed them to lay her new patient down on the operating table. He closed his eyes and sighed. Presently he eased his head to the side, his eyes focussing down the shapely cleavage of an attractive woman. Nurse Rosaline Highman was forty-ish with shoulder-length hair that might’ve been bleached blonde. She had light-olive eyes, a pert nose and full kissable lips. She was scrutinising the two-inch gash above and behind his left ear.

As she smiled reassurance he became aware of her *Wind Song*, a *Prince Marchabelli* perfume. “I’m afraid that this will have to be stitched,” he was warned, her compassionate voice soft and soothing.

“Go ahead Miss,” he nonchalantly replied.

The curvaceous nurse deftly threaded a surgical needle and lowered it to the wound. He tried to draw away at penetration but was pleasantly surprised to find that there wasn’t any pain. His skull was still numb from the concussion. Serendipity was the nurse firmly but gently cushioning his head against a soft breast to prevent similar movement. She placed three sutures, her mouth pursed with concentration.

"Can't you feel that?"

"No," he responded conscious of the bosomy earplug.

"You're very brave Mister King," her voice in a dreamlike lilt. "But I'm afraid that another suture will be required." She reached across his body to retrieve some silk thread. Her forearm brushed against his pelvis and she sensed his erection. "Feeling better are we?" she teased, sprinkling some antiseptic talc on the wound before applying a band-aid. "Go and lie down on that cot over there."

He gingerly edged towards the cot, lurching erratically. It was not entirely due to the ship's motion that he sought support from the nurse. He flopped heavily down on the mattress pulling the woman with him. A button popped open on her blouse top when she leaned forward to kiss him.

A soft knock on the surgery door diverted her attention and the blouse was hastily refastened. Big John's worried face peeked round the edge of the door his keen eyes noting the nurse's flustered appearance.

King's posture would've done justice to a death scene in a Shakespearian tragedy. 'Alexander Fleming must've had lads like this in mind when he invented penicillin,' he mused, watching the nurse straightening her attire before leaving the room. He drew a chair over to the bedside and sat down. "How are you lad?"

Fingers gingerly touched behind his ear. "It feels no' too bad just noo, Mister MacKay."

"Always keep in mind; one hand for the ship and one for yourself, especially in rough weather."

"If some folk would keep their hands tae themselves, Ah would dae much better, Mister MacKay!" the junior replied, quite forgetful of where his hands had been moments before.

"What do you mean, lad?"

"Ah mean somebody banjoed me in the upper airlock," was the indignant reply.

"Are you sure?"

"As sure as the egg startin' tae hatch in below this stickin' plaster!" he retorted, pointing to the wound.

"I'm going down there right now to check that out," promised the second and left.

The nurse returned to make him take a couple of pills before handing him a glass of water.

"Whit were they for?" he asked after swallowing.

"To help you sleep."

"Ah thought *you* were gaun tae dae that!" he murmured.

"Not tonight love. You've got a headache!" imparted the nurse. "Besides it's going to be like Piccadilly Circus in here before long. I've had four stewards in here already asking about seasick pills for their passengers. This weather doesn't seem to be getting any better." Before closing the door behind her she coyly glanced over to ask, "Why don't you invite me up to your cabin for a drink later on in the trip?"

"Ye're oan!" he chortled happily.

The liner ploughed deeper and deeper into the fury of the storm. Great waves broke heavily over the high bow, smashing across the fo'c's'le head in gushing torrents to cascade onto the well deck. She shuddered with each assault but stubbornly stayed on course.

He awoke to two worried expressions staring back at him; Jake White and Big John MacKay. "Whit's up?" he tried to sit up but a blinding pain behind his eyes put the kibosh on that effort. “Ooh!”

“The doctor just had a look at you,” said his boss. “He says that you just have mild concussion.”

“Just!”

“Mister MacKay told me what happened Gus,” said Jake, shaking with anger. “You didn’t - uh - get a glimpse at all of the person who hit you - right?”

Angus shook his head and immediately regretted it. He related his painful experience.

“Aye,” confirmed Big John. “When I checked, the airlock door was still ajar. I had to go round the long way to shut it.”

“He seems to know the ship pretty well - right?”

“Aye,” agreed MacKay. “He is, or has been a seaman at some time but not necessarily on this vessel.” He arose. “Anyway, we’ll just keep this under our caps for the moment. I’ll pass this incident onto the Chief Engineer. As far as the rest of the ship’s concerned the storm caused the door to slam into Mister King. He crawled along that catwalk seeking help when he fainted. Come on Mister White, let’s get some breakfast before they shut the mess. It looks like this young fellow is in capable hands.”

“I’m - uh - going to hang around here for a bit, Sec.”

“All right, have it your own way,” replied the second leaving the room.

“Are you hungry Angus?” asked Jake.

“Naw, no’ really,” he admitted. “Just tired.”

“Ok buddy. I’ll leave you then. I’m going to have a word with the nurse,” said Jake. “I was talking to her earlier. She’s - uh - going to get me some laxative. I’ve been constipated for three days.”

"Ah've always thought that ye were full o' it," giggled Angus.

"Really!"

The nurse returned and gave Jake a few pills. "These should fix you up. Now how about toddling along and let your friend get some rest." She fussed around tucking in the sheets. By the time she had got around to fluffing up the pillows Angus was fast asleep.

Confessions

0425 Monday

The storm's tail end masked their journey up the different levels of open decks from C Deck aft. Davis entered his quarters from the landing above Boat Deck. With keys in hand he peeked fore and aft, checking that the alleyway was clear before signalling his father to enter his nearby cabin.

He had an outboard cabin with twin bunks, a pair of easy chairs, the customary coffeetable and wardrobe with the combined tallboy-desk. His father sat down on the outboard bunk while Davis flopped into his chair with a sigh of relief. They both began to talk at the same time then stopped in laughter and prompted each other to tell their story first.

"Wait a minute Dad. When did you last eat?"

"I found a leg of cold chicken in one of the pantries about six hours ago. Someone's late snack, I guess."

The engineer stood up and said, "Hang on and I'll get us some sandwiches from the mess. If you're thirsty, help yourself to the coke and ginger ale there on the desktop. I'll try and grab some coffee although the stewards get pissed off if we take cups from the mess."

"No - no son, coke's fine."

Minutes later, Oscar was back with some sandwiches and fresh fruit. His dad looked at the curled-up sandwiches and laughed. "Nothing ever changes on the graveyard watch at sea. Never mind. I'm hungry enough to eat a horse."

He picked up a sandwich filled with pressed corned beef and began to chew. As his fingers clamped the bread slices together to keep the meat from falling out Oscar noticed the scrap of cloth wrapped around his father's left hand.

"What happened to your hand Dad?"

"Cut it on something," he mumbled through his chewing.

"D'you want some Elastoplast for it?" asked his son, lifting a tin out of his desk drawer. "I had to use some earlier for the same reason," he said, demonstrating similar injuries.

"Like father - like son," grinned Davison. "May I?" he gestured towards the wash hand basin.

"Sure Dad," replied Oscar, handing him a clean towel.

With the grime removed he scrutinised his fingers and palm. "Not too bad," he grunted. "More like paper cuts than anything. I won't need those Band-Aids."

The men smiled at each other until the face of the younger grew serious. "That engineer that you slugged is in our hospital," he stated, relating the gossip that he'd overheard in the mess. "MacKay, that's our walking second, reckons that the airlock door swung and hit him when the ship rolled. He thinks that King, that's the engineer, crawled along the catwalk before flaking out. They found him only about ten minutes after we dragged him there. Well - I would've 'found' him before the end of the watch anyway."

His dad bit into another sandwich and chewed reflectively.

"So why did you hit him Dad?"

His father swallowed before answering: "I was afraid that he might have recognised me."

"Why - have you met him somewhere before?"

"Yeah. We chatted together out on Boat Deck just about this time yesterday morning."

He gaped at his dad. "You're the one who is supposed to have jumped overboard?"

"Yeah," admitted Davison. "Pretty good stunt, eh?"

Oscar shrugged and gazed morosely into his glass.

Davison brushed crumbs to the carpeted deck. "What's up?"

His son remained silent before blurting out, "Dad, I've killed a man."

"Yeah? Who?"

"Mum's boyfriend. He's beaten the shit out of me for the last time."

"Whereabouts did you kill him?" asked his father.

"In a cabin down on B Deck for'ard." Oscar went on to explain that he'd caught a glimpse of George Brown shortly after the ship had sailed. "I went down to the purser's office on the pretext of getting a pay advance and took a butcher's at the passenger list." He placed both hands on his face before continuing. "I wanted to get even with that bully after he beat me up in front of Mum just before I joined the ship. Then - "

"Where is your mother, son?" Davison gently interrupted.

He uncovered his face and peered bleakly back at his dad through reddened tear-filled eyes. "Brussels I think," he replied. "Leastways that's where she was supposed to have been going. A conference I think. But I haven't seen her since that beast gave me a thrashing in Crewe Station."

"Mm."

"The more that I thought about him, the more I raged," said Oscar through clenched teeth. "The next thing that I knew was that I was dragging a great big knife from behind a shield in one of the public rooms. I hid it under my jacket and went down to B17. I don't think anybody saw me enter. Brown must have gone to dinner for the cabin was empty. I went into a walk-in closet and closed the door. I hunkered down in the dark and waited.

"I must have nodded off - the movement of the ship I expect - but some sounds woke me up. I opened the door just a crack and peeked out. It was quite dark because there was only one small table lamp lit in the far corner of the cabin. I could make out this great shadow of George Brown rogering some broad on the bed. I stabbed him in the back. The blade only went partway into his body. He collapsed immediately. I wanted to haul the knife out again and clean it before putting it back where I got it - but it was stuck. The dirk's handle was just too short to grasp it with both hands.

"I thought that it was safe enough to grab the blade with one hand because I was wearing gloves. But that edge was like a razor." He flexed his left hand gently, grimacing at both the pain and the memory. "There wasn't a sound from the woman underneath him. Whether she was drunk or had fainted I don't know, but I lit out of there pretty fast."

'Like a bat out of hell,' thought Davison, reflecting his surprise at seeing his son emerge from Cabin B17 to scurry aft at a great rate of knots. Aloud he asked, "What did you do with the bloody gloves?"

"I chucked them over the wall," replied his son. "But when I overheard King talking to the MA in our mess I thought that maybe one of them had blown back on board again." He removed the stolen glove from a drawer. "It's not mine," he continued. "Mine were the standard white cotton gloves that we use down below. This glove is made of silk."

Davison took the glove from his son. "Yeah, you're right son. It *is* made of silk, in fact it's mine." Their eyes met. "And it's also a fact that you didn't kill George Brown . . . I did."

Oscar Davis stared at his sire with astonishment then eyed the bloody glove in horror.

Davison's vehemence unleashed suddenly. "That bastard framed me. He stole my business and my wife - your mother - everything! And I've had twelve long years to brood about it."

He toyed with his glove. "When I found out that he was heading for the States I followed him aboard. After I saw you leave that cabin down on B Deck I went in. It was quite dark in there so I switched the lights on. Brown was moaning but not quite conscious. He was still alive anyway.

"So I grabbed that great big knife and hauled on it. But like you said, it was stuck. I wrapped one of my gloves around the blade and held it just like you did. He squealed like a stuck pig when I wiggled the knife. Suddenly it was loose and before Brown could move I slid it between his ribs and right into that bastard."

"Did you kill the woman Dad?"

"Nah. She was out cold."

"There's a rumour been going around the ship for the past couple of days now about a double murder. I've also heard that there's a great big coffin in the fish fridge with a man and woman in it."

"Is that right?" queried his dad, and lackadaisically stroked his chin. "Maybe I did kill her then. That's too bad - it was a pretty long knife."

"Did you know her?"

"Nah!" lied Davison. "She was probably just some floozie that he'd picked up somewhere."

Which wasn't true. He had recognised his ex-wife all right. She'd come to and screamed when she saw me. Calmly he'd just placed his full weight on the pommel of the dirk and down it went - right through her too. He relished the moment and smiled.

"What about King?"

"Who?"

"King, the engineer that you slugged." Oscar pointed out. "He could recognise you. Are you going to kill him too?"

Davison meditated for a while. "Nah, we'll be docking sometime tomorrow. When I slip ashore, that'll be the last I'll see of him."

"What about Mum?"

"What about your mother?"

"Are you going after her too?" asked Oscar concerned.

"I've had enough of killing," his dad replied easily. "There's no way that I'll ever get my business or my money back. Anyway, nobody gets through this world without something bad happening to them. What goes around, comes around." He nodded to the inboard bunk. "Is your bunkmate on the four-to-eight?"

"No Dad," replied Davis. "The water-softening engineer couldn't make it on this voyage because of appendicitis. It's yours for the rest of the night. I'll slip you out around 11:00 a.m."

"Is there any chance of getting a shower? I feel kinda grungy after roaming around the bowels of this ship."

Oscar objectively shook his head.

"It's kind of dodgy at this time in the morning. A lot of the guys will hit the showers in half-an-hour or so after their sarnies. Some of them will be chug-a-lugging beer for a little while before they shower. And then the stewards start showing up around six. Sorry Dad, you'll just have to settle for the old sponge in the sink."

"Fine," sighed Davison. "It's better than nothing."

The plate was empty.

"Would you like some more to eat Dad?"

"No thanks son." His father yawned. "I'll just have a quick wash and then I'll turn in. It's been a long day."

1015

A wee man with a big hammer was pounding inside his head. "Ooh!" he groaned. Cautiously he rose to a sitting position, his legs dangling over the side of the cot. The tattoo diminished to a dull throb. "Och, Ah've had much worse hangovers," he said, his eyes panning around the ward for his boilersuit. It hung over the back of a chair. He padded over, stepped into them and proceeded to don his socks and shoes.

"What on earth are you doing Mister King?"

His head swivelled in response to the query directed by a middle-aged nurse, or matron, he reflected before answering. "Eh - Ah'm feelin' no' too bad just noo, nurse. In fact Ah'm bluidy weel starvin'!"

"Get undressed and get back into that bed," was the prim response.

"But Ah'm feelin' ok, ye ken," he protested.

The door opened and the ship's doctor, carrying a clipboard, stepped breezily into the room. "What's all the noise about?"

"He'll not do as he's told, Doctor," she objected.

"Angus King?" the doctor asked, tapping a chart on his clipboard with his pen. "How are you feeling this morning, young feller?"

"Eh - no' bad, Doctor. Ah've felt worse."

"Are you ready for some breakfast?"

"Ah'm no' hauf!" he avowed. "Ah could eat a cuddy."

"Ok," laughed the doctor. He scribbled a note on the chart and said, "You seem healthy enough to me. Give him a few aspirins for later nurse. Take two at a time as needed. What watch are you on Mister King?"

"Ah'm oan watch again at noon."

"Well, tell your boss that I'm giving you the watch off. Take two aspirins after you've had your breakfast then go to bed. You should be all right for the midnight watch. Come back in ten days and we'll take your sutures out. Good day." And ending his prognosis left the hospital.

Angus went to the engineers' changeroom and put on his patrol suit before heading for the lift to go topside.

A knife of sunlight pierced the badly fitted chintz curtains over his porthole and awakened Davis. He got up to wash and shave. Gurgling sounds stirred his dad who eased his frame from the bunk.

"When you've washed and shaved Dad, I'm going to give you an old uniform to wear. I bought a new one last month and I've been debating on whether I should toss out the old one or not. It's just as well that I waited, I think," said Oscar, checking his watch. "It's nearly eleven o'clock. The stewards usually have their smoko about now and the storekeeper will be calling the watch in about ten minutes."

His dad wasn't long getting dressed. Oscar cracked open his cabin door and peered out. The passageway was empty. He glanced back and was worried to see that his uniform was far too snug on his dad but nothing could be done about it now.

"Let's go," he whispered.

They walked briskly aft to the end of the passageway and went out onto a scrap of deck space that some engineers used for sunning themselves during warm weather. Oscar gestured to a ladder that led to an upper deck.

"Up there is a bit of Sports Deck for engineers' use only. There's a tank room up there for domestic water. It'll give you a bit of shelter. I'm going for breakfast now. I'll bring you back something to eat in about half-an-hour."

He watched his dad scramble up out of sight before opening the steel door to go back inside. That new engineer seemed to jump right at him just as he stepped over the coaming. On the other hand Angus was just plodding along the alleyway, eyes down, his mind minutes in the future when he'd be feasting on ham, eggs and sausage with lots of toast.

"*Je-sus*!"

"Whit's the matter? Whit's the matter?" stuttered Angus, suddenly startled out of his reverie.

"What did you see?" blurted out Oscar.

The Scot's head slewed back and forth, up and down the passageway seeking for something out of the ordinary. "Nuthin'," he responded. "Ah didnae see nuthin' - honest. Whit have ye lost, Scar?"

It took a few seconds for Davis to realise that this was just a chance encounter. "Don't worry about it," he snapped brusquely and stormed off along the corridor.

"Ah think hauf the guys oan this ship are nuts," opined Angus, haggling at a slab of Virginia ham.

"You got that right," agreed Jake. "I'm glad to see that lump on your noggin - uh - hasn't displaced your usual buoyant personality." He spooned some sugar into his coffee. "What's the matter now?"

"Och, yon Scar Davis just aboot scared the livin' shite oot o' me." He related his unsettling byplay with the fuel-oil engineer. "Wheesht! He just came intae the mess."

White noted that the fuel-oil engineer ignored his usual table companions, Sudbury and MacAdam, the jenny room engineers and sought out an empty table at the far end of the mess. The other twelve-to-four watchkeepers came drifting in, some of them asking the floater about his wellbeing and chiding him to be more careful. John MacKay humorously remarked that some juniors would do almost anything to get a watch off before going to the head table.

The boiler room engineers of this watch also had a bit of a clique in the mess. They were respectively, Pete Eaton (1BR), Taffy Morgan (2BR), and Larry Treen (3BR). Air-conditioning engineers Charlie Benson and Dave Hedges sat at the engineroom juniors' table. Three electricians; Artie Berwick of the main jenny switchboard; Bill Danforth, HS switchboard, and Dave Armstrong, electrical shop, were seated at another table.

All of these officers were dressed in patrol suits with the exception of Charlie Benson who was required to dress in best bib and tucker so that he could haunt public rooms with his swing-ger as he called it.

This curious instrument, colloquially known as a Twaddle was a swing psychrometer, a gadget that consists of two thermometers that are fastened in parallel to a small board. The board was revolved like a football rattle. After a quick spin the wet bulb thermometer's reading was compared to the dry bulb thermometer. The former measurement was usually lower than the latter and when divided by the dry bulb reading the result was multiplied by one hundred so that air humidity might be determined.

For a comparison, if a reading was taken out on the open deck and both temperatures were the same, the weather was inclement; rain, snow, sleet, or fog. It is worthy of note that when both air and sea temperatures were the same, similar weather took effect.

Another curious fact about this instrument was that it attracted the curiosity of the passengers and if some of them were female and attractive so much the better for Charlie. Fine tuning individual cabin climate control was his speciality and he didn't have to go near fan room thermotanks either.

Stuffing an apple and a banana into his pockets Davis left the mess toting sandwiches wrapped in a serviette.

His breakfast finished Angus swallowed two aspirins with the last of his orange juice. Tiredness began to take effect as he left. Just before he entered his cabin Davis was observed exiting the engineers' quarters from the far end of the passageway but he never gave it any thought. He crawled onto his bunk whilst unbeknown to him a murderer was munching on a bacon and egg sandwich almost directly above his head.

Davis handed a key to his father. "You'll be able to go into my cabin shortly after two o'clock this afternoon. A brand-new John Wayne movie called *The Comancheros* is showing at two this afternoon in the First Class Cinema. It's a safe bet that any engineer who is not on watch and still awake will be there. The stewards don't come back on until the bar opens at six. So it should be safe to go back into our accommodation. "I'll see you at the end of my watch."

His dad was reading a paperback novel when Oscar entered his cabin with food nobbled from the high tea buffet set up for the four-to-eight watch going on duty and the twelve-to-four finishing their duties. Opening a couple of large table napkins revealed a chicken leg, a couple of corned beef sandwiches, a fresh tomato, a boiled egg, some lettuce and celery, a slice of apple pie, some petit fours, and a nice big chunk of Brie and assorted biscuits from the cheeseboard.

"Wow! You guys really live high off the hog. We have a veritable picnic here." He frowned at the decadent petit fours. "You eat them Oscar. They'll play hell with my diabetes."

"I'm sorry Dad, I didn't know that you had diabetes. When did it happen?"

"Oh, I've had it for quite a while now, son. They diagnosed it shortly after I went into prison. It's not too bad as long as stick to the Glyburide medication and I still got plenty of that." He thumbed at the duffle bag on the deck.

"Where did that come from?"

"I went down to the fan room where I had stashed it."

"Jeez, you took a chance Dad."

"Well, King is the only guy who can really identify me and he was on watch with you."

"No he wasn't," said Oscar. "I just found out in the mess that the doc had given him the watch off. He lives a few doors up from here. Christ, he could've got up for a piss or something and run straight into you." He rubbed his chin worriedly. "You were lucky. That guy seems to pop up all the time like a jack-in-the-box."

"Well, it didn't happen so there's no use worrying about it. My main worry is getting off this ship and past customs and immigration when we dock. I want to see an old shipmate of mine who was handling the stocks and shares in my companies before your mother took them over. I have to find out if there is any way of getting some of my money back."

"Don't worry about getting ashore Dad," he was assured. "I'll be bunkering on the first night watch after we dock. It should be quiet on the dockside then. I'll give you my pass when you leave. You can drop it in an envelope and mail it back to me after you get clear."

Relief lit up Davison's face. "Thanks son, I feel better now."

The Port of New York

1100 Tuesday

"Ten-ten WINS New York!" squawked a Japanese transistor radio as Angus and Jake passed the deck engineer's cabin on their way to the open deck. It was bitterly cold. A stimulating breeze purged tears from King's eyes as he leaned out from the starboard rail. Nearing its zenith the sun played peek-a-boo with a few clumps of high-flying clouds but failed to radiate heat with its light.

"There it is!" Jake pointed to a slender tower on the horizon. "Just off the bow!"

Angus wiped moisture from his eyes. The same motion shaded them to catch sight of the faint outline of a tower that jutted straight up out of the ocean. "Aye, Ah can see it noo!"

"It's - uh - the first thing we see coming from the east even before land is sighted. It's two hundred and fifty feet high - right?"

"Ye said it was the parachute jump at Coney Island?"

"You got that right. If you're still aboard in summer we can - uh - take a trip down and jump from it."

"No' me pal!" he said fervently. "Ah'm strictly navy! Leave yon shite tae the paratroopers!"

Jake's teeth chattered. "Let's get back inside," he urged. "Before our nuts drop off and shatter in the scuppers - right?"

The juniors were kept busy during the afternoon watch. The ship had been decelerating for the past eight hours. Both propeller shafts were turning at one hundred rpm when standby rang at 1415. The telegraphs were answered and they waited for the eight-to-twelve watch to take over the manoeuvring wheels.

When they were relieved Christie seized the floater's arm. "Get over there and look after the gland steam," the second ordered along with the warning. "Be ready for a complete stop in a few minutes."

"How dae ye ken that we're gaun tae stop in a wee while?" Angus asked curiously.

"Because we normally pick up the pilot at Sandy Hook around this time."

The pilot was not the only person to be picked up. Detective-Inspector David Cunningham and Detective-Sergeant Betty Stevenson along with four customs officers and two immigration officials waited uneasily on the wallowing tender. A shell door swung open and a pair of handline bitter ends were dropped down. When the tender came alongside the liner a wooden ladder was set up and held steady by three of the tender's crewmembers.

The pilot experienced in mid-ocean transfers scampered easily up the ladder. The American officials nervously took a bit longer to make the ascent. Cunningham with great reluctance groped his way up while Stevenson, on the other hand, was groped on the way up.

Hodgkin and Tilbury led the police officers to Cabin B17 and acquainted them with the latest events of the case. The ships' officers learned that the New York Police Department would be interviewing all passengers debarking at this time. It was likely that the CID detectives would be staying on board the vessel for the first cruise to interview all the crew and any remaining passengers.

The Sphere relieved Angus on time while he in turn relieved The Mekon at the port manoeuvring wheels. When Davis showed up the Scot was sent topside for thirty minutes.

By now the ship had already passed through the Narrows, the strait that runs between Staten Island and Brooklyn, and was presently entering New York Harbour.

The liner was navigating the channel between Liberty Isle and Governor's Isle when he stepped out onto the open deck. Directly ahead lay a panoramic view of the Battery on Manhattan Island. Snow-crested skyscrapers were etched against the clear winter air. From the port side the first tripper watched the massive green Statue of Liberty slip past. Ellis Island loomed out from behind the edifice.

The vessel's bow shifted a few points for the North River approaches. He went back to the starboard side to catch a glimpse of the famous Brooklyn Bridge spanning the East River. The frigid air sweeping across the harbour chilled his bones and ushered him back into the warmth for some hot food. Reasonably thawed out after his repast he went below,

Thirty minutes later it was darker on deck. Admiring the Manhattan skyline, he was disturbed to find himself sandwiched between DI David Cunningham and DS Betty Stevenson at the ship's rail. His head oscillated from one to the other in mute askance.

"Is your name Angus King?" the policewoman enquired, her voice soft and polite yet somewhat stern.

"Aye," replied a mystified Angus.

A nod from Cunningham sent Hodgkin scurrying back to the bridge. Flashing warrant cards accompanied introductions. Quite suddenly the Empire State and Chrysler Buildings diminished, melding into the glitter of lights that were twinkling on all over the city. His vivid recollections of the murder case were swiftly converted into Betty Stevenson's shorthand. The crossfire of questions made him wonder if he was going to be charged with the heinous crime.

His feelings hit a new low, almost to the depths of the Lincoln Tunnel, which the *Dalriada* just happened to be sailing over at the time. The interview only lasted twenty minutes or so and presently the two police officers were off on a search for further evidence. He sighed with relief and went back down below.

A third time on deck revealed the liner edging towards her berth at Pier 92 in the vicinity of West 53rd Street. Tugs were assisting the ship to ease her massive bulk against the powerful current of the Hudson River. At least Angus thought it was massive until he looked across to Pier 90 to gape at the gigantic RMS *Queen Mary* dwarf the sheds of her own berth. The famous liner's well-lit triple black and red funnels stood starkly against the New York skyline. The *Queen of Dalriada* inched towards the quayside where light lines, attached to heavy hawsers, snaked fore and aft into waiting hands on shore. Gangways trundled out of the big green shed spearing the open shell doors in the ship's side.

Jake tapped his shoulder. "Finished with engines."

"Ok thanks Jake," he replied absently.

"What's the matter?"

"Ah was just quizzed by a pair o' detectives."

"Oh? And what did New York's Finest want?"

"Naw. Yon twa were from Scotland Yard."

"Wah-ow! In the big leagues, eh?"

"Ah just telt them whit Ah knew," he said, dismissing this line of conversation. "When dae we go ashore?"

"Uh - you can't go until you get an immigration pass - right?" White told him. "Go down to the - uh - Tourist Class Lounge and - uh - see the authorities. They're waiting to check out the new guys - right?"

With the ship docked suppertime was moved back a couple of hours to five p.m. Davis overheard the pair discussing the police interview and quickly gulped down his food. He grabbed an apple and orange from the fruit bowl and went up to the tank room to inform his dad.

Davison thought about this recent turn of events while he crunched on the apple. His son had told him of the new difficulties of trying to move about in the accommodation. Also, there was a chance of being spotted going in and out of the tank room from the shore. He considered taking his chances with the fan rooms. It occurred to him that in reality he was imprisoning himself. What was it Samuel Johnson had said? Something about a ship was a prison with a chance of drowning. With a bit of luck he'd be able to nip ashore in the wee hours of the morning when the waterfront would be hopefully quiet.

Straight after supper King went to apply for a landing pass in the Tourist Class Lounge. He latched onto a long queue where a large black man soon singled him out because of his uniform. The Negro was dressed in a sky-blue shirt with multicoloured insignia on it, black trousers and shoes. In the space of a few moments he was fingerprinted, photographed, and interrogated which made him wonder whether he was to be integrated or incarcerated.

He peeped into Jake's cabin after the aggravating rigmarole and found his shipmate attired in civvies. A yellow woollen scarf encompassed his neck to drape the lapels of his heavy winter coat. He clutched black leather gloves in his left hand.

"Uh - how did you make out Gus?"

"Ok. Ah guess," he answered, flashing his temporary landing card. "Yon immigration guys are a nosy bunch. They kept askin' if Ah was affiliated with communists, radicals or unions. They seemed paranoid tae me."

"You got that right," agreed White. "Dress a Yank and a squarehead up in the same uniform and give them a little bit of authority and you've got the nucleus of an SS squad."

"Where are ye gaun?"

"I'm going to buy a record player in Macy's. I didn't have enough bread to buy it last trip. I'm going to Sam Goody's afterward for records. D'you want to tag along and give me a hand to carry the stuff back?"

"Ok. Hang oan a second until Ah get changed."

Shortly after, they were threading through the bustling crowds in the busy customs and immigration shed. Porters were everywhere shoving trolley loads of luggage. The dockside was an emotional affair where various groups of people met with much hugging and kissing. A general hubbub filled the building while the two shipmates weaved their way through the masses. Angus was excited by firsthand glimpses of the new country. His senses were becoming attuned to strange sights, odours and sounds as they approached the warehouse exit.

They stepped out onto a wide cobbled street with an overpass running the full length of it. The street was Twelfth Avenue and the freeway above was the West Side or Joe DiMaggio Highway. Like great wasps hovering around fruit preserves Yellow taxicabs jockeyed for position ready to pounce on the first succulent victim from the ship. Jake opened the rear door of one and ushered his buddy inside.

His eyes panned in every direction as the cab whizzed along Broadway. Bell-ringing Santas ho-ho-hoed on the doorways of department stores. Here and there breaches had been dug through the walls of snow that divided roads from sidewalks. Neon lights and Christmas trees decorated store windows. The cab sped past Times Square on its way to 34th Street. The cabby wished them 'A Merry Christmas' in response to the Canadian's tip. The engineers zigzagged through bustling shoppers into the cloying warmth of Macy's popular department store.

Inside, the pair bee-lined for the electronics department. Angus became bored and wandered off to the sporting goods area. He was perusing some fishing equipment when Jake, toting his purchase, found him.

A card of brightly-coloured tied flies absorbed his shipmate's focus. "Planning on doing some fishing?"

He looked up from his pondering. "Ah was just wonderin' if Ah might get a chance tae dae some fishin' when we reached the Bahama Islands."

"Would the fish take these flies?"

"Ah wouldnae think so," said Angus, dubiously studying them. "These are for bass."

"Well, you could always use 'em back home - right?"

Angus laughed heartily and shook his head. "It's kinda obvious that ye're no' a fisherman!"

"Couldn't you catch fish in Scotland with these?" asked a slightly peeved Jake.

"Och aye!" he hooted. "But it would be illegal."

"Really? Fly fishing is legal in Scotland - right?"

"Aye," he agreed. "But if Ah dropped a line o' these flies in the Clyde, a' the trout would fall oot onto the riverbank laughin' an' Ah could just chuck 'em them intae my creel."

"I thought fish would take any fly - right?"

"They will, but just at certain times o' the year. Trout are not daft enough tae go for a mayfly in September."

"Hey Gus, look at that!" Jake pointed to a complete fishing kit that seemed reasonably priced.

His companion cursorily examined it and agreed that it was a bargain. "Aye, that's a braw wee rod an' spinnin' reel. It'll dae me fine." He chose a number of spoons and other lures, an extra spool of heavy monofilament line along with some wire traces. "Ye never ken whit ye're gaun tae catch!" He did not realise just how prophetic his statement was.

The frigid air hit them outside the overheated store. The wind sweeping along Broadway forced the visitors to cower deeply into their overcoats. Snatches of Christmas carols could be heard from various stores.

"They get ready early for Christmas here," said Angus.

"You got that right. It's the same in Canada."

"That reminds me Ah'll hae tae get some Christmas cards an' post them afore we sail."

"You should've bought them in Macy's - right? Never mind there are plenty of variety stores between here and the waterfront - eh?"

The engineers continued north along Broadway past Times Square, only stopping occasionally to window-shop but eventually they reached the record store Jake had mentioned. They went inside.

Angus was amazed at their stock. "Jings, they must hae millions o' records in here!"

"You've got that right," replied Jake while they navigated aisles that displayed row upon row of records. It did not take long to make a selection for Jake obviously had some choices already in mind.

"Will that be all sir?" asked the pretty salesgirl, sorting out his selection of long-playing records on the counter. "Yeah, this'll do me for this trip," he said, reaching for his billfold.

Stamping his feet outside the record store Angus inquired, "Where tae noo?"

A high-pitched whistle flagging down a taxi partly answered his question. "Back to the ship with this lot first - right?"

The taxi whisked them back to the waterfront and dropped them off in front of a Market Diner that sat directly across the road from the ship.

"Hungry?" asked King.

"You got that right."

The busy diner was cosy and warm. Tantalizing aromas drifted from the stainless steel interior of the kitchen. Stevedores, truck drivers, and a policeman were mounted on bar stools around the counter. A lot of the tables were occupied with customers. Jake selected a freshly wiped Formica table and sat down. His buddy took the seat opposite.

A bleached blonde waitress sporting a bubble-cut was soon hovering at their table, pencil poised at the ready. Shifting a wad of gum in her mouth, she snarled, "*Whaddayawanna* eat?"

"Could Ah hae the navy bean soup please?"

"I'll have the same sweetie," said Jake.

"*Two-bowl-a-bean*!" the woman cried out loud.

Within minutes two bowls of piping hot soup were served with bread sticks and crackers.

"Ah enjoyed that." Angus beamed up at the waitress as she cleared away the two empty bowls.

"*Ja wan' enythin' else*?" A honeyed Southern accent escaped from the gum chomping teeth.

"Aye," he replied. "Could Ah hae the New York strip steak wi' french-fried potatoes please?"

"I'll have scrambled eggs on toast honey," Jake ordered politely.

"*Haddaya lak yo' stay-ik*?" she asked, scribbling on her note pad.

"Eh - oh -" stammered Angus, his brow frowning while he tried to decipher this gibberish. "Eh, weel done - if ye dinnae mind."

The woman yelled at the phantom in the kitchen again. "*Wan strip stayik - birrnt - n'frahs. Two 'n' a raft 'n' wreck 'em*!"

Jake grinned from behind his plate of scrambled eggs at the look on his friend's face when his steak arrived. The huge slab of beef overlapped the platter leaving little room for the chips, which were heaped on top along with a generous scoop of baked beans. With a puzzled expression on his face the young Scot sifted through the chips with his knife.

"Sumpthin' wrawng hunny?"

"No' really, Ah'm just lookin' for the horns!"

She giggled, "This is Noo Yawk nat Tixas! Gee, Limeys ah funny!"

The woman reappeared with a carafe of coffee just as he was finishing his steak.

"Yew boys lak moa cawffee?"

"Aye," said Angus with a sigh for he was feeling completely stuffed.

"Yo fram Scatland?" queried the girl topping up his cup.

"Aye," he repeated, casting an appreciative eye on her generous bosom.

"Ma Gran'pappy ciame fram they-ah," she informed him. "Ah cain remembah him teachin' me to speak Scattish when Ah wus jest a lil gal."

"Ah thought Ah could detect a wee bit o' an accent," he lied, and took a wild guess. "Frae the Hebrides?"

"That's riaght! Cain yo' guess which eye-land?"

"Skye?"

"No - farthah wist. Tra a-gain."

"South Uist?"

"Naw - still farthah wist. Tra one mo' ti-me."

""Newfoundland?"

"Aw, *yo're joshin' me*!" She laughed. "It's Barra!"

He paid the tab and gave her a generous tip. "Thaink yo' sugah! Ah don't know wha folks sigh-ay Scatsmen ah tight!" She flounced off to serve another table.

The two friends carried their purchases back to the ship. Angus wanted to grab a couple of hours of shuteye since he had the first port watch.

Oscar Davis was ashore while King was in Immigration. He'd observed the unusual degree of gangway security. Uniformed police were noticeable among the milling throng within the customs and immigration shed. Upon reaching Twelfth Avenue he walked across to the small stores that catered for seafarers where he purchased a large thermos

He went into the Market Diner, and had it filled with soup. Davis had a quick bite before ordering a takeout of steak sandwiches and coffee then he made his way back to the ship.

Though the crowds had thinned out considerably security was still very much apparent. The engineers' quarters was practically desolated which made it perfectly simple to go to the tank room unobserved.

Below the King Edward Hotel

0030 Wednesday

"Hey Oscar, did you get the watch off tonight?" asked Emsworth, the 2BR eight-to-twelve watchkeeper.

Davis froze, his key still in his door lock. "Oh hi, Hamish. Er - no, I just came topside for some tools."

"Too bad. I've got a date at the *Lorelei.*"

"Lucky sod," said Oscar, and waited until Emsworth was out of sight before opening the door.

His father was bundled up ready to go. "I'm sorry Dad. You can't leave right now. The dockside is chock-a-block with security. Try and grab a couple of hours of shuteye. I'll be back around four. Maybe things will be quieter then."

But the word had already gone out and security was beefed up. New York policemen patrolled the great sheds, company watchmen guarded the gangways on the dockside and MAs stood watches at all the open shell doors. They would remain on duty until the vessel left port.

1930

The day had been uneventful and only two items of significance had stuck in King's mind. The first was Boat Drill and the second was meals in port. The whole ship's company was frozen from standing around for almost an hour watching packice drift past in the Hudson River's sluggish current. The usual launching of lifeboats had been cancelled not because of the bitter weather but to prevent the freshly painted hulls from being scarred by the growlers. The cuisine had changed drastically in port. It seemed as if the chef had died suddenly, the cook had gone to the funeral and left his cat in charge of the galley.

Consequently Angus ate in the Market Diner. He was indulging in another strip steak dinner when Jake slid beside him and asked if he was interested in going to the British Merchant Navy Officers' Club. After swallowing a choice morsel of well-done beef, King said that would be ok since he wasn't too keen on roaming around alone in the city at night.

"It opens at eight o'clock but it doesn't liven up till later, right?" he was told. "That steak looks pretty good. I believe that I'll have that too."

Just then the girl who'd served them on the previous evening came to the table. "Ah see yo' friend is back a-gain, Aingus."

Jake's left eyebrow climbed a few millimetres in response. A glance at his shipmate brought a shrug and a brief smile.

The waitress went to Jake's side, notebook at the ready. "What would yo' liake?"

"Strip steak, rare, with a baked jacket potato, please."

"*One stay-ik - raw*! '*Tater in a tuxedo*!"

The colourful language made King splutter as something went down the wrong way. The waitress patted his back enthusiastically and anxiously asked him if he was all right. After clearing his windpipe with a few sips of ice-water he coughed and wheezed, "Thanks Corrine. Ah think that Ah'm ok the noo."

"Yo' haid me worried they-ah, Aingus!" Looking at Jake she said, "Ah'll get yo' order na-ow."

As she sashayed away Jake's left eyebrow quivered in its elevated position. "Corrine?" he queried before mimicking, "Aingus - eh? What's going on?"

"Och, we just got talkin' aboot Scotland," he explained. "Ye dinnae think that Ah fancy her, dae ye? She must be nearly twice my age!"

"Ri-ight," drawled Jake, his right eye drooping into a slow wink. "Well, she fancies you, old son. You know what they say: the older the fiddle the sweeter the tune."

"Knickers! Besides, Ah like tae tune up my ain fiddles."

"You know what? That, my friend, is a forced draught job!" he warned. "And if you're not careful she'll eat you bloody well alive."

"Och, your knickers are a' mince!"

Jake craned forward and whispered. "During your little tete-a-tete, did she tell you she came from Texas?"

"Aye, she does come frae Texas," he admitted. "How dae ye ken?"

"Elementary my dear Angus," replied White and cupped his hands toward his chest. "Everything is bigger in Texas!"

Both men burst out laughing. It was almost nine o'clock by the time they left the diner and grabbed a cab, which dropped them off outside the King Edward Hotel at 120 - 126 West 44th Street. The British Merchant Navy Officers' Club lay crouched in the hotel's basement. Upon entering the Canadian went directly to his left, heading toward an elderly lady who was playing a baby grand piano, the only musical instrument in the place.

He introduced King who politely smiled before scanning the room while Jake chatted to the pianist. Rectangular in shape with a well-stocked bar at the far end, the darkened room probably was four or five times bigger than the engineers' wardroom. The dance floor was of highly polished parquetry with tables and chairs forming its perimeter. Coloured lights flickered intermittently, revealing faces of dancers shuffling by. Many of the girls hailed from the UK and staffed offices in and around Manhattan. Often they sought out news by keeping touch, in more ways than one, with their countrymen.

Bright lights at the bar drew the two engineers like moths to a candle flame. A crush of people surrounded the bar and Jake was forced to call his order over the shoulder of a man perched on a stool. When the drinks came he reached over, dropped some bills on the counter and started to pick them up. The fellow in front had been conveniently leaning over conversing with a friend when he abruptly straightened up and nudged White. The drinks including the stranger's beer foamed across the wooden counter top.

Jake apologised. "Sorry buddy! I'll buy you another, right?"

"If thy say so myte," a broad Yorkshire dialect replied.

The bartender wiped up the spill and took his order.

With a grin the Yorkshireman lifted up his replenished glass. "Ta myte - cheers!"

"So-o, what line are you with?" asked Jake.

"Kunard myte."

"Cunard? Are you from the *Queen Mary*?"

"Reight again myte!"

"What's your job?"

"Feed man - after engineroom." He gestured his glass at a fellow nearby. "'Arry 'ere, is the lub-oil man."

"Feed man?" repeated Jake. "Boilerfeed water, you mean?"

"Aye lad," admitted the stranger.

"Do you mean to tell me that feed and lub-oil are two separate jobs?"

The Yorkshireman smiled in acknowledgement and pick-ed up his glass again. "Cheers!"

"Cheers!" Jake replied automatically. "Y'know, we're on the *Queen of Dalriada* berthed next door. I'm the only engineroom junior of the watch. Excuse me for asking, but what's your salary?"

"Eighty-four quid-a-month."

"Eighty-four pounds-a-month!" The Canadian all but screeched. "Eighty-four pounds-a-month, for doing half a job? Christ, I only get seventy-four pounds-a-month and I'm doing the whole damned job!"

The Yorkshireman drew himself upright on his stool and mustered as much prestige into his tone as he could. "Ah myte," he proudly beamed. "But I work fo' Kunard!"

"I work fuckin' hard too, buddy!" Jake bitterly retorted. "But I don't get no eighty-four pounds-a-month for it!"

Angus laughed at the witty remark his friend unconsciously made. He had been too envious to twig onto the East Pennine vernacular. The two friends moved to a vacant table and cast glances about the room scouting the talent. The pianist began to play, *Save the last dance for me.*

"Now there's a bit of romantic music, buddy," said White. "Are you going to dance?"

"No thanks," Angus simpered. "Ah'm sweatin'!"

"Prick! I didn't mean with me!" Jake exclaimed. He set off on a course towards a well-developed brunette in the far end of the room.

Angus had fetched in another round by the time Jake returned to their table. Anger marred the Canadian's face. He picked up a glass and drained it with one swallow. He slammed the empty glass down on the table with a curse. "Bastard!"

"Noo, whit's wrang?"

"Do you know what? That chick that I was dancing with is just raring to go and I have to turn to at midnight."

"How dae ye ken she was? Ye've only had one dance."

"I tell you buddy," gloated Jake. "I whispered in her ear 'I could eat you rare.' D'you know what her reply was? She said 'You mean raw, don't you?'"

The beat stepped up with a passable rendering of *Let's twist again* and Jake was off again in pursuit of the brunette. Two dances later he was back for his coat and scarf. "I'm off to get my jollies, I hope!" he crowed with a lecherous grin. "I'll be seein' ya pal - eh?"

"Hae fun."

About half-an-hour later Christie ambled in and made his way to the bar before drifting along to his table. He slid a glass of Scotch in front of his junior.

"Would you like a whisky Mister King?"

"Aye," replied Angus. "Dinnae mind if Ah dae. *Slainte*!"

"Slumming tonight Mister King?" the second leered.

Angus shot him a puzzled glance. "Slummin', Mister Christie? Ah wouldnae call this slummin'."

"I would. Only tarts and perverts frequent this den of iniquity."

"So how come ye're here then?"

The satanic grin widened. "Because as well as being an arch-bastard, I'm also a bit of a pervert."

He gazed thoughtfully at his swarthy face. "How lang hae ye been at sea Mister Christie?"

"Fifteen years," answered the second. "Ten on tankers." He shook his head as if recalling past tribulations and warned his junior. "Never sail on tankers. It's an awful lonely life sailing from one sandbar in the Persian Gulf to another desolate spot in the middle of nowhere to unload. Then you top up with ballast and sail back to the same bloody sandbar!"

"Didn't ye ever get intae a port?"

"Sometimes, but not too often. If you stay on tankers long enough, you either turn queer, alcoholic, or crazy."

Angus grinned. "Ye left yourself wide-open there Sec!"

"Cheeky young twerp! The only thing that saved my sanity was chess. I sailed for years with a chess master," he reminisced. "I ended up beating him too!"

"Aye," agreed King. "It's a fine game all right."

"Do you play?" Christie asked hopefully.

"Ah've had my moments," replied Angus, smirking.

"Let's go back to the ship right now and we'll have a game!" insisted the second.

Before he could reply a fairly attractive girl tapped him on the shoulder, which motivated him to look up into twin pools of come-hither eyes. "Ladies' choice," her mellow voice invited. "Would you like to dance?"

"Cer-certainly Miss," Surprised, Angus stumbled out an enthusiastic assent. Rising he led her onto the dance floor. They shuffled around the floor. Consumption of spirits had lowered his reserve and made him feel amorous. He boldly held his dance partner closer. Softly he hummed Buddy Holly lyrics in her ear and kissed the perfumed neck. He was interrupted when someone bumped into him. He swivelled his head round just in time to see Christie mouth 'jig-a-jig' as he waltzed by with another girl. He mouthed silent curses at him and continued to make romantic overtures to his willing companion. "*The weatherman says clear today*," he crooned softly.

A firm jab broke the spell.

Expecting another rude comment or vulgar gesture from his second, he turned to find a fist exploding on his chin. The sudden blow, accompanied by brightly coloured stars, drove him backwards into a vacant chair. With a glazed expression he gaped up to watch his aggressor seize his dancing partner by her arm. Christie appeared from the crush and stared daggers over his horn-rimmed glasses into the perpetrator's face then proceeded to belly bump him across the dance floor.

"Hey, that's my floater you've just hit!" he belligerently roared over the now-racing piano chords.

"He was trying to get off with my girl," the stranger retaliated. "Now piss off before you get the same!"

"Thou shalt not threaten a Second!" snarled Christie, bringing a massive tightly clenched fist down on the male-factor's skull. The man dropped pole-axed to the floor.

"Here, that's my shipmate you've just hit!" protested a bystander. "I'm going to flatten you!" The man was much bigger than the second and was obviously much stronger than his somnolent buddy.

Sizing up the new contender the second said, "You wouldn't hit a guy wearing glasses, would you? Hang on a second," he said and removed his spectacles.

The other man hesitated. That was his mistake. With a flourish the sturdy glasses slashed upwards like a blade and hit the bloke beneath his nose. Blood, snot, and tears appeared like magic. The man yelped and bowed over clutching his face whereupon he was dropped by a vicious rabbit punch. A girl screamed and the music stopped. The bartender-bouncer elbowed his way through the crowd. "What's going on here?"

Christie calmly polished the lens of his glasses. "These men have had too much to drink. Look, they can't even stand up!"

He stepped over the crumpled forms to help Angus to his feet. "Are you all right, lad?"

Gently rubbing his chin his junior replied, "Aye, Ah think so. Thanks Sec!"

"Call me Bob. Well I think that's enough callisthenics for tonight. How do you fancy a nice quiet game of chess?"

His junior grinned then winced.

"Does it hurt . . . Angus?"

"Only when Ah laugh," came the timeworn cliché. "Come oan Mister Chris - Bob. Let's go back tae the ship an' play a game o' chess."

"Bastard!" Christie vehemently exclaimed when he saw the NOT WANTED ON THE VOYAGE baggage sticker on his cabin door. "I'll bet you it was that get White who stuck that bloody thing on my door!" He tore the label from his door, stepped into his cabin and threw the offensive missive into his waste basket.

Angus was reluctant to say anything and before long the insult was washed into oblivion by generous tots from Christie's bottle of Scotch.

Fire Drill

1140 Friday

'Well Sammy Johnson - if a ship is a prison with a chance of drowning to hell with you. If I can't get off this scow I'll damn well make sure I'm going to enjoy the experience. This is a cruise ship, goddamn it!' Davison was mulling over his new predicament. 'There's only one guy on board who can really identify me and he's on the twelve-to-four watch. I'll just to stay out of his way for a couple of days and leave this barge in Nassau. I'll make my way back to New York from there.'

He stiffened, his eyes drawn to the sunlight as the tank room door opened. It was Oscar with fried bacon on a couple of Scotch baps and some fresh fruit. "That was a good idea getting this thermos son," Davison said pouring a cup of hot coffee for himself.

"Thanks Dad. Look, sometime during this watch we'll hit warm weather. This deck won't be safe anymore when some of the guys come up here to do some bronzie-ing."

"Yeah I know son," acquiesced his father. "Don't worry about it. I've got a pretty good handle on this ship now. I figure that I can go practically anywhere I like just so long as that young Scotchman doesn't spot me." He chewed hungrily and washed it down with the java. "Listen son, is there any chance that can you get me a couple of blankets? I'll need them for tonight. And oh - if you can get me a bit of tarp and some twine that'll come in handy too."

"Ok Dad. What do you need them for?"

"I'll tell you when you come off watch," promised his father eying his watch. "You'll be late if you don't hurry."

"Ok, see you later Dad."

Lounging against a ship's rail appeared to be a favourite pastime for seafarers since bygone days and Angus was no exception watching serried waves from Boat Deck. He'd remembered to mail his Christmas cards yesterday just before the liner sailed. The greys of sky and sea blended so well that it was difficult to see the horizon. The ship rolled and yawed slightly as it sliced through heavy swells. White horses were a fitting term for wave crests that reared up in feathers of glorious spume.

The first tripper tried to imagine the warmth of the Bahamas but could only recall the bitter-cold, snow-covered streets of Manhattan. According to Jake the ship would soon be entering the Gulf Stream and the fine weather normally associated with that latitude. A cold breeze buffeted him and a shiver ran up his spine. It was time to go below.

The watch changed over. The juniors slouched against the platform desk, drinking kye and smoking. Jake reminisced about his latest conquest. Christie strode across the plates to interrupt their conversation.

"Angus, stick around for a bit, will you? Mister White will be needing a hand shortly."

"Ok Bob," acknowledged King.

Christie ambled off to the port side of the starting platform. Jake stared at his receding stern before directing his indignant astonishment upon his shipmate.

"What's all this Angus - Bob, shit? Has he been showing you the golden rivet?"

Chuckling merrily his co-worker retaliated and placing his hands provocatively on his hips asked, "Could ye, by any chance, insinuate that my big buddy is a poofter?"

"Buddy? Whaddayamean - buddy? What's going on?"

"Well, after ye buggered off with yon whore last night . . ." Jake cut him off.

"What whore? She was a very nice girl."

"Did ye get your nasties?"

"Of course! It had to be a quickie though because I was on watch that night - right?"

"Aye, right. So Ah stand corrected then," confirmed Angus, and completed the interrupted sentence. "Wi' yon whore Christie, my pal Bob, brought a couple o' drinks tae my table an' we discussed a few things."

"Really? Like what?"

"Och, the manly art o' self defence, chess, an' . . ."

"Self defence?" interrupted Jake with a sneer. "And just who did he fill in this time, eh?"

"Ah dinnae ken," he replied ruefully. "A guy thumped me right oan the chin so Black Bob slew him an' his pal."

"Then what?"

"Then we came back tae the ship an' played chess."

"Chess? I didn't think that - uh - he was bright enough to play snakes and ladders!"

"Weel, he is!" King assured him.

"Who won?"

"Ah did, twa games oot o' three. But his bottle o' Haig's Dimple beat us baith." He grinned. "Noo he thinks the sun shines oot my arse!"

"Really? Well, it sure ain't the sun that he's shovin' up mine!" retorted Jake. "I'm going to start my checks.'

"Ok. Ah'll check oot the tunnel for ye."

The floater ambled along the tunnel feeling line shaft bearings as he went. The reflections of deckhead lights on the highly polished spinning shafts had a strobic effect against the cavern-like gloom. In the next compartment one of the black gang hung over a hand railing. This was his first trip also. "How are ye daein' the day Jones?" he asked pleasantly. "Are ye still lookin' for Hughie?"

"Oh - hi, Mister King." A pallid green face glanced back at him. "No, I haven't found him yet."

The engineer could feel a flutter in his stomach as the stern heaved up and down in the falling sea. There was a sensation of floating. Jones vomited bits of bacon, beans and fried egg into the bilge.

"Hewaaay!"

A taste of bile seeped into the floater's mouth, giving him the urge to follow suit. Not that he was seasick; it was just the act of witnessing someone spewing that gave him the same urge. 'Thank God Ah dinnae get seasick,' he reflected and left Jones with his misery.

An echoing halloo halted his inspection. He shouted a reply and Jake materialised in the frame of an open watertight door. "Come back to the platform," he bawled. "I need help now."

He hastened back into the engineroom to find White manipulating a valve on the port lube-oil cooling system. "Whit's up?"

"The lub-oil temperature - that's what's up - right? We must be entering the Gulf Stream. The sea temperature is going up and down like a whore's drawers! It's playing merry havoc with lube-oil temps. If we don't get it under control, we'll lose a main engine bearing for sure!"

He opened the valve another half turn and ordered: “You’d better - uh - monitor the starboard cooler and I’ll stay on this one. Try to keep the oil temperature on the cooler’s outlet side at 90° Fahrenheit. If the oil temp rises, open the valve more and vice-versa if it drops - right?”

“If ye say so. Why is it gaun up an’ doon?”

“Because the ship isn’t right in the Gulf Stream yet. We must be sailing through some alternating warm and cold currents. If the sea temp steadies soon, we should be ok.”

An hour was to pass before the temperatures settled. The engineroom air temperature had risen considerably causing them to perspire freely. “Do you know what?” asked White. “It’s time for smoko - right?”

“If ye say so.”

The two juniors indulged in a few moments of relaxation.

“Ah noticed that the ship’s stopped rollin’,” observed Angus. “That’ll make Jones happy.”

“You got that right,” agreed White. “And me too. Calm seas, bronzie weather, nubile women in scanty bikinis laying on the open deck and soaking up the sun - right?”

King pursed his lips and blew a long wolf whistle.

“Don’t let Christie hear you whistling in the engineroom,” Jake warned. “Friend or no, he’ll go absolutely bananas!”

“Why? Is he superstitious?”

“Not that I know of,” replied White. “But you can understand his point. A superheated steam leak might initially begin as a whistle and end up sounding like an express train. That whistle you hear may save your life someday - right?”

“Oh!”

“However, let’s forget about these mundane thoughts and consider other more interesting things - eh? For instance, at the end of our watch we should go out the deck above our quarters, sit in the sun with an ice-cold beer and do some bogging."

"Whit's boggin?'"

There was a lecherous reply. "Birdwatching . . . Ogling women."

The phone buzzer interrupted the conversation.

"What in the hell does Taffy want, I wonder?" asked Jake, snatching up the receiver and made the 2BR connection. "Macy's department store," he hollered. "Third Floor, Lingerie. Can I interest you in a pair of silk knickers?"

"This is the Senior Second speaking Mister and if I catch you answering the phone this way again I'll have your knickers!" He hesitated briefly before speaking again. "And your Gim-bals too! Now ask Mister King to come through!"

The line went dead.

The floater sped off in response to the summons. Noticing on his way through that every section had hoses and extinguishers neatly laid out for Fire Drill he assumed this was the reason why Christie needed him. Jake will just have to manage on his own he reasoned.

Upon entering 2BR he spotted MacKay and Morgan by the fuel-oil heaters. The second, reacting to the loud slam of the airlock door, noted his arrival. "Ah Mister King, just the man we need!"

He motioned at a sizeable cylindrical tank on the catwalk above the heaters. "This stokehold has been designated the Seat of the Fire. So we will be testing all the fire equipment in here to make sure that they all work. Now then, you'll observe that cylindrical tank up yonder on the catwalk above us?"

"Aye Mister MacKay," rhymed Angus

"Mister Morgan has already checked the equipment. The only thing left is that tank. The outlet line must be blocked. An agile young chappie like you should be able to scramble up there easily. I'm too old and the Welshman here is too fat!"

"Whit's in the tank, Mister MacKay?"

"Ox blood."

"Come again?"

"Ox blood," repeated Big John. "When it's mixed under high pressure with seawater it discharges from the fire hose nozzle as foam. It's for putting out oil fires," he added.

"Is it really ox bluid?"

"I don't really know. The damned stuff smells more like it came from their backsides."

King looked around for an access ladder.

"Come on laddie!" Big John urged impatiently. "Get a move on! The Chief will be through here directly to see this unit being tested."

Reaching for an overhead pipe Angus nimbly swung himself up and an instant later he was kneeling on the catwalk removing the lid from the tank. A pungent stench assailed his nostrils making him wrinkle his nose and shake his head in disgust. Accepting the inevitable he rolled up his sleeve and plunged his arm fully into the greyish-tan mess. He soon became aware of a clammy sensation drifting over his right shoulder and down his back just as his fingers located some object on the tank's bottom. He should have rolled up his sleeve further because the cloth was now acting like a wick and drawing the filthy mire all over his boilersuit. The slight turbulence caused by him hastily withdrawing his arm transposed the smell from horrible to indescribable. Almost gagging he slammed the tank lid back in position.

He was back at MacKay's side in a trice hauling a wiper from his pocket to begin dabbing at the congealing slime on his person. "Good lad! It's clear now!" he praised, his smile faded in the now-tainted atmosphere. He nudged the junior back a pace. "Stand downwind a bit laddie! What was causing the blockage anyway?"

"A wee bit o' wood."

The chief engineer strode into the stokehold in full regalia, two rows of multicoloured ribbons honouring his left breast. Four gold bars on the cuff of each arm proudly gleamed in the incandescent light. His small brown eyes darted over the array of fire equipment seeking discrepancies. "Are you ready Mister MacKay?"

"Aye Chief. Mister Morgan, activate the foam unit!"

Taffy picked up a polished brass nozzle and twisting it aimed at the bilge. A powerful jet of dirty foam shot out to permeate the air with its ghastly stench. Bilgewater swirled and slopped against the tank tops. "That's enough! There's too much water in the bilge already," complained Lindsey. "Get it pumped out immediately!"

The stokehold engineer waddled over to a bilge valve and began to spin it open.

"Hold it!" snapped the chief. "Why has that extended spindle been disconnected?" He glared at the steel shaft dangling freely alongside the bilge valve before motioning to Angus to reconnect it.

While the floater made the repair Lindsey asked him if he knew what purpose the spindle served. A glum headshake was the response. He was then told that every compartment was isolated from each other by watertight doors during the event of flooding.

Lindsey explained. "If this boiler room became filled with water an engineer could go to a higher deck, open this valve, and pump out the section. Then he could affect the necessary repairs. That is, of course, if the engineer knew the upper location of the extended spindle and if some idiot hasn't disconnected it!"

The chief craned his head upwards, tilting his cap farther back on his head, so that the path of the spindle could be traced. At deckhead level a set of right-angled mitre gears redirected another rod off to a similar set of gearing where the extension shaft disappeared from sight.

"Do you know where that comes out?"

"Ah dinnae ken sir."

Lindsey vigorously shook his head in disgust, inducing his cap to fall. It would've landed on the footplate but Morgan's frantic effort to catch it inadvertently kicked it into the bilge. All four engineers lined the handrail to view the cap serenely float upside down in a pool of filthy water.

"You blithering idiot!" roared the chief.

Taffy was very apologetic. "Sorry about that chief! I'll go down and get it, see you."

"You've done enough bloody damage! I'll get it myself!"

He ducked under the handrail and stepped onto a tank top cover that was about two feet below the floorplates but still above water level. He stooped down, retrieved his cap and glanced up just in time to see the floater cover his mouth in a vain attempt to conceal his laughter.

"You!" he howled. "Get topside right now! Find where that spindle comes out and open that damned valve!"

The chief wiped the plastic cap cover with a rag donated by Taffy. The second took this opportunity to whisper to Angus,

"In my office you'll find a blueprint of the ship on the after bulkhead. The spindle locations are marked in red ink."

For a brief moment Lindsey permitted himself a little smile. He knew where King had to go. That shaft ended up inside Number One Funnel casing amongst twenty-nine-years of accumulating dust and soot. This petty gloat was short-lived when he started to extricate himself from the bilge.

He grabbed a nearby fire extinguisher firmly to heave himself out. Ordinarily these canisters were securely clamped onto special supports that prevented movement at sea but now, because of fire drill, all units were left standing free in readiness for testing. A shriek of surprise and fear escaped from his lips, its Doppler effect ending with a splash when he fell backwards into the bilge water.

He lay full-length in the swirling foamy scum embracing the fire extinguisher that chose to go off at that very instant. Bellows and spurts of foam splashed upward prompting MacKay and Morgan to reach down and haul their commander from a watery grave. Angus fled the scene.

Inside the senior second's office he perused the blueprint that gave up its secret of the spindle locations. The hand wheel for that specific bilge valve was inside the casing of Number One Funnel. Tracing the circuit back to the pump he noticed that another valve, the main isolation bilge valve for 2BR, should be opened as well. The end of its spindle was inside the First Class Restaurant about ten feet from a specific column. It could be found under a brass plate in the deck.

What the chief failed to tell him was that this particular valve was always left open.

The floater set off on his mission. Partway along the working alleyway a steel door gave him access to the funnel casing. He opened the door, stepped over the high coaming, and shut it behind him. Blackness reluctantly retreated beyond the penumbra from his flashlight. It became apparent that he wasn't inside the funnel at all but on the perimeter of a large cylindrical casing of steel through which boiler exhaust gases passed. Low pipes were an encumbrance, which forced him to inch his way around the heated casing towards his objective.

This is it, he thought, after brushing away an era of soot in order to read the wording on a solitary valve wheel plate. The mechanism was stiff but he succeeded in opening the valve.

Curiosity stirred him to explore farther into the curved narrow recess. He came across a ladder, its rungs descending through a deck opening. His light shone down into the void and he could see a trapdoor secured by hinged lug bolts to the deck below. Chicken bones, serviettes, empty pop cans and other garbage were strewn about as if someone had sat on the trapdoor to have a meal. Strangely enough their labels were clean and legible as if from recent use. Perhaps one of the black gang had found a hidey-hole in which to goof off.

Back out in the working alleyway he brushed the sooty patches on his less-than-white boilersuit into long black streaks. A nearby companionway carried him up to the galleys on R Deck. Various aspects of food preparation daunted his quest briefly until his eyes alighted on a pair of swing doors bearing the legend, First Class Restaurant, in gold leaf. He eased through the doors and stood stock-still in amazement. It was if he had just stepped into a palace.

The restaurant was half-filled with fashionable people having lunch. The enormous room was square and took up the full width of the ship. The port and starboard bulkheads consisted of veneered panelling inset with large windows rather than portholes. On either side of the double swing doors, situated fore and aft, were large murals and tapestries. Eight columns were equally spaced throughout the restaurant. The pillars were a yard square and held up the mosaic ceiling.

Each support was completely covered by mirrors, the glass etched with birds, flowers and leaves. Small alcoves at the base of these supports contained chinaware, cutlery and tiny alcohol burners. A massive chandelier of gleaming crystal hung majestically from the beautiful ceiling.

Directly in front of him stood a catering officer, his watchful eyes surveying the peaceful scene looking for minor inconsistencies. It had been a trying day for the two-ringer. Earlier in the forenoon his well-practised diplomacy had pacified two irate passengers.

Sensing a presence behind him the catering officer casually glimpsed at Angus and calmly gazed forward again. A sliver of time later his head whipped aft and nearly snapping his neck in the process. His eyes bulged at the apparition that had the effrontery to enter this luxurious saloon. With slow shuffling motions the two-ringer edged back to the engineer and from the side of his mouth whispered, “Get to hell out of here - this is the First Class Restaurant!”

“Ah *ken* that,” he was assured.

The catering officer searched upwards imploring, “Why me oh Lord, why me?”

Deepening his voice almost to bass the floater said, “Because two-ringers piss me aff!”

“I beg your pardon?”

“Just a wee joke,” smiled the interloper. He espied a round brass plate that was sunk flush with the Korkoid linoleum deck. It coincided with the blueprint, which regrettably had neglected to divulge pertinent information in regards to the gentleman sitting in the chair above it.

"Ah-ha!" he happily proclaimed, and began ambling towards goal. "That's just the very thing Ah'm huntin' for!"

"Oh my Gawd!" squeaked the officer. "Come back!"

The engineer strode on confidently ignoring passengers who had temporarily ceased their repast to view this unusual interruption. The stench of ox blood wafting over their food would kill appetites for the rest of the day.

"Excuse me sir," he politely asked the diner seated above his objective. "Would ye mind gettin' up for a wee minute?"

The gentleman in question peered up at him, a skewered morsel of filet mignon hovering in midair some three inches from his open lips. The aquiline nose on his weathered face twitched when the delicate aroma of haute cuisine metamorphosed into . . .

He could not place the putrid odour although the word 'shite' was predominant in his mind. That thought vanished instantly when he realised whom and what was encroaching on his repast. "What in the blazes are you doing here?"

Angus' eyes riveted on the four bars of gold braid on the diner's epaulettes before stammering, "Ah'm really sorry Captain but Ah'm just followin' the Chief Engineer's instructions!"

"And that is?"

"Ah hae tae operate that valve under your chair."

"Doesn't the Chief know its lunchtime?"

"Ah wouldnae think that lunch in his uppermost thoughts right noo Captain," he answered humbly.

"Where is he?"

"Probably haein' a shower," he guessed.

"Having a shower? What the devil is going on?" demanded Captain Cowell, trying to keep his voice level for the benefit of the passengers. He turned his head this way and that before his eyes rested on the nervous catering officer. He stabbed a finger at him.

"*You*! Get me the Chief Engineer on the telephone immediately!"

The two-ringer came sprinting back with a telephone and plugging it into a nearby jack, spoke frantically into the mouthpiece. He handed the receiver to his captain.

"Chief?" grated the skipper. "So you finally got your revenge after all those years!"

A distant voice asked, "What in the blazes are you talking about, Skipper?"

The captain whispered hoarsely. "You know what I'm talking about. You never did forgive me for that practical joke that I played on you when we served as apprentices together. I never realised that you could be so vindictive, Alan"

"I still don't know what you're talking about!"

"At this very moment, I'm seated in the main restaurant with a - a creature standing in front of me and it belongs to you!"

"What is it?" came drifting faintly.

"I can only describe it as a red-maned Scottish zebra!"

"A zebra?"

"Well, it's wearing an off-white boiler suit with black sooty stripes on it!"

"Black sooty - oh my God!" exclaimed Lindsey. "Put him on the line please, Skipper."

The intruder was handed the receiver. "He wants a word with you."

He cautiously placed it to his ear. "Angus King here, sir!"

The forthcoming blast jerked the instrument away from his head. The tirade died down. He gingerly placed the phone to his ear again and asked, "Does that mean that ye dinnae want the valve opened?"

Another upbraiding message blasted the phone from his temple. "Ok Chief - cheerio just noo!" he acknowledged and hastily hung up. "It seems that this valve has already been opened." And more to himself than to the captain said, "He wants tae see me at the end o' my watch."

The master wholly agreed. "I darn well think so too!"

"Maybe he'll no' be so angry then," he said wistfully.

"I wouldn't count on that if I were you Mister," he was advised.

"Well, see ye," said Angus, and blithely ambled off.

Captain Cowell apologised to his table guests and said, "Y'know, about a hundred and fifty years ago that lad would have gone far - all the way around the keel!" His guests tittered and returned to their repast with a bit less gusto.

Back on station in the engineroom he recounted his adventures to Christie and White.

"Jeez!" Jake observed glumly. "First trip to sea and already you're in deep shit! Right?"

"Whit dae ye think the Chief will dae, Bob?"

"Oh, nuthin' much Angus." Then Black Bob offhandedly remarked: "A couple of dozen lashes. And don't forget to take your own grating!"

1620

The chief engineer's door swung open in response to the soft knock. The culprit, dressed in his best uniform, peered back at his senior as if butter wouldn't melt in his mouth.

"Come into my cabin," said the spider to the fly.

Engineer King crossed the threshold and the door closed behind him.

1655

Jake crouched forward in a pilfered deckchair, his eyes arrested by a lithe, bikini-clad body below. He sighed and cracked open another bottle of beer. A shuffling dragging sound drew his attention and he dipped his sunglasses for a better view. An uneven gait emulated a painful limp. "Cleared your haemorrhoids out - right?" he commiserated, handing his friend a much needed beer.

His recently chastised shipmate took a deep swig and resting both elbows on the oaken rail absorbed the panorama aft. There was hardly a cloud in the sky and a friendly sun warmed his face. A faint trace of funnel smoke drifted across a turbulent widening roadway of emerald and silver that stretched right to the horizon, a magnificent contrast to the deep blue of the sea. He let out a despondent sigh and bugled again before wiping his lips.

"Thanks Jake - Ah needed that. After the Chief reamed oot my arse, he gave me a pep talk aboot officers' dress code when in the presence o' passengers an' ended up cancellin' my watch aff when we reach the Bahamas."

There was just a mere hint of sympathy. "Tough titty! Still, it's better than being logged. Look on the bright side, it's only your first trip and already you're bloody famous!"

That remark invited a deluge of cold beer on his bare chest.

"Ooh! You bastard!" yelped Jake, then laughingly suggested: "Go and get your swimming trunks on and get some sun before it sets. And bring some more beer - right?"

King returned shortly toting four beers and a blanket, which was spread out on the warm planks. He flopped down again with a sigh. An hour passed and they were out of beer again.

Jake broke the silence with a wheeze. "Boy, it sure is hot! I'm going for more beer. Hey, I bet you'd like some ice cream, right?"

"No thanks Jake. Beer'll dae me fine. Ah'll tell ye whit though, get me the day's paper. Ah havenae read it yet."

"You got it Bud."

Having discovered that the bar was open he returned with two tankards of beer, a small plate of ice cream, and a newspaper tucked under his arm. He was relieved of the paper and a pint. White resumed his lookout station and dug into his ice cream.

His buddy lay on his stomach perusing the small newspaper. The news was brief, a little more than headlines plucked from ether by the ship's radio and published by the printer shop. Other articles gave insights into travelling, fashion, and certain leisure activities. A medley of anecdotes and jokes inspired its name: *The Pict-Wit Papers*. Soon tiring of reading he laid his head down and closed his eyes.

Recalling the beer spill on his chest revenge was repaid by flicking a blob of ice cream onto the small of King's back.

"Oo-ya! Arsewipe!"

Jake slapped his knee in delight. Angus glared up at him and rolled onto his back shading his eyes with the newspaper. Fifteen minutes later a warmer dollop splattered onto his navel.

"Cut that oot, Jake!" he warned, not bothering to look up.

A minute or so passed. "We must be near land."

"How dae ye ken?"

"A little bird told me - right?"

King drew the newspaper from his face, his eyes squinting against the glaring sky. He swore at the diminishing seabird that had used his belly button as a latrine.

"You know what?" Jake philosophically began: "Some people have good days and some people have bad days but you - uh - Gus ol' buddy, have had a real shitty day - right?" He proceeded to itemize on his fingers. "Oxshit down below, real shit from the Skipper, bullshit from the Chief, and now to round off your day - bird's shit! Right?"

Oscar was aghast at his father's plan. He watched him nibble on a thick slice of cold ham. The fierce sun had reddened his face and neck for he'd been strolling around Boat Deck acting like a tourist for most of the afternoon. He had even lolled in a deckchair and shared a pot of tea with an elderly couple on Prom Deck. Now he was proposing to spend tonight and perhaps more nights up the after funnel sleeping behind the ship's whistle!

"That foghorn is securely mounted on a steel plate with a roomy catwalk on either side," his dad had explained. "There's just enough room for me to lie behind it and sleep without rolling off. Nobody is likely to look up and I certainly can't be seen from the bridge because of the forward funnel."

"But what if there's a foggy?" he protested. "Your eardrums will be shattered if that whistle blows when you're up there."

"I'll be all right. It happened to me before in another ship," Davison reassured his son. "Most of the sound is projected forward. Anyway, I'll feel or see any fog before the bridge does. I didn't spend all those years in sail and not learn anything. And another thing the odds are three-to-one on that whistle blowing because there are two of them on the forward funnel."

"Each whistle is activated in rotation Dad," Oscar informed him. "And I don't know which one was used during the last foggy,"

"It's a chance I'll have to take."

"Have it your own way. It won't be for much longer. We'll be in Nassau tomorrow so maybe you'll get ashore there without any problems."

Shark!

1400 Saturday

While Angus King was on anchor watch in 1BR Homer Davison had slipped ashore on the tender using his son's pass. The ship had arrived that morning and being too large to go alongside at Prince George Wharf she had anchored near Paradise Island, which lies north of New Providence, the main island. The American had planned to keep a low profile until the *Dalriada* has sailed before he booked a flight to the States.

The twelve-to-four engineers and black gang who could be spared from watchkeeping duties were allowed to go ashore leaving a quasi-skeleton staff below.

Fireman-trimmer William Telfer viciously slammed an inspection door shut during the process of his burner check. The disgust on the rating's face was apparent.

"Whit's chewin' at *your* arse?" Angus asked moodily.

Telfer sighed. "They'll not let me ashore. I've been a bad boy. All this lovely weather and damn all t'do!"

"Why don't ye try a wee bit o' fishin'?" suggested Angus.

"With what?"

The engineer gazed at him thoughtfully before replying. "Dinnae worry about that. Ah'll soon fix ye up."

Selecting one of the torches used for igniting the oil fires he removed the kerosene-soaked rag leaving him with a steel rod about three-eighths of an inch in diameter. He stuck one end into the furnace. When it was red-hot he took the rod to the workbench and hammered the first two inches flat. He reheated the rod and continued to fashion an eyed hook. It was near the end of the watch by the time the double barbed hook was ready. Pleased with his work he handed it to the rating. "There ye go, Wullie, ye can start fishin' after watch."

"What about fishing line?"

"Use marline twine. Ah'll gie ye a chit for some."

The rating was dubious. "Will it be strong enough?"

"It's strong enough tae hang yoursel'. Ah would imagine it'll take the strain o' a barracuda or maybe a wee shark."

Telfer brightened. "Ok thanks, Mister King. What can I use as bait?"

"Ask the butcher for a chunk o' bloody fat or gristle."

Forging the hook had made the watch pass quickly and after a cool shower had sluiced away the clammy sweat of the engine spaces, he dressed into mufti. He grabbed a quick snack before heading ashore.

Armed with a camera he boarded the tender. Sunglasses filtered the tropical glare as he click-clicked away his shutter at nearby islands and the approaching shore. A brilliant green sea effervesced on sandy beaches dotted with palms and other lush vegetation. Strange but alluring aromas assailed his nostrils as the tender motored closer and closer to the shore.

The souvenir stands around Prince George Wharf were a good place for the working tourist to browse before strolling over to Rawson Square to relax for a few minutes. From a park bench Angus soaked up the beauty of frangipani, bougainvillea and hibiscus, all of which assailed his eyes and inspired him to take more snapshots. He basked in the late afternoon sun and scribbled frivolous messages on postcards for his family and friends in far-off cold and dismal Scotland.

A passing black lady, her head toting a basket of strange looking fruit, interrupted her journey to direct him to the post office in Bay Street. He found it easily enough beside the courthouse. With his postcards duly stamped and sent on their way he wandered into Shirley Street, a bustling thoroughfare of shops, cars and bicycles. Walking around in the heat made him feel thirsty. His sightseeing activities had introduced him to another section of Bay Street, and by happenstance, in the vicinity of a likely looking tavern.

This merited closer inspection.

It was cool and dark inside. Some Americans lolled around a low stage where a calypso band rippled out pleasing notes. He sauntered to the bar to edge onto a stool. Behind the liquor bottle display was a huge saltwater aquarium. A barkeep rustled up his order, a Cuba Libré in a tall frosted glass.

Lounging against the padded vinyl rail he sipped his drink quite mesmerised by the brightly coloured denizens of the aquarium. The soft music of the islands enhanced the feeling of euphoria so that Time seemed to have no meaning.

A tap on the shoulder jolted him from his daydream. Jake stood behind him grinning like a piano keyboard. "I'll have a drop of the local hooch, ol' buddy if you're buying - right?"

"A planter's punch please," alliterated Angus.

The barkeeper placed a rum-filled frosted glass with a slice of lime on the counter. "Thanks buddy!"

Jake focussed on the aquarium and slowly absorbed the soothing, rhythmic motions of the fish. Musing aloud, he stabbed a finger at a fish with black and white vertical stripes. "Here, that's nice - eh? I wonder what kind of fish that is?"

"It's called a Moorish idol."

"Really? How in the hell do you know that?"

"Ah used tae keep tropical fish," replied King. "No' these saltwater varieties but Ah've read aboot them."

"What's that?"

"A four-eyed butterfly fish," said Angus and revealed further knowledge on the subject. "*Chaetodon capestratus*."

"Ok smart ass. Let's see what you *do* know!" Jake jabbing at the glass as each fish swam into view.

"Marine jewelfish, Queen triggerfish, Blueheid, Common frog fish," he was told. "An' that's a sea anemone behind a' yon livin' brain coral."

"Do you know what? I knew that there were lots of different varieties of fish in the sea but I didn't know they all had such exotic names."

"An' that only touches the surface!" punned Angus. "The majority hae Latin names aboot as lang as your airm. Anyway, whit have ye been up tae while Ah was stuck oan board?"

"Seeing the sights. A drop here, a drop there - all from a connoisseur's point of view, of course."

"Aye right. Or tae put anither way - a bluidy pub crawl!"

"I have to get back on board and see the purser about a sub," announced Jake, supplementing, "I'm out of cash."

"Aye - Ah quite forgot aboot seein' the purser tae."

"Oh, I got a sub from the purser but it was all pissed against a wall."

The Scot placed a banknote on the bar. Waiting for his change he happened to notice a man's figure silhouetted against the tavern's sunlit entrance. There was something about him. The chap stepped over the threshold and waited until his sight acclimatised to the gloom. Realising that somebody was watching him, his eyes flickered briefly as if in recognition. The man about-faced and strode back out. Angus rushed outside, his eyes searching the street. Davison was nowhere to be seen.

Jake followed his friend after picking up the change. Sluing his head this way and that but not knowing what to look for, asked, “What’s up Gus?”

“That guy - did ye no’ see him?”

He shook his head and dropped some coins in his hand. “See who?”

“Yon man who just ran oot,” replied Angus, flushed and quivering with excitement. “He’s the guy that Ah was talkin’ tae last Sunday night - the same night that the ship turned aroond.”

“I thought that Treenie said he’d jumped overboard.”

“Ah thought he did tae,” he admitted. “But Ah’m pretty sure it was him that Ah saw there just noo.”

“Then he must be the world’s best swimmer,” considered Jake skeptically. “Fancy swimming all this way in the dead of winter and beating the ship to boot!”

“Piss aff Jake!” he retorted. “He must hae stowed awa’. Let’s go back tae the ship so that Ah tell yon cops.”

“Ok by me.”

Davison had nipped into a bazaar. ‘That damned kid,’ he muttered. ‘He pops up all over the place like a blasted jack-in-the-box.’

Hidden by racks of coloured fabrics and dangling gourds he could see the engineer out on the sidewalk searching for him. His buddy came out and checked the street for a bit before they walked out of sight. He considered his options.

What options?

As soon as that kid gets back on board, he’ll go straight those English cops. Now what? This was British territory. Jeez, an APB on this little island would nail him for sure. He’d stand out like a snowflake on tarmac. His best bet would be was going back on board the liner. Still, he had Oscar's pass and who in the hell would ever suspect his audacity?

The two engineers boarded the tender. Nearing the liner's counter King could see Willie Telfer lounging by the stern railing, his length of marlin twine drooping into the sea.

Jake nudged Angus, nodding towards two American girls in their early twenties. "Come on and I'll take your picture against that nice backdrop over there."

Terrycloth robes hanging over both girls' shoulders did little to hide their scanty bikinis. The Scot slipped unnoticed behind them and posed while they leaned over the port handrail to peer at the water surface, three feet below them.

By this time the tender had stopped in the shadow of the liner's stern and waited for a sister lighter to complete the embarkation of shore bound passengers. Jake snapped a picture. His friend's gaze swept the superstructure of the ship before coming to rest on the fireman.

The man's line had gone taut. With his experienced fisherman's eye Angus traced the line. It ran alongside the tender and entered the water directly beneath the girls. At first he had surmised that the yarn had fouled the tender's propeller but this was unlikely since the boat had been stopped for more than ten minutes. The girls were waving madly up at some acquaintance on the ship trying to attract attention. Suddenly he became aware of a large greyish shape just about to break surface right beneath the point where the young ladies stood.

On the spur of the moment he grabbed both girls by their beach robe collars and roughly hauled them inboard just as a large sand shark, antagonised by the homemade hook in its maw, leapt clear of the water with hardly a splash.

The girls screamed not because of the shark, which had dropped silently and unseen beneath the waves but because of his assault. In his prompt action to rescue the girls he had inadvertently seized their bra straps along with the terrycloth. Both bras had split between the ample firm breasts now jiggling unfettered in the warm sunset.

Never one to miss an opportunity Jake snapped shots away as fast as the camera allowed the film to index. The tender gently motored alongside the landing stage as this scene was being enacted, much to the delight of the male audience,.

Passengers trooped aboard their floating hotel. With scarlet faces and robes clutched tightly about them the girls trotted up the boarding ladder to complain to the MA on duty. Tearfully they gestured downwards to the tender. An ominous feeling swamped him.

A foregone conclusion hit Jake seconds beforehand and prompted his quite unnecessary remark: "I do believe the shit is on a collision course with the fan!"

The master-at-arms accosted the two engineers on the upper landing. "Hey you!" he snarled at Angus.

"Whit's this 'Hey you' shit?" he retaliated in anger. "Dae ye no' ken that ye're talkin' tae a ship's officer?"

"The officers aboard this vessel are gentlemen," sneered back the MA. "I'm talking to a pervert!"

Angus' temper soared to flashpoint. Bristling, he seized the MA's tunic. "Pervert am Ah? Ah'll show ye who's a pervert!"

Jake stayed the impending clenched fist before it landed on the MA's chin. "Cool it Gus," he warned. "You're in enough trouble as it is - right?"

His shipmate's reasoning made his ire wane. He released the man who promptly grabbed him just as another MA stepped arrived to assist his colleague. They frogmarched him in the general direction of the brig on C Deck for'ard. The lift doors slid open to reveal the captain. The great man recognised the culprit instantly and directed the men to release him.

"Now then, what's going on here?"

After the first MA reported his misconduct Cowell shook his head and advised, "All of you had better come up to my cabin right now."

Inside the captain's cabin Angus related his side of the incident. "This puts the matter in different light. Did anyone else see this shark?"

"Ah dinnae ken Captain," admitted Angus.

The skipper regretfully shook his head. "Well, in that case Mister King, you are confined to your quarters until I find out what actually happened. You will be allowed out for meals and duties only. Dismissed!"

The escorts departed with a crestfallen junior engineer who was too worried about this current development to recall his discovery ashore.

0005 Sunday, 17th December, 1961

On watch that night he asked Jake if he had seen the shark. "Sorry buddy," he said. "To tell you the truth, my attention was completely on those lovely titties you exposed. I thought that you were spinning a yarn about the shark. But just for you I'll fib at your logging. I'll tell the Old Man that I saw the whole thing, right?"

Relief showed momentarily on his countenance before reverting back to his glum state. "Thanks Jake, that means a lot tae me. But Ah dinnae want ye tae get intae bother by lyin'. They might think that ye were part o' the mischief."

Later that watch he sought out Telfer in 1BR. The rating said that when the heavy tug came on his line he'd been too busy trying to lash the end around a rail before chancing a look. He hadn't even seen the shark that had got away. The engineer opined that the rating could still be a witness just the same but when it was pointed out to him that fishing for sharks had been his idea in first place, that avenue of thought closed.

At 0830 that same morning the Chief Engineer sent for Angus to escort him to the captain's mast. The defendant was freshly shaved and dressed in his best whites. Lindsey mulled over the case while they sauntered along the boat deck in the dazzling morning sunshine.

"Your story is quite unbelievable Mister King," he said. "And yet I think that you're telling the truth. Seasoned hands might spin a yarn like that but not a first tripper. Still, it would be better for you if you had a witness."

A whimsical smile recollected some of the boggling salt-encrusted tales Jake and Wheelkey had related and his hopes rose slightly. The engineers lingered in the vestibule outside the captain's office. Two MAs stood on guard.

The usual bunch of malefactors, mostly engineroom ratings, loitered within awaiting just retribution for their run ashore during the previous night. One had his arm in a sling. Others sported Band-Aids on various parts of their bodies. Most of them had hangovers. Contusions and black eyes added colour to the scene as they sadly contemplated the error of their ways. The office door opened and Hodgekin beckoned the engineers.

"Rank hath privilege," said the chief. "You're first!"

Cap-in-hand he was marched into the master's office to stand stiffly at attention in front of a veneered desk. Captain

Cowell glanced up at him while the scribe, seated at his left, poised to take notes. The chief engineer and the second mate sat down behind the accused.

The captain shook his head and sighed, "I'm sorry, Mister King. There aren't any witnesses to substantiate your tale. Due to the seriousness of this offence I have no further option but to log you a month's pay and stamp CBC in your discharge book."

"Jings, Ah havenae been employed for a hale month yet!" he remarked then asked. "Whit's CBC Captain?"

"Caught Broaching Cargo," replied the captain. "Normally that means stealing or damaging cargo."

Chief Lindsay cleared his throat and said, "That's a bit stiff, isn't it? That means that he'll never get another ship with that in his book."

"I'm really sorry," replied Cowell. "But in this case, passengers are cargo and very important cargo at that. These girls are the daughters of a very important American admiral who also happens to be well connected with our head office. He wants blood. There is also the matter of assaulting the Master-at-Arms," he added.

"Ah was provoked," Angus objected sullenly. "The guy insulted me."

"Anyway," the captain sighed again. "You are restricted to the vessel until she docks in Southampton. You will not be allowed any of the ship's amenities such as the cinema, the swimming pool, the gym, et cetera. Case dismissed! Next!"

A couple of hours before the storekeeper called the midnight-to-four watch Will Keyes was draped across an easy chair in Jake's cabin, draining a bottle of lager. He reached for another from the handy crate nearby and performed his forté against the chair's wooden arm. The cap dropped quite ignored to the carpet. "I'm starting to feel better already. That was a tough watch," he announced, pushing the foaming bottleneck into his mouth.

Jake ruefully watched his purloined brew gurgle down Wheelkey's throat. "They're all tough according to you! But never that tough you'll ever buy your own beer! Right?"

"Bugger off. I bought a case just only last week!"

"Yes, and drank three of mine since!"

"Where's Gus?" asked Keyes, changing the subject.

"He's been in his cabin since his logging this morning except for going on watch. He's probably drowning his sorrows right now I should imagine."

"Well, after he hears the latest, he'll soon perk up."

There was a soft rap on the door. "If that's him don't say anything to him yet," whispered Keyes. "Let's have a little bit of fun and light a fire under him."

"Really! Well you know what? I don't think that's such a good idea," warned Jake. "His fuse is already lit and you want pour on gunpowder instead of sand?"

A depressed and bleary Angus crawled in to perch on the bunk. Keyes beamed a cheery grin up at him. "How's it gaun China?"

"Bluidy hellish!"

"Never mind pal. Here - have a beer on me!" invited Keyes, and generously offered him a bottle from the almost depleted beer case. He watched him open it. "You've achieved one helluva reputation for a first tripper." This first prod brought the newcomer's instant attention. "First, you start off the trip by trying to raise the dead. Then you get the ship to turn around . . ."

"Ah didnae hae the ship turned aroond. It was Larry Treen!" Angus protested indignantly.

The Glaswegian blithely ignored this rebuttal, continuing, "Then you kick the Chief's hat into the bilge and shove him in after it. Not satisfied with that you set off a fire extinguisher and chuck it at him - just as he's surfacing for the third time!"

"Ah didnae kick his hat in - Morgan did," he retorted. "An' the Chief fell in a' by his sel'!"

With sadistic delight Keyes kept up his goading, seemingly unaware of the warning signals; the voice rising half an octave; the reddening face; fists clenching and unclenching; the left knee quivering; and the eyes wide-open with pupils staring daggers. "Next, you went into the main restaurant - bold as brass - and farted in the Skipper's face! And I heard about the stink you caused - putting the Old Man off his grub. It must have been some fart. I heard that there were passengers barfin' all over the place! Are you trying to push Bomber Harris off his throne?"

"Ye're a bluidy liar!"

Keeping his face deadpan his tormentor protested, "Who - me? I'm as honest as the day is long!"

Then came the clincher. "And what about you're latest little escapade, eh? Go on, tell us about how you stripped two young dollies bollock naked - in broad daylight yet - and then played with their titties before you tried to have your way with them!"

The expected reaction was more like mortar fire than a bomb explosion. He pounced from the bunk and seized him by the throat. Wheelkey, being much larger, was quite confident that he could hold him at bay. He hadn't taken Sir Isaac Newton's Law of Momentum into account. This force knocked his chair backwards and gravity did the rest. “Ah’ll bluidy kill ye, ye ba-astarrd!” yelled Angus, falling on his tormentor’s chest and pummelled with all his might while beer frothed down onto the Glaswegian’s uniform.

Keyes held him by the shoulders. His longer arms broke the grip from around his throat. King’s fists ineffectively smote the air. “Jake!” he pleaded. “Show him that damned photo!”

“Maybe later. I want to see how you get out of this one.”

“For fuck’s sake, Jake!” Wheelkey rhymed. “Show him that fuckin’ picture!”

The Canuck let out an exaggerated sigh. “No problem Wheelkey. I would’ve shown it to him - eventually.” With exaggerated effort he slowly extracted a picture from a photographic envelope and held it in front of the angry face.

Angus focussed his eyes on the snapshot and stopped swinging. Keyes gingerly released his assailant who moved aside to sit cross-legged on the deck. Meanwhile the instigator dabbed his uniform with his handkerchief trying to soak up the beer. It took but a few seconds to reposition the furniture.

The evidence in Angus’ hand brought a smile to his lips. The snapshot had caught him in the act of disrobing the girls. Their shocked faces were directed at the camera’s lens, which also captured their full firm and desirable bare breasts. As interesting as they were, it was the background view between the girls that drew his eye for it clearly showed the shark’s head and gaping mouth?

“How did ye get this developed so fast Jake?” he asked, amazed and relieved at the same time.

“I still had your camera after the screws wheeled you away so I removed the spool and then toddled along to see Christina, right?”

"Who's Christina?"

"Christina Hastings, the ship's photographer - right? She's a lovely girl," he reminisced. "She gives me fast service and I, of course, reciprocate with stud service!" A glint appeared in his eye as he digressed.

"But how did ye ken the shark was in the picture?"

"I didn't. Everything happened so fast that I missed seeing their headlights properly. I'd rush developments made so that I could examine them closer. That reminds me, I'm going back later for enlargements!"

Having wrung the beer out of his handkerchief Wheelkey interjected, his voice dripping in sarcasm. "So you can pull your puddin' no doubt?"

Jake held up his hands palms outward. "That's a nasty insinuation! You don't see any hair there, right?"

"It's probably all worn off!"

"Anyway," Angus cut in. "This is grand! Ye've saved my bacon, Jake. How can Ah ever repay ye?"

"You can start with the film development cost," Jake replied succinctly.

"Shite!" swore Keyes. "You just bloody wanted these pornographic pictures for yourself!"

"The pair o' ye can argue a' ye want," said Angus, waving the snapshot in the air. "Ah'm aff tae show the Chief this photo." He swung the door open before casting an eye back at Keyes. "By the way, Ah'm sorry that Ah lost the rag, Wheelkey. Ah knew ye were just takin' the piss but the way that Ah felt a wee while ago, Ah wouldnae wish it oan my worst enemy."

"That's ok Gus," replied Keyes. "Right warned me but I wouldn't listen. It was too good a chance to pass up."

Angus left the pair minutely perusing the other photographs.

Exactly twenty-four hours after his logging he was back in the captain's office, this time under very different circumstances. Instead of two MA's guarding him he had two young ladies kissing and caressing him with Daddy looking on. Angus had a sick grin on his beet-red face. Nervously he allowed his right hand to be engulfed in the American admiral's massive paw. "Mister King, I'd like to apologise for the trouble I've caused you. Your quick-witted action prevented a terrible tragedy."

He gazed dreamily at the deckhead as if willing a phantom lantern to start swinging. "When I was sailing in the Pacific Ocean during World War Two under the command of your namesake my ship was torpedoed. I spent three days with some of my crew on a raft before being rescued. During that time one of my men had his arm dangling over the side. A shark chewed it right off! The ship's surgeon was with us and he treated it immediately. But it was no good, the poor fellow died of shock and loss of blood."

His train of thought moved on to the present. "It makes me shudder to think it could've happened to one of my girls."

"I've invited the Admiral and his daughters to be my dinner guests tonight," said Cowell. "He has requested your presence. It's against Company policy Mister King but under the circumstances I'm going to bend the rules. Please be at my table at seven thirty this evening." And with a twinkle in his eye added, "I know that you won't have any trouble finding it! Just make sure you don't have to work on the foam equipment today. I want to enjoy my meal this time."

"Aye-aye Captain," replied a solemn Angus.

2005

He lounged back in an easy chair with a balloon glass of fine brandy warming in one hand and a big cigar in the other. Sitting directly opposite was Rear Admiral Higgins USN (retired) regaling him in tales from the South Pacific. Angus was only half listening as the admiral droned on about fighting the whole Japanese Navy.

His eyes scanned the plush suite and contemplated if he had had a good day or a bad day. It had started off as a good day when he was being lauded a hero but things had deteriorated rapidly during dinner. The captain had glanced up from his Chateaubriand to acknowledge the police officers who had just stepped into the restaurant. This circumstance jogged the engineer's memory. His belated report was hastily whispered to Cowell. The master's safety valve feathered puffs of angry steam. He jabbed his knife in the general direction of the police officers' table and jerked his darkening face from the miscreant back along same compass bearing.

The hint was taken. He arose with an apology, scooted across the restaurant and spoke to the detectives. Cunningham telephoned to alert the Nassau Constabulary. The detective listened for a few more minutes before he hung up. Another cruise ship had left the previous evening and a passenger-freighter had sailed on the tide that very morning.

Dinner had lost its magic. Shortly after the captain drew him aside for a few terse words making him reflect that the earlier pat on the back was now rerouted south of his coccyx.

"Hello! Are you there?"

"Eh?"

A bony hand waving in front of him came into focus and into the admiral's suite on Sun Deck.

"I asked if you would like to go ashore with me tonight."

"No thanks, sir. Ah'm oan watch at midnight."

"You do have time for a few dances though," commented Donna, the eldest daughter, glancing at her watch. "It's only ten twenty-five."

"Don't forget me," urged her sister.

"Very well," conceded Higgins. "I'll go ashore alone." He kissed both daughters goodnight and left the stateroom.

Donna eased her bottom onto his lap. Loosening his tie she huskily said, "I don't feel like dancing. Do you Barbara?"

The younger sister who was in the process of relieving him of his drink and stubbing his cigar gazed straight into his eyes before replying. "Definitely not, we must reward our rescuer!"

Barbara sat on his chair's armrest and kissed him. In the meantime Donna had unbuttoned his shirt and was gently massaging his single-haired chest. The governor on the engineer's heart tripped out on overload to send his pulse racing. Blood coursed like steam into a turbine until it was dead-ended at a juncture under Donna's squirming bottom but like a hydraulic ram it soon rose to the occasion.

A mere tongue's length away Barbara's nipple, bare and erect swiftly squelched any technological thoughts that might have remained in his mind. He held her soft firm breast in his left hand and nuzzled the pink areola. Donna slipped off her blouse, thrust her larger bosom to his face and pouted its turn.

"There's a bedroom next door," suggested Barbara.

He gazed alternately into the girls' faces and smiled.

2358

Jake slouched on the platform desk, his fingers interlocked around a mug of tepid cocoa. He watched the eight-to-twelve floater check the engineroom clock for the umpteen times. The Mekon's lack of relief was making him restless. Topside there was a party going on without him.

"Where in the hell is he?" moaned Harding. "He's usually ten minutes early. I should be downing my second beer in Jazz's pad by now!"

"When you hear the pips it will be exactly twelve o'clock - right?" White intoned into his half-empty mug.

"Are you sure you didn't see him?"

"Look, I've told you before," grunted Jake. "I haven't damn well seen him since last watch! Right?"

It was precisely midnight when Angus scrambled down the engineroom access ladder. The Mekon, ascending three steps at a time, met him at the halfway level.

"Good job Gus!" he hollered, and not tarrying for an excuse, he continued his speedy climb.

"Ok Mekon," he acknowledged to nobody for Harding had already gone into the changeroom.

"You know what? You look like you've been dragged backwards through a sumac bush - right?"

"Ah've had an exhaustin' night."

"Why - what happened?"

"D'ye mind o' yon twa lassies oan the tender? Weel, they're bluidy nymphomaniacs!" He shook his head and with a sly grin complained, "A guy can only dae so much!"

"You screwed both of them?" Jake asked incredulously.

"Aye," he reconfirmed.

"Two of them!" his friend repeated with awe. "Really?" When he got over accepting this phenomenon White asked him to solve his new enigma. "Hey wait a minute, just yesterday you were sick with worry in case you got canned for hauling their bras off. Now, you smug bastard, you're on top of the world for a near hung-by-the-knackers offence! What gives?"

"That was different," replied Angus. "Ah dinnae mind gettin' nailed for somethin' Ah've done, it's gettin' punished for somethin' that Ah havenae done that pisses me aff!"

Christie's bellow from across the platform sent the juniors diligently about their duties. They reconnoitred again in the changeroom at the end of the watch. King was hauling off his boilersuit when Jake invited him to his cabin for a beer.

That offer was declined. "Thanks, but no thanks, Jake. Whit, with yon women an' this watch, Ah've had it! Ah'm gaun tae turnin' in for three or four hours then go ashore tae buy some souvenirs. Imagine sailin' a' this way tae the Bahamas an' not gettin' a single souvenir!"

"Ok Gus. I'll see you next watch."

He trudged wearily along the passageway, opened his cabin door and stepped into darkness. Flipping a switch, he was almost sure that his lights had been left on before his watch.

"Hi Angus!" a familiar voice welcomed him. He gaped at a stark naked Donna lolling in his easy chair with one shapely leg on the coffeetable, its twin resting on an opened drawer. Barbara, clad only in a black see-through negligee was in yoga mode, and perched upside-down on his bunk.

Perhaps he'd get his souvenirs on his second voyage to Nassau.

An in-depth Police Interview

0705 Monday

DS Betty Stevenson chucked another discharge book onto the untidy pile in front of her. She was thoroughly pissed off with this job or rather its instigator, Detective-bloody-Inspector David Cunningham, who at this very moment was probably sleeping off having 'drinkies' with the chief steward. The policewoman massaged the back of her neck before getting up from the pokey little desk in the pokey little office that was on loan from the pokey little purser.

She paced back and forth a few times before limbering her body up with some simple back exercises and leg stretches. It would have been a nice break going ashore in Nassau but her superior had denied her that. When she made the excuse that the recent evidence should be mailed off to Scotland Yard, her boss told her that he'd look after it. He went ashore to the Governor's House with the silk glove and sent it off in the diplomatic pouch. No doubt he had some plonk with the Governor while he was at it.

A week had passed since Stevenson had begun work on her fearless leader's theory. The DI had pointed out that in his experience most murderers were either related or acquainted with their victims. Well, that fact was known before they had taken off from Heathrow Airport. Davidson must have had help after his faked suicide - if it was fake. They had only a young engineer's word on that. They might be chasing a Will-o'-the-wisp for all she knew. Davidson might've had an accomplice to assist him before as well as after the fact. Her boss figured that most people lived, married and died within a ten or twenty-mile radius from where they were born.

This idea may have been valid when Cunningham pounded the beat thirty-odd years ago, but now? More than a hundred thousand Jocks stampeded over Hadrian's Wall every year seeking work in the Midlands or London. The void that they left was readily filled by the overflow of Irishmen from the 'Ould Sod'.

A list of propinquity was compiled by using an old RAC road map of Britain and the Seaman's Record books. The passenger manifest from the outward-bound trip had been examined. Fortunately there had been less than two hundred and most of them were elderly. The crew was a different story and there were nearly a thousand of them.

Another screw-up was discovered when they went to the cabins of the late? Homer Davidson and the definitely late George Brown. Both accommodations had been cleaned thoroughly for the cruise passengers destined to board for this trip. Hopefully their luggage, which had been sent back with the coffin, would reveal some clues.

She'd arisen at five-thirty that morning to go through the remaining books and wasn't any further ahead. Securing the last pile of little blue books with a large rubber band, she chucked the bundle into a cardboard box. She stuffed her notebook into her small handbag, vacated the office and went down to her cabin on B Deck aft.

"When are the electricians gaun tae fix that bluidy a/c fan?" Angus groaned aloud. Dan Dare and a pair of Treens oscillating before his eyes gave meagre comfort as he wafted a two-year-old copy of the *Eagle* comic book across the front of his face in an effort to cool himself. He heard the clump and banter of the eight-to-twelve going below to relieve the four-to-eight morning watch. He grabbed a blanket and bath towel and padded off down the passageway for a cool shower. Drying himself off he wrapped the towel around his hips kilt fashion and went out on deck for a couple of hours zizz.

The scrap of deck space on the starboard side of the engineers' quarters would be shaded until nearly ten o'clock. He lay face down on his blanket and revelled in the occasional cool zephyr that scooped past.

A toe nudged his side.

"'Mornin' Gus." It was Keyes. "Fucking knotholes in the deck are we?"

"Bugger aff!"

His tormentor grinned and sauntered to the rail to peer down onto Boat Deck's sun-drenched after end. A bevy of passengers congregated near the cradled whaleboat that was neatly labelled Lifeboat No. 25. One of the female gym attendants was preparing them for a session of callisthenics. A tannoy located a yard or so below his feet blared military music into the light morning air. Lustfully he watched young breasts and buttocks bounce, bump and jiggle to 4/4 and 4/8-march time music.

"Here comes Taffy!" he snickered, watching the Welshman dressed in singlet and Bermuda shorts puff to a halt just as a fanfare introduced a fresh march. His humour piqued his countryman's attention.

"Whit's so funny?" His question was partially muffled by a blanket.

"That tune could've written just for old Taff," he replied. "It's called *Solid Men to the Front*!"

Angus smiled briefly, his cheek caressing the warm blanket. The mainmast's shrouds thrummed a soothing soliloquy enticing him to slumber. Snatches of Keyes' tenor voice hummed an accompaniment to the music. The Grenadier Guards' rendition of *Blaze Away* induced him to sing lyrics that composer Abe Holtzmann had never envisioned:

"Missus McGwitty
had only one tittie
to feed her baby on.
The poor little mucker
had only one sucker
to rest his chin upon!

Awful a sudden,
a great mealy pudden
came flyin' through the air,
did she duck?
Did she f -

"Well, helloo there!"

A shapely leg stepped over the coaming from the shadow of the engineers' accommodation. "Hi! I was told that Mister Angus King might be here."

The sun worshipper rose onto his elbows and craned his head back to gaze up between a pair of gorgeous limbs, which seemed to vee up into infinity but actually ended inside a pair of white tight short shorts. Up and beyond this stunning apparel another vee was formed by twin hillocks, both cairned and encased in a red silk blouse. They framed an attractive face that beamed down at him. Her eyes sparkled in the warm air.

"Mister King?"

His lower jaw dropped open, his head bobbing up and down like a slinky puppy's. Stevenson, by now was squatting on her hunkers, a severe strain the stitched seams of her shorts. "Do you mind if I talk to you for a few minutes?"

With a gulp he realized that he was quite naked except for the towel. "If ye step back inside an' go tae cabin forty-three, Ah'll be alang presently Miss eh . . ."

"DS Betty Stevenson," she supplemented before vanishing into the gloomy interior.

He stood erect in more ways than one to hastily rearrange his towel.

"If you play your cards right Gus," leered Keyes. "You might get a bit of nooky before you go on watch."

"Wi' my bluidy luck Ah'll be in the slammer afore then!" he retorted morosely and stomped up the faint wake of *Evening in Paris* perfume.

Inside his cabin he found the policewoman seated comfortably in an easy chair flipping through an old Wizard. She looked up and smiled placing the comic book aside. "I'll step outside while you get dressed," she offered and stood up.

He wasn't so nervous that the physical attributes of the police officer couldn't be admired. The DS was taller by a couple of inches and she wasn't even wearing high heels. Her chestnut hair was slightly wavy, cut short with bangs. Her face was longish with clear skin that was devoid of makeup although her thin lips had been touched up with a hint of pink lipstick. She had large chartreuse eyes, a thin nose and was late thirtyish, perhaps forty.

Her shorts supported a little tyre of fat, that he guessed correctly that she had trouble getting into. Proof of this was confirmed by her thighs, which seemed to expand as they left the almost nonexistent legs of said apparel. Her well-stacked blouse, opened at the neck, revealed a generous cleavage. All in all her stature tended to disguise those few extra pounds.

"Is this gaun tae take lang?" he inquired, reluctantly for he was not too keen on changing into full dress just to sit in a warm cabin.

"No, I don't think so," Stevenson replied, and lifting her handbag from the coffeetable extracted a pencil and notebook. She flipped through some pages and waited.

"Weel in that case, Ah'll just stay the way Ah am then, if ye dinnae mind."

Drawing the chintz curtain across his open doorway made the cabin air feel even worse. He flopped into the other easy chair and surveyed those gorgeous legs as she crossed them.

"Now then Mister King," she began. "I believe you were the person who discovered that the murder weapon was missing from its original place."

"Well, actually it was Jake White who noticed that the dirk was missin'," he corrected her. "Ye see - he thought that the dockies had pinched it while we were still in port. But Ah pointed oot tae him that Ah had seen it just a few hours afore when Ah was explorin' the ship. This is my first trip." He added with a tense smile.

She drew a line on her notepad and scribbled something beside it. "Is it? What a wonderful experience for you."

'No' right at this minute,' he thought.

"Ok now, I believe that you were one of the few people on board to get a good look at the victims."

He shuddered as if a blast of Arctic air had entered the cabin. "Aye, Ah suppose Ah did," he conceded. "No' that Ah wanted tae mind. Horrible it was, just horrible."

Sympathy registered briefly on her face. “I’m sure it was an awful experience, Mister King. I’ve seen the pictures but they’re not quite the same things. I’m sure that we’ll get the post mortem results in a few days, but until then, we have to rely on witnesses. Any small detail that comes to mind could help us with our inquiries.”

He closed his eyes, his mind going back to that dreadful sight and began slowly. “It seems tae me . . .”

“Yes?”

Angus went on. “There might’ve been anither wound oan the man’s back.”

“What do you mean, might have been?”

“Weel, there seemed tae be a vertical cut oan the man’s back - right next tae the dirk.”

She stared quizzically at him.

“Whit Ah mean is - it was as if the blade had been used the wrang way an’ got stuck atween the ribs. Maybe it was hauled oot, turned ninety degrees, then shoved back in again - this time clearin’ the ribs tae go right through the body.”

“That is very astute of you Mister King. That might be very helpful to us. Anything else?”

He shook his head glumly.

She turned a page, re-crossed her legs, and went on. “Now, can you tell me a little about the passenger that jumped overboard?”

“Where are ye gettin’ all this information?”

“I interviewed the Chief Master-at-Arms and Mister Hodgekin, the ship’s Fourth Officer.”

“Oh aye - him!” he scoffed.

“We’re just making sure that you’re not in the frame,” confirmed his interviewer.

"That so-an'-so would frame his granny," Angus said dourly, recalling his first encounter with the fourth mate.

"Well, never mind about him Mister King," pressed the DS. "Let's go over your discovery of the blood-covered glove after your conversation with this er - Mister Richard Davidson. We've only your word that it was he whom you saw in Nassau."

"Aye, it was him, a' right," he assured her. "My eyes aren't painted oan, ye ken. Anyway, a wee while after Davidson supposedly jumped ower the side Ah found a silk glove layin' oan the deck. It had been cut wi' somethin' sharp an' there was some bluid oan it."

He jerked a thumb up at the scrap of clothesline rigged behind him between the washbasin light and wardrobe. "That's where Ah hung it up tae dry. But when the MA came aroond the damned thing had disappeared!"

Just then, the muffled sound of a fan motor starting up preceded cool air gushing from the pair of Punkah louvres.

"Thank God!" grunted the engineer and got up to adjust the direction of flow.

Stevenson savoured the welcome breeze and tugged at her damp clothing. She flapped her blouse lapels slightly to allow circulation around her neck. A button loosened enhancing her décolletage. His eyes darted down the tempting cleavage like ferret after a mole.

A stirring in his loins prompted him to think of something else before it became too evident. Then he exclaimed, "Och aye! The ither glove!"

"I beg your pardon?"

"The ither glove," he repeated excitedly. "Ah found the neighbourin' glove the very next day when Ah was oot oan deck huntin' for my cigarette lighter. See here," he said, eagerly opening a drawer and lifted out a brown paper bag that contained the glove.

Her face lit up. "This could be an extremely valuable clue Mister King," she said, reaching for the bag.

He kneed the drawer shut and in doing so, a corner of his towel became firmly snagged and left him stark naked when he stepped towards Stevenson. Like the jib of a dockside crane his tumescence suddenly became apparent.

Engrossed by its increasing size the interviewer's eyes bulged accordingly. It was as if his penis was a magnet and the lady's hand the keeper. Her hand took on a mind of its own and automatically grasped his organ like seizing a felon by the wrist. She pushed his foreskin back revealing the deep purple of the glans.

"Hey Gus, how did you make out with -" asked Wheelkey, peeking past the curtain to quip. "Oh, I see you've got everything in hand, Detective-Sergeant!"

She let go of the penis as if it was red-hot. It was, but not overly so.

"Can ye no' knock afore enterin' somebody's cabin?" snarled Angus, jerking the towel about his torso.

"I did," riposted Keyes. "I chapped on the curtain and I'm sure that I heard somebody say 'Come'!"

With a face first flushed with rapture and then with embarrassment the policewoman scurried from the cabin taking the evidence with her.

After a lengthy walk round the deck she went back to her office and slammed the door shut. With her back leaning against it she chastised herself.

"Stupid! Stupid! Stupid!"

She went over to her desk and threw herself into the chair. Taking a deep breath she recalled the entire incident in her mind. Suddenly being confronted by that young man's nudity had completely mesmerised her. And the size of his cock . . .

All of her previous affairs had been just that, a need to satisfy her sexual feelings. Acting on her dad's advice, don't mix business with pleasure, she'd stayed away from dating other cops and never any villains. Yet Angus King wasn't a villain, was he? Just visualizing his supple - his naked supple - body brought goose pimples.

There was some amount of truth to romance on the high seas. Probably the heat had a lot to do with it too. And that cock! She took the glove from the brown paper bag and examined it. 'Damn it!' she thought, stuffing it back into the bag. 'I need a drink!' She glanced at her watch. The sun was nearly over the yardarm in naval parlance and it was lunchtime.

1630

Scar was greatly surprised to see his dad sitting in his cabin. "What happened?"

"That kid - King - he saw me in Nassau. I couldn't take the chance of staying on that little island. The cops would've nabbed me in no time all."

"What are you going to do now Dad?"

"Back to doing what I was doing before I guess."

"Are you hungry?"

"Now that you mention it - I do feel a bit peckish," admitted Davison.

"I'll get some grub for you before the mess closes."

Davis closed his cabin door turned and walked directly into DS Stevenson. “Oops sorry!” she said as the engineer stepped aside to let her pass. Before making his way to the mess he watched her stop and rap King’s door.

Since there wasn’t any answer to her knock she tried the handle and went inside. The clean and tidy cabin was an attribute to Barnes’ ministrations rather than the engineer’s tidiness. A patrol suit was draped on a chair and a pair of black socks dangled on a length of brown string. She was tempted to nose around but her afternoon tea libation still left her a bit tipsy. Anyway he’d probably be in at any minute.

No sooner she had reached for a Hotspur when he entered, again kilted in a towel. She glanced up from the comic book and smiled.

“Ah, Mister King.”

Flabbergasted, he peeked back into the passageway to see if anyone was coming. Oscar Davis was entering his cabin with a serviette full of goodies. He stepped back into his cabin and closed the door. Within minutes the room was steamier than the engineroom’s hot wells.

The DS was wearing a watered silk blouse of pale-blue, a white pleated skirt, and low-heeled sandals. He stood there by the door like an automaton, a loofah in one hand and a facecloth in the other.

“Are ye lookin’ for mair information?”

“It sure is hot in here,” she said, wafting the bottom of her blouse about to catch some air. She stepped in front of him and taking the loofah from him said, “The size is right but the texture’s too soft.”

She reached down and manipulated the growing hardness under his towel. “You’re making a little tent,” she smiled.

"Lock the door. I don't want that friend of yours barging back in again."

"He's oan watch," he replied automatically, his mouth becoming quite dry.

"I don't want anybody watching," she said, removing her damp blouse and draping it over the engineer's makeshift clothesline. She was naked from the waist up.

He locked the door. With eyes riveted on her full breasts he moved closer and massaged her nipples to hardness until they rose as two tiny carmine cairns on areoles of blooming heather. She in turn released the towel to grip his tumescence. Using it tiller-like she steered the biological rudder on a course to his bunk.

"I'm telling you Dad, that cop is back again. She's just up the alleyway in King's cabin."

His father calmly peeled a banana before biting into it. He chewed meditatively. "Look son," he said after swallowing. "You and him are the only ones on board who know that I'm still alive and they can't be too sure about that guy. They've searched the ship a couple of times already and found absolutely nothing. The authorities must've turned over the island after he spotted me and still found nothing. I wouldn't be surprised if they were pissed off with him for leading them on a wild goose chase. As long as I stay out of his way then I'm ok." He lobbed the banana skin into the waste basket. "So don't concern yourself about it."

Oscar still was not comfortable with his father's explanation. "So why did that cop go back to his cabin?"

His dad just shrugged. "How the hell should I know? Maybe she fancies him."

With a practised aim he chucked the banana skin skilfully into the garbage pail.

Jake tried the handle of King's locked door then knocked. "I don't think he's in," he said to Taffy and Treenie.

"I'm sure that I heard somebody moving around when I walked by a few minutes ago," said Treenie. "Maybe he's taking a nap. Try again."

The door was rapped a bit harder. "Gus, are you in there?"

At that moment Angus felt that he was doing push-ups in a Turkish bath. He panted fit to burst and Stevenson, with lips pursed and eyes squeezed tight, was clawing frantically at his back. The couple were slipping and sliding against each other on a lubricant of perspiration.

Taffy rattled the door again. "I think that he's getting his jollies," he whispered, his Cymric ear flat against the slats.

"Maybe he's having a wank," opined Treenie.

"Are you having a wank in there Gus?" Taffy bellowed through the slats.

"Tell-them-to-bugger-off!" she wheezed.

"Bugger off!"

"Well gentlemen," Jake began. "We've established that his cabin is indeed occupied and that our shipmate is likewise occupied." He spoke down through the slats on the door. "Hey in there Gus - we'll see you in the wardroom after you've finished your dip!"

"Whew!" gasped Stevenson after his comrades had left. "I almost lost it there. How about you, Angus?"

He rolled away from her and almost fell off his bunk. "Ah did fine - just fine Betty," he groaned for they were, by now, on a first name basis.

They clambered down from the bunk and using the extra towels by the sink, the lovers gave each other a rubdown, which almost set them off again. “I’ve got to get back my cabin,” she said as they both dressed.

The passageway felt pleasantly cool when he escorted her to the exit above the Boat Deck. Davis heard them go by and peeked out his porthole to watch the DS descend the ladder. Her hair looked damp and her face was flushed. “Hey Dad,” he smiled. “It looks like you were right. They *were* having it off!”

A Typical Watch at Sea

1005 Tuesday

The sun inched up a cloudless sky, a beautiful contrast to the dark blue of the sea. The weather brought cheer to passengers and crew alike. Angus awoke feeling marvellous and cranked open his porthole to inhale the clean salt air. He performed his ablutions before taking a short jaunt on deck to blow away the last cobwebs of discomfort from his head. Feeling positively rejuvenated he banged on White's cabin door rousing him from a deep sleep.

"What the hell do you want?" growled Jake.

"Emergency Drill in half-an-hour. Rise an' shine! Come oan Jake, it's a smashin' day! Dae ye no' ken it's bluidy great tae be alive?"

"Waken me like that again and you won't be," seethed Jake.

Wheelkey bustled in and cheerfully hauled the sheets from White's prostrate form. "Jesus Murphy! What's the matter with everybody today?" he bellowed angrily, easing down from his bunk. He shuffled over to his sink, splashed some cold water on his face and carefully towelled it dry.

"Hey Jake, you'd better hide your beer," Wheelkey warned him gesturing to an open case of plonk.

"Why? Are you thirsty again or rather, yet?" jeered Jake, rummaging through debris on his dresser top. He found his cigarettes and matches and lit up. He picked up the box of laxatives and tossed them at Angus. "Give them back to - uh - Florence Nightingale. I spent over an hour on the can during the night, right?"

"I'm just trying to warn you," persisted Keyes. "Bomber is after beer so you'd better hide yours."

"You know what? That fart isn't going to drink any of my ale." White muttered vehemently. "He'll make enough stink on this drill as it is. Did you see what he had in his cabin last night? Garlic. He nicked a bunch of cloves from the galley."

"Holy smoke!" blurted out Angus. "If he shites today it'll be a real emergency!"

Jake's frown disappeared. "Wait a minute - as M said in that movie last night, 'I have a plan and I think it might work.'" He lifted a bottle of Guinness from a case beneath his coffeetable. "Here Wheelkey, do your thing and open this without damaging the cap and - uh - don't drink any of it. Gus, give me those pills back."

"Jake, you've got a right wicked mind." Keyes chuckled as he expertly popped the top from the Guinness bottle. He watched his shipmate gently pierce two soft transparent capsules before squeezing their contents into the bottle of Guinness. A practised thump with the heel of his hand resealed the bottle.

"Ye're a evil get," Angus chided. "Ye'll likely blow his arse aff!"

"He's just going to get a good run for his money - right? Now there's a beer. Stand in the open doorway sipping it."

Angus lounged lackadaisically against the doorjamb nursing on the beer bottle. It wasn't long before Harris noticed him. He shoved past into the cabin and jarred the resident.

"Sorry old son," lamented Jake. "I've just got Guinness left, right?"

"Guinness," repeated Bomber. "A lovely drink that - just the very thing for a backed-up system."

"You got that right Bomber," admitted Jake. He opened the doctored flagon and handed it to the victim.

"Thanks mate. That's right white of you," said Harris and began guzzling.

His so-called shipmates looked on impassively as the foamy dark stout gurgled down the dupe's throat. He belched rudely and dumped the empty bottle back into its case. "Thanks Right," he grinned. "Here, it's time for Emergency Drill."

He walked out the cabin. The other engineers followed him and rushed for their lifejackets so that they could reach the elevator before him.

When he pontifically trod through the emergency generator room's doorway dressed in full regalia, including war ribbons, MacKay was acutely aware that he'd been the last one to arrive. A full complement of engineers arced around the starting console waiting silently. There was none of the usual tardiness of personnel arriving at the last minute. He wondered briefly if the ship really was sinking and that everybody had naturally neglected to inform the man most concerned, himself.

All the engineers, except MacKay, the Chief, Slack Jack, and of course Bomber, had somehow been forewarned of the impending disaster about to descend on the victim's waste treatment system. As was his wont Harris was positioned at the far end of the generator forlorn and alone.

Uncle Miltie gleefully rubbed his hands together and proceeded to divulge the various idiosyncrasies of the engine on the theory that total amnesia struck all engineers on the completion of each drill. "I'll start the engine now by hand."

"No, you bloody well won't!" countermanded MacKay. "Press the button."

A mutinous glance withered from the HSE's countenance as his senior's wrathful glare dared him to contradict the order. He pressed the starter. The engine whined in protest, shuddered and banged noisily, demonstrating its indignation for being disturbed from its weekly slumber. With a final shrug of con rods it decided to run in order to pacify its tormentors.

Obnoxious tendrils of a poisonous effluvium stealthily assailed the nostrils of the congregation just as the electrician threw in the knife switches. MacKay sniffed, his eyes probing amongst the sea of white handkerchiefs for the offender.

"Who's shit?" the second bellowed over the engine's angry roar.

Behind his back a white linen handkerchief dipped briefly from a protected nose and a wag called out: "It's yours if you want it Sec!"

"There was something in the air that we could share Fernando," Taffy sang softly to the tune, *Perhaps, perhaps, perhaps*, his voice muffled by a sky-blue kerchief.

The engine stopped with a sigh. Engineers jostled and pushed each other out the doorway in their haste to vacate the emergency jenny room. Angus stumbled on the coaming where Jake grabbed his arm.

"Your lace is undone Gus."

Angus went down on one knee and retied his shoelace. Two four-to-eight engineers remained at the opening. He moved aside believing that their path was being blocked. They remained in position, apparently waiting for something else. A loud thunderclap came echoing from inside the jenny room and a scream followed by a puff of blue smoke advanced through the doorway. He observed one of the engineers place a West Indies' two dollar bill into his companion's waiting palm. Minutes later they escorted a pained HSE to sick bay. Angus trotted along the alleyway to catch up with White and Keyes who were stalking Harris from a discreet distance.

"He's still walking normal Wheelkey," said Jake, grinning at Angus as he caught up. "I don't think that he's fired a salvo yet. Hi Scar!" he called out when Davis drew near.

Davis ignored him, glared at Angus, and strode on.

"He looks thoroughly pissed off with you Gus," observed Jake. "What in the hell did you do to him - uh - steal the sugar out of his coffee?"

A shrug was his answer.

"He can't be far off," forecasted Keyes. "His safeties are feathering like crazy. Phew, what a stench!"

"The man is inhuman. My stern would've blown off ages ago," opined Jake. "His asshole must be plugged solid."

The trio approached the elevator, and as usual, Bomber was being forcibly ejected with the same consideration that the human race has for a felon convicted of murder. Keyes tallied the engineers remaining. "There are only eight of us left, including Bomber, we'd better wait for the lift again."

The elevator descended. The doors slid ajar and in rushed the last batch of engineers, except Harris, who had the doors slammed in his face. Up top the group lingered by the notice board and watched the elevator return for Maxie. Doors could be heard slamming shut at the bottom of the shaft. Jake's eyes strained through the observation port into the darkness. The steel cables began to flex and sway.

"Right!" he yelled and Dave Armstrong, a shop electrician, threw the elevator's power switch. From halfway down the shaft, banging was heard.

Moments passed until a muffled voice drifted up from the gloomy depths. It called again, louder. The third hail, its tone noticeably pitched with desperation, could be heard: "Start up this lift. *Pul-leese*!"

"Any time now," predicted Jake.

"*Oh no-oo*!" shrieked the voice.

"*Jesus Christ Almighty*!" blasphemed a deeper voice.

"Jings! Some puir bastard's in there wi' him!"

With the compassion a mariner might show for a shipwrecked sailor Dave hurriedly re-established power.

The elevator glided to a halt on Sun Deck, its doors crashing open to release a retching chief engineer. Lindsey staggered off to his quarters, his parting words advising, "For God's sake Harris, see a bloody vet!"

Bomber remained inside the lift, misery marring his countenance. He stood in an ever-widening puddle of ebon faeces that trickled over his shoes. From then on he refrained from Guinness and flatulent foods.

The juniors assumed their normal stance lounging against the stoic platform desk. It was the start of a typical watch that had changed over with the usual minor amenities. They were discussing that morning's events, mainly Bomber's hard luck. Their routine inspections completed, the pair gossiped waiting for the coffee to arrive. They watched Dave Hope, a member of the leading hand's black gang, brasso-ing the telegraph that served the boiler rooms.

Rated fireman-trimmer Hope's duties were cleaning, polishing and general gofer in the engineroom until the leadhand said otherwise. It wasn't a bad assignment when one considered scouring and painting bilges or whitewashing boiler tops as alternatives. He diligently worked on bringing lustre into the pedestal. Brass gauges glowed like halos along the manoeuvring platform's instrument board.

Christie was a stickler for cleanliness and his section proved to be vastly superior to the other two watches. The checkered floorplates had been scrubbed to a greyish hue by the rating burnishing the telegraph. On the day after leaving Southampton he had directed him to clean out each individual diamond impression on every steel plate by hand using a wire brush. The poor man had painstakingly scoured and scrubbed in soul-destroying drudgery. Ten days later the present standard was deemed acceptable.

The other two watches simply washed off their floorplates with coal oil then wiped dry with a potato sack. Their blackish hue bore a grim contrast to the twelve-to-four's section.

Everton, the bilgediver, clambered up onto the platform, coffee lapping over the rim of his fanny. He alternated his trips fore and aft so that the same watchkeepers would not be served cold beverages all the time. He peered into the unwashed mugs and dropped the fanny in disgust. Ignoring the brew that had puddled on Christie's pride and joy he went to rinse the mugs at a water fountain on the platform's starboard wing.

The second stepped out from the opposite wing to edge his way across the platform, his eyes intent on various dial readings. He stopped when his foot collided with the pail of coffee. He glared down at the offending object that had served his shoe and immaculate floorplate with a generous splash of piping hot coffee.

"*Hoi*!"

Charlie craned his head around a steel column.

"Come bloody here you!"

Crestfallen the rating slogged despondently toward Christie and stood in front of him. The engineer blasted him for his carelessness then followed with a lecture on the wastefulness of food and drink.

"Sorry Mister Christie," he mumbled. "I'll clean it up right away."

"You'll do no such thing," retaliated Black Bob. "You've done enough damage. Serve the damned coffee and get to hell out of my engineroom!"

The juniors commiserated with the rating while their cups were being filled. Meantime Christie hunkered down to rub away the insult to his cherished floorplate. The accompanied obscenities changed to surprise and wonder as he gaped at the refurbished spot. The leaden hue was magically all a-glitter, almost like chromium in fact. He leaped jubilantly to his feet and seized the fanny from the thunderstruck rating. The contents were strewn right across his cleaning section. The eyes of the others bulged, their mouths agape.

"He's gone bananas! Right?" whispered White.

"You!" Christie gestured to Hope. "Get some clean wipers and start polishing these plates. And you," he stabbed a stubby finger at Charlie. "Get more coffee!"

Everton hesitated.

"Now!" roared Christie.

The rating scooted off and was back in a trice with another load of coffee. The contents were sloshed over a broader area. "More!" was bawled at Everton who promptly fled down the ladder, his empty can rattling against the steps.

After three or four gallons of coffee the second was satisfied. He sent the bilgediver off for more coffee for drinking. When he returned the plates had developed a sheen that disconcerted one's eyes.

"Shades of Medusa!" croaked Jake. "Look at Black Bob's face. You'd swear that he was having an orgasm - right?"

The second swaggered to the desk and took a sip of coffee. "That's amazing," he said. "I didn't think coffee could polish steel plates like that. Just imagine what it does to your stomach." His own imagination did not deter him from taking another appreciative sip of the questionable ambrosia. He locked his spectacled eyes on White and said, "I want them kept clean. No grimy shoes are going to dirty my platform. Ok?"

"You'd prefer us to wear carpet slippers Sec - right?"

"None of your snazz, Mister. Just remember I've got my eye on you. Now piss off and take the log."

His juniors abandoned the manoeuvring platform. Out of earshot Jake gave his shipmate an explicit opinion of his antagonist's sexual prowess, lack of toilet training and questionable parentage in one terse phrase. Angus grinned and offered to check the tunnel for him.

Stepping over the guides of an open watertight door the noise changed from a pitched hum to the hollow rumbling and re-echoing vibrations from the propellers as they droned monotonously through the vessel's hull. He slowly walked aft feeling each bearing block on the starboard prop shaft with the back of his hand. Christie had advised him that the palm of one's hand was not sensitive enough to distinguish slight temperature variations.

He smiled, reflecting on his yarn about the platform junior who had left the tunnel blowing on his hand. Upon enquiry that individual had moaned that he had burnt his fingers. The only steam lines in the tunnel were well insulated so Black Bob curiously prompted him for an answer.

'I burned them on one of those black things,' was the casual reply.

'What black things?' he'd asked. 'Them black things that the shaft runs through!'

When it dawned on him that there was a lineshaft bearing showing a serious intent to disrupt an otherwise peaceful watch by seizing up, he had dashed up the tunnel screaming for oil. Angus grinned when Christie showed him a minute gap between thumb and forefinger - a symbolic distance on how close the miscreant had been to signing off in mid-ocean.

The shafts' rumbling gradually increased as he continued through each watertight section all the way aft. He checked the stern glands for leakage, crossed to the other side to proceed forward again and check the port driveshaft bearings.

In the section just before re-entry to the engineroom a strange noise could be faintly heard over the thunderous pounding. A telephone was buzzing somewhere. He explored the compartment and found the instrument on a steel column. *Swimming Pool* glowed in its light indicator.

He cautiously lifted the receiver: "Hello?"

"Could you fill up the pool please?" asked a female voice.

"Eh?" he hesitantly responded. "Aye - ok."

"Thank you."

The light went out when he hung up.

He considered going back into the engineroom and seek out Jake for advice when he noticed a vertical pump waiting like a lonely sentinel.

A brass plate bolted to its housing bore the legend: Ballast Pump. Valve manifolds were connected on either side of the pump. On the left assembly each valve wheel clearly described its function; Ship's Side Suction; Ballast Suction; Bilge Suction; Pool Suction. The other set of valves was just as explanatory: Overboard Discharge; Ballast Discharge; Pool Discharge. All were closed.

'Seems simple enough,' he mused. He opened the ship's side suction valve, started the pump and spun the pool discharge valve wheel open. The pump's steady pace added harmony to the sonority in the tunnel.

Jake popped into the compartment drawn by the woof-woof of the pump. "Filling the pool?"

"Aye."

"Did you -?" The telephone's raucous buzz broke off the question. He snatched up the receiver. "Hello?'

"Who's this?" asked an angry male voice.

He recognized the voice. "Don't you know who you are?"

"Who's that down there?"

"Oo dat up dere sayin', 'oo dat down dere?" His tone assumed a not unreasonable imitation of the gravelly voiced Louis Armstrong.

"Jake, you bloody idiot, stop pumping!"

"What's up?"

"You're pumping all sorts of crud into the pool," yelled Wheelkey. "The water is dirty brown with all kinds of thing swirling around; fag ends, orange peel, caramel wrappers - Christ!"

"What's up?" repeated White.

"There's even a French letter!"

"Used?"

"No, it's still got a prick inside it. Oops! Sorry Daphne. Didn't you flush the lines out over the side before you started filling the pool? Jesus Murphy, even a first tripper could've figured that out!"

He peered round at his shipmate. "Evidently not."

"It was Gus? Well never mind - get this swill out of the pool. Daphne's pulling her hair out!"

"Don't get your knickers in a twist Wheelkey," soothed Jake. "We'll have her pumped out in a jiffy - right? Save that safe for Daphne."

"Piss on you White!" snapped Keyes. "Next time do the job right!"

The phone went dead.

From the gist of the conversation Angus realized that he was in trouble but his friend soothed his anxiety and told him that it was not such a big deal. "Some asshole has been pumping the bilge and was too lazy to flush the goddamn lines. In future, always flush overboard before filling the pool, right?"

A few hundred tons of clean seawater later the pair was back at the platform desk drinking lukewarm coffee. It was just another typical watch. 3BR interrupted their repast. Jake took the call. "That was Larry. He's got a leaky burner for you to fix - right?"

The bitter dregs of his coffee were gulped down and he went forward. Inside the stokehold he noted that Treen was giving the console desk his full support. "Which one is it?"

Larry gave him a bored glance and jerked his thumb over his shoulder at the delinquent oil burner. "That one, sitting on its slide."

Resigned from its duty of injecting boiling-hot Bunker C into the furnace the burner patiently awaited TLC. The floater squatted behind the unit to scrutinize the seals and hose connections for leakage. Although it was covered with sticky black residue there was no indication of its source. He would have to investigate further. He pushed the shutoff cock's handle to the open position and was rewarded by a thick warm stream of gooey oil.

He staggered back in surprise, slipped, and rolled into the puddle created by the leak. With hands on his hips Treen glowered down at the drenched Scot asking, "Now why in the hell would you go and do a silly thing like that?"

Slithering unsteadily to his feet he futilely tried to wipe himself clean.

Treen reproved him. "All you had to do was ask," he said. "Since you've found out the hard way that the packing sleeve has blown, you might as well get a new one at the stores when you go topside to clean up."

"Ok," he said glumly and squelched towards an airlock door.

Returning garbed in clean coveralls he noticed that mess had been cleaned up. He also perceived the chief engineer. That worthy's attention was directed upwards to some object in the boiler tops. Treen was nowhere to be seen. He was about to effect repairs when the chief became aware of the unserviceable burner. "Why in the hell is this fire off?" and threw the cock handle open.

His junior didn't say anything because he knew that a valve above the burner block isolated the leaking cock. When the fire didn't ignite the chief reached up and spun the isolating valve open before Angus had the presence of mind to warn him. This time, he knew better than to laugh when misfortune visited his superior. Black filth saturating Lindsey's uniform had seemingly demoted him for some oil congealed on his cuff, hiding three of his golden bars.

"Why didn't you warn me?" he growled.

"Ah was gaun tae but ye were just too quick for me."

"Huh!" grunted Lindsey in half-disbelief. "Well, fix the bloody thing!" He snatched up a wiper and proceeded to smear oil over his face before storming from the boiler room.

The stokehold engineer descended from his eyrie, sweat streaming down his temples. He dabbed at his brow, his head craning fore and aft. His peripheral vision took in the fresh oil spill. "Don't tell me that you did it again. I just had that cleaned up. Where's our illustrious leader?"

"He just went chargin' aft," revealed Angus.

Larry thumbed the spill. "I hope that he didn't see this lot."

"Och, he saw it a' right," he was laughingly assured. "In fact, it was starin' him in the face, so tae speak."

"What do you mean?"

"These mishaps just dinnae happen tae lowly juniors," he explained. "They afflict the mighty tae."

"Hell, I hope that I don't get in shit for this."

"Och, these wee things are sent tae try us."

He went aft and resumed his station in the engineroom. It had just been another incident in a typical watch. The clump-clump-clump of somebody clambering the ladder to the manoeuvring platform drew his interest. The chief's writer appeared with a male passenger in tow. There was a short discussion with Christie before he was beckoned into their company.

"Mister King, I want you to show this gentleman around the tunnel. Answer all his questions if you can."

The tall stranger returned the floater's smile. With shoulders square and back straight the gentleman stood at ease as if on parade. His sparse white hair had been cropped fairly close to his well-shaped head. His eyes were pale, pale-grey, like ice. The foreign-sounding name was missed by him, swept away unheard in the eternal cacophony of the engine spaces.

Nordic, he thought. "Would ye like tae come this way sir?"

He was followed aft, the scribe coming to heel in short jerky steps. After a few paces the guide stopped, his outstretched arm gesturing to the engineroom's expanse. "The main engines," he stated unnecessarily.

"Ja."

'Scandinavian maybe,' he thought.

Inside the tunnel the hollow throbbing had lowered the decibel level to make conversation just slightly better than the engineroom. The chap had many technical queries for the young engineer who was glad that he had asked similar questions during the voyage. Jake's thoroughness elaborated with his usual flair for the trivia had borne fruit. These facts were passed on to the visitor. Even the chief's writer, a crewmember of many years, showed a glimmer of interest.

In heavily accented English the passenger asked the engineer if he was aware of the similarities between his vessel and the *Queen Mary*. He wasn't but pointed out the fact that the Mary had three funnels while the *Dalriada* had only two.

"Ah," beamed the fellow. "But duringk ze vor, ze Eenglish feeted a doomy foonil to zis sheep makingk her look like ze *Mary*."

"Ah," repeated Angus. "So both ships would look the same from a distance. Now the *Dalriada* must look like the *Queen Elizabeth*."

"Nein!" the visitor denied. "Ze *Elizabeth* haf no vell deck."

"Ye seem tae be very knowledgeable on ships," said Angus. "Were ye in the navy by any chance?"

"Ja," he admitted. "I nearly had zis sheep duringk ze Second Vorld Vor."

"Oh, is that right?" asked a sceptical Angus. "Is it no' a wee bit unusual for a foreigner tae be skipper o' a British ship?"

"Nein - nein," protested the passenger. "You don't oonderschtand." He shook his head despairingly to begin again. "I vos Kapitan - ja - but not on Britisch sheep. I am Cherman!"

He thumped his breast with pride. He would've clicked his heels had his flip-flops permitted but instead came to attention. "I vos unterseebooten. U-boat, you oonderschtand?"

"Ja! Ja!" stuttered Angus. "Ah mean Aye! Aye!"

"I can zee zis sheep in my periscope," the German told him wistfully. "I fire last t'ree torpedoes. *Los* - *los* - *los*! Acoustic, you know? Nein bloody good! Zay blow up too soon. Poof! Poof! Poof! He shook his head sadly. "I t'ought she vos *Queen Mary*. I vos hopingk Der Fuhrer vould gif me ze Iron Cross wit' crossed swords und chools."

"Noo these propeller shafts are turnin' at one hundred an' sixty-eight revolutions a minute."

"Ja? Und vot is her top speed?"

"Weel, she's gettin' auld but Ah've been telt that she might dae thirty knots wi' a stiff tail wind, a followin' sea, an' the Chief gaun oan leave at the end o' the trip."

"Ja, that vos wot she wos doingk ven my leettle feeshes exploded. Zen, voosh! Off she went ofer der horizon like an E-booten - you know?"

There was a bleak smile. "Just as weel - itherwise Ah might be unemployed."

The ex-U-boat commander shrugged his shoulders. "Ja, chust as ze French say, '*C'est la guerre*.' But," he added wistfully, "I vould haff liked zat Iron Cross wit' crossed swords und chools."

"Are ye gaun' topside noo?" enquired Angus at the end of the tour.

"Nein," replied the passenger. "I go now to look at boilers."

"Ok," said Angus. "Enjoy the rest o' your trip. Cheerio."

"*Auf weidersen,*" replied the German, holding out his hand. "Danken for ein eenterestingk tour."

He took his hand automatically. "Ye're quite welcome sir." He left them at the airlock doors and resumed his station on the platform.

"Thank God, it's nearly quitting time," sighed Jake. "And so, dear Diary, ends another absolutely boring watch aboard the good ship, RMS *Queen of Dalriada*."

The floater smiled at his shipmate. "Naw Jake, it wisnae really."

At that moment MV *Eithne* was gliding past Ailsa Craig in the Firth of Clyde.

The Race

2215 Wednesday

His Munificence Alan Lindsey, the chief engineer, had decreed that only a skeleton crew would be required to staff each of the three evening watches. Archie MacAdam, the HSGR's watchkeeper, was out of luck since the ship still needed turbo-electric generators to operate the lights and pumps. Pete Eaton, 1BR engineer, lucked out too since said boilers had to supply steam for said jennies, calorifiers, galleys and air conditioning. A third engineer was needed for fire watch and to make sure that the ship's sprinkler pressure system was topped up. This assignment was to be either volunteered or drawn by lot.

His Malignance Mister Robert Christie, the platform second engineer, had decreed that Jake White would volunteer for the twelve-to-four watch. The Canadian, considering his lot, sought out Jazz Johns and asked him to stand an extra hour for him. Jazz agreed since his night would be wasted because he had drawn the short straw for the eight-to-midnight watch.

He cowered deeper into his overcoat and pulled his woollen scarf tighter around his neck. It made little difference. The piercing wind sucked greedily sucked the heat from his body. His feet were numb after an icy walk from the dockside. Standing on the corner of Broadway and Fifty-Ninth Street he stamped his feet on the packed snow and waited for a walk sign to condescendingly flash its permission to cross. Halfway across the wide street it angrily glared: *Don't Walk*. It was at this point when he was introduced to the peculiarities of Manhattan drivers.

When traffic beacons signalled *Go*, obstacles in their immediate path are studiously ignored. Crossing Broadway during rush hour he discovered was not an experience for the fainthearted. He clung weak-kneed and panting to the electronic Siren that had tried to lure him to his doom. A decade had passed since he'd shown such alacrity. A muckle black-and-white bull had taken umbrage at his shortcut through that far-off summer meadow. But this time, fortuitously, there had been no hawthorn barrier to impede his way to sanctuary.

He journeyed along West Forty-Fourth Street until he reached the King Edward Hotel. This renown establishment sat like a broody hen on the British Merchant Navy and Airline Officers' Club. Inside he breathed a sigh of relief and made his way to the bar. A tot of *Cardhu* stoked some heat into his shivering frame.

Christie stepped from the dance floor, slapped him on the back and bade him welcome. "You look like a snot that froze and broke off an Eskimo's nose," he rhymed.

"Ye would tae if ye howfed for miles in this weather."

"Are you crazy? Why didn't you take a cab?"

"None o' the bastards would stop for me."

"Where's your sidekick White?"

"Ah dinnae ken," he replied, feeling a little warmer. "Maybe he's dippin' it intae somethin' warm an' juicy. Ye ken, he's pissed aff at gettin' the evenin' watch again. He thinks that ye're shovin' it tae him."

Christie chuckled an evil chuckle. "Angus, do you honestly believe that I'm as nasty as that?"

The abrupt answer Aye was ignored and he switched the subject by asking his junior's opinion on his second visit to the Big Apple.

There was a keen response. Rockefeller Center and Radio City had consumed most of his day. He questioned Christie for further information on these edifices but only the sexual potentialities of the Rockettes were of interest to his friend. He gave up. "Whit are ye drinkin'?"

"Same as you. I'll have another single malt, laddie."

He drained his glass and caught the bartender's eye. "Twa single malts please," he called holding up two fingers. A young lady sitting near him threw him a shocked glance. Quickly he transposed the gesture into the V-for-victory sign.

The second downed his shot in one swallow. Angus just sipped his drink savouring each drop.

"Nice drop of Scotch that," said Christie, smacking his lips. "Same again please bartender."

"How dae ye ken it's guid? It must've raced by your taste buds at the speed o' sound."

"My taste buds got a whiff of it all right," Christie assured him, moving onto a stool and sighing. "Ah! That's better."

He drew out a thick wad of banknotes and peeled off a couple when the bartender plunked down the fresh drinks.

"Here, that's a lot o' money ye're totin' aboot," observed Angus.

"You need lots of brass to have a good time in this city."

The warmth of the club combined with the malt whisky had dispersed the chill from the junior's bones. Garlands, wreaths of holly and coloured fairy lights festooning the walls and ceiling blatantly announced that Christmas was not too far away. A large spruce decorated in the time-honoured tradition stood next to the piano, its tinselled branches hovering over an array of gaily-wrapped boxes. The Spirit of Christmas and a feeling of well being saturated the minds and souls of guests and hostesses.

Except Black Bob.

Muttering under his breath Christie slipped off his stool. King caught his elbow to ask where he was going. “I’m going to tell that old hag to play some decent music,” he grumbled.

“But she’s playin’ Christmas carols,” protested Angus. “Everybody likes them includin’ me.”

“I bloody well don’t,” snarled the maritime Scrooge. “I’m going to tell her to play something else.”

Fingers reached out in feeble restraint. “Dinnae make a scene or we’ll get chucked oot.”

“We can go elsewhere. Who gives a damn?” The grip was shaken off and he strode through the dancers toward the piano player. The young Scot shrugged and ordered another *Cardhu*. His eyes panned around the C-shaped bar looking for familiar faces. He thought that a couple of them were pursers from the ship but he wasn’t sure.

At one end of the bar just beyond its bright lighting was Scar Davis. He was wedged against the counter and the wall staring morosely into an old-fashioned tumbler cradled in his hands. Without further thought he swivelled around on the barstool and eyed his second’s approach to the piano player. Would sparks fly? He wondered.

The dowager never missed a beat. She continued to play calmly, quite indifferent to Christie’s expletives. The artistic fingers poised in midair after the line Seven pipers piping and coldly gazed up into her tormentor’s eyes. At five go-old rings the old dear nodded almost imperceptibly to someone in the throng. At this point Angus fully expected to hear the scrape of knuckles dragging across the floor when the proverbial gorilla-type bouncer responded to the signal.

The creature that answered the summons was quite unlike any simian that he had ever seen. It was an entirely different branch of the genus, *Homo sapiens* in fact - and female to boot. King knew that he would have to search far and wide to find such a choice specimen. Her voluptuous stern wiggled seductively beneath her tight crimson dress as she click-clacked across the parquet floor in stiletto heels. Her tall lithe form moored alongside the piano. The old pianist introduced her to Christie.

The second's face changed colour with the savour-faire of a chameleon. Dull red anger paled to dirty beige before glowing to a rosy blushing hue. A lopsided grin responded to the beam of the enchantress. She took his hand and lamb-like he was led onto the dance floor. The siren nuzzled against his shoulder and whispered something in his ear. He grinned wickedly and returned a confidential reply. The girl laughed. He could contain himself no longer.

"Five go-old rings," he bellowed as if piloting through a pea souper. "Four calling birds, three French hens, two turtle doves, and a partridge in a pear tree!"

That delicate melody *Silver Bells* filled the room and he waltzed out of sight. Angus was dumbfounded. The old lady's diplomacy had defused the situation. He swung around on his stool and reordered. Two dances later Black Bob jostled him from behind him. "Sorry to leave you Angus," he apologized, gulping down his drink. He gloated and rubbed his hands together. "Tonight's the night! I'm off to get my jollies!"

"Weel then, the best o' British luck tae ye!"

"Oops! She's looking for me," noted the second. "I'm off! See you!" He dashed into the crowd.

A few sips later Jake nudged him. "Hi Gus."

King's face lit up and slapped his friend's back heavily. "A Scotch-on-the-rocks for ma pal, bartender."

Jake protested. "Hey, steady on Gus. It sounds like you've had a few too many, right?"

"Och, Ah've only had a couple o' wee drams."

"Where's that four-eyed buddy of yours?"

"Who - ma big pal, Bob?" he mumbled. "He's hooked intae a real smasher. The lucky bastard!"

"Well - I don't know about lucky," said Jake craning his head across the slow-moving dancers. "But you've certainly got the bastard part right. Oh, there he is over there. Ha!"

"Whit ha?"

"He's dancing with Tina."

Angus peered myopically at the dancing couple. "Aye, that's her."

"If he gets off with her, I'll show my ass in the middle of Gore Park."

"Where's Gore Park?"

"Downtown Hamilton, Ontario, where I'm from - right?"

"If ye say so," was the bleary reply.

"You're going to have a sore head in the morning."

"Ah'm no' bluidy drunk," King declared indignantly.

"Oh yeah? Repeat after me - I'm not a pheasant plucker, I'm a pheasant plucker's son, I'm only plucking pheasants till the pheasant plucker comes."

He tried to focus his mind on his pal's doggerel. "Ah'm no' a pleasant phucker, Ah'm a . . . Och, it's just a daft tongue twister."

The bartender slid a glass of Scotch-over-ice across the counter top. Jake sipped his drink slowly.

"Who's this Tina anyway?"

"Goodtime Tina?" The Canadian innocently repeated. "She couldn't date a nicer guy, right?"

"Whit dae ye mean?"

"She's a gold digger. She promises guys a good time until they run out of money."

"Och weel, maybe Ah'd better warn Bob then," he suggested, sliding unsteadily from his stool.

Jake slipped a hand under his armpit and repositioned him smoothly back onto the stool.

"Damn!" he said, with little feeling. "They've gone. You've just missed them. Now isn't that a damned shame? And here was me - uh - just thinking about strolling over to warn the big guy, right?"

"Liar!"

Jake sniggered.

"What's the joke?"

They turned and beheld the Welshman, Morgan.

"Hello Taff," said Jake.

"How's it gaun rare?"

Taffy did a double take. "Eh?"

Jake translated. "He said, 'How's it going there?'"

"Oh - er - fine, thanks Gus."

"Whit ur ye fur havin'?"

"Eh?"

"What would you like to drink?" asked the interpreter.

"Oh - er - a beer please, Gus."

"A gless o' ale fur ma pal here, bartender."

"A glass . . . "

"I understood him that time Right," said Morgan, shutting off the flow. "What's up with Gus? I usually can understand him on board the ship."

"It appears that the intake of Scotch brings out the Gaelic in him."

"Say, how come you can comprehend his brogue, boyo?"

"I honestly don't know," admitted Jake, swirling the last few drops of whisky around his glass. "Maybe it's - uh - this stuff or maybe it's because I've being working with him for too long. After all, he's been aboard for about two weeks now - right?"

"If you say so. Hey - there's old Scar over there," said Taffy. "Hey Scar!"

Davis lifted his glass in acknowledgment. "Come on over here, boyo. Bartender, refill that gentleman's glass and bring it over here."

Davis reluctantly slid off his stool circumnavigated the bar and merged with his colleagues. Small talk and some banter ensued. He put in a comment or two but mainly stayed withdrawn until Morgan suggested, "Hey chaps, how's about us getting a table? My feet are sore just standing here."

"Aye," said Angus, his eyes twinkling when he prodded his shipmate's generous paunch. "Ah would be wantin' tae sit doon tae if Ah had tae support a' that."

"He is a cheeky blighter, isn't he?" Morgan said to White.

Jake laughed. "You don't seem to have any trouble understanding him now."

Noticing some customers vacating a table the engineers swiftly laid claim to it. Angus sat down and promptly flaked out. Nudging him roughly the Welshman grumbled, "Now then - would you look at that, boyo!"

"Oh leave him, Taff," censured Jake. "You know what? Let him sleep it off, right?"

Davis departed about an hour later just as Black Bob cruised back in to berth alongside the somnolent Scot. Chagrin marred his face. He vented some of his ire on Jake by grumbling, "What the hell are you doing here, White? You're supposed to be on watch in half-an-hour and here you are boozin' like a sot. Get back to the bloody ship or I'll have you logged."

Jake's eyes screamed silent retaliation across the table. He clenched his fists, arose and left the club in fury. Taffy tried to pacify his senior by offering him to buy him a drink.

"You can't bribe me Mister Morgan. Slowly and distinctly he said, "I-can-buy-my-own-drink-with-my-own-money."

Taffy shrugged and set sail for the bar to get himself a drink. Christie shook Angus, awakening him from a sound sleep. The junior yawned and blearily gazed up. "Hello Bob," he said, his faculties returning. "How did ye make oot?"

"That bitch took me for nearly every cent that I had. I went for a piss and when I came back she'd buggered off and left me with a whopping great tab. Luckily, I keep five bucks hidden in my spectacle case. That was the price of cab fare from the *Lorelai* to here."

Black Bob mournfully shook his head. "Can you lend me twenty bucks?" Peering through the gloom into his wallet King extracted two bills. "Thanks Angus. I'll pay you back tomorrow after I see the purser."

"Nae hurry Bob."

"What would you like to drink?"

A furry tongue probed around the vile taste in his mouth. "A shandy, Ah think. My mouth tastes like the bottom o' a parrot's cage."

"Ok Angus," said Christie, getting up just as Taffy rejoined the company with his drink.

"Awake are you, boyo?"

"Aye."

"That Christie's a real bastard, isn't he?"

"Is he?" he asked, smoothly. "Ah haven't noticed."

Christie returned with the drinks. "I see that old cow's playing better music now," he said. "I've a good mind to give her shit for lining me up with that Tina."

Feeling much better after his snooze Angus just grinned. He espied a likely looking girl sitting alone at another table. Since she seemed more attractive that the run-of-the-mill type that usually frequented the club, he asked her dance. After a couple of numbers she remained unreceptive to his charms. Romance wasn't in the cards for him that evening.

All was quiet along the waterfront. The security guard barely acknowledged Davis when he flashed his crew pass before striding up the gangway. There wasn't a soul around the engineers' quarters. Only the faint sound of a woman's laughter could be heard from some chap's cabin on the far side of the ship. His dad looked up from a paperback when Davis entered his cabin.

"It's pretty quiet now Dad," he said. "This is a good time to go ashore."

His father stuffed his belongings into his duffle bag, put on his shoes and overcoat. "Ok, I'm ready son - lead the way."

Davis opened the door then closed it hurriedly as Wheelkey furtively tiptoed past, an armful of beer bottles clinking together. When the passageway was clear Oscar signalled the ok. They stopped at a corner and waited until an electrician entered his cabin. He pressed the button for the elevator and on hearing voices within as it came up dashed towards the stairs leading to the pantries below.

"Christ," he swore. "One minute it's like a ghost ship. Now, it's like Piccadilly Circus."

Eventually they made their way down to open shell door where the gangway was located. The guard was flapping his arms trying to keep warm. Someone was leaning on the rail at the bottom of the gangway.

Night wore on without further incident. By one in the morning when the club closed, the three engineers were feeling no pain. A cab was hailed from the hotel's front entrance. It darted towards Pier 92. Taff burst into that Welsh favourite, *Men of Harlech*, much to the occupants' chagrin.

The taxi driver was only too glad to pour them out onto the Market Diner's sidewalk. The Cymric repertoire continued as they staggered past the diner with the intention of encroaching on the hospitality of the tavern that lay next door. The caterwauling induced a beat police officer to order Taffy to shut up or else he'd be run in. Christie, perturbed that a Colonial had the temerity to order a Britisher to be quiet, took instant offence. "Who in the hell d'you think you are?" he slurred. His eyes blearily focussed on Morgan. "Ignore him Morgan - sing!"

A sharp prod in the ribs from the cop's nightstick brought a squeak from that lyrical larynx. "That's enough I said," he growled. "No-aw move along."

"Right," snapped Christie. "We'll see about this."

And so he began his standard windup in preparing for a fight by removing his spectacles. He carefully folded them before placing them in their case. Opening his coat he tucked them out of harm's way in his inside jacket pocket. When ready he raised his fists in a John L. Sullivan stance.

Well, almost ready.

The cop, a veteran of more New York street fights than the second had raised steam, was intrigued by these antics. Without a word he took the initiative with a lightning crack of his billyclub across Black Bob's breast pocket. The resultant crunch, accompanied with muffled tinkling, stole his fire. Christie stared bleakly at the cop.

"Are you gonna move along na-ow?"

Without another word they set course for their ship and anchored in deep shadow until the cop continued on his beat. Retracing their steps they entered the tavern to witness its closing at 3:00 a.m. Decanted from there with senses reeling, the trio wove their erratic way back to the ship.

"Wanna drink in m' cabin?" mumbled Christie.

Taffy tottered on ahead.

"Naw - come tae my cabin."

"No - mines," insisted Christie.

"Na, na," argued his friend.

"I know how t' set-tle thi-is."

"How?" grunted Angus, grabbing at him for support.

"We'll have a race," beamed the second.

"A ra-ace? Where tae?"

Waggling a finger vaguely in the ship's direction Christie stressed, "D'you see those two gangways over there with a guard on each of them?"

King squinted hazily past the wavering digit and nodded.

"Last one up drinks in the other one's cabin. Ok?"

"Ok."

His second shouted, “Ready - steady - fire - go!”

They took off stumbling and lurching, occasionally colliding, which made them shoot off on tangents only to clash again further along on their erratic courses.

Taffy clung to the steep gangway’s handrail. The long walk had taxed his system. His obesity and excess beer forced him to stop so that he could catch his breath. Wheezing spasmodically he peered myopically down into the murky water between the liner and the dockside. Ice growlers mingled with garbage, were trapped by the huge baulks of timber that buffered and prevented damage to hulls and dock pilings.

An object flooded his view and quickly decreased in size as it flailed helplessly in midair to disappear with resounding splash into the frigid depths. Before the plunging water had subsided and the singular guard at the singular gangway had uttered, “What the -?” a piercing shriek rent the freezing night air from the opposite side of the gangway. Sure enough the scene was re-enacted as Angus King hit the water.

“This is our chance Dad,” urged Davis, picking up the duffle bag. “Grab that life ring there and follow me.”

They toddled down the gangway past Taffy. Davison tossed the life ring into the water and handed its rope’s end to the guard. Grinning, he reclaimed his bag from his son and strolled off. “Hey!” yelled the guard but was distracted by Davis taking the lifeline while pointing to another life ring mounted nearby on the building’s side.

Angus and Christie floundered about panting, shivering, and entirely sober. They clawed at ropes that were attached to the wooden battens and shouted for help. Taffy sat down on the gangway quivering with near hysterical laughter. Black Bob managed to clamber onto a batten and haul the chittering Scot from the water. Luckily there was a ladder handy. It took them huffing and puffing up onto the wharf.

Tears rolled down Taffy's fat cheeks and he pointed wordlessly at the dripping-wet engineers. Even Davis and the guard joined in as Morgan released wee choking squeaks and frantically gestured at King's feet. Angus peered down at the tiny moats that had formed in the turn-ups of his trousers. He too had to laugh, which triggered Bob's booming mirth.

"Crazy Limeys," chuckled the guard, watching the engineers board the ship.

His stockbroker's face was positively grinning when Davison walked into his office. Barney Rogers jumped to his feet and came from behind his desk to bear hug his friend and client. He stepped back and looked him up and down. "You're looking pretty good Om. When did you get out?"

"Nearly a month ago," replied Davison, returning the hug. "Say, you're looking good too, Barney. How's Sarah and the kids?"

"Just doing fine Om. Julie and Debbie are in college. How's Oscar doing?"

"He's doing all right too. He's an engineer in the British Merchant Navy."

"So how can I help you Om?"

"Well Barney, you can tell me what the score is on my companies for a start," replied Davison. He was told that Cathy Davis had laid claim to most of the companies held worldwide. "What do you mean, most?"

"You still own that electronics business in Marseilles, France - on paper anyway. By strange coincidence they've came up with a new transistor that's drawing the attention on the stock market. You really should go over to France. With your expertise, things would really take off."

"Thanks Barney. I might just do that but I'll need money to get there."

"Sure thing, Om. How much cash were you thinking about?"

"At least ten grand - cash."

"Fine. Why don't you stick around here for a bit while I drive over to our bank."

Davison smiled and sat back as his friend went out the door. He stuck his hand in his coat pocket and felt Oscar's boarding pass. "Damn!" He tucked it into a blank envelope that he found laying on Barney's desk.

Barney soon returned with the cash. "Are you sure that's enough to keep you going?"

"I'll tell you what. How's about you giving me a blank cheque?"

Barney laughed. "You know Om, you're the only person in the world that I'd trust with a blank check." He picked up a pen and began writing. "Who do I make the cheque out to?"

"I'll do that Barney. It's better that you don't know."

"Ok Om," replied Rogers. "Now I've got something for you to sign."

"I figured that," smiled Davison, bending over the desk and began signing a sheaf of transfer and loan documents.

Later that day Davison popped into a post office on West Thirty-Second Street to buy a stamp and mail off his son's boarding pass. He went to a counter for a pen to address the envelope. Some wanted posters draped the notice board behind the counter. One of them displayed a prison mug shot of him. He left in a hurry. By the time he'd reached Broadway he had considered his options. He stepped into the next phone booth and looked up the address of the Pict Line agents' office in Manhattan.

He filled in the blank cheque to pay for the next two cruises on board the *Queen of Dalriada*. He'd also booked up on its next Atlantic crossing to Cherbourg, France. Using his real passport he boarded the liner that morning. He decided not to tell his son of this latest development because any day now Oscar would be notified of his mother's death. The lad would soon realise that his dad had murdered his mother.

The Syndicate

2120 Friday

Ennui is a common condition suffered by seafarers, the smaller the ship the bigger the problem. Reading alleviates the symptom but on extended voyages the written word is devoured by questing brains at an alarming rate, so that other outlets are sought during the off watches to salve the boredom. On a large vessel like the RMS *Queen of Dalriada* that ailment was less apparent because there were more interests such as reading, cards, chess, draughts, dominoes, darts, ping-pong, swimming pools gymnasiums, female companionship, listening to radio and records, cinema, making models and curious other hobbies. Gambling was frowned upon but even so . . .

An ugly bronze face twitched for third time in a corner of Morgan's desktop. Multiple eyes scanned its surroundings seeking signs of danger. Oscillating antennae stiffened, the sensors detecting nourishment nearby. Only a few inches away a pool of spilt draught lager was wafting minute eddies of yeasty temptation towards the voracious animal. Caution was cast to the winds and six legs marched boldly in unison. Strong mandibles were soon bailing hop-flavoured nutrients into a greedy maw. A moving shadow triggered a warning to the ganglion brain.

"Gotcha!" A pewter tankard slamming on black painted woodwork accompanied the exalted Welsh cry.

"No you didn't," replied Keyes, gesturing with his own pint pot. "Look, he's still alive."

A pair of heads collided as they tried to peer down into the bottom of the empty tankard. Incarcerated by a hollow formed by the glass base, a roach sped in panic-stricken circles.

"Look at that bastard go boyo!" cried Morgan.

Keyes rubbed the tender spot on his head and scoffed, "Huh, You think that's fast? You should see the one in my cabin. He'd leave this bugger standing."

"Well, I'm going to leave this one standing see you," promised Taffy, removing his slipper.

"Hang on a second!" urged Jake. "I've got an idea."

"Oh Right, here we go again," moaned Taffy. "What weird and wonderful plan has tobogganed down from the Great White North."

"You know what? Since everybody and their brother-in-law has got roaches why don't we capture one from each cabin and race 'em?"

"Noo Ah've heard everythin'," scoffed Angus.

"Hang on - hang on," said Keyes, his imagination astir. "We could make a few bucks out of this if we play it right. Pardon the pun Right."

"How?"

"First of all we need more roaches and then train 'em." grinned Keyes.

"Dinnae be daft man," criticized Angus. "How in the blazes can anybody train cockroaches?"

"These little buggers are smarter than you would think Gus," replied Keyes. "They can live anywhere, from the equator to the poles. Heat, cold, it doesn't make one damn bit of difference to them. I've seen 'em skitter across boiler-tops and steam pipes where neither you nor I can stand for a couple of seconds, even wearing leather-soled boots. Yet this wee guy and his pals do it all the time."

"But that's just like Darwin says in his theory o' evolution," concluded Angus. "The one that can adapt will survive tae pass it ontae their descendants."

"You're right Gus," agreed Wheelkey genially. "That's a mark of intelligence too, isn't it? It's partly because of adaptability that Man is where he is today - where we are today, in actual fact."

"You got that right," Jake said and laughed. "All at sea!"

"Anyway," said Keyes. "Let's collect a stable of roaches and we'll go from there."

"What about this one, see you?"

"Leave him there Taff," replied White, but reconsidered. "No, you'd better not - he might run off with your pint pot."

Taffy produced a metal cashbox from a drawer. "This'll be his new home and serve as a stable for the others too."

"Good idea Taff," concurred Keyes. "Ok that's it, meeting is adjourned until we have a full stable."

And so, some leisure time was devoted to the pursuit of likely candidates. The next night a conglomerate of oddly shaped containers had accrued on the Welshman's desktop. "Now what?" asked Taffy, the self-appointed racing steward. "Are we going race 'em out the centre of a circle, see you?

"Nah," said Keyes. "That's only for amateurs. We need a bit more class. Let's find out how to make 'em all run in the same direction at the same time."

"I was - uh - strolling past the printers' shop just this very morning when I - uh - happened to find this," said Jake, holding up a roll of glazed cardboard and began to unravel it.

"It didn't seem to belong to anybody so I - uh - just helped myself to it, right?"

"Have you got any sticky tape and scissors, Taffy?" asked Keyes. "Thanks."

He snipped off a length of cardboard so that the ends touching it formed a circle four feet in diameter on the carpet. "Hold these two ends together Gus." he said, and deftly bound them with Sellotape. A slightly smaller hoop was constructed and placed inside the other. "There you go - one racetrack."

"Whit aboot them tryin' tae run up the sides?"

"Good point Gus," conceded Wheelkey. "Hey Taff, have you any roach killer?"

"No," replied Morgan. "It was no bloody use anyway. That stuff just got them stoned."

"No problem. I've got some," volunteered Jake.

"Well, don't hang around here, you Colonial twit," growled Keyes. "Bugger off and get it." When he came back the track's inner walls were sprayed. "That'll discourage 'em."

"Here," intervened Angus. "How are ye gaun tae identify the roaches? They a' look alike tae me."

Keyes, beginning to become exasperated by his countryman's pessimism, blasphemed. "Jesus Christ Gus! Why are you always looking for faults?"

"He's right, see you," agreed Taffy. "How in the bloody hell do we identify them?"

Mulling this over Keyes said: "Taffy, you're a good pal of Emsworth, aren't you?" He nodded. "Ok then. Nip along to his cabin and borrow his model paints for a wee while. We'll need a brush too."

He came back with four vials of Revell's enamel paint. They were given them a cursory glance. "Red, white and blue. Very patriotic," was Wheelkey's sarcastic observation. "And green? Is there a bit of Irish in you Taff?"

"Watch it boyo!" riposted Taffy, simulating an *en garde* stance using a paintbrush.

Keyes snatched the brush, opened the cashbox. "Your horse is first, Taff. What colour do you want?"

"I'll settle for the green."

"Right, open the paint bottle will you?"

In a trice Taff's roach was anointed with a dab of emerald green upon its wing casings.

"Who's next?"

"Me, white for White," replied Jake, holding out the bottle containing his roach.

"Dump him into the box and take the cap off the paint bottle," commanded Keyes. "Angus?" The cockroach was daubed crimson. "I guess that leaves me with blue. Damn!" he swore softly because the brush's tip had gone off target to mark the insect's posterior. "Oh well," he grinned. "At least I've got a ready-made name for him: The Blue-Arsed Fly!"

The engineers indulged in Taffy's beer chatting until the racing strips had dried.

"Let's put 'em through their paces," said Keyes.

The insects were dumped into the make-do racetrack. King's roach ran clockwise, Taffy's anti-clockwise and the blue chased the white in ever-decreasing circles.

"It's no damned good," Wheelkey groaned in disgust. "Another great idea gone for a Burton." He hauled off his slipper and towered over the milling insects.

"Wait!" squeaked Taffy, restraining the impending blow. "Leave 'em with me for a bit. I'll try again."

"Och, ye'll just be wastin' your time Taffy.

"Rome wasn't built in a day, see you," quoted Taffy.

Angus concurred. "That's true, an' Ah think that maybe we a' would've been better aff if it hadnae have been built at a'."

"How's about another beer Taff," bummed Keyes.

"Bugger off," replied Taffy, firmly planking a foot upon his dwindling supply of beer. "I'm going to kip for a couple of hours just as soon as I've rounded up our investments."

"Fancy some darts lads?" Keyes asked the other two.

Jake glanced at King who nodded. "Ok. Let's go."

"I've got a bit of bad news Jake old son," warned Jazz at the change of watch.

"What have you screwed up now Jazz?"

"I didn't screw up anything up," was the indignant denial. "It just happened."

"What did?"

"The De Laval has sheared a pin again. The Mekon is down there now lining up Gus," explained Jazz. "There's still a broken piece inside the driveshaft that'll have to be drilled out."

"Really? That's bloody marvellous!" groaned Jake sarcastically.

"Have fun," grinned Jazz. "I'm off for a few cold ones."

Jake found the floater sweating profusely by the De Laval lub-oil purifiers, which were located between the main engine reducing gearboxes. He was concentrating fiercely leaning a portable electric drill. Presently the machine's whining protest stopped. He beamed a smile of satisfaction up at his shipmate. "Ok Gus?"

He nodded and pointed. "Pass ower that tapered reamer an' dwang, will ye?"

"What's a dwang?"

"A tap handle. Dae Colonials no' ken anythin'?

White tersely sucked in his breath at the insult. "I'll remind you that only two weeks ago a certain Colonial showed a dumb Jock how most of the machinery in this fucking engineroom worked!"

"Och, ye're right. Ah'm sorry Jake."

"Ok then, I'll bite. Why do you call this tap wrench a dwang?" asked Jake, handing it and a tapered reamer to his workmate.

"Because that's the sound the tap handle makes if ye're stupid enough tae break the tap," Angus cheekily replied, adding. "Dw-wang!"

Jake laughed.

With the unit repaired and up running the juniors began their usual ritual by propping up the platform desk. Jake discovered a section of the New York Times that was dated from their last port visit. "Here what's this?" he asked stopping to leaf through the pages. "Aha, a crossword."

"So?"

"A crossword that hasn't been touched."

"Gie me a section o' the paper tae read then."

"Here," said Jake, sliding out a sheet. A quick rummage through his pockets produced a pencil stub. He settled down to try his skill with the puzzle. Within minutes, his shipmate disturbed him again.

"Gie me anither bit o' the paper, Jake."

"Hang on a second!" Jake urged. "Here's one you can help me with; twelve across, six letters, Britain without England and Wales."

"Heaven!"

"Smart ass! Typical bloody Scotsman," complained Jake. "Come on, what's another name for Scotland? The third letter is O - ends in IA."

"Utopia," snapped Angus. "How's aboot the ither page then?"

"Not until you answer the question."

"Scotia. Noo gie me anither page"

Jake jotted in the solution. "Shit! I should've known that. Like in Nova Scotia, right?" He drummed his fingers on the desk prompting Angus to look up from his newspaper.

"Stuck again?"

"Uh-uh. Twenty-one down, six letters. Spring flower that begins with C."

"Tulip," said Angus with a smirk.

"Tulip?" echoed Jake, taking the bait. Tulip's only got five letters and it starts with a T."

"C-H-U-L-I-P," Angus slowly spelled out the Scottish pronunciation.

"Fifty comedians out of work and you have to be funny."

It presently dawned on Christie that his juniors had been idle for quite some time. In his usual manner he suggested that they go about their duties. "Are you pair going to hold up that desk all watch?" he roared. "I wish that I had bugger all else to do but solve crosswords."

Both juniors vanished down the platform ladder.

"Twenty-one down, six letters. Spring flower, begins with C," muttered Christie. 'C-R-O-C-U-S,' he printed neatly. "That Colonial is a real dumb bastard. Imagine not knowing that. Let's see, twenty-nine across . . ."

The floater decided that a stroll forward was in order. He chatted briefly with Larry Treen, ignored Sudbury, and checked in with Taffy. The Welshman was industriously fabricating a miniature starting apparatus complete with traps for his charges. King idled with him for a few moments before going next door into the Hotel Service Generator Room.

There, an unusual sight confronted him. Dressed in shoddy denims, a lean figure lay hunched over a workbench vise. He sped to the pain-stricken rating's aid.

"Leave that sowel alane!" bawled Archie MacAdam, the watch engineer. "Let the bugger suffer!"

"This man's in agony!" retorted Angus over the whine of the generators. "Ah'm gaun tae help him up tae sick bay."

MacAdam cackled through a toothless grin. He was a runt of a man in his early forties, dour and hard-faced. "Ye're welcome tae try pal," he taunted in a Govan dialect before disappearing behind one of the turbo-generators.

"Try an' stand up," coaxed Angus.

The rating's frame rose to a stoop. He groaned and clutched at his midriff with one hand. The other wrist was handcuffed to the vise. Bending over the workbench's edge he vomited a brown foamy stream of foul smelling bile. King's nose wrinkled in disgust when a stench of stale beer permeated the jenny room's oily-warm air. His retching finished, the greaser drew a grubby fist across his lips to face him again. His pallor, dishevelled hair and bloodshot eyes with pupils like an eagle's in a vertical dive betrayed all the characteristics of a hangover.

"Still here?" MacAdam yelled upon his return.

"Oh Mister MacAdam sir," implored the rating. "Please let me go to my bunk. I'm dying. I don't care if I'm logged."

"Weel, Ah dae," MacAdam roared into his sensitive ears. "Ah've never had tae log onyboady yet an' Ah'm no' aboot tae stert the nicht."

Most of MacAdam's rapid-fire dialect was lost to the rating although the gist remained. "Please Mister MacAdam. Log me. Log me," beseeched the guy. "I'll never come on watch drunk again. Just let me get to my bunk."

MacAdam growled. "I ken ye'll no' dae it again because if ye dae, Ah'll bluidy weel chain ye up again! Suffer, ye bugger, suffer." Turning to King he warned: "Mind yer ain business in future. Ah'll decidse how tae discipline my men."

He unlocked the handcuffs from the vise. "Are you going to send me topside?" the miscreant asked hopefully.

"Naw," was the gruff reply? "It's time for roonds. Bring yer ile can. Ah'll bet that ye'll thank me for this oan peyday." A rabid glance abruptly changed to pain when MacAdam viciously tugged on the empty cuff to drag the man to his duties. "Here boy - walkies!" he cajoled, until the greaser reluctantly shuffled after his merciless master.

"Yes. Little Archie can be a right miserable so-and-so," agreed Eaton after Angus had entered 1BR and described his experience in the HS jenny room. "No, it's not clear yet!" he trumpeted up to a bedraggled figure near the top of B1 boiler, his voice competing with the banshee noise of escaping steam "Give it another half-hour at least then carry onto the next."

In that hellish steamy atmosphere desperation marred the fireman-trimmer's filthy countenance. He was slumped over a soot-blower's operating wheel sweating pink rivulets down his sooty cheek.

"*Hoi*! No sleeping up there. Snap to it!" bellowed Eaton.

"That guy looks like he's just aboot had it," observed Angus. "Ah thought firemen usually relieved each ither when blowin' tubes."

"They normally do," said Eaton. "Except that fellow up there is the drinking partner of the enchained malady next door. This is his punishment. He has to do the whole job by himself, and though he doesn't know it yet, he going to do the next watch's too."

"That's cruel."

"True - true," the tall Englishman sadly agreed and then he beamed, "It don't half sober 'em up though!"

"Ah'll bet it does. See ye later Pete."

King breezily marched into the messroom to take a pew beside Jake who was moodily contemplating some curled up sarnies. "Whit's up?"

"Look at them sarnies. Christ, you could lay a patio with them - right?" he complained. "You didn't happen to see our steward in your travels, did you?"

"Nope."

"Do you know what? He's probably got his head down somewhere," surmised Jake. He reached for a silver teapot and filled two cups with diluted bunker C. He added milk and sugar and took a sip. "Yech!"

The connoisseur's opinion was loyally respected and the freshly poured brew was left untouched.

"Where's Taffy?"

"Puttin' his stable through their morning sprints."

"Let's go an' see how he's makin' oot."

Jake's eyes roved over the unpalatable food. "Might as well, there's nothing for us here - right?"

They caught him crouching over a cardboard racetrack. He'd scrapped the original circular type and settled for a straight one.

"Any luck Taff?"

The Welshman bubbled over with enthusiasm. "Oh yes! It's really quite amazing. These cockroaches are very intelligent, see you."

"I suppose they would appear to be smart - to a Taffy," goaded Jake.

"Cheeky blighter, we should've let the bloody frogs keep Canada."

His guests seated themselves and politely listened to him pontificate on the idiosyncrasies of training cockroaches. "Now watch this," he said, lowering his ponderous frame onto the deck.

At one end of the revised course he'd set up his patent starter's box that contained the roaches. Halfway along the track was an upended bottle cap filled with beer. A fat finger depressed a small lever to activate a spring-loaded gate. All four insects scurried along the track to home in on the beer. King's beast won by a short antenna. They watched them guzzle down their reward.

Jake was astonished. "That's bloody marvellous! What a great job you've done - right? Can you get them to run over a longer distance Taff?"

"Yes," replied Morgan. "But it will take some time, see you." He shifted his cashbox to the bottle cap and obligingly the cockroaches scurried inside ready to be moved back to the starting gate.

That act prompted a comment from King. "That's amazin'! How did ye train them tae go back intae their bothy?"

"I think that they omit a scent," guessed Morgan. "They've come to recognise my cashbox as their home and the bits of grub that I drop in on a regular basis helps too. So these chaps are quite happy about being recaptured." He reinstalled the roaches inside the starter's box and shifted the cap a few inches further away. "We'll have to hang on a second or two. They're still quite strange to the gates, see you."

The insects soon settled down. Up went the gate and they charged off only to stop at the cap's original position. They milled around as if disappointed and coursed back and forth like miniature beagles retracing a lost spoor. Gradually, and in zigzag fashion, they rediscovered their prize. When Taffy repeated the operation the cockroaches raced all the way. "That's it for today fellows," said Taffy. "I can't get them to go any farther. I'll try again at the end of next watch."

"You've worked wonders Taffy," extolled Jake.

They left Morgan basking in their praise.

1700

The afternoon watch had been uneventful though the machinery spaces had heated up because the *Dalriada* was steaming into warm weather. Just before the watch ended Angus nipped up to the engineers' change room and dumped a set of dirty overalls into the washing machine. At the end of the watch he hung them over a handrail in the upper regions of the engineroom to dry. He planned to retrieve them after going to the hospital to have his stitches removed.

The voluptuous Nurse Highman was only too glad to perform this task before she went off duty. Soon his head was clamped in her curious vise. With his right ear against her left breast, his chin cushioned on her right and her left arm cuddling his head securely against that magnificent bosom, the sutures came out all too soon.

Shortly afterwards in the cosy little cubby of a cabin on B Deck aft, his ginger head was re-clamped - this time between the nurse's white muscular thighs. Under his nose forming a moustache was pubic proof that she was a natural blonde. His prehensile tongue flicked in and out between the unique folds of her vulva before deftly probing the mysterious depths of her slippery crevice.

Rosie, the formalities having been resolved only but a moment ago, writhed and rested and pursed her lips until the next stage of her pleasure crushed his face tightly against her crotch. Little pants of rapture elevated into a crescendo similar to the scream of the Royal Scot's steam engines *wheeching* through Carstairs Junction on the way to London in the dead of night. Not that Angus could make that comparison because he had become temporarily deaf by those aggressive thighs. At last she relaxed, her eyes rolling back to breathe heavily through a lopsided smile.

Rosie found it necessary to reciprocate and she did, literally, using another variation of the clamp. Sitting on his legs she lay forward cushioning his rigid penis between her pillow-like breasts and moved up and down. At the top of each stroke her lips nuzzled him, her tongue darting along his member as if it was an exceptional length of extra-thick Dunoon rock candy.

Before long her endeavours had achieved the desired effect. "Did you enjoy that Angus?" she asked, wiping away the excess fluid from her lips with the back of his hand.

"Och aye Rosie," he groaned in ecstasy and with a wicked grin said: "There's mair where that came frae!" Her reaction to that comment was to wiggle her body up onto his pelvis and impale herself on the still turgid member. Once more little squeaks, moans and groans of lovemaking filled the overheated cabin.

Morgan had passed the word. It had been decided that the impending race would be held in Jake's cabin since it was longer than the majority of others. Post time was nine-thirty that night. When the messroom closed the four-to-eight watch, sated by that night's sumptuous dinner, filed into Jake's abode where other off-watch engineers were imbibing. Friendly chatter abounded as they jostled for the limited amount of seating. Periodic rumbles from Angus' stomach drew the odd look. His amorous callisthenics with the nurse had caused him to miss dinner. He didn't even have time to shower.

Keyes, standing right behind him wrinkled his nose. "Hey guys, Smell Gus' cologne: *Eaŭ de Pussy*!"

Each officer had brought his own beer supply and a festive air impregnated the cabin. Before too long the racing stewards had to turn away tardy punters. By hailing at the top of his voice the host managed to get relative quiet. "Hold it fellas - hold it! Ah, that's better. Now I can hear myself think."

"So can I Right," shouted a chap. "I can hear your gears grinding."

A searing glance of scorn silenced the heckler. "Now uh - gentlemen and I use the term loosely," announced Jake. "In a moment the *Queen of Dalriada* Sweepstakes will take place. Mister Morgan will race the runners to that chalk line, a distance of twelve feet. Mister King here'll call out the winner and his decision will be final. Mister Keyes and I will take the bets. There are four clearly marked horses in the paddock.

"I will now call - uh - out their names as Mister Morgan enters them into the starting box. Since we've never raced them before . . ." Boos and catcalls filled the cabin. "Honest Injun fellas! Since they've never raced before the odds will be three-to-one the field."

The hubbub commenced again only to be hushed instantly with Wheelkey's succinct "Shut the fuckin' hell up!"

Jake grinned. "Thank you Mister Keyes, for your eloquent choice of words." He motioned at Taffy. "Mister Morgan if you please."

Taffy entered a cockroach, its carapace daubed with red paint. "Red Biddy; Mister Angus King, owner. Next, White Lightning, owner, yours truly. Next, Mister Henry Morgan's Green Gobbler and last but not least, The Blue-Arsed Fly belonging to Mister Wilberforce Keyes. Place your bets please."

Pouches, purses and wallets flashed and presently notes and coinage of three different countries were being exchanged between bettors and bookmakers. Jake stretched over Morgan to relieve a ten-shilling note from a prospective customer.

"How are we doing?" Taffy asked softly.

"Great!" whispered Jake. "We've got three horses in our favour. Most have bet on The Blue-Arsed Fly."

"What?" Morgan all but screeched. He lowered his voice again. "It's going to win the race. We'll all be taken to the cleaners."

"Whadayamean it's going to win?" Jake hissed in his ear. He smiled up at a client. "Five-bob on the Blue-Arsed Fly? You got it friend."

"It's his turn," replied Taffy hoarsely.

"Jesus!" swore White. "All bets on? Ok - are you ready Mister Morgan?"

Taffy nodded gloomily.

"Right!"

Jake rolled an old *Film Fun* into a cone and in a nasal tone began commentating as if he was at Flamborough Downs.

"They're under starter's orders. *A-and they'rrre off*! In the lead it's - uh - the Green Gobbler followed by Red Biddy. Next comes the Blue-Arsed Fly with White Lightning trailing . . . Red Biddy is beginning to move up. He's neck-and-neck with Green Gobbler.

"Now the Blue-Arsed Fly is moving up and White Lightning is dragging his ass. Get a move on you lazy bugger you," he urged. "At the halfway mark, it's Red Biddy shifting into the lead with Green Gobbler trailing but he's tiring folks! The Blue-Arsed Fly is passing the Green Gobbler and drawing up fast on Red Biddy . . . Now punters we're one furlong from home now. That's about the length of Gus' dick!"

King was in a quandary on whether to be insulted or pleased but he also wondered how Jake knew of his endowment.

"They're neck-and-neck! The Blue-Arsed Fly has just taken over the lead . . . And now, he's streaking away in front of Red Biddy. And at the post it's - The Blue-Arsed Fly followed by Red Biddy. Green Gobbler ran third and White Lightnin', the lazy git - also walked," sighed Jake miserably.

The engineers cheered and a forest of hands was felled in the bookmakers' direction. Keyes and Jake sorrowfully doled out the winnings. Angus sidled up next to the turf accountants who were comparing their losses while Taffy filled the paddock for the next race.

"How much did we win?" he gloated.

"Win?" squawked Jake. "I'm down twenty big ones and Wheelkey's down twenty-three."

"How come?"

Jake moaned. "Because everybody bet on Keyes' nag before that stupid Welshman told me that it was going to win - right?"

"How did he ken?"

"Now that's a good question," Keyes affirmed. "How did he know?"

"Well - uh - we certainly can't discuss it here in front of this lot - right?" expressed Jake. "We'll have to change the odds. Angus, nip over and ask Taff which horse is going to win this time."

"Ok." He edged through the happy mob and returned in a trice. "It's gaun tae be your horse again."

"Right. Here it is: the Blue-Arsed Fly, four-to-one on; Red Biddy, two-to-one against, Green Gobbler has same odds; and that speedster of yours Right will be ten to one against. Ok?"

"Fine," said Jake and called out the new odds.

Money changed hands again and the race was run with Wheelkey's cockroach winning just ahead of Green Gobbler. Cheers erupted from the excited punters. With bankruptcy facing the worried bookmakers Keyes decided to convene an emergency meeting of the Syndicate.

Inside Taffy's cabin he demanded an explanation. With arms akimbo Morgan shrugged saying that he didn't think that it would make much difference whose turn it was to win. "After all," he said. "They could've just as easily picked White Lightning to win."

"You blithering idiot!" scolded Keyes. "We could've changed the odds around so that we wouldn't have lost as much. We might even have gained." He shook his head. "Anyway, how in the hell did you know which cockroach was going to win?"

"I wasn't sure at first see," he hesitated. "It was only at dinner that I figured out that a pattern was starting to emerge each time they raced."

"Uh - d'you mean to tell me that you can think - uh - of other things when stuffing that fat gut of yours?" Jake jeered derisively.

"Rotter," snarled Taffy. "Of course I can, boyo."

"Well then," sighed Keyes. "Give us the form for Christ's sake. Who's going to win next?"

"Green Gobbler," forecast Taffy. "Then Red Biddy and after that, it's going to be White Lightning."

The floater derisively snorted, "White Lightning! That's hard tae believe."

"Damn right," concurred Keyes. "That moke has been dragging its arse for the first couple of races."

"If that's the case," Jake asked in reflection. "Why did the Blue-Arsed Fly win twice in a row?"

"That's the pattern," smirked Taffy. "They all take a turn at winning until the last one in the sequence wins twice. At the end of the next sequence Green Gobbler will win twice in a row then Red Biddy followed by White Lightning."

"Christ," sighed Jake. "I can't imagine my nag winning twice in a row."

"Never mind that," snapped Keyes. "What about place? Is that a sequence too?"

"Dunno. We'll have to keep a record, see you."

"We'd better get back," said Keyes. "I'll need a tenner from each of you to build up the kitty again."

Morgan's prediction was correct. His cockroach romped home easily much to the chagrin of punters who'd bet on the favourite. Keyes, whose mathematical skills had barely met standard for engineering blossomed where money and odds were involved. The depleted fund rose slightly but was kept in check by a few adventurous souls who bet long shots.

A quiet tête-à-tête with the syndicate prompted Jake to announce the last race so that the middle watch would have time to change and have supper before going on duty. The real reason was of course before the shrewder engineers cottoned onto the sequence of winners.

After Red Biddy won Jake informed the audience of a marathon race, which would be held in the wardroom in the near future. This raised a question from a punter who'd jarred Morgan earlier about the rudiments of cockroach training.

"If any of us manage to train a horse in time, can he enter it in the race?"

"Sure thing buddy," smiled Jake. "Taffy will have to give them a trial run first. We don't want a strange roach screwing up our trained ones." Under his breath he reflected: 'We don't want any ringers either.'

The spectators evacuated the cabin. Although the portholes were open and the air louvres were blowing their best Jake still had to flap a towel trying to dissipate the blue haze of cigarette smoke. With the team retrieved, empty bottles and glasses were hastily cleared away.

"Hey Taffy, how will the strange roaches affect ours?" asked Keyes, dumping ashtrays with a clatter.

"Dunno," replied Morgan. "I'll capture a couple and try 'em out."

"Make sure those butts are out," warned Jake. "I don't want my cabin to catch fire."

"I should set you on fire," commented Wheelkey.

"What for?"

"Why did you mention the bloody wardroom?" Keyes said. "Charlie will go nuts if we take a whole slew of cockroaches in. He hates the damned things."

"We'll do it when we come off watch. Six o'clock should wrap us all up. Charlie will never know the bloody difference."

"Exactly where do you plan to race them see you".

"Around the ping-pong table Taff," replied Jake. "It's big enough and the height is convenient. It'll allow everyone to get a decent view. I've got enough cardboard to make a track that size. Maybe we can make huddles for them for them to jump over."

Taffy was dubious. "What makes you think that they can run that far?"

"That's up to you," replied Jake. "After all, you're the trainer - right?"

"Huh! Boy, talk about passing the buck and a Canadian one at that. Hurdles, he says, the bloody Grand National says I. I suppose you'd like water jumps too, boyo!"

"Talking about money," said Keyes. "Where's your takings Right?"

"We weren't talking about money."

"We are now. Where's your takings Right?"

Jake emptied his pockets onto his bunk. Keyes added his spoils. Presently notes and coins of different denominations were stacked into four equal amounts on the chintz canopy.

"Let's see, thirty-nine pounds eleven shillings each. Twenty pounds each to start the kitty with ten pounds extra because our fat friend here forgot. That leaves a total profit of nine pounds eleven shillings each."

Reaching for his share Jake observed, "Not a bad night's work, right?"

Gone Fishin'

Sunday, 24th December

It was ten fifteen on a bright sunny morning when the great liner's sweeping wake disturbed the tranquil waters of North West Providence Channel with a resounding splash from her starboard bow anchor, nearly half-a-league from the low laying coast of the Grand Bahamas. Swarms of small craft besieged the huge vessel. A light zephyr bearing exotic fragrances slowly swung the ship parallel to the shore. Green and white water suddenly boiled beneath her counter. A loud hail from the bridge warned off a tiny speedboat, which sheered away just as the port anchor plunged down with a clanking roar of chains that accompanied a huge splash. The starboard hook dropped shortly after.

The twelve-to-four engineroom juniors shaded their eyes to gaze across the placid water towards a low sandy island. "Christ!" swore Jake. "It's just a spit of sand."

A few tallish buildings disrupted the horizon's shallow curve. Here and there the odd coconut palm drooped its green umbrella in the tropical heat. Construction cranes stood like sentinels, their booms stilled over the somnolent canary-yellow earthmovers. It seemed that the towns of Lucaya and Freeport were growing rapidly. Keyes stopped to eye the digging. "That's Freeport, in ten years it'll be a tourist trap."

To which Jake answered, "Let's get through the sixties first - right? What has this place got to offer us right now?"

"Golfing, fishing, scuba-diving and plenty of bronzie weather," intoned Wheelkey, as if reading the info from a travel brochure. “It’s also got a casino, plenty of cheap rum, lots of absolutely useless souvenirs, and I would imagine more than a few dusky maidens to satisfy the pent-up passions of horny engineers.”

Jake laughed. “You’re just a treasure house of useful information, aren’t you?”

“That’s because I read a lot of interesting books,” said Keyes. “Not like you lot. All you guys do is drool over pornographic magazines.”

“Ah read a lot tae,” chimed in Angus. “But Ah’ve never heard o’ this place.”

“Where did you find out about it?” asked Jake.

“From a pamphlet on the purser’s deck,” replied Keyes.

Gazing soulfully at the temperate coastline Angus sighed: “It’s hard tae believe that the morn will be Christmas Day.”

White jokingly chided him. “What’s the matter Gus? Are you homesick? Would you rather - uh - be at your fireside hanging up your Christmas stocking?” He chuckled before suggesting, “Why don’t you hang it from the funnel?”

“Huh, it wouldnae be hard for ye tae hang up your stockin’,” he retorted. “A’ ye’d hae tae dae is chuck it at the bulkheid. It would stick oan there for sure.”

“Really? Cheeky bugger!”

“Aye,” agreed Wheelkey. “How else would he find out if they were needing washed or not?”

“Christ, all you Scotsmen are all alike.”

“Aye,” replied Wheelkey in agreement. “All brains and big cocks. Not like Colonials and Sassenachs with both organs in the same small place.”

White scowled then pointed outboard. “Look! Here comes the passengers’ tender. Let’s try to get aboard it.”

"Oh-kay yew guys," growled Keyes in a passable John Wayne drawl. "Let's hit the beach!" and threw an imaginary hand grenade onto the tender. "Ka-boom!"

"That lighter is flying the Red Duster," admonished the Canadian.

With hooked thumbs in his belt he spat from the side of his mouth. "Goddamn Limeys are always gittin' underfoot."

The tender slid alongside the floating landing where a temporary stairway had been rigged for the liner's passengers. A courier with an enormous brown envelope tucked under his arm bounded up the steps to the landing by C Deck shell doors and asked for a British Police Detective-Sergeant Stevenson. Behind him came two young natives toting bundles of newspapers from New York, Miami, and Britain for display on R Deck Square. A steward purchased one of each for Homer Davison.

King went to Betty's office to ask her if she wanted to go ashore with him at the end of his watch.

"I'd love to Angus but I've got tons of work to do." She pointed to the large envelope on her desk. "That lot just came for me a few minutes ago."

"Whit is it?"

"Hopefully it's the information that'll help me solve this case. You go ashore with your friends. Maybe I'll have a better handle on things by this evening."

"Ok Betty," he replied and gave her a hug and a kiss before leaving to have breakfast.

The large envelope was slit open and its contents were carefully sorted out. There were eleven titled folders in all:

Folder 1. Pathology Report on George Brown, QC

Folder 2. Pathology Report on Katherine Lesley Davis

Folder 3. X-rays

Folder 4. Photographs

Folder 5. Forensic Report on Murder Weapon

Folder 6. Blood Groups Found

Folder 7. Forensic Comparison between Glove Cuts and Knife Edges

Folder 8. Findings on 3 Batches of Luggage

Folder 9. Forensic Report on Davidson's Passport including Fingerprints

Folder 10. Dossier on Homer R. Davison

Folder 11. Information on the Deceased's Next-of-Kin

She certainly had her work cut out for her. This was her second murder case as Cunningham well knew. She still didn't know if she was being used as a scapegoat or being thrown into the deep end. Either way her boss had made a terrific holiday out of it and had gone home, flying out from Idlewilde last time in New York. He'd decided that the case was cut and dried by concluding that Davidson had done the double murder and had committed suicide in remorse. Case closed. It was just a matter of her dotting the i's and crossing the t's as far as he was concerned.

The detective-sergeant wasn't so sure. Angus had been very dogmatic about his observations but then he was dogmatic about everything. Her mind drifted to their lovemaking for an instant until she sternly reproached herself.

Betty reflected on the administrating work that she'd done during her first murder case when still a simple constable in uniform. She remembered how confused some of the detectives had been with the phraseology that pathologists used in their findings. She had spent a lot of time translating those baffling Latin terms into language that laymen could comprehend. Her efforts were recognised and had earned promotion.

Now she had to format all this information in front of her for easy cross-reference. With a fresh sheet of foolscap she opened the first folder began:

Subject: George Albert Brown

Nationality: British

Weight: 184 pounds

Height: Five feet eleven inches

Hair: Sandy

Born: August 1, 1926 in London, UK

Eyes: Brown

Complexion: Fair

Other characteristics: None

Blood Group: A negative

Marital Status: Single

Occupation: Queen's Councillor

Present address: 212 Abbey Street, Rhyll, UK

Next-of-kin: None known

Initial Findings: Since subjects had been frozen solid during the trip from the US of A, post mortem results took longer because time had been wasted waiting for cadavers to thaw. Also the times of death couldn't be established accurately. See Death Certificate completed by ship's surgeon and documented witnesses' reports.

Obviously this was a snide remark in regards to the shipment and preservation of the subjects until they reached their destination.

Stevenson read on.

Cause of Death:

The first subject had been stabbed twice in the back by a Scottish dirk with a blade some 15-1/2" long. The initial wound almost penetrated the chest cavity between second and third ribs and jammed there by the thoracic vertebra, severing some thoracic nerves and azygos veins. This wound paralysed the subject.

The weapon had then been roughly extracted, turned 90° and reinserted forcefully the second time between the third and fourth ribs. It had plunged through the left lung and left atrium and came out between the front fourth and fifth ribs. Death was instantaneous at this point (See the attached documents for further details including x-rays and photographs).

The graphic evidence that she'd been mulling over all morning hadn't curbed her appetite by any means for by lunchtime she was feeling a bit peckish. There was plenty of time for her to go down to her cabin to tidy her hair and touch up her face before heading for the main restuarant.

An hour later she was back in her office feeling bloated. Ship cuisine was just too tempting and once again she promised herself to watch those calories. Choosing another sheet the detective began to make out an agenda for the female victim.

Subject: Katherine Lesley Davis
Nationality: British
Weight: 102 pounds
Height: Four feet eleven inches
Hair: Auburn
Born April 23, 1915, in Coventry, UK
Eyes: Blue
Complexion: Fair
Other characteristics: None

Blood Group: O
Marital Status: Divorced
Occupation: Electrical Engineer and Businesswoman
Present address: 157 Butterton Road, Rhyll, UK
Next-of-kin: Oscar Davis - son
Cause of Death: This subject had been stabbed in the chest by the same dirk that was used to kill the first victim. After exiting the male's chest via the fourth and fifth ribs the blade entered the female's chest between her second and third ribs. The remaining part of the blade was just long enough to partially sever the superior vena cava, which caused her to bleed to death - probably within minutes.

She placed the second folder aside and glanced through the x-ray folders. They didn't seem to hold much interest for her at that time. The photographs on the other hand were excellent but she felt that Christina Hastings had given a much better insight because of the drama of the murder scene.

However, the ship's photographer was unable to take views of the victims after separation. The view of Brown's chest showed an en or an inverted u handwritten in blood on his left shoulder. There was a close-up of this unusual clue. There was also a close-up of the female's index finger showing the first digit coated in blood. Obviously it was she who had written the en just before she died.

She riffled through Hastings' photographs. One showed Davis' right arm dangling down almost touching the floor and sure enough when she looked closely, blood could be seen on that finger. She wondered if it would've helped her case if the photos were scrutinized earlier with a powerful lens glass.

She now turned her attention to Folder 5: Forensic Report on Murder Weapon. She had previously studied its mate from the

Long Gallery and knew its size and weight. The murder weapon was a fifteenth-century Scottish dirk with a carved staghorn handle and cairngorm pommel. Its overall length was twenty inches and weighed one pound fourteen ounces.

The hardened steel blade measured fifteen-and-a-half inches, a bit longer than an average dirk from the same time period. The width of the blade at the hilt was one and five eighths inches. Minute traces of silk and cotton were found on the upper section of the blade (see attached lab reports). No fingerprints were found although a partial bloody palm print was found on the pommel cap (see attached lab report).

Most of the twelve-to-four engineers were dressed in their civvies by the time the tender was ready to cast off with another load of passengers. It didn't take Angus long to discover that Jake and Wheelkey were hardly the ideal tourist companions. All they did was wander from bar to bar sampling Cuba Librés, Planter's Punches and other rum variants. He could safely bet that every photograph in his camera had a glass or bottle somewhere in the scene.

A visit to the casino abruptly ended their sojourn when dextrous croupiers lightened their wallets. They returned to the ship at little wiser and skint.

Blood Groups Found headed the next folder and details of the blood groups were found not only on the bodies but also on those sheets and blankets that had been sent with the corpses. Most of the blood was A negative and presumed to have belonged to Brown. The bloody en on Brown's left shoulder was determined to be A negative as was that on Davis' right forefinger.

The blood groups on the murder weapon were by far the most interesting. Two different types were found on both the blade and the hilt: A positive and B negative. The bloody palm print on the pommel was also B negative and diabetic to boot. A further check on the blade discovered a mingling of B negative types, one normal, the other was diabetic. There was a mixture of A positive and O types on the female's breast. The appropriate information was added to the victims' sheets.

It was time to call it a day. It *was* Christmas when all was said and done. She yawned and stretched and wondered how Angus was getting on. Perhaps a quick shower would perk her up then she could go and see her paramour after dinner.

That evening, the three friends stood out on open deck under a black velvet sky. One star shone brighter than the rest and the Canadian in a melancholy mood mused aloud. "You know what? I wonder if that's the Christmas star."

"Why don't ye ask one o' the guys oan the bridge?" asked Angus.

Keyes scoffed. "Don't be daft - they're liable to think that they took a wrong turn and ended up in Bethlehem."

"Do you know what? I wish that I had a girl with me," mused Jake, somewhat forlornly. "I could go places with her. It's nights like this that make broads feel romantic."

"And not just women y'know," replied Keyes. "I feel kinda romantic too." He leaned over and planted a great slobbering kiss on the Canadian's cheek.

He was outraged and rubbed his handkerchief furiously against his face. "Ooh! You-dirty-rotten-queer-bastard! Now I know why all you Scotsmen wear kilts. Ooh!" he repeated. "That was fucking disgusting, right?"

"Now - now Jake," soothed Angus. "It's Christmas. Guid will tae a' men, y'ken."

"Right - towards men," Jake allowed, his loathing directed at Keyes. "It doesn't say anything about Christmas fairies."

He gradually calmed down and the trio slumped on the ship's handrail listening to the faint warbles from a male voice choir emitting from an open port in the engineers' wardroom.

"Ye ken," began Angus, staring out to sea. "Ah once read aboot a legend that said a' sheep face east at midnight oan Christmas Eve."

"Now you know why young Lochinvar came out of the west!" Jake shot back, slapping Keyes on the shoulder. "Come on inside and buy me a beer, sheep-shagger."

Drawn by the singing they met Betty Stevenson. She wore a light-green pantsuit with a cardigan draped about her shoulders. King wished her a Merry Christmas with a kiss.

"All right for some," muttered Keyes, and was rewarded with a thump on the arm from Jake.

They entered the wardroom where a bushy conifer filled one of its corners; its lights purloined from stokehold consoles twinkled intermittently among tinsel strips. Streamers of crepe paper bellied from the deckhead and sprigs of holly, acquired from God-knew-where, festooned the bulkheads. In front of the tree a tubby Welshman was conducting a semi-inebriated quintet of engineers who softly hummed *The First Noel.*

Taffy's expertise had been garnered from some obscure college of music located near Cardiff. In actual fact the college wasn't in the village, it was under it - five thousand feet under it. For reasons only known to Welshmen it is necessary to practice singing in deep underground caverns. Possibly they do not wish to disturb their English neighbours.

While some of the men sang, other perfectionists roamed around the caves improving the acoustics by removing pieces of a dark insulating substance called coal. This coal was sold in large quantities to England's industries that strived to enhance the planet's atmosphere with that wonder gas: smog!

The choral group was finally arranged to Morgan's satisfaction. After all, hadn't an insurmountable challenge been overcome by teaching barbarians the rudiments of song and harmony? Before too long Christmas carols were seeping through the wardroom's portholes to drift across the sleeping channel.

Alan Lindsey showed up to buy a round for his lads, his usual gift at this time of year. The sudden bounty of free beer from the chief engineer quenched the music and drew cries of protest from the Boat Deck. Angus, with Betty clung to his arm; peered out to find some elderly passengers blanketed warmly in deckchairs awaiting a second encore of carols. Jake invited them in but they declined, preferring to watch the stars and remember Christmases past.

With larynxes well lubricated the choir recommenced to everyone's delight. The first tripper was not to forget this Christmas Eve for a long, long time and he rued the fact that he had to go on watch instead of spending a night of rapture with his paramour.

Christmas Day dawned and found three friends shoreward bound on the tender. Keyes, having wangled the watch off, challenged Jake to a game of golf. King on the other hand wanted to try out his new fishing rod. The engineers split up on the jetty and Angus headed for Pinder's Point on the estuary of Hawksbill Creek.

With practised ease he set up his equipment and soon a spinning lure was being dispatched seawards. Wavelets lapped around his shoes were tempting enough to persuade him to go barefooted and paddle in the warm tidal waters. Tiny fish tickled when they nibbled at his pallid toes.

On his fourth cast a largish fish rose to his lure and missed. His heart jolted with excitement. The nylon line snaked out again to drop his spoon out past the spot where the fish had risen. Slowly he rewound his reel and trolled through his quarry's territory.

This time the fish hurtled clear of the surface, the treble hooks firm its maw. Immediately it twisted and turned heading for deeper water but he skilfully played it until the victim lay helpless and gasping in the sand at his feet.

'A bonefish,' he concluded, guessing the weight to be in the region of five pounds. He carefully extracted the hook and tossed the fish back into the sea.

Behind him, and laying prone amongst a stand of pine trees that abounded that area, Jake and Wheelkey spied on their shipmate. The Canadian surveyed the estuary and noticed a bit of a reef further out past a peninsula of rocks near Angus. "Right buddy, do you see - uh - where the water is swirling above that - uh - gap in that sunken coral there?"

Wheelkey shaded his eyes and nodded.

"That's where I'm heading for - right? Give me about twenty minutes to sneak among those rocks over there then go down and distract Gus' attention until I get into the water."

Keyes looked dubious. "Are you sure it's safe?"

"Sure, I used to dive around the wrecks at - uh - Tobermory on the tip of the Bruce Peninsula lots of times, right?"

"Who in the hell is Bruce Peninsula when he's at home?"

"It separates Lake Huron and Georgian Bay," he was told. "This'll be a piece of cake."

He picked up the flippers and aqualung that he'd rented and said, "His casts seem to be quite accurate. Get him plop his lure into the gap that I pointed out to you just now."

Wheelkey waited the allotted time before sauntering down to the waterline. His countryman was in the process of removing the hook from a small barracuda when he noticed his shipmate's shadow. He glanced back in surprise. "Whit are ye daein' here?"

"The golf course was shut."

"Where's Jake?"

"Reconnoitring."

"Whit for - booze or dames?"

"All of the above."

A smile turned into a grimace and a loud click followed by searing pain signified that the pan-sized barracuda had grown impatient for its release. With a curse he bashed the creature about the gills with a rock before slitting its belly open. He rinsed his hand then examined the extent of the laceration. The skin was barely broken, though the flow of blood made it seem worse.

"Bastard!"

Saltwater made the wound sting like hell.

"Bastard!" he repeated.

"That's quite a vocabulary you have," observed the Glaswegian. Out of the corner of his eye he observed a bronzed figure stepping carefully over a host of greenish rocks before wading into the sea to submerge beneath the waves.

"What are these Gus?"

He hunkered down to get a better view of the lure tray in the tackle box. Angus bent down too and regaled his friend in the lore of angling.

Over his friend's shoulder Keyes observed the would-be prankster sinking below the waves. He rose to his full height flexing a minor cramp from his leg muscles. "I'd like to see how you cast."

The glossy coloured lure soared into the air and plopped into a trough about one hundred yards out. Slowly it was reeled back to shore.

"That's pretty good. You should try near the sunken pinnacle of coral there. I could've sworn that I saw a big one near there."

Angus squinted against the glare coming off the water. "Whereaboot? Och aye, Ah can see - where yon bubbles are."

His shipmate's jaw dropped in response to this startling observation. "Er - yes," he muttered whilst thinking: 'He's got the eyes of a fucking eagle!' "Eh, what do you suppose causes those bubbles Gus?"

"Ah dinnae ken," he admitted. "Back home it's usually marsh gas. He laughed and said, "Maybe it's a scuba diver."

"Ha ha," force-laughed Keyes. "That's a good one. Come on, let's see you cast through the bubbles."

The Mepps arced over the water beyond the bubbles. He reeled in slowly allowing his line to bisect the stream of bubbles. Two-and-a-half fathoms down Jake White floated weightlessly behind an enormous clump of brain coral. A rotating red-and-white flurry zipped towards him. He grabbed the line just in front of the spinner and give it a swift jerk.

The tip of his rod twitching got Angus excited. "Ooo! Ooo! Ah think Ah've hooked one." The reel's clutch squealed.

Resetting the tension he wound in again. Below, Jake tugged the line sharply. The clutch shrilled in protest. “Ooo! Ooo! It must be a right big one!”

Keyes cupped a hand to his mouth to hide the grin as the strain on the line suddenly relaxed, parted by Jake’s diving knife. Angus groaned his disappointment and wound in the slack. He examined the end and exclaimed.

“Christ!” he exclaimed. “Would ye look at that? It’s been cut clean as a whistle.”

“That fish must have very sharp teeth.”

“Aye,” he growled, bending on a wire trace. “The fish will need tae hae awfy sharp teeth tae bite through this.” A larger spoon was clipped on. Off went the new lure to plummet almost in the same spot where it was snatched with ease.

Jake unclipped the lure from the trace and hung it on his belt with the former one. The opened fastener was meticulously scrutinised upon retrieval. “It must be one helluva big fish. It must’ve taken the whole spoon in its mouth an’ sprung the clip wi’ its teeth.”

“Maybe it’s got prehensile teeth.”

This merited a sidelong glance. Another spoon was attached. His stock of lures was gradually depleting.

A squadron of barracudas slowly cruised into the estuary as if searching for the wayward member that lay at the fisherman’s feet. The school hovered about twenty-five feet from the prankster with predacious curiosity. Oblivious to his uninvited audience Jake gleefully continued to arrest his friend’s line and purloin the lures.

King shook his head with chagrin as he clipped on the very last decoy. Never before had anything like this ever happened to him. Fastidiously he jammed a sliver of driftwood into the fastener's eye and bound it tightly before condemning the lure off to the briny deep.

The spoon was grabbed as it sped past. After a few quick jerks to tease his friend Jake tried to unleash it. His fingers were working feverishly at the intricate binding when suddenly the line heaved. The treble hooks bit into his hand and an extra large surge of bubbles escaped from his facemask along with a muffled yell of pain. He hauled angrily on the wire trace, cut the line and extricated the hook from his finger.

Tendrils of blood drifted away to dissipate in the current while the surrounding sea turned a deeper shade of blue as air bubbles escalated profanities that burst on the ocean surface. Incited by the scent of blood the barracudas' pectoral fins became quivering blurs. Powerful muscles flexed caudal fins that swept the fishes around each other jockeying for position. Under starters' orders they impatiently waited for the leader of the pack to begin his attack.

White came about and began to retrace his path to his original point of entry only to stop when confronted by the predators. Still facing them he slowly back-pedalled away and passed through the reef.

The disillusioned angler cursed the severed end of his line while Keyes successfully managed to curtail his mirth. Fed-up, his friend dismantled his gear and squatted down on the warm sand to replace his socks and shoes. Thoroughly discouraged he arose and snarled a pointless curse at the dead barracuda, its gills coated with congealed blood. "Ye can hae your pal tae," he shouted and tossed the carcass, entrails flailing at the waves.

Continuing to stalk the diver the family of barracudas had just cruised through the reef when their cousin splashed into the water and drifted down in front of them. They surged forward, a greyish-silver mass with countless rows of snapping teeth.

"*Holy shit*!" gurgled Jake. He spun immediately and began to work up maximum revolutions towards the beach. The predators, having quickly devoured their cousin, milled around snapping at each other before setting out for their original quarry who happened to be travelling in the manner of an Olympic gold medallist.

He broke surface in a welter of frothing water and muffled screams, much to the astonishment of his two shipmates who gaped on from about thirty feet away. Two barracudas leapt clear of the disturbance created by his panic-driven flippers. His fingers touched sandy bottom and he bounded to his feet in about fifteen inches of water. Lifting each flipper clear of the surface he high-stepped like a monstrous duck to collapse in the damp sand with sobbing panting gasps of relief.

Seeing his lures dangling from the prankster's belt Angus now realized what had been happening. He laughed heartily saying, "Serves ye bluidy right, ye dummy!"

Directing his shipmate's attention to one of the gnawed flippers he added, "Ye're lucky that wasnae your foot."

He calmly redeemed his property, set up his rod and resumed fishing. The barracudas fought each other to get onto the hook only to be devoured alive by their companions. Every fish caught was severely mutilated before reeled in.

Having regained his breath and some of his composure Jake doffed the scuba gear and stormed off to where he had hidden his clothes. Wheelkey escorted him. By the time the pair had returned the run of fish had diminished completely, much to the fisherman's disappointment.

"Hey Jake, would ye mind daein' me a wee favour?"

There was a sullen response. "What's that?"

"Would ye mind gettin' back intae yer scuba gear an' try tae entice some mair fish back here?"

"Screw you! I'm off - coming Wheelkey?"

The Glaswegian nodded. Sighing, King conceded to the majority. "Och, just hang oan a second an' Ah'll join ye."

By the time Angus had settled down to fishing, Christmas Day was just dawning for his girl friend. After a continental breakfast she perused forensic photographs of microscopic views of filaments of silk and cotton.

Enlargements showing the ridges on the murder weapon's edges were examined carefully. The next folder was more interesting for again those two unique B negative mixtures, normal and diabetic had shown up on the silk glove that her lover had found.

Other macro shots, according to the CID experts, determined that the cuts on the glove had probably been made by someone adapting it to grasp the blade.

The examinations of the victims' luggage proved that they had indeed owned it. Money and jewellery had been found, which ruled out robbery as a motive. Davidson's luggage was a different matter. The fingerprints found on toiletries and shoes belonged to one, Homer R. Davison: ex-convict.

This led to the passport of the fellow who'd supposedly jumped over the ship's rail a fortnight since. This passport with the name R. Homer Davidson was not current at all. The original holder was Homer R. Davison and it had expired in 1952. There were three major differences: the Davidson surname had been overwritten as Davison; the five in 1952 had been changed to a six, and the R had been shifted. Powerful bleach had been used to eliminate unwanted script.

Now we're getting somewhere, she muttered.

Subject: Homer Richard Davison

Nationality: US citizen/British subject

Weight: 240 pounds

Height: Six feet two inches

Hair: Grey and greatly receding

Born January 14, 1899, in Ripley, West Virginia

Eyes: Light blue

Complexion: Fair

Other characteristics: Full grey beard with a moustache

Blood Group: B negative

Marital Status: Divorced

Occupation: Businessman

Present address: No fixed abode

Next-of-kin: Oscar Davis - son

Accompanying his prison report were copies of his fingerprints, mug shots, time served and certain other information. He had been a model prisoner and kept to himself. He worked out regularly in the prison gym, specializing in weight training and weightlifting. His wife Katherine Lesley Davison, née Davis, divorced him while he was incarcerated. The prison physician had diagnosed him with type two diabetes. And last but not least, the motive for the double murder was in his court case transcripts, George Brown, KC, had been Davison's defence lawyer.

This sheet of foolscap was pinned beside the others.

It had taken her all morning to read through and condense Davison's dossier. All that remained was the folder on Davison's son. Perhaps she'd begin it after lunch but then again it was Christmas Day. Surely she was entitled to a little bit of a holiday.

'To hell with it,' she thought. 'I'm going ashore to do some shopping for an hour or two.'

A leisurely jaunt through the quaint streets of Lucaya was a welcome break and she was back at her desk by three thirty.

Subject: Oscar Harold Davis

Nationality: British

Weight: 145 pounds

Height: Five feet eight inches

Hair: Brown

Born: Coventry, UK

Eyes: Blue

Complexion: Fair

Blood Group: Unknown

Marital Status: Single

Occupation: Marine Engineer

Present address: Atlantic House, Liverpool

Next-of-kin: Homer Davison (father) Katherine Lesley Davis (mother)

Fingerprints: None available

There was a footnote saying that inquiries were being made to the Board of Trade to find out which shipping line was presently employing him. 'Davis' she thought. 'Did I see that name in the Seaman's Record Cards?'

She stood up to check through the D's when Angus sauntered in. He embraced his girlfriend and kissed her cheek.

"You stink of fish!"

He sniffed the arm of his patrol suit. "That's guid honest sweat hen," he said. "Ah just popped in tae see whit ye were wantin' tae dae tonight afore Ah had my shower."

She put her hand down his trousers. "What do you think?"

"That's as guid a way tae spend Christmas as any," he smiled reaching for the door. "Ah'll be back in a wee while."

"Oh by the way, Angus, have you ever heard of Atlantic House? It's in Liverpool."

He rubbed his chin. "No, Ah cannae say that Ah have. Ah'll tell ye whit though, Ah'll ask Wheelkey. He seems tae ken everythin'. Why dae ye want tae ken?'

"I want to find a fellow called Oscar Davis is."

"Oscar Davis? Weel, look nae further lassie. He lives two or three doors frae me. Whit dae want him for?"

"Remember that double murder? The woman was his mom."

His face fell and with genuine sorrow said, "The puir man."

"Yes, now I'll have to go and break the sad news to him."

"Surely no' oan Christmas Day!"

"Perhaps you're right Angus. Well, tomorrow then."

"Ah dinnae envy your job hen," replied Angus.

Christmas dinner on board the luxurious liner was something to behold. The first tripper had the traditional turkey, stuffing, cranberry sauce, roast potatoes, gravy, and garden peas. Two helpings left him more stuffed than the original bird. The menu carried a larger variety of foods than usual to celebrate the occasion. Jake opted for the baron of roast beef with Yorkshire pudding.

Across the mess Oscar Davis appeared to in a bit of a festive mood because there was a lively conversation interspersed with bouts of laughter between him, Beresford Sudbury, Pete Eaton, and Archie MacAdam. Taffy Morgan stoically endured macabre witticism on cannibalism as he keenly wired into a haunch of roast suckling pig.

Christmas pudding ablaze in brandy was the highlight of the meal. Every officer on board was offered a choice of a half bottle of port or sherry with his repast. The festive cheer enlivened Angus' first Christmas away from home.

Junkanoo

0500 Boxing Day

Eaton popped his head in the mess doorway, interrupting a technical discussion. “Aren’t you guys going ashore?”

“Now why in the hell would anyone want to go ashore at five in the morning?” shot back Taffy, peeved at the debate being interrupted just as he was getting the upper hand.

“Aren’t you going to the parade?” Pete asked.

“What flamin’ parade?” Jake snapped.

“The Junkanoo Parade. It starts at six.”

The floater, a mere spectator to the technical argument chimed in, emphasizing his Scots brogue much heavier than usual. “The whit-the-noo parade?”

“The Junkanoo Parade,” repeated Pete. “It’s a type of Mardi Gras. The locals have it each year on Boxing Day. It starts an hour from now and lasts for twenty-four hours, sometimes longer. There’s supposed to be one held on New Year’s Day when we get to Nassau.”

“Well, what are we waiting for?” Jake gave him a big grin; his chair squeaking as he swiftly arose. “Let’s go!”

“Hang on a second,” protested Pete. “Have you guys got any costumes?”

“What do we need costumes for, boyo?”

“It’s a masquerade. Everyone wears masks, clown suits and things,” explained Pete. “By the way, has anyone seen Scar?”

The trio shook their heads in unison. Jake said, “That guy’s been - uh - acting strange since he signed on this trip. What’s the matter with him?”

Pete shrugged. “I dunno. There’s something eating at him. He’s not his usual jovial self. I’ll nip along to his cabin and try to coax him into joining us. Maybe we can cheer him up.”

Jake stopped him. “Hey! Where will we get costumes?”

“They’ll probably sell stuff like that oan the island,” volunteered Angus.

“Here, you seem to be a little bit smarter than the average Scotchman,” said Eaton.

“Scotsman, ye daft Sassenach,” corrected Angus.

Taffy jumped in. “He’s a Musher, see you. That’s a Sassenach with a lobotomy. What are we hanging around here for? Let’s hit the beach.”

Three engineers formed a huddle on R Deck Square watching passengers, attired in bizarre costumes and masks, board the tender. Taffy, Jake, and Angus quietly chatted while waiting for Pete who was furtively approaching them from the companionway leading up from C Deck. Mustering a gruff tone he jabbed Morgan’s back with a genuine policeman’s truncheon. “Now then, now then! What’s this? An unlawful assembly - break it up there.”

Taffy yelped. “Ooh - that was bloody sore, see you! How would you like that thing stuffed up your aah -!” he gasped from another sharp prod.

“It’s not nice to threaten an officer of the law.”

The other two beamed with delight.

Pete really looked the part for he was clad in his patrol suit sans epaulettes and wearing an English bobby’s helmet.

“Where did ye get the hat an’ stick Pete?”

“I got it in a free house in Eastleigh last year when I took some of the lads out on a tour of Mushland,” answered Eaton. “During a bit of a scuffle the landlord called in the local constabulary. Anyway a copper laid his helmet nearby my table and a truncheon flew out of the melee to land at my feet. I sat around there for ages but no one came to claim them so I brought them back to the ship."

"Maybe the owner got hurt," opined Jake. "That's probably why they weren't claimed, right?"

"Could be," allowed Pete. "I hung about for two seconds."

Even Taffy laughed at that.

They tailed the passengers onto the tender. When they disembarked the shipmates left the wharf to join throngs of garishly dressed folk all heading towards the little community of Lucaya. Angus was proved to be right for natives were selling carnival paraphernalia from two-wheeled carts parked along the colourful street. The engineers dallied at a stall to examine its wares.

Taffy bought a black tent-like shirt sporting palm trees and bongo drums in yellows, greens, and reds. Parting with some West Indies' dollars he pulled it over his head and slid on a pair of sunglasses. Sucking on an olive-green cigar he let a balloon of acrid smoke into the air. "How do I look boyos?"

"Like a brothel keeper from Piraeus," said Eaton.

The engineroom juniors settled for ponchos, bright red and green respectively. An African devil mask completed the floater's costume whereas Jake was happy with a Panama hat with a ragged brim. "Come on!" Eaton urged impatiently, brandishing his truncheon. "The parade's starting soon."

Davis knocked on the chief engineer's door and entered when he heard "Come in."

He still felt a bit drowsy because the chief's writer had awakened him from a sound sleep.

"Ah, Mister Davis, this is Detective-Sergeant Stevenson of Scotland Yard. I'm afraid that she has some very disturbing news for you."

"Good morning Mister Davis,"the DS started solemnly. "Tell me - is your mother's name, Katherine Lesley Davis?"

Oscar nodded.

"Then I'm sorry to say that your mother is dead."

Shock filled his face. "When? How?"

Referring to her notes the police officer read, "Sometime during the eighth of this month she and a man named George Brown was savagely murdered on board this very ship."

That awful night rushed forward into his consciousness and he slowly let his body sag onto the chief's sofa, his head buried in his hands. Lindsey looked his junior with sorrowful eyes. Brandy splashed into a glass.

"Here son, knock that back."

Davis took a swig and coughed. The tears that sprang to his eyes were not entirely due to the chief's fiery liquor. His mind was in a spin as memories of that awful night tumbled through his mind. It had never dawned on him that the female might've been his mother. After all, Brown had always been a notorious philanderer. He had seen the lawyer in the company of different women but it never seemed to bother his mother when she'd been informed. She kept right on going out with the bastard.

The young man sobbed in despair. Stevenson sat down beside him, her hand on his. Minutes passed and he peered back at her through reddened eyes. It had been in the back of his mind that he'd get caught sooner or later.

'His grief seems genuine enough,' she pondered. 'Or else he's one helluva good actor.'

She waited for a few minutes until he seemed to grasp a hold of the situation. “I suppose that you’ll put in a request for compassion leave,” she opined and glanced at Lindsey for confirmation.

“Yes lad, I’ll radio Head Office to have arrangements made for you to fly out of New York when we dock. Of course, you could fly directly from here if you wish.”

“No, that’s all right sir. I’ve got nothing to go home to anyway. My Dad . . .” he broke off realizing that it was his father who’d killed his mother. ‘I wonder if he knew? Of course he knew. Talk about killing two birds with one stone.’

Mentioning his dad brought up that timeworn question from Stevenson. “When did you last see your father?”

He thought for a moment. What did it matter now if he told the truth? Or some of it. His father was long gone and he still loved him. Without referring to the murders he related how successful his dad had been moving around the ship as stowaway and how top security had prevented him disembarking in New York. He had tried again in Nassau to no avail. Still, he’d got away with his second attempt in New York and Davis hadn’t the slightest idea where he was now.

So Angus was right, Stevenson reflected, and nobody had believed him. “Did you know George Brown?”

“He was the company lawyer. I’ve met him on a few occasions.”

If that’s true, thought the policewoman, then I’m going to have trouble putting this chap in the frame. “Do you happen to know your blood group?”

“No.”

“Very well, we’ll leave that for now,” she replied and placed a tender hand on Davis’ arm. “Please accept my condolences for your loss. If you decide to stay on board do you mind if I interview you in a few days when your mind is more at ease?"

"Whatever," replied Davis, the word choking in his throat. He dabbed his eyes with a handkerchief, and shrugged. "I don't really care."

"Get along lad," the chief said kindly. "Try and get some rest. Take the watch off if you want. I'll tell Mister MacKay. Maybe tomorrow, you'll let me know if you want some compassionate leave or not."

A calypso band accompanied by cowbells, horns, whistles and other noisemaking instruments led the procession off. Everyone went wild. Natives danced back and forth across the street and in amongst those who came to watch the parade. It was impossible for anyone not to participate.

Instrumentalists and singers kept merging into the growing throng and the cacophony was complete. The Lucayan dancers' agilities were amazing. Many seemed to be disjointed, their callisthenics becoming wilder and wilder. The scenes were a glimpse into the past that had originated on the Dark Continent. Like a kaleidoscopic river masses of people tumbled along overflowing into the quaint streets and byways of Lucaya.

And then there was booze - a high proofed concoction of local rum. Bottles of it drifted like flotsam on the tide of dancers and spectators. It wasn't long before the engineers became tipsy from the potent liquor. Many streets later they ebbed into a shady alley to founder on the kerb.

A tall black man materialized behind them. His costume consisted of a light-khaki shirt, matching shorts, white knee-length hose, and blanco-ed canvas shoes. He wore a white pith helmet and a white lanyard completed his attire. He called to someone across the street. Realizing that the revellers were drowning his voice out, he hauled on his lanyard and drew a dried-pea whistle out of his breast pocket.

An ear piercing blast caused Angus to blearily look up at this disturbance. “Hey Constable Eaton, tell Jungle Jim here tae shut-the-hell-up.”

Eaton grunted onto his feet and authoritatively ordered the chap to be quiet. Ignoring him, the man whistled across the street again. A fumbling search produced the phoney cop’s whistle. Pursing his lips he blew it right at the stranger’s ear.

The offended man protested. “Hey Mon, doan do dat!”

“Hey mon!” mimicked Eaton. “Doan do dat eedah.”

A nightstick confronted Eaton and started to prod his belly. He retaliated with his truncheon. The pair jabbed at each other until the black took a wild swipe at his head. Pete dodged the blow and punched his opponent on the chin, knocking him flat on the street.

When he arose, so too did the other engineers who watched the combatants circle each other warily. The Lucayan, under the impression that all four engineers were going to accost him, blew his whistle again. So did Pete.

Acoustic shots reverberated between whitewashed walls until Angus slowly became aware of two black men in similar garb as the first. They were trying to force a way through the milling revellers, presumably to aid their companion.

“Hey Pete! Would ye like tae ken somethin’?”

Focussing on his opponent Eaton responded from the edge of his mouth, “I’m busy right now. Don’t bother me Gus.”

“Ok pal.” he replied huffily. “Ah just thought that ye’d be interested tae ken that yon’s a real cop that ye’re tanglin’ wi’.

There's two mair o' the sowels heidin' this way tae help your sparrin' partner there."

A surprised expression flooded the Englishman's face and he pointed instantly to some object beyond the policeman's right shoulder. The constable made the mistake of craning his head in that direction and his chin received the resultant uppercut for that error. The two constables approaching were in a quandary as to whether they should see to their comrade or detain his assailant first. Eaton took advantage of their momentary hesitation and steamed into the crowd.

Seeing that their colleague was just dazed the pair dashed off in Pete's wake. Brushing street dust from his uniform the first policeman regained his helmet and limped off in pursuit of his companions.

There wasn't too much the engineers could've done to assist Eaton, even if they had been sober, so they just blended back into the undulating swarms of merrymakers. At some point they became adrift again from the main crowd and found themselves in an open area. In his inebriated state Angus imagined that he was at some tropical gala day.

Marquee tents, stalls, and the inevitable two-wheeled carts all stocked with island delicacies, were set up sporadically in the area for the convenience of the boisterous participants.

Tiring at last of the festivities the engineers set a meandering course in the general and sometimes reciprocal direction of their ship. They wove their way into what seemed like a public park near the jetty and flopped down on the lush green grass to bask. The late morning sun had long since evaporated the last vestiges of dew.

After a while Jake reluctantly lifted his befuddled pate in response to distant shouting. He nudged Morgan who in turn awakened Angus. Shading their eyes they watched a drama about to enfold.

Arrays of bougainvillea in full bloom loosely formed a hedge at the far end of the grounds. In the forefront, crouched amongst a vivid display of pink bracts, Eaton monitored the movements of his pursuers. Two of them were slowly heading his way pushing thorny twigs aside with clubs as they neared. He began to creep away in the opposite direction.

One of the policemen hailed his buddy to indicate that their prey had been flushed from cover. Pete broke into a sprint parallel with the hedge, the constables in hot pursuit. At a wide gap he dithered uncertainly on which course to take. He decided to retrace his steps on the opposite side of the hedge. Not long after the policemen followed him round and disappeared behind the shrubbery.

At the far end of that same section of hedge Eaton's original opponent came on the scene. Paralleling the hedge he stepped slowly seeking either his companions or his aggressor. He stopped for a breather, his back to an enormous clump of purple bougainvillea. He doffed his helmet and glanced about him. Standing at ease he squinted upwards at the relentless Bahamian sun high in the sky. He withdrew a white handkerchief to wipe the moisture from his sweatband.

By this time the engineers were sitting upright their eyes glued on the only character on the scene. Presently a shock of blonde hair loomed out from the underbrush. Head down he started to haul the rest of his body through the hedge. Eaton stopped short at the sight of white canvas shoes; one a side, each containing a white woollen stocking fluffed around a black knobbly knee. The policeman donned his helmet, looked down and froze, his eyes bulging on the apparition that had suddenly appeared between his legs. A cry of exaltation switched abruptly to one of agony when Pete head-butted him at the apex of his legs. The poor fellow crumpled slowly onto the grass clutching his groin.

Like a startled stag Eaton was up and away. The other two cops had crawled through the hole and commiserated with the unfortunate while helping him to his feet. In the meantime their quarry was well past the hedge and down onto the beach. He kept waving frantically at a native chugging past on a little steamboat, which seemed to have been built to the same specifications as C.S. Forester's *African Queen* - perhaps even in the same yard. Having got the native's attention and alarmed that the pursuit was resumed, he dived into the surf and swam out to the steamboat to be hauled aboard. A bribe of soggy money warranted a change in course to the *Dalriada*.

Three breathless policemen stood on the shore shaking their fists before storming down towards the jetty with a gaggle of giggling engineers hot on their tails. Their colleague had already embarked by the time the lighter had cast off from the dock with the constables and his friends.

"They'll never catch him now," prophesied Jake, tapping his wristwatch. "It's five past eleven now and we sail at one." The engineers tittered to leeward well out of earshot.

Green indicators swung from *Standby* across the telegraph faces then back to their original settings denoting that anchor watches were finished and manoeuvring was about to begin. The incessant clamour of bells was stopped and soon the eight-to-twelve engineers were back down to await the first movement. Their complaints about having lunch interrupted fell on the deaf ears of the watch below who hadn't had one of those sumptuous meals all that trip. Happily for the fellows on standby there were only two movements, one to point the cruise liner's bows out to sea and *Full Away*.

Christie's usual glower killed any chance of conversation as they worked up revs. "Here White," he said, right of the blue. "I saw that pal of yours from 1BR stepping off an old puffer today. Is he sitting for his steam ticket by any chance or was it just a busman's holiday?"

"I haven't the foggiest Sec. Maybe he's just an old steamboat man at heart - right?"

And thus another nickname came into being.

The messroom steward plunked a tray of fresh cheeses onto the buffet table while Angus was loading his plate with goodies for afternoon tea. He watched the rating gather the remnants from the cheeseboard and place them aside.

"Here there Steward, whit are ye gaun tae dae with a' these bits o' cheese?"

"I'm going to toss 'em over the wall, Mister King."

"Ye'll dae nae such thing," admonished Angus. "Ah'll take them if ye dinnae mind. Ah'm very partial tae a bit o' cheese noo an' then."

"Very well Mister King," said the steward. "I'll scout up a paper bag for them and bring them to your table."

"That's very kind o' ye. Thanks."

"What's that Gus?" asked Jake when the steward placed a brown paper bag by his friend's side.

Beaming his thanks up at the steward he laughed quietly and said, "Cheese - Ah just love the stuff."

The Canadian spooned into a slab of strawberry shortcake. "To each his own, right?"

Strange, he thought opening his cabin door, he was almost sure that it had been locked before going on watch.

Betty coyly glanced up just as he entered the room. "Ah-ha! There you are!"

"How did ye get in here with my door locked?"

Holding up a straightened Kirby grip she quoted Richard Lovelace: *Stone walls do not a prison make nor iron bars a cage.*

"Mm," he replied, leaning over to kiss her, his paper bag dropping on the coffeetable. "So how's your case gaun?"

"Oscar Davis was pretty shook up when he heard of his mother's death," replied Betty.

"Ah'm no' surprised. Naebody likes tae hear that their Mammy's deid. So ye're no' gaun tae go after him then?"

"I didn't say that. There may have been some bad blood between him and his mother's lawyer."

He slid out his jacket and hung it up on a coat hanger. "How are ye gaun tae prove that?"

She stood up and put her arms around him, her fingers nimbly investigating every bulge and curve on his naked torso. "I don't know. Maybe I'll think about it tomorrow."

She loosened his belt and his trousers dipped like the colours at sunset. His Fruits of the Loom gave chase. He kicked off his shoes and stepped out of his clothing looking manly in his black cotton socks. He reached for a fresh towel.

"Ah'm gaun for a shower first," he said, picking up his loofah and soap.

"No, you're not," whispered Betty, taking a firm grip of his tumescence. "I'm placing you under arrest. You can shower later. Now lock that bloody door before one of your shipmates come a-gawking."

"I see old Scar is hitting the sauce pretty hard," observed Treenie, nodding toward the fuel-oil engineer who was sprawled out dead drunk on an easy chair at the far end of the wardroom.

"Aye," concurred Angus. "He just found oot this mornin' that his Maw was bumped aff."

"Nae shite?" MacAdam was eavesdropping as were some of the other engineers slouched at the bar. They perked up to hear the juicy details.

"Weel, ye already ken aboot it," said Angus. "She was the woman in the double murder oan the voyage oot. Her boyfriend who got stabbed wi' her was the family lawyer."

"Nae shite?" MacAdam repeated, craning round to stare at Davis. He took another swig of lager. "Puir bastard!"

Whodunit questions and guesses consumed the next few minutes until Arsenal took over the general conversation.

The watch was handed over without any problems. The juniors were just finishing their kye when Christie approached them after his speedy tour round the engineroom and tunnel.

"Angus, you'd better get up that tunnel and pump the sprinkler before MacKay shows up. White, your lub-oil coolant water temps are too high. See to them - now!"

The floater bent down to check the pressure gauge on the fire sprinkler ballast tank. It read one-twenty psi instead of one-thirty. He tapped a knuckle on the gauge, no difference. He went over to the wee horizontal reciprocating pump, opened two valves and started it.

Chi-chi-chung! *Chi-chi-chung*! *Chi-chi-chung*! the pump stoically clanked as it had since Jonah had gone deep sea. He lolled against a handrail acutely aware of the eerie presence of the dimly lit tunnel. Both driveshafts droned, their shiny surfaces reflecting strobe-like glimmers from the handful of forty-watt incandescent light bulbs jiggling above. The swish of empty potato sacks draped over a line shaft to polish it added to the din.

A Lesley valve farted and hissed like a snake until its diaphragm was satisfied that the proper steam pressure was feeding the saltwater calorifier. An hour dragged by. The needle on the sprinkler gauge had barely moved. The tunnel seemed to close in on the young engineer. He sighed and paced up and down between the watertight doors.

Chi-chi-chung! *Chi-chi-chung*! *Chi-chi-chung*! Echo upon echo carried hollowly along the tunnel above the droning and hissing, the chuckling of water lapping against the bilge cofferdams and a myriad other little sounds that might fire the mind of an overly imaginative young man. An eternity seemed to have passed when a tap on his shoulder made him jump. “Shite! It’s *you*!”

“And a Good Morning to you too,” replied The Sphere. He looked at the pressure gauge: 122 psi. “It looks like I’ll be here until crow piss.”

Before heading for the changeroom he handed over the watch with the typical laconic statement. “Guid job Sphere!”

“D’ye fancy a beer Jake?” said King, donning his patrol suit.

“No thanks, Gus. I’m pooped. Your pal Christie ran me ragged again.”

“Och weel, Ah’ll just hae a couple mysel an’ maybe hae a wee nibble oan my cheese.”

“You know what? Don’t eat too much of that stuff before turning in or else you’ll have nightmares, right?”

"Och - that's just auld wives' tales," scoffed Angus.

A Tennants lager gurgled into his beer mug. A few days earlier King acquired a Douglas Reeman novel, *A Prayer for the Ship*, from the wardroom library and was by now a few chapters into it. He eased into his comfy chair put his feet on the coffeetable and with a sigh dipped into the bag of cheese. He was pleased to find that the steward had the presence of mind to add a small variety of biscuits to supplement the cheese. He plunked a sliver of Stilton onto a Peek Freen biscuit and sampled the other cheeses.

After a while his head was beginning to droop, his eyes seemingly filled with sand. He decided to call a night or a morning because sunup wasn't too far away. Although not realising it nor could he have named most of the cheeses, he'd nibbled his way through Camembert, Brie, Cheshire, Wensleydale, St. Ivel, Danish Blue, Port Salut, Edam, Roquefort, Caerphilly, as well as Cheddar. He had consumed over a pound of cheese.

He was back in the storage room again. The man lay on the woman, the dirk still pinning them together. The man's hand moved and clutched the woman's bare shoulder. Her eyes opened as she turned her head to stare at him. The man gasped, his buttocks heaving up and down in the sexual act. He withdrew the blade from his back and climbed out the coffin. Suddenly he was clothed. The woman was clothed too when she vacated the coffin. She screamed. A cloud of vapour blocked his view and when it cleared the scene had changed.

He could hear the impatient sigh of steam panting from beneath a railway engine. He was sitting in an LMS carriage looking across a station platform. The man was stabbing someone in a waiting room and the woman was still screaming. The knife disappeared and the man punched his victim instead. It was a young fellow with lank mousy hair. His face was bruised and bloody and he stared back across the platform into Angus' eyes. It was Oscar Davis. The man seemed to leap into his compartment and grab him before punching him. The woman was screaming something.

Chi-chi-chung! *Chi-chi-chung*! *Chi-chi-chung*! The train was leaving the station. The woman was screaming and screaming and screaming . . .

"Angus! Angus! Wake up Angus!"

"Lemme go! Lemme go!"

"Wake up Angus!" urged Betty, shaking his shoulder. "You're having a nightmare!"

Roused to a brightly-lit cabin he blinked his eyes. "Oh jeez! Oh jeez!"

He was soaked in sweat and shivering. His heart was palpitating like a demented sprinkler pump. He took a deep breath, relieved to be back in the real world.

"Are you all right?"

He shook his head to clear it. "Aye," he sighed. "Aye hen, Ah'm a' right the noo. Ah guess Jake was right aboot the cheese."

"Cheese?"

"Och dinnae fash yourself aboot that hen,' Angus reassured her with a weak grin. "Yon dream reminded me aboot an incident that Ah witnessed in Crewe Station oan my way tae join the ship." He related the experience saying that the couple in the coffin were the same people in the waiting room. "Noo ye've got a motive for Oscar Davis."

Relieved that he was ok Betty mulled on his story. "I don't think that a nightmare will stand up in court."

"It's no' the dream itself Betty," he said. "Ah really did witness the incident. The dream jogged my memory. Weel, it didnae just jog it - it scared it right oot o' my subconscious."

She grinned and gave his a kiss. "You're right Angus - that definitely puts Davis in the frame."

"Are ye gaun tae arrest him noo?"

"No," replied Betty. "We need a lot more pieces of the puzzle before we have the full picture."

"Whit time is it?"

"Eleven-twenty Mister King," said the storekeeper, peeping round the door and ogling the policewoman.

"I'm here on official police business!"

The storeman's head disappeared abruptly his voice drifting in from the passageway. "No cop looking like that ever gave me such business!"

Dhobi Day

0025 Wednesday

It was during second middle watch out of New York that the floater appeared to be confronted with death once more. He was propping up the port engineroom desk absorbed by Christie's annals from the dreaded tankers when Jake received a call from the main generator room asking for assistance.

"That was Beery. He's moaning about a hydraulic leak in the starboard stabilizer compartment and needs a hand."

Off he went giving Larry Treen a wave as he passed through 3BR. Beresford Sudbury was nowhere in sight when he reached the main jenny room. Four giant turbines whined harmoniously quite oblivious to their operator's absence.

A voice hailing from above drew his attention. Artie Berwick's stocky form shimmered through the invisible vapours that rose from the turbo-generator glands. The main switchboard electrician urgently beckoned him up to the mezzanine.

Angus stamped up the port ladder to ask, "Where's Beery?"

Artie's sky-blue eyes weighed up the first tripper. A little taller than King the 'leckie had chubby cheeks, a ruddy complexion and usually sported a ready grin but today he looked a bit downcast. His curly locks were sandy-ish, almost strawberry-blonde.

With a deadpan face Artie pointed down over the jennies to an opening on the far side. He spoke with a Northern English accent. "He's over there in the starboard stabilizer compartment. Keep him talking will you? I heard that he just received bad news from home. I've never seen the feller looking so depressed."

Sympathy marred King's face. "Aye, sure. It always helps tae talk tae somebody when ye're feelin' a wee bit doon."

Berwick watched him descend. The sly electrician quickly gestured to Sudbury who stole out from behind the switchboard. "Look Beery," he sniggered. "He's just going in now."

"Betcha ten-bob he shits himself," the third engineer cackled in a strong Birkenhead brogue. "It's been a long time since we pulled t'is one."

Nobody was quite sure how Beery came by his sobriquet. It might have been the Beres in Beresford or the bury in Sudbury or even the suds in his surname, but an observer witnessing this third engineer downing a couple or six pints to replenish his beer barrel paunch would simply put it down to galloping consumption.

A notice board outside the stabilizer compartment warned him that its watertight door would close and a red light would flash prior to the equipment being activated. There were dogs in place so that the door could not be closed automatically while someone was inside inspecting or performing repairs.

Angus stepped over the high coaming and entered the compartment. To his right crammed amongst snakes of copper tubing, directional valves, flow controls and gauges he spotted a minor drip. He tightened a loose union with his adjustable. 'Maybe there's anither leak tae,' he considered.

A drop of hydraulic oil splashed on the back of his hand and he glanced up. About three inches above the hexagonal stabilizer shaft a pair of shoes with legs attached swung in cadence to the motion of the ship. Having heard somewhere that a hanged man's countenance was a gruesome sight to behold he deigned to look above the lower section of the white boilersuit.

But curiosity tempted the frightened junior to gaze higher. He noted that the corpse wore cotton gloves. His eyes became riveted on the tightened noose. The dead man's peaked cap had slipped forward, masking his face. Nervously, he beheld this whole ghastly scene and felt his hair becoming erect on the nape of his neck.

In eerie light the lifeless figure swayed with the motion of the ship. The junior's knees became rubbery. *Deja vu*, his mind sensed with horror. He half-turned, ready to dash from that fearful place when common sense struck him like a lightning bolt.

According to the electrician, Beery couldn't have been in there much more than a couple of minutes. He leapt up onto the stabilizer shaft to take the body's weight. His arms encircled the stocky frame, and heaving upwards, he lost his balance and nearly fell off. The 'body' weighed but a few pounds. The cap dropping to the grating below revealed a ball of rags where the head should've been.

"The bastards!" screamed through his mind although his body trembled with relief. "Ah'll get them for that!"

Through a space formed by the door and its runner he espied Artie and Beery sniggering in anticipation. There was no way that he could sneak out of the compartment without being seen by these two. There's nowhere to hide either, he thought, his eyes panning around the machinery space. Then an idea came to mind.

He dismantled the dummy and dumped the rag filling behind the shaft. Tying the rope about his waist, he donned the old boilersuit over his own while allowing the rope to run up his back and out from his neck. Putting on the cap and gloves he scrambled back up on the stabilizer shaft. With the rope's free end a double clove hitch was bent around an overhead beam.

Holding the beam with one hand he hauled himself up while taking in the slack with the other. Slowly he eased off until the hitches became snug and the rope bore his full weight. Making sure that the cap covered his face he dangled there, waiting . . .

Up on the mezzanine the practical jokers were puzzled by the delay. "Maybe he's fainted!" suggested a worried Beery.

He doffed his cap to smooth back the hair that didn't exist on his scalp. Only greying thatch on the sides and back of his head, alleged that he once possessed black hair. He took off his rimless specs and squinted at the lenses. Replacing the glasses back on his podgy face merely proved that Artie was right. The floater was not in sight.

He plodded over to a ladder and said, "I'll go and see. You wait right here."

The third slid down the ladder's handrails and clumped over to the open door. He glanced around the compartment ignoring the dummy completely. There was no trace of the floater. He stepped outside and spread his arms akimbo and shrugged at Berwick who descended to see for him.

"Where in the blazes did he go?" Artie shouted over the whine of the turbines.

"How in t'e 'ell should I know? Maybe he slipped out when I came down t'e ladder."

"No bloody way! I've been watching it all the time."

"'Ere!" Beery bellowed into the jenny room greaser's ear. He was polishing some brass work near the forward airlock door. “Did you happen to notice a young engineer leave here a few minutes ago?”

The rating just shook his head and carried on burnishing a tachometer gauge. “I’d better phone t’e engineroom and find out if he went back t’ere.”

He frowned, looking even more perturbed. The duo hurried over to the mezzanine’s port side. Berwick hung around impatiently while Sudbury phoned aft.

Back inside the compartment the floater released himself, rebuilt the dummy and hung it back up again. He risked a quick peek. Beery had his head stuck in the soundproofed telephone housing. The electrician’s back was towards him so he seized his chance and was soon out of sight by scampering up a convenient escape ladder.

Quite perplexed, Beery shook his head as he slammed down the phone. “T’ey haven’t seen ‘im since the start of t’is watch. T’ey’re going to get MacKay.”

The escape ladder took him to a fan room on C Deck. A few seconds passed before he became accustomed to the dimness emitted by a solitary light bulb. He crossed the room and carefully cracked open a door, just in time to witness the walking second heading towards his office. He discreetly tailed him.

From a watertight door’s recess he could safely watch the second’s office. Two minutes passed later his senior dashed out. His next port of call: the engineroom. Angus went into the office and sat down. Pleased with himself he poured himself a cup of tea.

Black Bob was adjusting the port rev counter when MacKay strode toward him. “Right Mister Christie, what’s this about losing our floater?”

"You'd better check with Mister Sudbury," he was advised. "He was the last one to see him."

"Ok. I'm going for'ard to talk to him," grunted MacKay. "Meantime, phone through and tell everyone to check their areas. You search the engineroom and have Mister White scout around the tunnel."

In the steamy heat of the main generator room Big John interrogated Sudbury. "One more time Mister Sudbury," he commanded, his voice tense with impatience. "Let's go over it again."

Supplemented by Artie the story was retold. Any reference to the dummy was carefully omitted. MacKay strode to the stabilizer compartment to check for himself. "He's definitely not in t'ere Mister MacKay," exhorted Beery in an effort to prevent the inevitable.

The walking second ignored him and looked up. "*Jes-us Chri-ist*!" He stepped back clutching his chest.

"It's all right Mister MacKay," Beery declared hastily. "It's only a dummy."

"Only a dummy!" gasped Big John. "Only a dummy! Only a dummy would pull a stunt like this. No wonder the floater has disappeared. He's probably still sitting in a shitehouse somewhere." Gradually his breathing got easier and he beckoned the two of them nearer. "Er, Mister Sudbury and Mister Berwick -"

"Yes Mister MacKay?" the pair chorused.

"You're a pair of stupid bastards!"

He stormed out the jenny room.

Wearily the senior second shoved his office door open and was confronted by a perfectly relaxed junior in the process of lighting up a smoke. “Ye’re late Mister MacKay,” the audacious floater chided him. “Your tea will be cold. Would ye like me tae get ye a fresh cup?”

The second flopped heavily into his chair. Taking a sip of tea he meditatively studied him over his cup’s brim. “The tea is warm enough thanks. Did you get a fright, lad?”

“A fright? Mister MacKay,” echoed the young man innocently. “Whit dae ye mean?”

“Don’t play games with me Mister,” warned his boss, banging the cup down on his desk. “I saw that dummy and I know what happened. What I don’t know is - how in the hell did you get out of that stabilizer compartment without those two idiots seeing you?”

Angus divulged his clever ploy. The second heaved back in his chair laughing uproariously at the thought of a neophyte bamboozling two experienced men.

“That’ll teach the silly bastards!”

A thought struck him as he sipped his tea. His face lit up with mischief. “Ah-ha! Their education hasn’t finished yet.” Downing his cup he picked up his phone.

“Those practical jokes have got to stop. Hello - engineroom? John MacKay. Get Mister Christie on the line please. Aye, I’ll hang on. Hello Bob, couldn’t find him eh? Well you listen to this: I want the machinery spaces thoroughly searched. Check particularly around any steam leaks, in case the lad got burned. He might be laying unconscious somewhere.

“Aye, the boilertops, bilges, everywhere. And you pass the word that if I find anyone who isn’t as black as the golly on a Robertson’s jam label when I take my rounds I’ll have his guts for garters. Ok Bob? Oh, and by the by, I want a list made out of all steam and oil leaks that are found.”

He slammed rubbed his hands with glee. “This’ll be the first proper check we’ve had since lay-up. While we wait there’s a wee problem I’d like to discuss with you.

“I’ve smelled liquor on Mister Davis’ breath over the last few watches,” he began. “And today I caught him red-handed knocking back some booze in the fuel-oil lab. I reamed him out good. I know he’s going through a tough time right now but if he keeps this up he could be a danger to himself or the ship.”

“Er - whit dae ye want me tae dae Mister MacKay?”

“Keep an eye on him. He’s probably found himself a new hidey-hole to drink on the fly. If you catch him, let me know.”

“Dae ye want me tae clype oan him Mister MacKay?”

“Well, that’s putting it a bit strong son. Just make sure that he’s not getting into trouble. So far he seems to be doing his job all right. Just keep a weather eye open for me. Ok?”

An hour later MacKay pulled himself to his feet. “I’m going to the engineroom first then I’ll walk through. You wait in the main jenny room’s upper catwalk until I arrive. I’ll keep those two clowns distracted while you sneak back into the stabilizer room. And don’t forget to fix that leak.”

“It’s fine by me Mister MacKay.”

The hydraulic leak repair didn’t take long and during that time the two miscreants were being lambasted by the walking second. When the floater reappeared at the doorway he pointed and announced, “There he is, right over there!”

Two heads swivelled in unison, their mouths agape at Angus’ sudden materialization. He strolled easily towards them, a wiper sponging residue from his hands.

“Where have you been lad?” MacKay asked easily. “We’ve been looking all over for you.”

He jerked a thumb over his shoulder. "Ah've been in yon compartment for the last wee while."

The fib came smoothly.

"Did you manage to fix that hydraulic leak?"

"Och aye. It'll be a' right noo."

"But - but," stuttered Beery.

"Whit happened tae ye?" King glibly interrupted him, his eyes roaming over the third's filthy boilersuit. "Did ye no' hae oan a clean boilersuit when oor watch started?"

"I've been looking for leaks," was the sullen reply.

"Oh aye," recalled MacKay, proffering his hand. "I almost forgot. Give me your list of leaks, Mister." He eyed the tally. "That's grand! I got some fine lists from Mister Christie and Mister Treen and I'm expecting a lot more during my rounds. And it's all thanks to you, Mister Sudbury. I'm very pleased."

Beery's lips formed a convex slit.

Yes," he continued. "All these repairs will be done next time in port. It'll keep everyone out of mischief for a bit. And I'll tell them that it is all thanks to you Mister Sudbury."

The slit became concave.

"Come on Mister King," boomed MacKay. "Let's see what jobs Mister Morgan has for us."

The floater trailed him to the airlock door. With the dying hiss of air escaping from the airlock Big John hesitated before looking back. "Oh by the by Mister Sudbury, you'd better hang on at the end of the watch."

"Why is t'at Mister MacKay?"

"Every engineer on this watch has got dirty for some reason. I think it's entirely possible that there might be a bundle of boilersuits for you and Mister Berwick to wash." Their laughter echoed in the airlock as the door slammed shut.

The pile of grimy coveralls grew higher on the jenny room floorplates as their watch progressed. The pranksters glowered morosely at the heap. A rating brought a note for Beery and dropped more laundry on the heap. "What does it say?"

"It's from Taffy. Get t'em clean or else!" read Beery and crumpled the missive before tossing it onto the heap. "It'll take us hours to wash t'is lot," he moaned. "T'at bloody washing machine of ours only takes two sets at a time."

"Hey!" exclaimed Artie. "I've got an idea. I read a book once where a sailor knocked some holes in a barrel and dragged it over the arse end with his laundry inside.

"D'you t'ink it'll work?" the engineer asked dubiously.

"Nothing ventured, nothing gained," was the blithe reply.

The volume of extra work was weighed against the volume of beer-drinking time. "I've got an empty forty-five gallon drum behind One Jenny. We'll use t'at."

The remainder of the watch was consumed by the fabrication of a maritime washing machine. The soiled boilersuits were heaved in and clipped the lid shut just as his relief showed up. Some daunting projects had been inherited from this man's watch. George Forgan, the four-to-eight engineer, had leerily decided long ago that he neither liked nor trusted him.

"What in the hell are you up to now, Beery?"

Sudbury told him. Forgan grinned knowingly and slapped him on the shoulder, "And the best of British luck, mate!"

With less than two hours to sunrise and a gibbous moon setting, stars twinkled mirthfully as if anticipating a humorous grand finale to end their blissful night. Hardly a swell marred the oily purple-black surface of the sea.

Beery found some rope neatly coiled near the after end. Berwick helped him bend it onto a rod that would become the axle when passed through the barrel's centre. The engineer hoped that the barrel would spin in the ship's wake without coming adrift. The moment of truth arrived when they lifted the barrel onto the stern's handrail. "Are you sure t'is'll work?" asked Beery for the umpteenth time.

"Of course, it'll work. Have you ever known me to be wrong before?"

"Maybe we should take a turn around t'at t'ere bollard," Beery indicated with a nod. "T'ere's one helluva turbulence down t'ere in t'at wake."

"Ok," agreed Artie, bending a hitch about the bollard.

"Right? Off she goes!" The barrel swooped to the sea in a graceful arc to bounce alarmingly upon the boiling surface. "Run it out more!" urged Beery.

Leaping like some rotund dolphin on the phosphorescent wake the container's leash strained intermittently until it sank out of sight. Only the thrum on the taut line signified that the barrel ever existed. Berwick made the rope's end fast. The dim-witted pair lolled against the ship's rail enjoying the night air. "So - eh - how long did t'at chappie have his dhobi spinning in t'e ocean?"

"About two or three minutes," replied Artie.

"We'll give ours eight minutes more," said Beery, squinting at his watch. Time dragged by and a seed of doubt germinated in his mind. "What was the name of t'at book?"

"I can't remember," admitted Berwick. "It was about a frigate or some ship like that."

"A corvette?"

"No-o."

"A destroyer?"

"No, nothing like that. It was like a Hornblower book."

"Hornblower?" A niggling thought kept skipping elusively across the neurons in Beery's brain. "Wasn't he t'e captain of a sailing ship?"

"Yes, that's right."

"*Jesus Christ*!" hollered the third, and rushed to the handrail to haul on the rope.

"What's the matter?"

"You-uh-are-uh-an-uh-idiot!"Beery gasped, sweat bleeding from every pore. "Don't-uh-just-uh-stand-there. Pull!"

Hauling hand over hand the two men sweated and heaved until the barrel hung vertical. When it cleared the sea they secured it with a half hitch until the barrel drained off the seawater. Beery clung to the rail puffing like an overactive steam trap. Artie still wheezing repeated his question.

"A sailing ship only does about four or five knots," panted the flabby engineer. "We're steamin' at twenty-five plus!"

"So?"

"So, you've worked on our washing machines," he was reminded. "What's t'e motors' horsepower?"

"Less than a quarter - oh!"

"Yeah - oh! And t'ere was seventy-five t'ousand pissing t'rough ours. Come on, let's haul t'is bleedin' barrel up."

The barrel ascended easily enough now that it had drained. Sitting there on the deck it looked like the test piece in a sledgehammer factory. Beery loosened the clips and the lid sprung into the air to be whisked off by the breeze, a prototype for a latter year Frisbee.

The men slid the barrel under the nearest light to inspect the laundry. It positively gleamed the whitest of white. He reached in and withdrew a cloying mass of lint and thread. His eyes met Berwick's. "What are we going t' do?"

"What do you mean - we?"

"You're in it wit' me!"

"Not me," denied Artie. "I didn't bloody chuck 'em over the wall - you did."

"You both did - and you're both in the barrel."

Startled by the unexpected interruption the squabbling pair cringed involuntarily before Treen's unexpected presence. When he had passed through the main jenny room after being relieved late on watch Sudbury's relief had gleefully enlightened him of the stupid stunt.

"Tell me Beery, what did your village do for an idiot when you went to sea?"

"You can't talk to me like t'at Treenie," Beery indignantly replied. "I'm t'e SeniorT'ird."

"Senior T'ird?" mimicked Larry. "More like senior turd! You pair better visit the purser today or you'll both be in that barrel." He spun on his heel and stomped away leaving the miserable pair arguing with one another.

Larry peeked in on King. "How's about a beer, Gus?"

Jake glanced up from a Playboy and gestured down at a crate of Tennants. An opener dropped into a clean glass was handed over to the newcomer. The welcome pop and hiss followed by the musical gurgle of beer filling a glass are ambient sounds in a engineer's cabin after a steamy watch.

"Ah!" sighed Larry drawing a sleeve across his lips. "That's better. Here Gus," he said to his host. "What's this I hear about you hanging yourself then jumping over the wall?"

When the other two laughed King related his story.

"I meant to ask you Gus," said Jake. "Whatever did you intend to do after you sneaked out of the jenny room?"

Angus shrugged before responding. "At the time Ah wasn't too sure. But somehow Ah was gaun tae get even wi' yon two. It a' sort o' snowballed frae there."

"Did you give Beery some overalls to wash?" Treen asked White.

"Yeah - why?"

"You'll never see them again mate," replied Larry, and proceeded to tell them about the fiasco on the after deck.

"No problem. It doesn't matter - uh - not to me anyhow," said Jake. "I put on an old set when the word came down from MacKay - right?"

"Me too," smiled Larry. "And probably the other guys did as well. Big John wanted to see dirty boilersuits. Well, we had 'em ready-made!" He took a swig. "But that's not the point, those twits have to be taught a lesson. How much are boilersuits going for these days anyway?"

"I paid thirty-seven an' a tanner for a set last month," said Angus.

"Right, that's two quid each for everyone on watch."

Opening time was brisk for the wardroom's bartender. Most of the middle watch eagerly anticipated the arrival of Sudbury and Berwick. Some eight-to-twelve engineers were there to watch the fun. Jeers and catcalls greeted the would-be jokers who reluctantly wormed through the jostling crowd.

Thirsty engineers with outstretched palms formed a circle.

"Drinks on the house!" piped up Jake. "Beery and Artie are buying! Right?"

"Like hell we are!" Beery contradicted.

"Like hell you are!" chorused the mob.

"We'd better," said Artie. "We'll be lynched otherwise."

Beery sullenly conceded and counted his change from the round. “At least you’ve got something to count,” muttered Artie, patting his pockets. “I’m stony broke.”

Beery showed an open palm: Two florins and three coppers nested on a ten-shilling note. “T’at’s all I’ve got,” he said sadly. “Fourteen bob and t’rupence.”

Artie’s eyes gleamed.

“Correction Beery,” he grinned, whipping the ten-shilling note from under the loose change. “You bet me ten bob that the floater would shit himself. You lost. He got you in shit!” He turned away to order a pint of lager.

Halifax, Nova Scotia

0020 Thursday

The port door of the darkened wheelhouse slid open letting in a blast of icy rain and a heavily muffled figure. The master greeted the newcomer warmly and a bridge boy hastily slammed out the near gale. The pilot smiled in response, his face rouged by the dimmed red night light. He shivered and unburdened his body of the moisture-laden checkered jacket. "It's a miserable night Captain," he informed Cowell unnecessarily.

The captain nodded. "I didn't think that you were going to make it."

"Neither did I," groaned the pilot, shuddering at the recollection of his hair-raising leap from the buffeted tender to hang helplessly on the shell door coaming, spotlighted by the ship's searchlight. Profuse thanks had flown from his lips, eternally grateful to the seaman who had whisked him inboard so smartly.

"I'm getting too old for this."

"Nonsense," chided the skipper. "You've got years left left in you yet."

Now that his eyes had become accustomed to the ruddy gloom the pilot moved to the Clear View Screen and peered through the thick glass that was constantly being wiped clean by three rubber blades rotating at high speed. Intermittent squalls thrashing an angry black sea allowed him fleeting glimpses of the Sandy Hook lights which were flickering at irregular intervals off the port quarter, some five miles away.

He made a decision. “Half ahead . . . Both engines,” he drawled. Telegraph handles clicked and were answered almost immediately by jangling. “Quartermaster, bring her left about five degrees . . . Ok, hold her there! What’s your heading?”

“Three-oh-two degrees sir.”

“Make it so.” The American spun on heel and gazed into the lighted binnacle to confirm the helmsman’s statement. “Oh, by the way Captain, there’s word that the stevedores might strike at midnight tonight.”

“I hope not,” was the response. “That could be very awkward for us. How would you like a cup of piping-hot coffee to take out the chill?”

“Why, thank you Captain,” smiled the pilot. “I’d appreciate that very much.”

Cowell stared pointedly at a bridge boy who was standing stiffly at attention by a telegraph before flashing his eyes aft. The transitory gleam of incandescent light signified the fellow’s hasty departure.

“Watkins - take over that telegraph,” the officer-of-the-watch commanded and another rating complied instantly.

The bridge boy scampered into the deck officers’ pantry. “A pot of coffee - quick!” he urged the attending steward. “It’s for the Old Man and the Pilot.”

“All right me old cock. Don’t get into a fluster,” advised the steward. He lifted a silver coffeepot down from a cupboard and stuck it under the tap of a coffee urn.

“So what’s new?” he asked conversationally, laying out China cups and saucers onto a silver salver.

“I hear that the stevedores will be on strike by the time we are docked.”

"Just our luck," grumbled the steward. "Now we'll have to tote all bloody luggage ashore for all the bloody passengers."

He cursed and slammed the coffeepot onto the tray. The bridge boy reached for the salver and made for the door. "Hang on a second," he said irritably and dumped a sterling silver sugar bowl and cream jug beside the coffeepot. The bridge boy started for the door again. "Jesus wept," quoted the steward. "Will you hang on another second? Where's the bleedin' fire?" He laid a teaspoon in each saucer. "You'll need these. Now . . ."

"Yes?"

"Piss off!"

When the lad had gone the steward pondered on the impending strike before phoning one of the assistant bakers. "Hey, Fred? Rusty - just reminding you of those special croissants the Old Man likes for his breakfast. If you forget to bake 'em again, he'll have my guts for garters tomorrow."

"Right mate. I won't forget. What's new?"

he Pilot's on board. He says the dockies are on strike."

"No shit? I hope that the tugboat men don't come out in sympathy like last time."

"Why should a tug strike affect an assistant baker?"

"Because this assistant baker has got a piece of crumpet waiting for him on the dock side. Last time we docked without tugs and we were more than two hours late getting alongside? With my luck it'll probably take even longer in this filthy weather."

"I see," said Rusty. "Well, the best of British luck mate. And don't forget those croissants."

"I won't."

Click.

An irate Chief strode across the wheelhouse deck, a flimsy sheet of paper flapping in his fist. “Here’s the latest fuel-oil consumption report. Tell me Captain, why is it that the man most concerned is the last to know?”

“You seem a bit tense tonight Chief. Please calm down,” soothed the captain. “Tell me what all this is about.”

“Halifax!” Lindsey remonstrated. “Where in the hell am I going to find enough Bunker C to get us to Halifax?”

“Halifax?” echoed Cowell; cautiously asserting that there were enough men available to restrain him on the remote possibility that he might run amok and disturb the serenity of the bridge. Engineers, he reflected, are a strange but necessary evil at sea. The thought died as he quietly answered the angry engineer. “We’re not going to Halifax, Chief.”

The engineer ignored this statement. “If we make a quick turnaround here I might, just might, be able to scrape up enough fuel to get us to Canada.”

“But we will not be putting in to Halifax Chief,” insisted the master.

“We’re not? But - but,” stammered the engineer. “But my writer received a message that we were.”

“I don’t know where he got his info from but it’s rubbish!”

“Excuse me Captain, I’ll check,” he replied. After a few minutes of explanation he roared down the phone at his writer. “I’m sorry Captain,” he apologised. “My writer was repeating gossip. He got the story from the junior engineer of the watch who’d heard it from the bilgediver. When the bilgediver went topside for cocoa, the crew’s cook passed it onto him from the lead hand.”

He paused for a breath.

"He in turn picked up the rumour via the butcher, the baker, and probably the candlestick maker. It appears that the New York stevedores have been on strike since the day after we left the Hudson. The tugboat crews have come out in sympathy and blocked off the East and North Rivers. No ship can enter or leave. And even if they could the tugs have refused to bring fuel-oil barges alongside. I honestly don't know how the rumour got started."

The captain looked at the pilot who grinned, and then he directed his glance at the youth by the telegraph. The bridge boy flinched under the master's terrible glare and fearfully anticipated forthcoming retribution. With an 'I'll see you later' look at the instigator the captain faced his engineer again and with an offhand remark said, "Well Chief, I guess that the only people on board that don't know are the gym instructress and the Valet Service."

"As a matter of fact Skipper, I happened to bump into that young lady on my way here and she inquired if we'd in Halifax be long enough so that she could visit her aunt in Dartmouth. The chap in the Valet Service who'd been informed by an a/c engineer told her."

Captain Cowell drained his cup and exclaimed, "God bless my soul, all that in the space of an hour. I suppose we should be grateful that you didn't mention abandon ship, Pilot!" He turned on heel and ordered, "Stand fast people!"

It turned out that the seedling of rumour that had spread its roots of fallacy throughout the vessel grew into a tree of truth. The stevedores *did* go on strike. The tugboat men *did* come out in sympathy and they *did* block the North and East Rivers - to a certain extent. Insomuch as any tug master who was caught red-handed attempting to create hazardous conditions would be severely reprimanded by the United States Coastguard.

Next to the *Queen Elizabeth* and *Queen Mary*, and of course their own *United States* and *America*, the New York populace had always shown a sincere affection for the venerable *Queen of Dalriada*. Tugboat operators were no exception and accordingly, they steered their powerful little vessels to allow free passage.

They had no other option. Fifty thousand tons of Scottish steel bearing down on them and showing every inclination of steaming over them at fifteen knots was a great incentive to make the tugs back off. The pilot relinquished control of the vessel to the captain when she approached Pier 92 since the master bore the ultimate responsibility of command anyway. The ship docked in good time without the use of tugs.

On the manoeuvring platform the standby engineers waited impatiently for the telegraphs to ring *Finished with Engines*. A telephone message from the bridge requested them to keep steam up because the ship was leaving directly after the passengers had debarked with their luggage. The destination would be Halifax, Nova Scotia, for refuelling. The chief engineer put a damper on the groaning and ordered the standby engineers topside. A serious discussion now ensued between his second in command, Phillip Edwards, and himself about the fuel reserve or lack thereof.

An hour later Lindsay was invited to the captain's cabin to review the problem. The captain's tiger served a fifteen-year-old Dalwhinnie, a tactful attempt to pacify the engineer. The single malt's warm glow achieved the desired effect and the chief relaxed in his soft plush easy chair. He surveyed the luxurious cabin and compared it with his own. He concluded that it definitely had a significant edge over and above his living quarters.

When the problem first arose at Sandy Hook the chief, wise in the ways of bridge officers who tend to neglect their engineroom staff, knew that he had enough fuel for the five-hundred odd nautical miles jaunt to Halifax but it would use up all his reserve. Like every conscientious chief engineer he kept a few tons up his sleeve for just such a contingency and submitted slightly higher daily fuel consumption in the bridge report than had been actually used.

Lindsey had been a chief for many, many years and forgotten that as a junior climbing the ladder of promotion he'd flogged the fuel log to cover his backside.

Phillip Edwards (Ettie), the First Senior Second Engineer, flogged the daily fuel log before he sent it to the chief's office. He compiled the account at eight o'clock each morning when the logs of the six previous watches accumulated on his desk. Naturally John MacKay, the Second Senior Second, and Jack Williamson, the Third Senior Second, the walking seconds of the twelve-to-four and four-to-eight watches respectively did the same thing to keep a step ahead of Ettie.

The lowly fuel-oil engineer on every watch did the same to keep two steps in front of their seniors so consequently, seven engineers were wandering around the ship with enough oil up their sleeves to take them to Goose Bay or perhaps even circumnavigate Newfoundland and Ellis Island.

After receiving a reluctant affirmative Cowell said, "Now then Alan, if the fuel problem's settled there's just the passengers to contend with."

"What about food, Bob?"

"I was talking to our Catering Officer just prior to your arrival. Our New York staff had some refrigerator vans loaded when they heard of the impending strike. The crew's bringing the stuff on board now."

"Too bad they didn't lay on an oil barge!" Lindsey morosely remarked.

"Ah - yes," replied the skipper. "We can't have all ways it seems. However, I've been made aware that there are only about thirty American passengers and they've all been contacted. According to our Manhattan office they'll be boarding directly. All the other passengers are Canadian, mostly from the Maritimes. Telegrams advising them to meet the ship in Halifax are going out to them as we speak."

Bob accepted a replenished glass from the steward and splashed in a minuscule drop of water. "What about water?"

"Get the Chief more water," the captain told his tiger.

"No," countermanded Lindsay. "I mean freshwater - for the ship. Have we enough to get to Halifax?"

"Oh, I'm sorry Alan. I misunderstood. Yes, I've seen the Carpenter's report. We'll manage all right."

"Good. I'd visions of burning more fuel for the saltwater evaporators," smiled Lindsey and drained his glass. He rose from his comfortable position to breathe out a sigh of euphoria and fifteen-year-old malt vapour. "I'd better get back and line up my men. By the way, when do we sail?"

"I'm figuring on a six-hour turnaround," replied Cowell, rubbing his chin in thought. "So it'll be about eight or nine and it'll be as fast as we can there. As soon as we bunker I want revolutions for top speed so we can arrive in Nassau in time for our passengers to celebrate the New Year."

0440 Thursday

The snow-covered hills of Pennant Point gleaming under a frosty moon were sighted off the port bow. Angus was on deck taking a break from his standby watch. His thinly clad body shuddered when the icy remnants of a breeze penetrated his patrol suit. Flakes of snow sporadically struck his face with hail-like force bringing tears to his eyes. A faint tap on an access door drew his attention. Taffy's uneasy face, framed by the porthole, beckoned him inside.

"You're crazy boyo!" Taffy gaped at his shipmate's rosy cheeks, their hue brightened by the Canadian blasts. "Now, what in the bloody hell were you doing out there, boyo?"

"Just gettin' a breath o' fresh air."

"Fresh air?" shrilled Taffy. "Fresh out of the bloody fridge, see you! You'll get pee-neumonia. Don't you know that it's minus twenty-five out there, boyo!"

"Man, that's invigoratin'! Just the thing tae gie a body an appetite for breakfast," grinned King. He clutched a chubby arm and pushed heavily on the door to open it. "Here, try it!"

"Let go of me, see you!" retorted Taffy, brushing off the grip. "Let's grab a cuppa and a sarnie. We've got people to relieve y'know."

"Aye, ye're right. Ah dinnae want Jake mad at me. He's been a bit under the weather lately."

It had been a short standby. The great liner sailed majestically into Halifax Harbour and slid easily alongside Ocean Terminal. She tied up adjacent to the CNR Station. White was reluctant to go ashore with him. He'd complained of a headache and a runny nose. So shortly after nine that morning Angus, encumbered in his heaviest winter gear, went off on his own to explore the city.

Taxicabs were delivering passengers to the ship. He climbed into one that had just emptied only to realise that he'd no idea of his destination. "Where to Bud?"

"Eh . . ." he hesitated. A flash of inspiration struck him. "Eh, Woolworth's please."

"The one on Barrington Street, Mac?"

"Eh - aye."

Ok," nodded the driver, edging out into the traffic.

Unknown landmarks whizzed by his eyes, some partially hidden by walls of snow. Never in his life had he saw so much snow. Snow, that even yet, was continuing to float heavily down when he entered Woolworth's. He browsed around the store and purchased picture postcards of Halifax and Nova Scotia without the shroud of winter.

Trudging through the deepening snow the bright window display of a bookstore beckoned him inside. He stocked up on literature for the next step of his odyssey. Works of Ian Fleming, Sir Arthur Conan Doyle and a Hammond Innes, *The Land God gave to Cain*, went into his shopping basket.

Daylight illuminated few colours on the drab grey waters of Halifax Harbour. Davison peered out of his cabin porthole, his mind's eye seeing row upon row of freighters, iron-ore carriers, tankers, armed merchant cruisers and corvettes, all jockeying for position in the roads. They were preparing for the long, long gauntlet to Britain. He'd sailed on one or two HX convoys in his time. How did that ballad go?

> From Halifax one cold, dark night,
> some ships got under way.
> Group HX84's sad plight
> is quite a tale they say,

when merchant ships met Nazi might,
and it, the *Jervis Bay*.

Gone were the days of rich resorts,
and folk who sought the sun,
she'd plied the planet's pleasure ports,
her time was almost done.
The navy sadly lacked escorts
when war had just begun.

They fitted her with six-inch guns,
one fore, one aft, they say,
they were out-gunned these mothers' sons
who died with *Jervis Bay*.

The War had waged for but a year
on that November day,
a host of ships felt naked fear
on cold, cold seas of grey:
in wait, here lay *Admiral Scheer*
to fight the *Jervis Bay*.

This battleship had little fear
when stalking easy prey,
convoys were flocks of sheep to *Scheer*,
to slaughter, sink, and slay;
till one old ewe bleats, "Fegen's here -
aboard the *Jervis Bay*!"

"Convoy dispersing." signals say,
they flee like hell from here,

as *Jervis Bay* steams through the fray
to ram the mighty *Scheer*.

Poor *Jervis Bay* has gone below
as though she'd never been,
she's gone to where good sailors go
for berths in Fiddler's Green.

Ships are foundering here and there,
a few ablaze I think,
men are drowning everywhere
in bunker C's foul stink.

That frightful cry: *Abandon ship*!
Loud klaxons vent their spleen,
and ships begin their final trip
below, to Fiddler's Green.

There was more but he'd forgotten it. There was a knock on the door and his steward came in with a couple of Canadian newspapers: The *Halifax Daily News* and *Toronto Star*. He tipped the man and sat down to peruse them.

The voyage was going well so far. He only went out on deck during the twelve-to-four watches. He'd shaved his head and had cultivated a Van Dyke beard, a big difference from his old mugshot. Still, it paid to play safe. He'd discovered that the policewoman preferred to have a light lunch and was prompt when the First Class Restaurant opened at 1:00 p.m. She rarely stayed more than twenty minutes.

On the other hand he went in after one-thirty and lunched heavily. He took his other meals in his cabin. Davison usually had coffee and a croissant for breakfast and for dinner, perhaps a steak or chicken sandwich with a beer. Just the other afternoon he had met her on the Prom Deck. There hadn't been any flicker of recognition and they passed as strangers might in any street. He wondered how his son was faring . . .

Oscar was sitting in the *Buckingham Tavern*.. A burly waiter placed a couple of ten-ounce glasses on his table with a flourish and waited for his money. A US one-dollar bill was dropped onto the badly scored table. The change machine on the waiter's belt clicked out some coins. Salt was sprinkled into the beer before he left in search of another customer. Davis sipped some beer and stretched out his legs. There was a distinct click of bottles when his feet contacted his grip.

A flurry of snow ushered Angus into the same tavern. With the door hastily closing patrons soon lost interest in the newcomer. His eyes panned the room and came to rest on the only familiar face there: Davis. Thumping snow off his boots onto the coconut mat he crossed over to where Scar was sitting. "Dae ye mind if Ah sit here?"

A languid flourish over a nearby captain's chair was taken as acceptance and he sat down. The waiter returned, dumped down two beers and lifted some of the coins from the table.

"Ah'll get that." King waved a US five-dollar bill.

"Dontchya have anythin' smaller?"

He shook his head. The man picked up the coins necessary. "You'll have to break that bill at the bar," he said, sprinkling some salt into the beer before leaving.

"Here! Whit are ye daein?"

"That's how they drink beer in Canada," said Scar.

"Weel - it's no' how Ah drink it."

"When in Rome do as the Yanks do."

He took a test sip and decided that it wasn't all that bad. "Whit Ah really wanted was a wee dram tae take the chill oot my bones."

"You'll be lucky. They only sell beer here."

"Where dae ye get liquor then?"

Scar's grip chinked with a touch of his toe. "In a liquor store."

"Ah dinnae want a whole bottle - just a wee dram."

Davis thought for a moment. "You'll have to go to a lounge bar for that and I don't know if there's one nearby. Anyway," he said, glancing at the bar clock. "You've just got enough time for one more before we go on watch."

"Aye, ye're right," agreed Angus, and took another sip. "Ye ken, Ah'm awfy glad that ye're talkin' tae me. Ah didnae think ye liked me. Ah feel like ye've been sendin' me tae Coventry a' durin' this trip."

"It's funny that you should say that King. I was born in Coventry but I've lived in Rhyll mostly. You'll find beautiful sandy beaches there. My mom and dad used to take me down to the beach on picnics."

He shook his head and sighed heavily.

"Ah'm really sorry tae hear that ye'd lost your Mum."

"Thanks King. But it's worse, much worse than that."

"In whit way?"

"I believe that Dad murdered my Mother. I think that he killed the family lawyer too. But there's no great loss there. He deserved to die."

"Naebody deserves tae die."

"That bastard did!"

"Och weel, whit's done is done. Ah hope that everythin' works oot a' right for ye."

"Thanks King," said Davis. "I appreciate that. But I have other problems that I have to work out as well."

"Aye well, Ah ken that it's nane o' my business but . . ." His toe chinked the grip again. "That's not gaun tae help."

Davis said nothing.

"An' by the way, Big John has telt me tae report ye if Ah find ye drunk or sleepin' oan watch."

"Will you?"

"Ah dinnae think so. Unless ye're a danger tae yourself or someone else," he answered in all honesty. "Ye ken, Ah think ye should talk tae some professional person - the doctor maybe. It's a long way out o' my league Ah can tell ye."

Scar held out his hand and with a sad smile said, "You know, you're not a bad chap even if you are a Scotsman."

Angus grinned and shook his hand. "Like Ah said, Ah hope everythin' turns out fine for ye but ye ken, Ah think we should heidin' back tae the ship."

Scar asked the waiter to phone for a cab, which arrived by the time they'd finished their beer. The Canadian coins were left on the table as a tip.

At the races

1220 Saturday

The floater on a mission: find the bilgediver. The platform second had noticed one of bilges in the tunnel was flooded and was out for blood. Charlie Everton was found in 3BR oiling the bilge pump.

"Charlie, ye'd better get your arse aft fast. Your services are required by Mister Christie, like yesterday."

Everton seized his wheelkey and sped past Brian Halliday, one of Treenie's firemen. Halliday seemed puzzled. King asked him what his problem was.

"There's something wrong with this whitewash," he complained, scrutinising his paintbrush. "It won't stick to the side of the boiler."

The engineer kneeled closer to the boiler casing. Instead being the usual white the steel was bare and turning black. Sure enough, when the brush touched it the whitewash just spluttered. Maybe it was just his imagination but the steel appeared to be slightly pinkish.

He went round to the console and casually mentioned the phenomenon to Larry. Treenie's eyes bulged. He grabbed a pair of green goggles and gazed into the furnace of the afflicted boiler. With a yelp he began pulling off some fires. He increased the fuel-oil pressure before scribbling a note to send through to Morgan. "Whit's wrang, Larry?"

"The brickwork has fallen down from the back of that furnace. I'll have to shut down the boiler. Get a hold of Big John, will you?"

MacKay didn't take long to put in an appearance. He concurred with Treenie and told him to shut the boiler down right away.

The complete back wall was a pile of rubble on the furnace floor. The walking second paced up and down fretting. He'd heard on his radio that there was an unusual amount of weather disturbances in the East Atlantic - possible embryos for hurricanes. He'd leave word for the chief to see about repairs in Nassau.

In the meantime he'd get the floater to pull off a burner assembly to get more air into the defective furnace so that it would cool down quicker. The snag was that they might lose too much draught for the other fires to combust properly. But the large forced-draught fans were adequate for the task.

Jake's cabin door burst open to reveal the huffing puffing figure of the indomitable Taffy Morgan. The Cymric chubby jowls were all a-quiver with excitement.

"I've done it! I've done it!"

"Well don't do it again," commented White, annoyed with the boisterous intrusion.

"Whit hae ye done Taff?" inquired Angus curiously.

"Did," said Jake, showing off his Canadian education in grammar.

"Whit hae ye done did?" asked Angus.

"The cockroaches," wheezed Morgan, after his marathon run from the wardroom. "I've managed to get them to run twice around the ping-pong table."

"Really? You've - uh - been trotting roaches in the wardroom at five o'clock in the morning?" asked a disbelieving Jake. "You must be nuts, right?"

"Nuts am I?" retaliated the Welshman. "We'll see who's nuts when we're all rich."

"That's guid news Taffy," commended Angus. "Dinnae mind Jake. He's just pissed aff because Christie gave him a rough time last watch."

"Oh tough luck," consoled Morgan. "Anyway boyos, pass the word that I'll be trying out contenders in the wardroom shortly after sixteen hundred hours today."

"Ok Taff, we'll dae that."

"And tell the guys that I've only got a limited amount of paint for their racing strips. So it'll be a case of first come - first served."

"Ok."

By four-thirty that afternoon a temporary racetrack had been erected on the ping-pong table. Morgan, being starter and trainer, operated the gates while King resumed his role as steward. Jake with pencil and clipboard was the official recorder. A handful of engineers showed up either with prospective candidates or simply from plain curiosity. Taffy lovingly ushered his team into the starter's box. "Ok, who's up first?"

"Me," said Larry Treen, handing him a matchbox.

"That'll be one pound please."

"A quid! What for?"

"To go towards the purse for the winner," explained Morgan and carefully enticed the applicant into the trap with the seasoned runners. "That looks like a fine specimen Larry. Gus, just place the beer trough at the end of the table. That's fine. Are you ready?"

With his assent Taffy raised the starting gates, letting them loose. Larry Treen's cockroach was first past the post.

"Well done Larry," Jake congratulated him while Morgan appropriated the money. "What colour do you want?"

Larry picked up a bottle of silver paint and handed it to Jake who hailed over to Angus in a phoney western drawl. "Hey thar po'tnah, hawgtie thet ther mustang so Ah cain brand the critter."

"How in the hell dae ye hogtie a cockroach?"

"Jest grab his horns an' flip the critter on his back."

"Listen Hopalong, just put a wee dab o' paint oan his arse while he's busy suppin' beer."

"Oh - ok."

With the cockroach knighted Jake asked the owner if he had a name for the beast. "Silver Streak," said Larry.

"Next!" cried Morgan.

"Hang on, hang on!" objected Larry. "What in the blazes is going on?"

"Nothing's going on," countered Morgan.

"I want my cockroach back."

"You'll get him back after the race."

"I want him back now."

"What for?"

"I have to feed him."

"We'll feed him."

"He's on a special diet," insisted Treen.

"Give us the recipe and we'll see that he gets it," promised Taffy, determined to keep the insect for illicit trials that night.

Treen impounded his horse. "No Taffy," he said. "I'm very fond of this little guy and besides . . ." he paused.

"Besides what, Larry?"

Treen stuck his face right up against the Welshman's. "Besides I don't trust you bastards!"

The matchbox was stuffed into his pocket and he sat down to watch the rest of the proceedings.

Taffy glumly placed the veterans back into the starting compound. "Next!"

Beery strode forward brandishing an aspirin bottle that housed his cherished hope. The cap was unscrewed and the contents dumped unceremoniously in the trap with the others.

"Hey, steady on," Beery remonstrated.

"Sorry," Morgan apologized without too much conviction. "A quid, please."

The matriculation fee was reluctantly transferred into the waiting palm. Pandemonium erupted - Lilliputian style when the competitors were released. Roaches milled everywhere. They darted up and down the track until the Welshman corralled the offender beneath a glass tumbler.

"Sorry Beery," he apologized again. "But I'm afraid we'll have to disqualify your horse. It upsets the others, see you. Do you mind if we put an extra special mark on him?"

"What kind of a mark?" Beery asked suspiciously

"Oh, just a mark denoting that it's too highly strung. It's just to make sure that he doesn't get mixed up with the others. You might call it insurance, boyo."

"Oh, all right t'en."

"Right Gus. The extra special mark if-you-please."

"Ok," beamed Angus. In the blink of an eye, the tumbler was lifted and swiftly swapped by the heel of a size 8 shoe.

"*Hoi*!" shouted an indignant Beery. "What kind of a mark do you call t'at?"

Inside a deep zigzag groove insect remains were still twitching. Angus held the rubber heel under Beery's nose and hollowly intoned, "The Mark o' Zorro!"

"Give me my money back!" bellowed Sudbury.

He was handed a ten-shilling note.

"Here, what's t'is?"

"That's your change."

"What change? I gave you a quid!"

"Oh, didn't I tell you boyo?" Taffy murmured in all innocence. "There's a ten-shilling forfeit for upsetting our thoroughbreds and causing them unnecessary distress."

"That's extortion!"

"No, exertion," laughed White.

"Bastards!" roared Beery and stormed out the room.

"Next."

Maxie Harris proffered a handsome snuffbox.

"Gee Maxie, where did you get this guy? Windsor Castle?"

Maxie giggled.

"I like my nags to travel in style."

He watched the crushed remains of the previous entrant being wiped from the table. "That's pretty final insurance, isn't it?"

With bated breath, he observed his hopeful breeze past the post with flying colours. Jake was asked to daub the nag with purple and name it Purple Prince. Taking his cue from Treen, Harris retrieved his chattel and stood back to watch the remainder of the trials.

"Next."

The Mekon came forth, or fourth, toting an Embassy crushproof cigarette packet and a one-pound note. The starting gates went up and his roach performed like Sudbury's.

Havoc rent the track.

"DUM, da-dum, DUM!" he groaned sadly. "The Mark of Zorro?"

There was a grave nod and a heavy thud vibrated the table. "We try to keep it as painless as possible, see you. Here's your ten-bob back."

"Thanks," replied a crestfallen Mekon.

"Next."

Artie Berwick placed two matchboxes into Morgan's hand. "Sorry Artie, only one nag per head, see you," came a Welsh censure.

"Mine is in the Swan Vestas box. The other belongs to my relief."

"Ok, two pounds please," said Taffy, emptying the Swan Vestas box into the trap.

"Disqualified!"

Thump!

The team was regrouped along with the next entrant, which ran like a champion.

"Colours and name please."

"Golden Goy."

Taff echoed. "Golden Goy? That'll be Cohen's nag! Next!"

A pair of engineers was politely offering each other the honour of being next when Christie barged in on the scene and belligerently shoved a path to the head of the queue. With his roach successful in the trial he egotistically named it Black Bob and departed as abruptly as he'd arrived.

Mike Finney, the deck engineer, had come upon an exceptionally large roach behind an oven in the first class galley. Inside the trap this insect, which had dined *cordon bleu* all of its life, dwarfed the veterans.

"It looks like you'll need a saddle and jockey for that one Mike," joked Taffy. "Hey Jake, if this one is disqualified Gus will need help to kill it before the rest of the herd is mangled."

Up went the gates and the humongous cockroach immediately lumbered into the lead. The other four trotted behind at a discreet distance as if recognising the potential hazard of being trampled. The great beast trundled up to the trough and greedily guzzled all the beer. The Syndicate's team milled around in dismay. "Colour and name, please."

"His size will distinguish him so he doesn't really need a colour," reasoned Mike. "Just call him Big Bronzie."

"Right," said Jake, scribbling in this latest entry. "Oh I almost forgot - here's Jazz James' entry Taff," he said, handing over a pillbox.

"I hope that you didn't forget about his quid."

"Oh yeah - here it is."

Mumbling something about no honour among thieves Morgan set them off. Jake daubed the insect with a bright fluorescent orange and named the successful participant, The Flaming Phoenix.

"Trust Jazz to come up with something flashy," commented Morgan.

Like Judas, the Syndicate received another thirty pieces of silver when Angus auctioned off the next three rejects to the fourth horseman of the Apocalypse.

Bob Emsworth entered the last contender, which he'd previously painted with bold yellow stripes. 'Hornet' initially caused some alarm with the other roaches but they soon settled down and the trials came to a successful conclusion.

"That's it fellows," announced Taffy. "The races will begin tomorrow afternoon at four-thirty. The first one will be a regular flat race and the second will be the Grand National. The forfeit money will be used to buy beer for the owners and spectators."

The wardroom was soon tidied up. Some engineers loitered around perhaps to play darts or table tennis until the bar opened. Angus peered across two tankards of ice-cold lager into Jake's face and asked him if he had worked out some kind of form for the upcoming races. The Canadian studied the list of entrants for the umpteenth time before shaking his head.

When he came off watch Keyes was brought up to speed. The solution to the problem wasn't readily available to him either. "The only thing I can think of is that we have four nags against seven," he told them. "That's in our favour. Also, our team is more experienced than the rest."

"Yeah right," agreed Jake. "And what about the odds?"

"Easy, just give me their times and I'll work it out."

"Times?" repeated Jake, quite aghast.

"Don't tell me that you chumps didn't time each race." The pregnant silence was his answer. "Bloody idiots!" snorted Keyes. "If brains were a disease you three would have permanent immunity!"

"See now, what do we do?" asked Morgan.

"Fortunately I've got enough brains for all of us," bragged Wheelkey. "Going by the results you gave me and combining them with my superior mathematical skill and logic, plus a little inspiration that borders on pure genius, I have arrived at a foolproof solution."

"What's that Wheelkey?" asked Taffy, impressed by his colleague's verbal diarrhoea.

"Elementary, my dear Morgan, we lie!"

"Wheel that by me again?" requested Jake.

"Who's to know that you didn't time them?" proposed Keyes. "I'll make out a betting form and set a bogus time against each nag. If you're boned about it - tell 'em that there was a stopwatch under your clipboard."

"Ah just thought o' somethin'," chipped in Angus. "Every horse tested was first by the post."

Keyes chortled. "Better still! Jake, me old son, give us a bit of paper and a pencil. We're in business."

1300 Sunday, 31st December, 1961

"I want all the bricks out of that furnace by the end of the watch," MacKay ordered the floater. "Stack all the good ones and have the rest of them chucked over the wall. When that's done, have the furnace floor swept out ready for the brickies in Nassau."

It was hot and muggy enough in 3BR and the junior didn't relish the thought of working in an even hotter and dusty space. Reluctantly he crawled through the hole left by the Number Seven burner assembly. Halliday followed him inside. They were pleasantly surprised to find it was much cooler inside - thanks to the great fans that had blown most of the dust up the funnel. The rubble was extricated from the furnace and piled up to be bagged later.

Presently the job was finished and Scar Davis was waiting when they eased their bodies through the narrow opening. "Hot in there eh?" he speculated through a haze of gin.

"It's no' really Scar," replied Angus. "It's so cool in there that ye'd think that it was air conditioned."

"No shit?"

Seeing that the reusable bricks had been neatly stacked the floater decided that it was time for smoko. Davis watched them go round to the control console which was out of sight. Since he'd made all his transfers for the watch and there weren't any more settling tanks to change over, the time for right a little snort. He decided that the furnace interior was an ideal place to hide from the walking second. He knelt down and crawled inside.

1640

Morgan and White were relieved early the next afternoon, which left them plenty of time to prepare for the race. Upon entering the wardroom Angus was pleased to find that the track and accessories were in the final stage of completion. Slips of writing paper, plundered from public rooms, occupied the bar along with pencils from the same source. The desk was commandeered for Jake, the chief bookie.

Encompassing the tennis table's entire perimeter the racetrack was a work of art. Walls impregnated by low-grade insect repellent stood eight inches apart. At two feet intervals flagged swizzle sticks denoted furlong markers. Owners and spectators arrived and soon chattering filled the room. Engineers congregated in front of racing forms that had been stuck at random onto the bulkheads. Diverse opinions were floated in response to the entrants' disposition as formulated by Keyes:

HORSE	OWNER	TIME (inSecs)	ODDS
Silver Streak	L. Treen	15.5	8-11
Big Bronzie	M. Finney	15.7	Evens
Golden Goy	B. Cohen	15.9	5-4
Flaming Phoenix	Jazz Johns	16.3	11-4
Black Bob	R. Christie	16.7	3-1
Purple Prince	M. Harris	17.0	7-2
Hornet	H. Emsworth	17.5	4-1
Blue Arsed Fly	W. Keyes	17.6	9-2
Red Biddy	A. King	17.8	5-1

Green Gobbler	H. Morgan	18.4	8-1
White Lightnin'	J. White (who cares?)		20-1

The merits and flaws of insects and owners were discussed and bets made accordingly. Betting slips and banknotes were waved at Jake who was furiously recording the wagers. Off track betting was handled from telephone calls from the machinery spaces. The tumult died down when Taffy called the owners to the paddock. The competitors were loaded into the starter's box without incident until Hornet made his appearance. There had been quite a flurry when Big Bronzie performed push-ups on the striped carapace. Remarks about the legality of copulation before the race buzzed through the crowd until the roaches came under starter's orders.

A hush blanketed the room as a pudgy Welsh finger pressed the release button. With a cry "They're off!" the roaches galloped lustily towards the first marker. Morgan removed the starting box and replaced it with a spare corner section of track. The nags were bunched up at the first furlong with Big Bronzie trailing by three lengths. Steamboat, primed by a gill of 160° proof Bahamian rum, began an imitation of Richard Dimbleby through a cone made from that day's issue of *Pictwit Papers* just as they approached the two-furlong marker.

"Good afternoon viewers!" welcomed a rich plummy voice. "This unusual race is being brought to you from the engineers' wardroom on board the luxury liner *Queen of Dalriada* somewhere in the Atlantic. At the moment the runners are beginning to thin out as they near the third furlong. In the lead is Purple Prince, followed by Black Bob and Golden Goy. About four lengths behind and bunched up are Green Gobbler, Blue-Arsed Fly, Flaming Phoenix. Favourite, Silver Streak, is trying to break through. Big Bronzie is last but is slowly gaining on White Lightnin'.

"They're coming into the first turn now with Purple Prince still holding the lead. Black Bob and Golden Goy are closing fast. The others are still bunched up. Now . . . Big Bronzie looks like he's going pass White Lightnin' to port. No, starboard. He ran over the top of him, by George! Foul! White Lightnin' is down! Get up you lazy beggar. This is no time to fall asleep! Ah, he's up and running again but he's got a lot of ground to make up."

Steamboat paused for a swig of beer. White Lightnin's loss of ground was no understatement. The insect had just approached the second bend when the leaders completed the first circuit. The bunch had thinned out between the second and third turns allowing Silver Streak to move into third place. Big Bronzie hadn't been lagging either as the stragglers discovered to their dismay. His great bulk, and ever increasing in speed, either bowled them over or spun them aside.

His thirst slaked for the time being Steamboat resumed his commentary. "Going into the first turn again, it's Golden Goy, then Blue-Arsed Fly, Silver Streak, Purple Prince and now Big Bronzie. He's still accelerating folks. Oops! There goes Purple Prince. That big beast is just churning up the dust.

"Now, Silver Streak just went under those big hooves. Into the straight before the final turn Golden Goy has just lapped White Lightnin'. The Blue-Arsed Fly is safe because Big Bronzie passed him to starboard. They're going into the last turn and Big Bronzie has just lumped the limpin' White Lightnin' - the rotten sod!

"At the last furlong Golden Goy and Big Bronzie are neck and neck. Big Bronzie's neck is above Golden Goy's. He's being run down. No, Golden Goy's carrying him! No, it's not that either. Holy shit! Big Bronzie is literally screwing the race. And at the post, it's Golden Goy, or should I say Golden Gal. In second place: Big Bronzie by a short stroke and in third, The Blue-Arsed Fly."

Cheers and groans resounded through the wardroom. Jake elbowed his way back to the writing desk and paid out the few happy winners. The Grand National was announced and the only change in the betting was White Lightnin' which went to thirty-to-one. Angus and Jake raked in the new wagers while Taffy methodically reloaded the battered contestants. "Hurry up with the fences, Jake," he ordered.

"Ok, ok," shouted Jake. "Are there any more bets?"

Nobody answered.

"Right, hand in your pencils," commanded Jake.

Flights of pencils shot over him like the English arrows at Agincourt. He gathered them all up to be placed at intervals along the track to become miniature hurdles.

Post time: Off they went. To everyone's amazement, most of all Jake's, White Lightnin' came beetling out first with Red Biddy close on the former's cerci. Big Bronzie came third followed by the remainder. At the first fence White Lightnin' unshipped his wings slightly and jumped, half-gliding over the obstacle.

Red Biddy hesitated momentarily before doing the same. Big Bronzie made the mistake of just stepping over the pencil and got stuck. His first four legs made it but his rear legs just kicked helplessly in midair. In a frantic effort to complete the hurdle the large insect gave a Herculean heave with his forelegs. Although he didn't succeed in releasing his body, Big Bronzie's great strength caused the pencil to revolve.

The other cockroaches baulked at this hazardous impediment. Golden Goy waited for the pencil to roll further along the track before giving a quick spurt in order to negotiate the huddle. The unfortunate roach completely misjudged the speed of the rotating pencil. His magnificent leap was in vain for although his effort got him to the far side the gilded creature neglected to maintain his momentum and was crushed mercilessly beneath the oncoming juggernaut.

Black Bob was next to brave this perilous hurdle and annihilation was his penalty for failure. Undaunted the royal roach, Purple Prince, proved his mettle against the deadly hazard and raced on, though still in Red Biddy's wake. The other roaches saw their chance when the first fence collided with the second. Big Bronzie's head had cushioned the point of impact leaving the pencils undamaged.

By this time White Lightnin' was on the backstretch with Red Biddy two lengths behind him. Four fences in the rear Purple Prince was gamely closing the gap while back at the first corner the residue were beginning to increase speed quite unhampered by the most recent casualty.

The excitement became too much for Flaming Phoenix who at the next fence spread his wings and glided over it. Preferring to stay aloft he flew over the next two fences to the cries of Foul! whereupon disqualification was signalled. The insect soared over a corner where Angus swiped but missed. However at deck level the Mark of Zorro swooped directly on target and the last flight of the Phoenix was duly recorded.

White Lightnin' completed the first circuit with Red Biddy a close second. Both were galloping towards a scene of carnage. When the leader reached the double fence he paused momentarily to wrench a limb from Big Bronzie's corpse.

With vengeance sated the roach bounded along the track with a leg dangling from his mandibles. Red Biddy had managed to steal the lead during the mutilation but White Lightnin' was swiftly closing the gap despite his gruesome burden.

Whether by accident or realizing his indiscretion Jake's roach dropped his payload and zoomed past Red Biddy on the last corner. On the opposite side of the track Purple Prince duplicated his daring leap by taking both fences simultaneously but he collapsed on the other side.

An onlooker pointed and called out, "What's the matter with 'im, then?"

"Winded, by the looks of him," opined his neighbour. "Maybe his lungs gave out."

Morgan, now an authority on the family *Blattidae*, hailed back. "Roaches don't have lungs."

"Jeez, no wonder he's gaspin'!" exclaimed a wag.

"They breathe through their skins," Taffy supplemented.

"It looks like he's got dermal emphysema," diagnosed Jake.

"He's deid," said Angus, deliberating the prognosis. "An' there's White Lightnin' wheechin' past the post!"

"Wheechin'?" questioned Taffy.

"Ok then - rushin'," translated the Scot.

"Red Biddy is second and Silver Streak will be third if he gets there," announced Jake. "Line up all you fellas who backed the winner."

Shouts of abuse and insults greeted this last remark and a few engineers collected place money. Jake laughed heartily at the cries of resentment knowing full well that nobody had ventured on the outsider.

"We'd better clear up fast Taffy," warned Angus tapping his timepiece. "Charlie'll be here ony minute."

In the twinkling of an eye the track was swept away, papers and pencils neatly stacked on the writing desk and empty beer bottles dropped back into their crates before Charlie entered the wardroom. The bartender raised an eyebrow at the unusual amount of engineers waiting but diplomatically kept silent.

Jake had the track bundled under his jacket and the starting box behind his back. With a clandestine motion, he sidled behind Morgan who was propped against the bar with his cashbox stable tucked under his arm.

"I'm taking all this stuff back to my cabin," whispered Jake. "Do you want me to take the nags as well?"

"No thanks Jake," replied Morgan. "I'm going to have a couple of jars before I go back and feed 'em. 'Ere, what about the money?"

"We'll square up when Wheelkey gets relieved."

"Ok, see you later."

Morgan grandly plumped his rear end on a barstool. "When are you going to open Charlie?"

"I can draw you a pint right now Mister Morgan."

"Thanks Charlie, I'd appreciate that."

There were parched cries with further orders for beer. After serving everyone the bartender started to fill the small sink behind the bar with scalding hot water. Steamy vapours billowed about and Morgan gently admonished the rating. "Steady on Charlie," he said, placing his cashbox on the bar counter to take a sip of beer. "We could get another couple of knots with all that steam, see you."

The water was shut off.

"I'm sorry Mister Morgan but I've had to wipe up a lot of dried beer marks that have been mysteriously appearing on my bar counter since the day before yesterday."

He dipped a wiper into the water and gingerly squeezed out the excess and proceeded to attack an offensive stain right in front of Taffy. While he scoured Charlie's attention focussed on the cashbox. He stopped cleaning to pick it up and admire the ornate exterior. He fiddled with the fancy hasp, cracked open the lid slightly, and got a whiff of the contents.

"Begorrah, what a rotten stench!" His Irish brogue suddenly became more pronounced. "Never you mind, Mister Morgan sor, I'll soon get rid of that for you," and plunged the box into the scalding water.

It was at that precise moment that a swig of lager was in transit between Taffy's mouth and stomach. It reversed course, a drop or two heading for his lungs. He coughed and spluttered while Steamboat, a chagrined loser who happened to be standing nearby thumped him none too gently on the back. Tears welled in the Welsh eyes and Scottish lager dribbled down his ample chin.

"Dear me, what's gthe matter Mister Morgan?" asked Charlie. "Did some beer go down the wrong way?"

"The box!" Taffy wheezed. "You put my bloody box into the water."

The container was removed from the sink and wiped dry. "Was there something in it?"

"No - it's all right," lied Taffy. "I just remembered that I'd left my documents in my cabin."

"Thank goodness! I thought that I'd destroyed something very valuable. Oh, by the way Mister Morgan, I can't get under those corrugated recesses with my chamois. You'll have to leave the lid open and let it air out for a little while."

"Ok," breathed Taffy and noticing Jake's return said: "Pour a pint for Mister White please."

"Hi Taff, crying in your beer again?"

Charlie moved off.

"You'll be crying too, boyos, when you hear the latest."

"Hi guys," Angus greeted Taffy and Jake. "Who's buyin'?"

"Make that two Charlie! On second thoughts," said Taffy, draining his glass. "Make it three."

"Thanks Taff," said Angus. "Treenie came oot wi' a guid one. When are the chariot races gaun tae start!"

"More like pulling biers than chariots, see you."

"How can cockroaches pull beers, Taff?"

"B-I-E-R-S," he spelled out. "Gone. Dead. Kaput!"

"Deid?"

"Dead?" echoed Jake. "What happened?"

"Charlie committed them to the deep," answered Taffy showing the clean and seemingly empty cashbox.

"There you are gentlemen, three lovely pints."

Coins were placed in his hand. "Thanks Charlie."

"You're very welcome Mister Morgan. Now I can get on with my cleaning." Charlie looked into the sink. "Bejasus! Whir did all t'em bleedin' roaches come from?"

Jake leaned over the counter to watch the lifeless insects drift around. "They must've come up the plughole Charlie."

"I guess you're right Mister White," rhymed Charlie. "It's funny how I didn't see 'em when I filled the sink."

"No wonder with all that steam," Morgan pointed out.

"Per'aps. Well, they're all going back down that same plug'ole!" he said, hastily withdrawing the stopper and a vortex formed to spin the roaches into a watery grave.

"Come on Taff, cheer up!" said Jake, laying a sympathetic hand on his sleeve. "Let's have a game of darts. Gus, ask La Treen over there if he'll partner you."

"I heard that, you cheeky bugger!" retaliated Larry. "Come on Gus. I'm game! Let's thrash 'em"

Angus and Larry warmed up while Jake was scaring up another round. Taffy sat at a nearby table gazing dolefully at his cashbox.

"For God's sake Taffy, snap out off it!" Jake cajoled him. "Nothing can bring them back."

The intake of two more pints and winning the first game cheered the Welshman considerably and halfway through the second game, he strolled jauntily to the bar to buy another round.

Inside a dark recess formed by a corrugated plate attached the cashbox's inner lid a bronzed creature crawled painfully towards the light. During its passage it stumbled over two companions that were awakening from a scalding nightmare.

They seemed to communicate by rubbing their antennae against one another. What thoughts, if any, passing through those ganglion brains were unknown but possibly the hazardous Sport of Kings was considered a price too high to pay for the dubious benefits.

The will to escape was unanimous. Handicapped with severed or broken limbs the cockroaches struggled valiantly up the wall of their prison to poise quite exhausted on the very lip.

Taffy distributed the tankards and took a deep quaff from his own. He quickly slammed it down adjacent to the cashbox, his reaction to his shipmates reproaching him for taking too long.

The earthquake tremor panicked the insects into taking what seemed to be the safest way out - across his beer mug. One by one the roaches dropped in and slowly sank beneath the soft thick foam.

"It sure is hot in here boyos," remarked Taffy, taking a great swig of beer. His face took on a peculiar expression caused by two unknown objects squirming in his oesophagus. Carefully he lowered his tankard.

"What's the matter with you Taff?" asked Larry.

Silently Morgan stared blankly at the bulkhead, his mind focussed on the foreign body awash in his mouth. His tongue sensed twitching where there shouldn't be any and reacted accordingly. He spat the object out.

Treen analyzed the strange projectile that had rudely erupted from the Cymric maw. It was a section of carapace, a cockroach's carapace, and it still carried a trace of silver paint.

"You swine!"

"What's the matter?" Morgan managed to cough out.

"You bit my cockroach in half!"

"I what?" snapped Taffy, and gaped down at the remnants of Silver Streak. "Oh my God!" His face went from pale to a greenish hue as it dawned on him that he'd swallowed other roaches. Clamping a plump hand to his mouth he bolted for the door clumped along the passageway to the open deck and barfed into a scupper. The sight of White Lightnin' wallowing belly up in the beery residue induced another surge of vomit that included a three-legged insect with blue markings. "Ooh!" he moaned, resting his head on the ship's rail. A clammy feeling enveloped his body and he shivered.

The dart players rallied out on deck to see how their shipmate was faring. They viewed the brown foamy mess swirling in the scupper with disgust.

Angus grinned. "Look at that Jake. Taffy came out lookin' for Hughie an' found White Lightnin' an' The Blue-Arsed Fly instead."

"Taffy Morgan!" chided White. "You ate my cockroach. You ate the damned winner."

"For goodness sake, fellows! Don't bloody talk about roaches," he pleaded. "You'll make me puke again."

"It's your own fault Taff," Jake blamed him. "It was you who brought the subject up, so to speak."

"Ooh!" groaned Taffy. "Hugh - aayy!"

"Come on Gus. We've got time for a game of one-oh-one before dinner. I'll need to find another partner, of course."

New Year's Day, 1962

1825 Sunday

A bank of cloud chilled his skin. He felt a sensation of movement, floating or flying perhaps. Fog billowed around him like ethereal gossamer. Where was he? Now he was soaring in a clear blue sky. Directly below him a little boy was playing with his bucket and spade beside a lady who was sunbathing on a sandy beach. He was that little boy, the woman his mother. His dad came running up from the surf, grabbed a towel and dabbed at the glistening beads on his skin.

Dad's dark hair was thinning even then. His father picked up the lid of his mother's plastic trifle bowl and flicked it so that it skimmed through the air. The boy scampered after the lid and tried to emulate his father but it wouldn't fly for him so he sulked. His dad patiently demonstrated the wrist action and soon the little fellow had got the hang of it. His dad motioned him to stand down by the water's edge while he threw the lid to him. The cloud closed in.

Davis was awakened by a loud long sonorous blast from the ship's whistle, which announced the *Dalriada*'s arrival in Nassau. He sat up, reached for a bottle of brandy, and took a swig before realising that he'd missed standby.

2350

He was sprawled out on his bunk with a book when Keyes looked in on him. "So you managed to get the watch off did you?" Angus peered over the top of his book and nodded. "It's nearly time for the bells Gus," the Glaswegian reminded him. "To friends across the water?"

A drawer slid open and a bottle of *Cardhu* was liberated from its cocoon of thick woollen socks. "Ah'm ready."

"So am I." Keyes flashed his hoarded bottle of Glen Morangie.

Retrieving a couple of empty glasses from his desktop, the pair went out on the open deck. The reflected lights of Paradise Island twinkled on the satiny waves that undulated between ship and shore. Only a couple of hours earlier the liner had anchored after a high speed run from the cooler northerly latitudes. The night was calm and clear with stars glistening in the velvety sky. Keyes poured a generous measure into each glass.

They waited silently, each dwelling in thought. The ship's bell on the bridge chimed out eight crisp clear notes. A pause - then another eight chimes floated across the deserted deck. Sixteen chimes: eight to ring out the old year and eight to welcome in the new.

"Happy New Year Gus!"

"An' a Happy New Year tae ye pal," was the response.

They shook hands and their glasses clinked.

"Wha's like us?"

The traditional reply followed.

"Very few an' they're a' deid!"

There was a faint cheer from the shore and the strain of American voices broke into *Auld Lang Syne*. Single malt slid down easily warming their gullets. Angus replenished the glasses from his bottle. Both men held their drinks over the sea and the old Jacobite sentiment was intoned, "Tae friends across the water."

"Ah haven't seen that done in years," came a female voice.

Their eyes focussed on a small silver-haired lady who stepped from a lifeboat's shadow. A drawl threaded through her strong Scottish burr. "Ah've always found yon saying tae be very movin'," she said with a tear in her eye. "Are ye baith engineers?"

Keyes nodded.

"Aye, Ah thought so. It's awfy funny how so many Scots turn oot tae be engineers."

"You're kind of far from home," said Keyes. "It's a long way from here to Scotland."

"Scotland?" she echoed. "Ah haven't been there for ower forty years. Ah've stayed in Canada all that time."

"Ye havenae lost your accent anyway," Angus observed with a smile.

"No," the old lady admitted. "Ah'll talk like this until the day they pu' the sod ower my heid."

"You remind me of my Mum," said Keyes, the drink and the mood made him feel a little bit melancholy.

"Why thank ye young man," replied the lady who softly began to hum the melody.

Keyes had been imbibing since the end of his watch and the booze was having a melodious effect on him. His clear tenor voice caused tears to spring from her worldly eyes and roll down her gaunt cheeks.

"That was smashin'!" she praised him when the song had ended. "Would ye like tae first-foot my friends in the Port Garden Lounge?"

"Certainly ma'am," he said. "Hang on a second please."

He rushed back into the engineers' quarters and was back presently with a black rock.

Angus chuckled. "Coal! Did ye pinch that oot the Welshman's suitcase?"

"No," laughed Keyes. "Actually, it's a lump of carbon from an oil burner. But it'll serve as coal."

The lady clapped her hands. "Ye'll make a perfect first foot because ye're tall, dark and handsome."

"Come oan then," urged the lady, taking each engineer in arm. "Ah dinnae want tae keep my friends waitin'."

The Port Garden Lounge was like an old folk's reunion. Most of the ladies were members of a Canadian women's rural institute. All were Scots-Canadians. Chattering died away when the engineers ambled in to wish them a Happy New Year.

Introductions took place with much handshaking and soon everyone was conversing once more. Standing beside a piano the engineers' new acquaintance rippled her fingers along the keyboard calling for silence.

"Och, that's better! This young gentleman is a wonderful singer," she announced, pulling Keyes closer to her. "Maybe we can encourage him to sing a few songs for us."

He stroked his throat and rasped, "I don't know if I can. My throat is pretty dry." A large glass of whisky was thrust into his hand. "Aye, that might help."

"Jessie, will ye accompany the officer on the piano?"

Another grey-haired matron arose and made her way to keyboard and Wheelkey whispered. "D'ye think this piano can hold both o' us?"

"Och, awa' wi' ye, laddie!" Jessie shrilly chided. "Whit would ye like me tae play?"

"*Auld Scots Mother Mine*," prompted the first matriarch. "He sings it so beautifully - just like Robert Wilson."

There wasn't a dry eye in the room when he had finished.

"Encore! Encore!"

The Canadian song, *When you and I were young Maggie*, brought the house down. With his throat further lubricated he sang a series of sad Scottish airs. Angus was asked if he could sing.

"Like a rusty hinge," he told them but did admit that he could recite poetry.

"Rabbie Burns," shouted someone. "Give us some o' Rabbie Burns."

The poem *To Mary in Heaven* was followed by Keyes' rendition of *The Road and the Miles to Dundee*. Handkerchiefs fluttered across teary faces like sodden cabbage butterflies. "Christ," he muttered aside to Angus. "We'd better phone down and tell Jake to start up a bilge pump. We'll be sinking soon if we don't cheer this bunch up. D'you know any jokes?"

Angus pondered for a moment. "Ah'll cheer 'em up. Ah'll tell them a Bible story that my Grandfather told me. He cleared his throat and in a loud clear voice began to recite Grandfather Tells the Story of the First Ne'erday, a Scottish term for New Year's Day.

"Noo accordin' tae some devout mathematician who counted back a' the years recorded in the Holy Bible, the world was created in the year 4004 BC at nine o'clock, oan the mornin' o' October twenty-third. But that's no' quite true. Ye see, the guy never took leap years an' such things intae account because there wasnae any guid wind-up clocks then.

The maist accurate calculation tae date turns out tae be December, the thirty-first, four thousan' an' three years BC.

So if we go back tae yon time, we might get an inklin' o' whit happened:

"If bells had've been invented then they would've been just aboot ready tae ring midnight when Archangel Gabriel came sloggerin' alang the road. He noticed Our Lord sittin' oan a mountain lookin' all pecht oot."

The company presence and booze was having a noticeable effect on thickness of Angus' brogue so that the tale continued as follows:

Gabriel had been awfy busy practisin' high notes oan his new horn an' quite forgot that his Master had started a new project just six days afore. He felt fair ashamed o' himsel' for no' offerin' tae help. Still, it was never too late.

"Ah've come tae lend a hand wi' your project, Lord."

"Och, ye're too late Gabe," rebuked The Lord, feelin' fair knackered. "The job's aboot done." He swept His Hand across the heavens, the seas, an' the Earth an' said, "Ah've just got this wee handful of stour left an' Ah've been wonderin' whit tae dae wi' it."

"Man, a' yon looks braw," whispered Gabe, his eyes wide-open in awe at the stars an' the moon an' a' the planets birlin' their way through the black infinity of Space. He gazed up at His Lord an' pondered for a minute afore makin' his suggestion. "Ye ken Lord, a' great artists sign their work once they're done. Why don't ye dae same?"

"Gabe, that's a rare idea," announced The Lord. He opened up His Mighty Hand an' looked doon at the one or twa ounces o' dust layin' in His Palm for a wee while then blew life intae it. Right away a young man came intae bein'.

Gabriel was astonished at the lad who stood there, ballock naked. "Oh my Lord, he's the deid spit o' yersel'."

"Aye, Ah ken Gabe," said The Lord. "Ah've made him in My Very Ain Image. He'll be my legacy tae this braw world that Ah've just created wi' My Ain Twa Hands."

He sighed wearily.

"Ah've been puttin' in triple shifts oan that lot for the past six days an' Ah'm fair wabbit. Tomorrow, Ah'm gaun tae take the day aff."

Adam, for that was the name His Father gied him, stared aboot his strange surroundin's in amazement an' wondered whit tae dae.

"Here laddie," saith The Lord, yawnin'. "Dinnae hang aboot like a lang drink o' watter. There's some trees ower there. Awa' an' cut some branches an' build yersel' a wee bothy. Ah'll see ye first thing Monday."

Monday came alang an' The Lord gave Adam a few pointers on livin'; like whit kind o' animals gied the best meat; whit kind o' fruit an' tubers tae eat, how tae make fire, how tae grow corn, an' such like. Three months went by an' it was spring. No' that Adam knew, for the weather in Eden was always guid.

He had been lazin' aboot all yon time because he'd nuthin' tae dae. Adam would kill a cow or a sheep once in while. So he was a' right for fresh meat - an' there was plenty o' fruit oan the trees an' bushes for his dessert. When his bothy got dirty an' untidy wi' bones an' such like he just moved awa' an' built anither one.

Some time later Archangel Gabriel came daunderin' alang the road an' noticed Our Lord sittin' oan his mountain lookin' teed aff. 'Whit's the maitter Lord?"

"Och, Ah'm fair upset wi' Adam. It turns oot he's no' like me at a'."

"In whit way, Lord?' Gabe asked, his heid cranin' aboot tae see Adam. He was up on the ither side o' a glen. "He's the very spit o' ye, can ye no' see?"

"Aye, he does look like me right enough," admitted The Lord. "But he's no' as industrious as Ah am. He doesnae seem tae any ambition."

"Whit dae ye expect him tae dae, Lord?"

"Weel, Ah thocht that he'd maybe roond up some kye an' build up a dairy herd. Or maybe learn how tae make a ploo an' till the land tae plant barley, corn, wheat an' ither cereals. He could make breid frae the wheat, make butter frae the dairy, an' maybe jam frae the fruit trees. There's nuthin' better than a doorstep laden thick wi' butter an' lashin's o' strawberry jam."

"Maybe he doesnae ken how tae dae these things."

"He kens, a'right! Ah gied him brains. Did Ah no'?"

Gabe stroked his chin an' pondered on this irrefutable logic. 'That's a' very well, but it's obvious that he's no' usin' them. Maybe he needs some incentive."

"Mm, maybe ye're right Gabe! Ah'm gaun tae gie him the greatest incentive ever."

"An' whit might that be Lord?"

"Ah'm gaun tae gie him a wumman!"

"Whit's a wumman?"

"That's a question Adam will be askin' himsel' for the rest o' his days, startin' tomorrow."

The very next mornin' Adam woke up with an awfy pain in his chest. Too mony ingons in the mince, he thocht. He sat up an' saw this young thing grinnin' at him. "Who are *you*?" he asked in amazement.

"Ah dinnae ken."

The Lord showed up just then an' told Adam that he noo had a companion who'd stay wi' him for the rest o' his days. Her name was Eve an' they had tae be fruitful an' multiply. Adam wondered how he could multiply withoot a slide rule. The Lord, readin' his thochts, telt him that he already had a six-inch one but he just didnae ken how tae use it yet.

So Eve took charge an' put Adam tae work. She was smart enough tae make him think it was a' his ain idea. So everythin' went hunky-dory until the day afore the first anniversary o' the world's creation. Whit happened that mornin' had a lot tae answer for.

Ye see, Eve was quite happy drivin' Adam tae get oan in the world. That is until the Lord told them no' tae partake o' the Tree o' Knowledge. That was only fruit in the hale o' Eden that was forbidden tae them. Noo Eve, bein' the prototype o' original wummun, didnae like anybody tae tell her whit tae dae, or in this case, whit no' tae dae. An' of course the Serpent in the guise o' Auld Nick, just egged her oan.

That afternoon the Lord watched Adam an' Eve set up the banquet table with black bun, shortbread, sultana cake, an' ginger wine. 'Gabe," says Himsel'. "Keep an eye on things for me. Ah'm gaun awa' tae yonder stars."

"Rho Coronae Borealis? That's sixty light years awa'!"

The Lord nodded his heid. "Ah ken that! Ah made it - did Ah no'? But dinnae fash yersel'Gabe, Ah'll be back by Ne'erday."

Sure enough that next mornin', the Lord found Gabe sittin' on his usual mountain wi' his heid in his hands.

"Whit's the matter Gabe?"

"Och Lord, Ah've let ye doon. Yon Serpent pu'ed a fast one oan me. He talked Eve intae pu'in' fruit frae your Tree o'

Knowledge. She gave it tae Adam, an' when he ate it, a bit stuck in his thrapple. So that it widnae happen again she boiled some fruit tae make it saft. Then she baked a sponge cake oan top o' the stewed apples an' ca'ed it Eve's Pudden."

"Gabe, noo ye've got me angry!"

"Och, that's no' the hauf o' it Lord."

"Ocht Gabe - whit next?"

"The De'il spiked the ginger wine an' they a' got steamin', fa'in' doon drunk. They talked Eve intae daein' a dresstease. It's amazin' whit ye can dae wi' a couple o fig leaves. When Adam's turn came he put oan a docken leaf. Everybody kens whit the proper use o' a docken leaf is."

"That's it! Ah've heard enough! Where are they noo?"

"Och, they're a' sittin' ootside the bothy haudin' their sair heids an' too sick tae eat their Ne'erday dinner. Man, how onybody can turn doon steak pie wi' tatties, neeps an' pickled beetroot is beyond me."

"So-o,' saith the Lord, standin' ower them. "Ah turn My Back for a minute an' a' yon-other-place breaks loose. Weel, ye had your chance an' ye blew it. Your life o' Riley's ower."

"Aw gie us anither chance Lord," pleaded Adam.

"Na, na. Ye'll be celebratin' next Ne'erday oot in the boonies. Awa' doon the road wi' ye!"

An' so Adam an' Eve were cast oot o' Eden. 'Never mind,' the Serpent shouted. "Ah'll be your First Fit again next year."

The Almighty glowered at him. 'An' Ah'm thinkin' that ye'll find it awfy hard tae First Fit wi' nae legs, ye handless creature ye!"

An' so the Serpent crawled awa' oan his belly. But some o' the curse must've hit Adam an' Eve tae because followin' generations have been found legless at Hogmanay!"

There were cheers, laughter and hand clapping when he had finished. Keyes announced that he would just have time for one last song because he wanted to grab a bit of shuteye before going on watch.

The sighs of dismay diminished and he sang *Scots Wha Hae.* He bowed to the audience. "Coming Gus?"

"Aye, Ah'm gaun tae wish Jake a Happy New Year."

As they made to leave the passengers began to sing *Auld Lang Syne* and slowly a circle formed by clasping hands. The engineers completed the circle and the haunting melody floated through the open windows toward the silent shore.

The huge grey cloud evaporated as quickly as it had appeared. The strange disc spun toward him growing larger and darker. The sky around it had become dull yellow-red like a sunset about to be swallowed by deadly black night. The disc hovered just in front of him. It seemed to be made of hardened leather with concentric rings of thumb-sized rivets of brass.

A long spike of sharp gleaming steel marked its centre. The disc had stopped spinning now and was oscillating up and down slightly.

"Hey mon! Is it ok to start work in here now?"

He blinked at the black face grinning at him from the burner opening on D3 Boiler. With the ship at anchor there had been little for Scar to do. He'd sneaked inside the furnace guessing MacKay would never think of looking for him there.

Without waiting for an answer the hard hatted Nassauvian hauled his body past the opening to survey the damage.

"What time is it?" asked Davis, getting to his feet.

"Just after three o'clock mon," replied the black in a deep melodic voice.

"How come you're here so early?"

"Oh mon, I'm heah to assess damage and see how much brick and mortar we need fo' de job. Den I go ashore and tell contractor so material arrive heah with brick gang at six o'clock." He took a pencil from behind his ear and jotted some notes on a scrap of paper. "Aren't you goin' to Junkanoo today mon?"

Davis gave him a blank stare.

"Junkanoo is big carnival," explained the workman. "I will be playin' de saxophone in de parade when I finish work on this here furnace."

"How long will it take to repair the furnace?"

"Maybe a day," the black opined indifferently. "If brick gang go to Carnival, then maybe two."

The fuel-oil engineer vacated the furnace.

Early afternoon found Angus focussing his *Halina* camera upon the sun-soaked wharf of Prince George Wharf. The shutter flipped and the TSTS *Queen of Dalriada* was captured on film for the umpteen time.

"Come on Gus," urged Jake.

"Alright, alright! Dinnae get your knickers in a twist. Whit's a' the rush? We've got eight hours, ye ken."

"Seven hours and fifteen minutes," Jake corrected him. He tapped his wristwatch for emphasis before turning to join the flow of tourists heading for Nassau's beautiful centre and the New Year's Junkanoo Parade.

He jogged a little to catch up. "Where are we gaun anyway? Surely we're no' gaun tae another pissup parade?"

"Shantytown," replied his shipmate. "Wheelkey said that he'd meet us there later. He managed to wangle his watch off."

"Sounds guid."

The pair quickly bypassed the town ignoring the swarms of revellers in Bay and Shirley Streets. Presently their feet were crunching along a gravelled lane, reddish because of its volcanic origin. It led them through delightful tropical woodland that opened intermittently into glades, tiny meadows of curious vegetables or fruit laden shrubs. Coconut palms were plentiful and made the Scot secretly wish that he could have the chance to climb one to harvest one or two of the luscious green nuts.

"Whew! It's awfy hot!"

"You got that right," agreed Jake, and pointed down through the branches of some oak-like trees that overhung the road. "I think that's it Gus - eh?"

The partially hidden frond-covered roofs emerging below turned out to be the native village that they sought. Shacks raised on stilts bounded a dusty street. Shaded verandas hosted wicker rocking chairs while here and there snow-crested Negroes slumbered in the afternoon sun. On an intersection a dilapidated sign with the faint inscription *Bar* dangled precariously by one wire.

Both men gazed up at it, looked at each other and agreeing without comment climbed the six warped planks, which took to them to the veranda.

It was surprisingly cool inside. Their eyes gradually discerned a bar, some rickety tables, and chairs scattered in the dimness. The welcoming buzz of a fly broke the silence of the room. Selecting a table the engineers sat down.

`"Christ, what a dump," muttered Jake.

"It disnae look like anybody's here - an' certainly no' Wheelkey," said Angus in a hushed tone.

"Chances are he's likely shacked up behind there somewhere," grunted Jake, nodding at the decrepit oil-lit bar.

Four straining eyes panned across the darkness, its graveyard silence now complete with the six-point landing of the fly. A huge dark shape suddenly arose from a corner table.

"*Jesus*!" erupted from Jake, his shipmate aping him.

"Hokay!" beamed the apparition; his Colgate-white teeth gleamed in the darkness. "What you want mon?"

"Uh - two beers please," said Jake, his voice tense.

"Hokay mon," repeated the waiter-bartender and padded off into the gloom.

A long sigh of relief wheezed from Angus' lips, rupturing the stillness. "Jings! He gied me quite a turn."

"Me too likewise. Watch it - here he comes again."

A dim shape became silhouetted against the flickering oil lamp. Four thuds on the shaky table heralded the arrival of two bottles of beer with corresponding glasses.

"Three shillings mon," stated a deep resonant voice.

"Thank ye," replied Angus, placing a couple of florins in the outstretched pink palm. "Keep the change."

"Ta mon," said the Negro and softly merged into the gloom.

"Ah think that we should finish these beers an' bugger aff."

Jake declined, saying that Keyes would show up sooner or later. Cool beer gurgled into their glasses and they drank deeply, licking froth from their lips. The clicks of glasses resounding on the table disturbed the fly, which resumed its irritating whine. A loud slap terminated its epic flight and signified the proximity of the hidden bartender.

Footsteps clumping up the outer stairs disturbed the quiet ambiance. Stark against the brilliant light the familiar outlines of Taffy Morgan and Will Keyes were framed by the doorway.

"Come on in you two," hailed Jake.

"Oh - there you are," said Keyes. "We'd wondered where you pair had got to."

The newcomers moved hesitantly through the gloom and took their places at the table. Like a wraith the bartender materialized by Keyes' left shoulder.

"Yes mon?"

Startled Keyes exclaimed, "*Holy shite*!"

Jake grinned. "Four beers please Sunshine."

The man shot him a sullen glance.

"Hey mon," he objected. "My name's Arleigh, not Sunshine."

"Uh - sorry. Ok then, four beers please, Arleigh."

"Where in the hell did he come from?" hissed Wheelkey, after the waiter had merged with the background once more.

"Christ knows," shrugged Jake. "He just shows up whenever you need a drink, right?"

Clinking bottles and glasses forewarned them of the Negro's impending reappearance. Jake paid. "Wait for it," whispered Keyes. "The next thing will be whores oozing out of the cracks in the walls."

And sure enough a pair of dusky ladies of the evening imposed on their company. One sat between Taffy and Wheelkey, the other separated the engineroom juniors. "Hey mon, buy us a drink," cajoled the first girl.

"Sure sweetheart," smiled Keyes. "What's your name?"

"Tricia," said the coffee-skinned girl. "An' dat's Lena."

Lena at that particular instant was unashamedly groping the private parts of Angus and Jake. The resultant erections prompted her to squeal "Ooh! Big banana!"

Meanwhile Tricia was similarly manipulating the other two engineers who thus encouraged began to fondle a breast each. They were served two rums and coke with another four beers. The Welshman footed the bill.

When Arleigh had gone Morgan resumed his original vocation. His plump hand trembled with excitement and dropped on Tricia's knee to begin edging up her skirt. She firmly grasped his wrist and pushed it away. "Hey mon," she protested. "It cost you five dollah to touch me up der."

He pondered on that offer. Her thin cotton dress did little to hide the rounded attractions of her body. He extracted a West Indies five-dollar bill from his fold and pressed it in her hand. The woman squinted in the feeble light emitting from the bar to check the note's authenticity before nodding her consent.

Taffy's hand slipped under the table to rest surreptitiously on the inside of her thigh. His body quivered, jelly-like with anticipation, as a hand slid minutely higher and higher savouring the tender warm skin. Fantasy and reality were becoming one. Two inches from his target he could contain himself no longer. With a quick movement his hand was fumbling at the female's groin.

An astonished look enveloped his face when his little fat digits sensuously groped the crystal face of an Ingersoll watch that was securely anchored to a thick hairy wrist. His eyes met Wheelkey's who fluttered them demurely, pouting his lips. Morgan withdrew his hand in anger, and snatched up his beer, muttering obscenities.

The Glaswegian chuckled happily and called for another round including one for the bartender. Upon his return Arleigh sat at the table and tossed off a tumbler of clear liquid with relish.

"What was that you just drank Arleigh?"

"Rum mon!"

"How much is it?"

"One dollah a bottle."

"Ok. Bring us a bottle."

A bottle of rum was duly brought along with seven glasses. Keyes did the honours and replenished the women's glasses too. "Say when," he said automatically, pouring into Arleigh's glass and stopped when it was half-full.

"I not say 'when' yet mon," cautioned the black man. The liquid transfer was resumed. "When!" Only the meniscus' natural formation prevented the glass from being totally filled.

"Cheers mon!" The natives chorused and sent it cascading down their throats.

The engineers copied them with their single shot glasses. Coughs and spasms overcame them. Keyes wheezed, "*Holy shite*! Now we know what they keep in those forty-gallon barrels before they're converted into calypso drums."

Angus spluttered. "Jings! It's like bluidy paraffin."

"I wonder how many knots we'd get if this stuff was used instead of bunker C - see you?" mused Taffy.

"About sixty," figured Jake. "Straight up - eh?"

"What proof is this firewater Arleigh?" Keyes asked, gingerly inspecting the volatile remainder in his glass.

"Dat' just one hundred an' sixty mon," grinned Arleigh. "Fo' de tourists, y'know. We keep de strong stuff fo' ourselves."

A few more natives descended on the place to loll around and imbibe on the potent liquor. The afternoon wore on taking its toll on the engineers' faculties. The tropical night swooped down swiftly. Coloured bowls, each containing a lighted candle, were placed on every table.

Three young Negroes who were part of Gus Cooper's Junkanoo group, The Valley Boys, dropped by on their way home to Centreville from the New Year's Parade. They trouped in through a beaded doorway near the bar carrying their musical instruments to set up on a low stage in the far corner of the room.

The lads were dressed in ruffle-sleeved floral shirts open to the waist and shin-length skintight trousers. Their feet were bare and tattered straw hats adorned their kinky hair. A calypso drum set was centred on the dias. A fellow with a pair of bongos drummed on the port side and a guitar player thrummed to starboard. Soft primitive music began to fill the room.

"Gotta go now mon," said Arleigh, and he moved towards the stage. He waited until the trio had finished before whispering something to them. The calypso drums rippled *Yellow Bird*, which was accompanied in his deep baritone voice. Many island songs including Harry Belafonte hits; *Island in the Sun, Scarlet Ribbons*, *Mary's Boy Child*, *Woman is Smarter* and *Hole in the Bucket*, filled the room, much to the visitors' enjoyment.

Both women ran to the dias for a pair of bamboo supports and a long willowy rod. Coaxing some patrons to move their tables to create some floor space they set up what seemed to be a pole vault for leprechauns. A primeval tattoo emitted from the bongo drums and the audience clapped in time.

Arleigh leapt high in the air to land near the flimsy structure with a fearsome yell and gracefully limbo-ed beneath the rod. Each time he passed under the girls decreased the level until it was about eighteen inches from the floor. The crowd cheered each time that he successfully managed this difficult feat. Arleigh invited the visitors to emulate him. Ably encouraged by the consumption of high-octane rum all the engineers with the exception of Taffy were game to try.

All failed.

The bar was raised six inches. All failed again. At the three-foot mark most of the engineers were successful but only by cheating. Tricia kept badgering the Welshman but Taffy was adamant.

"You're wasting your time with him love," said Keyes. "He couldn't get under there if you pulled him on a trolley."

"You cheeky Scotch twerp!" snapped Taffy.

"Hey mon," oozed Tricia, meaningfully sliding her body against Taffy's. "Yo' get t'ru dere an' yo' cain have me."

This offer put the dare in an entirely different perspective. Keyes commented on Tricia's remarkable generosity. With such an incentive Morgan would've gladly limbo-ed through the Severn Tunnel. So while he perspired and grunted and heaved she shrugged, mumbling something about having been already paid. Finally Taffy's vigorous efforts paid off. He got to his feet. He approached the bamboo frame in the manner of an elephant contemplating back flips.

Slowly his trunk, Taffy's not the elephant's, bent backwards his feet ponderously shuffling forward. Miraculously the lower body had navigated the obstacle.

The band's tempo had slowed to a dirge and Morgan wondered if this might be his last strenuous act on earth. It was just no good. He was absolutely spent. He couldn't move forward anymore but neither could he stand erect. He just hung there as if in suspended midair until gravity decided to haul him back down to the floor.

Tricia edged to his side and whispered in his ear. "Yo' want me help, mon?"

"It's no good lass," wheezed Taffy. "I've had it. I've run out of steam, see you."

"No, no," persisted Tricia. "I help you mon."

"How?" Taff huffed and puffed. "How can a slip of a girl like you-move-my-great-weight?"

"No problem mon," Tricia airily assured him and moved in between his wide-open legs. "I move yo' - yo' see."

She took a firm hold of the Morgan family jewels and hauled lustily. Taffy's ankles adopted the function of his knees as his splayed feet pounded up and down like tappets on a Morris Minor in an effort to maintain pace with his testicles. Little squeaks of pain burst from his lips as his obese frame juddered beneath the bar and his colleagues wondered if they were watching a limbo or the launching of a supertanker.

Tricia released her fierce grip and he collapsed on the floor with a soggy thud. He sat up and gingerly stroked his groin. Tricia attempted to help him but was roughly shoved away. "Gerraway from me, you bitch! You've ruined me for bloody life, see you."

"Come wid me mon!" She coaxed amorously. "Let's find out if it still works."

His face flipped from loathing to lust. Helped by his dusky paramour, he struggled to his feet and was steered through a doorway at the back of the room.

"Did you - uh - get a picture of that Gus?"

“Aye Jake,” he replied. “But Ah’m no’ sure that they’ll come oot. It’s awfy dark in here. Ah had tae use the camera’s B exposure.”

“Something might come out then,” laughed Wheelkey. “Old Taffy was as steady as a statue for a wee while. Boy, that was funny.”

The music had diminished to soft restful island ballads and love songs. Jake glanced at his watch and nudged Angus. “You know what Gus? It’s five after eleven, we’d better make tracks back to the ship.”

He nodded in agreement and finished his drink just as Taffy reappeared beaming like a sunrise.

“You dirty fat little Welshman you,” leered Wheelkey. “We thought that you were going to have an all-nighter.”

“Jealously will get you nowhere, boyo” sighed Taffy, ruffling the hair on the Glaswegian’s head.

“Gerroff!” he shouted, pushing the hand away. “I bet that you never washed your hands.”

“It’s better than Brylcreem, see you, boyo!” Taffy shouted back as he waddled toward the exit. His shipmates followed astern.

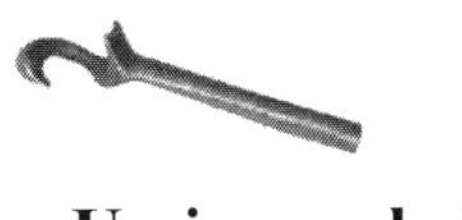

Up in smoke!

0001 Tuesday

The steel spike popped out and inverted itself and in doing so changed into a knife, a long sharp knife with a brass pommel attached to its stag horn hilt. The disc was becoming paler and was elongating. It was still oscillating up and down those last few inches like a naked man's back in the throes of sexual intercourse. He plunged the knife in. Now the knife was stuck. He wiggled it back and forth pulling at the same time. It remained in place. Blood, his blood, trickled down the blade and splashed on that fleshy pallid skin. Suddenly the knife came free. He stabbed again. This time the blade went all the way in. He was glad, very glad, that it was finally over.

"*Oscar*!"

A woman's voice shouted.

"Oscar, what have you done?"

He looked down past the murdered man's head and saw his mum staring up at him.

The sky was no longer blue just a dirty bronze canopy. The elongated targe made from human skin was shuddering so that the flecks of blood reflecting an expiring sun seemed to shimmer into tiny blobs of candlelight. The knife plunged down.

"Oscar, what have you done?"

Eddie Wainwright's hazel eyes viewed the gauges on 3BR's control console. The telegraph needle was set on *Standby* for the ship was still swinging on her anchor. All the gauges were reading normally except the fuel-oil inlet pressure gauge. The filter needed to be cleaned again. He lifted the off-white beret, an old peaked cap cover, from his balding head and wiped away the sweat. The stokehold thermometer read 122° F. He couldn't wait to get his squat flabby body under a shower. A rush of air from the engineroom airlock announced his relief. He grinned gratefully when Larry Treen strolled in towards him.

"Boy, am I glad to see you Larry."

"Hi Eddie, what's up?"

"Low pressure on the fuel-oil filters," Wainwright told him. "I was just about to change them over. That'll be the third time on this watch. We must've sucked up all kinds of crud from the settling tank that we're running on at the moment. It'll probably be changed over in a little while anyway. Hopefully, that'll resolve our problem."

He removed his beret to wipe his head again. "Whew! Am I glad to get out of here? One fire all round, except D3, of course. I would've had it boxed up but our floater was too busy to come and sight it."

"Ok Eddie. Piss off and have a cold one."

"Right Larry. By the way, we're sailing at six a.m."

"Bloody great! I'm to be hauled out my cart again for a ten-minute standby."

He watched Wainwright leave. The boiler room ratings were relieved and one was assigned to change over and clean the dirty filter. The stokehold filled with the roar of rushing steam when the walking second stepped through the airlock from the engineroom. He edged along the after end gazing up at the smoke glasses on each boiler in turn. Noticing that burner unit for D3 was still out on the floorplates he sought out Larry Treen who was supervising the tube blowing operation on B3

Boiler. MacKay spoke to him. Treen made a sign that he couldn't understand. He yelled up at the fireman on the second catwalk and the tumult of steam died away. "That's better, what were you saying Mister MacKay?"

"I want to know why D3 Boiler isn't boxed up yet."

"Dunno Sec," replied Treen. "Mister Wainwright said that he couldn't get anybody to sight it. He should've done that job himself anyway because it's his boiler."

"I don't give a damn whose boiler it is," growled MacKay. "Just because the eight-to-twelve cleans and maintains the port side and we do the same with the mid-section, every boiler affects the running of the whole bloody ship! So let's start getting that bloody boiler on line."

"Ok Sec."

The second stormed forward.

Treen phoned through for the floater. A few minutes later he breezed in. "Whit's up?"

"Hi Gus. Big John wants the furnace front put back in on D3, toot sweet. Nip inside the furnace and make sure there's no rags, tools, or any other crap there."

"Ok Larry." He walked between B3 and E3 towards the port side then aft to D3. An electrical extension cord supplied light through the furnace opening. Raising his hands in the manner of a swimming dive permitted his shoulders to pass easily through the narrow port. The wall had been repaired and the bricklayers had made sure that the furnace floor was free of debris. He came back to the console to report to Treen.

"That's fine Gus," said Larry. "Take . . ."

Oscar Davis swayed into sight, an ominous bulge tucked under the armpit of his coveralls. "Gonna changesh over shettlin' tanksh," he slurred through a cloud of rum vapour.

"Jesus! Scar, if MacKay catches you stoned again, you'll be for the high jump."

The fuel-oil engineer leered and stroked the side of his nose. "He won't catch me again, Treenie boy. Old Shcar's got a perfect hidey hole."

He staggered out of sight, changed over settling tanks and went to D3 boiler. He entered the boiler in much the same manner as Angus - just in time for Everton to catch sight of his legs disappearing inside the furnace.

Brian Halliday, the fireman who was supposed to be watching the water levels for the port boiler, should have seen Davis too, but he was half-dozing on his feet until the rush of air signalling the arrival of hot cocoa drew his attention to Charlie Everton and his welcome burden. Halliday lifted his mug from a nearby workbench and held it out. Everton filled it from the fanny of kye and continued to where the engineers were standing. He filled three mugs then served the other two ratings before disappearing aft.

Inside D3 boiler furnace Scar crawled over the length of the brick floor and sat down with his back to the after wall beside number one burner. He let go a sigh of relief and placed his forty-pounder of Bahamian Screech to his lips. The blast from the forced draught fans was lovely and cool. He took another slug before stuffing the cork back in his bottle. Sighing again he leaned his head against the brickwork and dozed off. His grip relaxed on the bottle. It rolled across the smooth floor and came to rest in the centre of the furnace.

Larry swallowed the dregs of his cocoa and wiped his lips. "Right Gus, let's get this show on the road. Grab a couple of my strongos to lift that burner assembly in place. I'm going circulate the fuel-oil header."

The extension cord and light was hauled out of the furnace and soon the burner assembly was in place and aligned. When the retaining nuts were tightened and the oil supply hose reconnected, he reported back to Larry at the console. Halliday was ordered to get a torch. Treen was satisfied that the circulating oil was at ambient temperature. "We might as well check this burner out to see if there are any leaks."

"Ah noticed that there's only an inch o' water in this biler's gauge glass," said Angus, watching fireman-trimmer bringing a torch and a bucket of paraffin.

"Trying to tell your granny how to suck eggs?" scoffed the stokehold engineer. He nodded to the rating standing ready to ignite a torch with his Zippo lighter.

"Flash off Number Seven."

Halliday lit the torch and threw over the fuel-oil supply cock lever for the burner. He opened the inspection plate, shoved the fiery brand into the furnace, and opened the burner supply valve on the fuel-oil manifold. When the burner fired he withdrew the torch and slapped the inspection plate shut before quenching the flame.

He saw a little boy below him as he glided through a clear blue sky. It was a hot day and the sun was blazing down. He squinted up at the blazing orb. It seemed to be getting nearer and nearer. The little boy's skin was bright pink from sunburn. It must have been sore. It was sore, he recalled, pure agony and his skin was all blistered for days and days. He'd never felt such pain - until *now*!

Davis opened his eyes and hastily lifted his hands against the searing glare. Just a few feet away flames from the burner farthest from him bathed the furnace in brilliant light. His skin was reddening from the tremendous heat. He was being roasted alive! He screamed . . .

"Tell Mister King why you lit the fire that way Brian," prompted Larry.

"So I don't get a flashback," said the rating.

"Right. It's good practice to get into, Gus. You see, not all stokeholds are pressurised like this one. So there's - what was that?" He cocked his head in response to an unusual sound.

"Whit was whit?"

"I thought I heard something," replied Larry. "Like a distant squeal or scream. I hope my FD fan shaft bearings are ok." He nodded to Halliday. "Ok Brian, flash up Number Four."

The rating flashed off the centre burner. Treen followed Angus towards the after end of the boiler. "You mentioned the water level a few minutes ago Gus," said Larry. "If you keep an eye on the water gauge, you'll soon see the level rising as the water expands with the heat."

Seeing that the centre fire was burning successfully Treen decided to check that the repaired furnace wall was still ok. He slid open the inspection plate for Number One Burner.

"*Help me*! *Help me*!" shouted Davis.

Just then the heat from the centre fire caused the rum bottle to explode. Davis was instantly enveloped in blue flame, some of which escaped through the inspection plate orifice. Treen's reaction was immediate. Startled he drew his face away and tried to stand erect at the same time. The crown of his head smacked against a valve wheel knocking him out.

Inside the furnace Davis was doing a macabre dance in agony, twirling and birling, until he waltzed into the flames of the centre fire to be completely consumed.

Halliday was quenching his torch when he noticed Treen laying on the floorplates. "Mister King!"

Angus rushed over and knelt down to examine his friend. There was a growing lump on the top of Treen's head but little blood. "Just knocked oot," he surmised, just as the telegraph bell on the console sounded. 'Mustn't panic,' he muttered to himself. He gazed up at Halliday and beheld the rating's burly frame. "Brian, dae ye think that ye can gie Mister Treen a fireman's lift up tae the hospital?"

"Sure thing," was the breezy reply, and stooping down, the rating swept the unconscious man across his ample shoulders. He headed for the engineroom airlock. Angus led the way to open the door for him before rushing back to the console to press the acknowledgement button below the telegraph. The phone buzzer went. "Number Three."

"Gus," said Jake. "Where's La Treen?"

"He's oan his way tae Sick Bay. He managed tae knock himsel' oot."

"Ok I'll try and get - uh - a hold of Big John and tell him," promised Jake. "Look, the bridge just called down - right? That weather front is coming in quicker than expected. We'll be moving as soon as they haul up the hook." The telegraph rang again. "Oops, here we go!"

"Hang oan a second!" he yelled down the receiver. "Whit dae Ah dae here?"

"Don't worry about it, Gus. It's easy. Slow means two fires on each boiler. Half means three, and Full is four fires all round. Gotta go!" and the phone went dead.

He glumly hung up the receiver and went to the front of the console. *Slow* jangled on the telegraph. He pressed the button to stop the clamour. He held up two fingers and the other two firemen scurried around igniting fires. He noticed the fuel-oil pressure dropping when the extra fires were lit. During the trip he'd watched other stokehold engineers manipulate the bypass valve located dead centre on the console desktop. He adjusted this valve until the fuel oil pressure gauges were at their original settings. *Half.* He held up three fingers, pressed the button and adjusted the oil pressure. He smiled. Jake was right. It *was* easy. *Full*, four all round.

The engineroom airlock gushed aggressively and Eddie Wainwright barrelled in. He was decked out in tropical whites. Halliday followed in his wake. Eddie swept right up to the console, elbowed Angus aside and started spinning four small handwheels on the console desktop. "Where in the hell's Treenie?" he thundered, dialling up the amperage so that the needles were soaring on four gauges. The forced draught fans began speeding up and eardrums could sense the rapidly increasing air pressure in the boiler room.

"Larry had a wee accident," he shouted over the increasing noise. "He's up in the hospital."

"Huh - that's no excuse. Scar Davis could've taken over for half-an-hour or so."

"Weel, Ah did the best Ah could under the circumstances."

Eddie just shook his head but calmed down after a few moments when everything was copasetic. He turned and faced him. "I'm leaning against the ship's rail, enjoying the cool night air and suddenly, there's white water at the arse end. Then I get a whiff of pork roasting. And pretty soon there are big gobs of black shite floating gently down on my whites and I wonder: 'What the hell is going on?'"

He pointed to the greasy ebon smears on his freshly laundered jacket for emphasis. "So as I wonder where might this crap be coming from. I looks up at the after funnel to see thick black smoke trickling over its rim and dribbling down the outer casing like bloody treacle!"

One of Morgan's firemen came through and handed a note to Angus. "When full away rings doon, go tae seven fires a' roond," the Scot read off. "An' get D3 boiler oan line ASAP."

"Old Taff writes with a Scotch accent, does he?" gibed Wainwright. "I know I shouldn't ask this but what state of readiness is D3 in right now?"

"There's twa fires oan an' the steam pressure is fifty pound."

"Is its stop open?"

Angus shrugged not knowing what a stop was. Eddie shook his head again and went to check for himself. He ordered one of the ratings to flash up another couple of fires. He gave Angus a shout to get his attention and beckoned him by crooking his finger. He answered the summons. Wainwright observed steam gushing out a drain line. He closed the valve and pointed upwards. "D'you see the big valve above this little un?" The floater nodded. "That's the boiler stop valve. Get your arse up there and open it full."

While he complied the telegraph double rang *Full* and MacKay entered the stokehold. He took stock of the situation immediately. With all fires lit and the fuel-oil and stokehold air pressures stabilized Wainwright was ready to go topside, providing the second would sanction it. MacKay only had one question: "Where in the hell is Davis?"

Both his juniors shrugged.

MacKay pondered for a moment. "Ok Mister Wainwright, you can go topside now. Mister King and I will look after things now that we're full away." He ambled off to check the flue sight glasses.

“Well - good luck kid,” grinned Eddie. “Better you than me. Boy, I’m feeling a bit peckish. I’m going into the mess and see if I can get the night steward to rustle up some roast pork sandwiches for me.”

After he left the walking second instructed Angus on how to put a boiler on line. By the time they had finished that task the bilgediver had came by carrying a fanny of coffee.

“Everton,” said MacKay. “By any chance have you seen Mister Davis recently?”

“I saw somebody climbing into D3 when I first came through with the cocoa Mister MacKay,” he replied. “It must have been Mister Davis inspecting it I guess.”

“Ah inspected the biler,” said the floater. “It must’ve been me that ye saw climbin’ in.”

Everton vigorously shook his head. “No Mister King, if you recall, you were here by the console with Mister Treen when I poured out your kye. See look, Mister Davis’ mug still there. It looks like he never touched it because it’s still full.”

The engineers’ eyes met as if mutely questioning each other. “You don’t suppose . . ? The second hesitated. “No, there must be another explanation.”

He paced up and down, his face drawn in thought. “Mister King, everything seems to have settled down for the moment. I’m leaving you to look after things while I go topside to check on Mister Treen.”

He was back presently, his face quite ashen.

“How’s Mister Treen daein’ Mister MacKay?”

“He’s - eh - he’s all right,” the second replied absently. “He’ll be able to stand his next afternoon watch. In the meantime I’ll have to make a few personnel changes.”

“Whit dae ye mean Mister MacKay?’

The second related Treen's awful experience.

The young engineer slumped against the console, horror marring his face. 'Cremated alive,' he shuddered and all but puked.

The second laid a hand gently on his shoulder. "Just look at it as another lesson in life son," he said. "Mister Treen told me that Davis was sozzled. If you must drink, make sure you do it with moderation."

At the end of the watch Angus went to the hospital to see Treen but he'd already gone.

He found him sitting in the mess staring morosely into a cup of milky-white tea. His head had a miniature tonsure with a round Band-Aid stuck in its centre. Angus occupied a seat directly opposite, lifted a pewter teapot and filled up a cup. The smoky aroma of Scotch drifted his way.

"It all happened in less than a second Gus," slurred Larry. "But every time I close my eyes it seems that it lasts for hours and hours."

"Whit did ye see Larry?"

"Scar was trying to squeeze past the burner screaming for help when I heard a loud pop. It must have been his rum bottle exploding because shards of glass were hitting his body and face. Almost instantly he was enveloped in blue flame. The blood from his wounds was congealing to light brown. Y'know, like the way a steak goes after a few minutes in a hot frying pan. Some of that blue flame blew out the inspection hole. When I felt the sudden heat I jumped up and hit my nut of that valve. Christ, it's sore!"

He gently touched the wound. "It all happened in less than half a second yet that memory will stay with me as long as I live." He pushed back his chair and stood up. "I'm going for another few snorts. Maybe it'll help me get a couple of hours zizz without dreaming," he said, without much conviction.

"Hey, Gus!" It was Jake calling from the next table. "Our steward has done himself proud tonight. Look! Roast pork sarnies instead of the usual spam and cheese. You'd better grab a couple quick before they're all gone." Biting into one he gestured at the laden tray.

Most of the watch Christie, Steamboat, MacAdam, Morgan, Sudbury, Benson, Hedges, and electricians, Berwick, Danforth, and Armstrong, were devouring the sandwiches with relish - and mustard - and HP sauce - and ketchup - and sliced onion . . .

Angus shuddered recalling Eddie Wainwright's remark about smelling pork being roasted. He decided that he wasn't hungry after all. He knew it wouldn't take long for the grapevine to do its work. Tomorrow morning he'd tell Betty that her suspect was no longer aboard or wouldn't be after they blew tubes on the eight-to-twelve tonight.

The East Coasters

0915 Thursday

Although it had been a short turnaround in New York DS Stevenson had managed to gather a lot of evidence from Oscar Davis' cabin. It was sent off in the diplomatic pouch for Scotland Yard. The next afternoon she met Angus coming from the mess and together they went to his cabin. Inside they embraced momentarily. Betty was excited, but to his chagrin, not by sex. "I'm a lot closer to solving our mystery," she bubbled. "Did you know that Oscar Davis doodled?"

"After a month oan this ship hen," he said laconically. "Nuthin' surprises me."

"What do you mean?"

"Al Somers, one o' our electricians, has a pet alligator in his cabin. Then there's Archie MacAdam - he's got a talkin' parrot for a pet. The funny thing is - the damn thing's deaf - an' only Archie kens."

"Then how do you know it's deaf?"

"Wait till Ah tell whit some o' the ither engineers have been daein'," he grinned. "It seems that the parrot learned tae talk afore it went deaf. Although it could repeat a few phrases, its favourite was "Come awa' the 'Gers!"

"So?"

"Well, every time Archie went on watch some o' his pals would sneak intae his cabin an' say - pardon my French - 'Fuck the Gers!' ower an' ower again, hopin' it'll repeat it."

Betty laughed and asked, "So how did you find out the parrot was deaf?"

“Weel, Archie borrowed a few bottles of beer aff me the ither day an’ last night I bumped intae him just ootside his cabin. He invited me in tae gie me my beers back. They were on his tallboy proppin’ up a steel tray. When Ah lifted the bottles awa’ the tray drapped wi’ a clatter right behind the parrot. It never even batted an eye. It was then that Archie swore me tae secrecy because he knew whit the ither engineers were tryin’ tae dae.”

“That sure is funny Angus,” giggled Betty. “I guess if one is at sea long enough you could go nuts.”

He touched her thigh. “Talking aboot nuts . . .”

She reluctantly pushed his hand away and opened a folder that she’d brought with her. The first page of standard letter size paper had a few doodles on it. A couple of them were more like sketches than doodles. His eyes widened at the enormity of those pencilled abstracts. One showed a likeness of a man and woman copulating in missionary position. Both were naked. The other sketch was similar but this time a knife protruded from the man’s back. The memory of his first night out came rushing back.

The next page had some geometric designs comparable to those on the dirk’s hilt. The third sheet displayed a man with a dagger above his head as if ready to plunge it down into something. There were two insets attached to this sketch. One was a vague likeness of Oscar Davis, the other Homer Davison. Other pages had many manifestations of imaginative or mythological creatures. The final one depicted a fire-breathing dragon incinerating a likeness of Oscar Davis.

“Jings! These are scary.”

“Yes,” she agreed. “The shrinks will have a field day with this one. We can safely say that both father and son shared in the murder." She flipped back to the second page and handed it to him along with a photo of the murder weapon.

"There's nae doobt here Betty," breathed Angus. "The designs are awfy close. Noo, whit are ye gaun tae dae?"

"Well, since one of the suspects is dead and the other could be anywhere," began Betty moving over to squirm on his lap. "I think that I'll just take advantage of the remainder of this cruise."

He put his arms around her and smiled. "Tae quote my Canadian pal, 'Ye got that right!'"

0035 Saturday

Chin in hands, the floater slouched against the second's desk half-listening to Black Bob's sagas about the Indian Ocean. Wisps of steam bled sighs of relief from the main engines after their lengthy jaunt from Nassau. Only the hum of running pumps could be discerned in the engineroom.

'One does not listen to units running normal' the second had taught him so that his ears had become attuned accordingly. The bridge phone's raucous blast disturbed the harmony.

"Engineroom," intoned Angus.

"Please get ready for a movement on the port engine. The tide is turning and we wish to swing the ship round on the anchor."

"Ok," he replied and hung up. "They want tae swing her roond oan the hook Bob."

"Fine Angus, I'll warn the stokeholds."

King went to the port manoeuvring wheels just as the telegraph needle swept to *Dead Slow* astern. The order was acknowledged and the astern wheel was spun open. The slumbering turbines awoke with protests of fluffy clouds of steam erupting from their glands. A mighty roar persisted for a time until *Stop* jangled and peace was resumed. "We're in position now, thank you," a disembodied voice from the bridge phone told him.

"Ok."

"By the way, a small oiler will alongside in about ten minutes. We'll be sailing for Cherbourg as soon as we have refuelled."

"Ok," he repeated and passed the message to Christie.

The hollow sounds of feet clumping up a ladder warned of Jake's hurried appearance on the platform. "What's going on?" he asked breathlessly. "I heard the engines turn over."

"We're docking at Pier 92," said Christie sarcastically.

"But we're in Halifax! Right?"

The second sneered, "By the time you took getting here we could've been in New York."

"Jeez! I was at the far end of the tunnel," lamented Jake.

Christie jeered. "What tunnel? The Lincoln Tunnel?"

The Canadian was in the process of retaliating when the walking second's head materialized at floorplate level. He crooked his finger. "Mister King?"

"Aye, Mister MacKay?"

"Come with me laddie. I've got a wee job for you."

He followed his descending senior. They ambled forward and took the elevator up to the working alleyway. Still going forward on C Deck, they kept walking until they reached an open shell door. Pete Eaton, the replacement fuel-oil engineer, was leaning out into the cold night air peering down at something. A spiral of hemp rope flew up which he caught and drew in the slack.

"Give him a hand," ordered MacKay.

He stepped behind Steamboat, grabbed the rope's end, and took the strain. Both men began to haul on a heavy object. Soon the brass maw of a six-inch diameter, wire-reinforced hose came into view. Gradually a black serpentine thing lay obscenely on the steel deck. Pete manhandled the hose end and awkwardly slipped it onto a fuel-oil tank inlet. A quick-witted Angus moved in to swing down and clamp home the dogs thus securing the hose, its tail anchored to the oiler. Grabbing a wheelkey Steamboat cranked open the valve that would allow the black fuel to charge the bunkers deep in the ship's bowels. He hailed a crewman on the small tanker. "Whenever you're ready!"

There was a pause before the heavy hose began leaping around as if in agony. The fuel-oil transfer had commenced. After a few fits and starts the hose died. "What's the matter?" MacKay yelled down to the oiler. Mutterings between the crewman and the pump operator drifted up through the frigid Canadian night air. The diagnosis relayed back to him implied that the pump's sexual capabilities had achieved complete climax prior to some dextrous ascent. He hollered down again. "Can you fix it?"

This time the middleman was left out and the negative reply, accompanied by even choicer Maritime phrases, was hailed directly to the walking second. He absorbed this information, and ruminating briefly, looked at his floater. "Jump down there and see if you can fix it for them Mister King."

"Ok Mister MacKay," was the keen reply. He leapt down onto the tanker's steel deck some four feet below.

His shoes contacted this new plane and his vertical momentum changed unexpectedly into lateral motion. He accelerated across the icy deck on his back past the astonished crewman. Presence of mind made him grab a rung on the weather-scarred handrail and prevented him from going over the oiler's outboard side.

"Hey buddy, why didn't you tell me that you were coming on board?" asked the Nova Scotian. "I coulda put a ladder up for yah."

"Ah didnae ken the deck was icy," gasped Angus, shivering from fright and cold. "It disnae look icy."

"Decks never do after freezing rain. Say, dontcha have a parka?"

"No," replied Angus. Having never before heard of the phenomenon asked, "Whit's freezin' rain?"

The crewman scratched the grey stubble on his chin. "It's just like ordinary rain when it's falling but as soon as it hits anything it freezes instantly. It's practically impossible to see in the dark but I guess you know by now that it can be a pain in the ass at times."

"Ye can say that again pal!" was the response and he ruefully rubbed his posterior. He shivered again. "Where's this pump that's givin' us a' the trouble?"

"Come with me."

The Canuck swung open a nearby hatch that emitted blesséd heat. The engineer was shown down a ladder into a tiny machinery space. The vessel's propulsion unit was a Cummins diesel motor not much larger that the *Dalriada*'s emergency engine. About three times bigger than a washing machine, the oiler's auxiliary boiler stood next to the engine.

"Is that your jenny system?" he queried, jerking a thumb at the Cummins.

"What generator? That's the main engine!"

"Oh, sorry!" he gasped. "Eh, where's the pump?"

"This's it," replied the fellow, slapping a hand on what seemed to be the world's most archaic pump.

"Are ye the Second Engineer?" asked Angus, his head craning from side to side trying to grasp a better understanding of the pump.

"Yeah," said the Canadian. "I'm the Second, the Third and the Fourth. The name's MacLean. Jim MacLean."

"Angus King. Whit's wrang wi' your pump?"

An exasperated reply was not long in coming. "Damned if I know Scotty! I'm just a goddam car mechanic trying to make an extra buck by moonlighting. I know sweet FA about pumps!"

"Weel, let the dog see the bone," said Angus, crouching down. "It's just a simple reciprocatin' pump. A bit weird maybe but it shouldnae be too hard tae get gaun again."

The steam pump's supply valve was opened to reward him with a vaporous fart from the piston rod gland. Otherwise it ignored him completely. Closing the valve again, he mulled over the pump's elaborate linkage. "There seems tae be somethin' missin'."

"Is that right?" rasped MacLean. "Have you worked on this type of pump before?"

"No, but Ah'm willin' tae bet that its very first job was pumpin' birdshit an' elephant pish."

"Eh?"

"I think this pump began its life oan the Ark."

"Smart ass! Can you fix it it?"

"Maybe," he replied absently. "Ah-ha!" came a triumphant cry. He picked up a strip of soft red rubber. It was badly deteriorated. His eyes fell on a section of truck tyre inner tubing hanging nearby. "Have ye got a knife oan ye?"

"Sure - here."

"Ta," he said and trimmed away a cross-sectional slice of tubing. "This is the missin' link." He stretched the oversized rubber band and coupled a trigger to a hook then restarted the pump. With a smooth motion the piston hissed up and down and soon bunker C was being transferred to the great liner.

"Gee, that's swell Angus. Would you like a beer?"

"No thanks Jim. Ah'd better get back tae the ship. Could ye maybe arrange tae get a ladder for me?"

"No problem."

MacKay watched him clamber over the sill of the shell door. "Well done lad!" he lauded the junior. The supply hose pulsed rhythmically. "What was it?"

Angus chuckled. "The rubber band broke!"

The second frowned. "Don't get flippant with me Mister! I asked you a civil question."

"Ah'm no' kiddin' Mister MacKay!" he objected. "The shuttle valve's operated wi' a bit o' kahoochie!"

"Is that right? Jeez! What a way to run an outfit. Come out of the cold and we'll have some hot kye."

He'd just finished his cocoa and was about to light up when the phone rang. "That pump's conked out again. Nip back down onto the oiler and get it going. Stay there and keep it going or we'll be here till hell freezes over. And that won't take long in these latitudes."

The floater boarded without the earlier gymnastics. He found MacLean thrashing angrily away at the pump with a light hammer. "Noo whit's wrong?"

"Darned if I know!" yelled MacLean. "The damned thing just stopped suddenly. The rubber band is ok."

"Dae ye hae a Monday hammer?"

"What the blazes is a Monday hammer?"

"A sledgehammer."

"Oh yeah, there's one right here somewhere," said MacLean. "But take it real easy, I don't want the pump to get completely smashed."

"Dinnae fash yersel' man," he soothed, minutely inspecting the shuttle valve casing. Brushing away some rust revealed a faint x etched on the metal. "A wee tap right . . . there! Ah! There she goes."

The piston rod glided smoothly up and down as if nothing had happened. MacLean was flabbergasted. "How in the hell did you manage that? I've been pounding at that damned thing without any success."

"Ah, but ye only used a toffee hammer," the floater explained, knowingly.

"But you barely rapped with the sledge."

"That wisnae a wee tap," replied King, well versed in the psychology of stubborn pumps. "That was a big threat!"

"Anyway," sighed MacLean. "At least you got the damned thing running again. Are you going back to the ship?"

"No. My Second has ordered me tae stay here until we've finished bunkerin'."

"Fancy a beer?"

"Aye sure."

He was taken to a small cabin aft and slightly above the engineroom. There was barely space for the twin double-tiered bunks inside. "Sit up there Angus," MacLean directed. "That's my bunk. I'll get the beer."

He knelt down and opened a plastic box, which was on the deck between the heads of the bunks. He withdrew a couple of beer bottles from their nest of melting ice. The visitor took in the rude decor of the cabin. His eyes settled on a prone shape on the opposite lower bunk.

"Who's he?"

MacLean glanced back at the unconscious figure and said, "The Chief Engineer."

"He looks dead tae the world. Is he sick?"

"Yeah. You could say that," replied MacLean. "He's got the forty-ounce flu." The Scot caught his drift and accepted the newly opened beer bottle. His patron hopped up beside him. "How's the beer?"

"It's really guid," he said, noting the white schooner on the label.

The door swung open and a slovenly dressed man entered the cabin. He nodded a silent greeting and clambered up onto the bunk above the chief. The dark shifty eyes on the newcomer's swarthy face were noted. "Angus, this is Kip. Kip, this is Angus. He fixed our pump."

"Hi," said Angus.

Kip grunted.

"I meant to ask you something Angus," said MacLean. "Why do you call a sledge, a Monday hammer?"

"Because if ye swing it a' day oan Monday, ye're buggered for the rest o' the week!"

"I see."

"Maybe ye could tell me somethin' Jim. How did ye get a marine engineer's berth when ye said that ye were just a motor mechanic?"

"I was the only one who knew about Cummins' engines. I work in a little garage just off Jubilee Road and things tend to get slack at this time of the year. Before that I repaired bulldozer engines and other earthmoving equipment. When this job fell into my lap I decided to do a little moonlighting. I need extra money so that I can buy a scuba outfit."

"Scuba? Ah didnae think that ye would've had much opportunity for divin' - wi' the sort of weather that ye get aroond here, I mean." He reflected for a moment. "Unless ye plan tae go tae Sable Island. Ah'm in the middle o' a book right noo aboot a' the shipwrecks a' alang yon coast."

Jim grinned. "Well, I do plan to dive for treasure right enough but not where you'd expect." He elaborated after asking him if he'd ever visited the City of Halifax during winter. Nodding his head Angus recollected his first shore leave in that port. "Well, every year after a big snowstorm hits us, the city's snowploughs shove the snow all the way down to the docks and dump it in the harbour. Each spring the city has to replace all the parking meters that were ripped out. I figure that an enterprising guy like me could dive down into the harbour and bust them open for all the pennies, nickels, and dimes. I'm betting that there's quite a few grand down there in coins."

"That's a rare idea. Guid luck tae ye."

The crewman that he had met initially entered the cabin and was introduced as 'Curly'. Curly passed the message that his boss wanted to talk to him. Angus went back on deck.

"Can that pump be bypassed?" MacKay bellowed.

"Aye," he said. "Ah noticed a bypass valve when Ah was fixin' the pump. Why, whit's wrang?"

"We've been loading for half-an-hour now and took on about forty tons. We'll be here until Doomsday at this rate. Open that bypass valve. Mister Eaton has tied in the two big Carruthers transfer pumps to the suction line. They'll shift that oil in no time at all."

"Ok. Ah'll open the valve."

"Right Mister King. Stay there in case I need you again."

He changed over the appropriate valves and a deep rushing sound could be heard from the pipe as the liner's massive pumps began drawing oil aboard in large quantities. Satisfied all was well, he went back to the tiny cabin. Jim revealed some interesting facts about the closemouthed Kip. Some months previously he had lent money to an acquaintance with the understanding that the debt would be honoured the following week. The debtor reneged and consequently Kip, who needed money badly at the time, became perturbed and struck the fellow a couple of times (according to Kip). When interviewed in hospital by the Mounties the man put the finger, the only part of his body that could be painlessly moved, on him. Word drifting along the grapevine prompted him to sign on. He'd been there ever since.

"Is this whit is known as 'bein' oan the lam'?"

The fugitive scratched his nether regions absently, nodding.

"You'll notice that Kip scratches frequently."

"Aye, now that ye mention it," admitted Angus observing a gnarled hand creep under Kip's left armpit searching for some minute antagonist. "Dae ye hae hives Kip?"

He shook his head. A gleam of triumph lit his face momentarily to be quenched to sullenness as he glared at the translucent tormentor trapped between his thumb and forefinger. With a word he stretched out his arm so that Angus could see the irritant. Two tiny pincers clawed the air in vain.

"Holy shite - crabs!"

The chief engineer snuffled, rolled on his back, and began to snore loudly. Kip withdrew his hand, studied the bloodsucker, peered down at the slumbering engineer, and gazed at his tormentor again. A yellow toothed grin spilt his face and he dropped the tiny louse onto the chief's body. Kip's face regained composure.

"Man, ye should get yersel' intae a bath o' hot water wi' a gallon or twa o' Dettol in it," Angus advised him. "That'll shift yon bastards."

"This scow doesn't have the facilities for Kip to have a bath or a shower," explained MacLean. "The best that he can do is sponge off in a bucket of water that's been heated by a steam drain. He can't go ashore," he reminded him. "The Mounties'll grab him."

"Man, Ah'd raither let the polis put me in jail than stay wi' yon parasites." Revulsion made him shiver.

Kip disagreed, his head lolling from side to side while his fingers sought another host near his scrotum. This most recent capture was given new accommodation aboard the chief's body.

A bottle of *Moosehead* and two parasitic emigrations later the chief's mouth emitted sucking chirrups when he turned over on his side. His new hosts seemed to be whetting their appetites. He scratched instinctively and squirmed over onto his side leaving the cabin in blesséd silence.

The rest of his watch was enjoyable and educational. MacLean's anecdotes about Canada, particularly Nova Scotia, were both amusing and informative. Kip actually spoke and gave a personal insight, although bias view of the Canadian penal system. MacLean was telling him about the SS *Mont Blanc*, an ammunition ship that blew up Halifax Harbour during World War One and killed thousands of Haligonians, when a faint call was heard.

It was Big John.

When he went on deck, Angus noticed that the second was now slightly above him. The liner had gained in draught while the oiler had risen quite a few feet due to the fuel-oil transfer. “We’re well on our way to being topped up,” announced MacKay. “You can come back on board now, I’ve told your relief to come through here.” And disappeared inboard.

MacLean beckoned the young engineer from the bottom of the hatch and nimbly he descended. “Here,” said the Canadian, offering a bunch of multicoloured banknotes.

“Whit’s that for?”

“That’s for you - for helping us to unload.”

“Ah dinnae want it! Ah’m just daein’ my job.”

“Look Angus,” persisted MacLean. “If we weren’t able to refuel your ship, another oiler would’ve done it and our bonus would’ve been lost - right? So take it.”

He was given an emphatic no. MacLean was disappointed, and then, he brightened. “Kip, bring that bottle you’ve been hoarding.” Kip displayed a bottle before wrapping it in an oil wiper. MacLean reached over and handed it to him. “Here take this,” he said. “Look on it not only as a token of our appreciation, but as a Canadian souvenir as well.”

“Well if ye put it like that. Whit is it? “

”Newfie Screech,” grinned MacLean. “Just go easy with it. It’s pretty potent.”

“A’ right Jim,” he thanked him and stuffed the prize inside his boilersuit. “Ah’ve a Canadian pal oan board who’ll really appreciate this.”

“Have a safe trip Angus. See you around maybe.”

They shook hands and he climbed aboard the liner where The Sphere stood, his rotund frame shivering in the chilly air. “Guid job Sphere,” he said. “Dinnae bother gaun doon there.

Just hang aroond an' wait until Steamboat's relief shows up. Find a warm spot somewhere."

"Jeez Gus, you don't have to tell me twice. Here," he said, tapping the bulge in his boilersuit. "What's that?"

"Just some Canadian gratuity."

"Mm - liquid no doubt?"

Angus beamed. "Ye got that right!"

Jake wasn't in his cabin so he went out onto the landing above Boat Deck. Across the bay the shadowy snow-covered hills of Nova Scotia beckoned. The sky was jet-black and studded with glittering stars. They seemed so close. Some unknown engineer must've had an overheated cabin or perhaps he was just getting rid of cigarette smoke. In any case somewhere near, a porthole had been cracked open and Glenn Miller's rendition of *The Story of a Starry Night* drifted out, a fitting accompaniment to the cold clear night. A breath of Arctic air told him that a thin patrol suit was not the attire for the open deck so he went back inside.

He rattled White's cabin door again and peeped in. The Canadian was flipping pages on a thumb-worn copy of *Reveille*. "Hey Jake, whit dae ye mix with Newfie Screech?"

"I just happen to have a few Pepsis here. A ready mix so to speak, right? Now how did you manage to - uh - lay your grubby Scotch hands on this stuff?" he asked, freeing the bottle from its ragged cocoon. He listened to his friend's adventure while rinsing out a couple of tumblers. He opened the bottle and sniffed it, his face in rapture like some connoisseur discovering the ultimate wine. By the time a couple of snorts had slid down their throats the storekeeper announced standby. King wondered if he'd be able to see the telegraph face because his eyes were watering like a golden eagle's in a vertical high dive. Jake slurped down the remainder of his drink.

The telegraph's glazed face stared back at him. The green indicator suddenly swung to Half Ahead spurred by the clamour of bells. Angus reached out to answer the jangling summons but a red-hot stab of pain redirected his hand to a sensitive part of his anatomy.

"Answer the bloody thing and stop clawing at your balls!" The indelicate command bellowed across the platform from the chief engineer.

"Ooh!" groaned the floater, shifting the handle. He opened the ahead manoeuvring valve with his left hand, his right still seeking relief in his nether regions.

"Jesus Christ!" blasphemed Lindsey. He turned to Slack Jack. "I don't know about these youngsters nowadays. They come on board with their cocks in their hands; they run down the gangways with their cocks in their hands, and now here's one driving with his cock in his hand! I really don't know what the Merchant Navy is coming to these days."

The painful itch eased momentarily but when he reached to acknowledge the latest movement, the scourge returned with a vengeance. He clasped his private parts for a second time. Slack Jack answered the telegraph. "What's wrong with you young feller? Have you got crabs or something?"

Understanding glimmered in his eyes until another biting torment nearly dispersed that thought. The wiper that hid the bottle must have come from Kip's bunk. It was probably infected with the parasites. He cursed the generosity of the Canadians. He glanced over to port manoeuvring wheels. Jake was in stitches with laughter. Angus muttered obscene oaths and fervently hoped for a short standby. His wish was granted although it seemed that an eon was to pass before the telegraphs rang *Full Away*.

He galloped up the access ladder three stairs at a time. Tears welled in his eyes and he fidgeted impatiently inside the elevator bemoaning its lackadaisical progress to Sun Deck. Bursting into the first vacant bathroom he feverishly sloughed off his clothes. The hot shower's saltwater spray brought instant relief. He plugged the drain and after a while sat down in the bath to soak. Half an hour later he rushed wet and naked towards his cabin.

The timing was uncanny. An instant before he turned a corner an engineer stuck his head into the passageway and signalled the all clear before ushering three stewardesses from his cabin. Trills of surprise and delight escaped from their lips as the naked Scotsman ran slap-dab into them.

"Ooh," cooed one of the women. "It's Eric the Red."

"Perhaps he's Irish. Peter O'Toole maybe."

"His beacon is red too!" giggled another.

"Who wants to play pin the tail on the donkey?"

"He's certainly hung like one."

A woman began to whistle Rudolf Friml's *Donkey Serenade*.

"Brings a lump to your throat."

"Going in any direction."

"Jings! Lassies!" erupted from Angus, much, much too late.

With the discovery of his nationality, witty ripostes and comments flew fast and furious as the women surrounded him. "Donald, where's your troosers?"

"I can see your sporran, where's your kilt?"

"I thought that Scots had tartan bagpipes."

"Cock of the North is pointing south."

"Let's see you toss your caber."

"Is that a haggis basher?"

"Red is the colour of my true love's hair."

He drew his threadbare cloak of dripping dignity about him, squeezed between two stewardesses who gasped in pleasure, and stalked off up the passageway.

A parting shot came just before he turned the next corner: "See Isabel, there goes another Scotsman who rolls his R's!"

Inside his cabin he donned a bathrobe, collected a bar of soap, scrubbing brush, and a plastic bag. Checking that the coast was clear he made his way back to the same bathroom and used freshwater to ruthlessly scrub down his body. Satisfied that the vermin were gone he began drying himself. He heard a sudden slam and rushing water from an adjacent bathroom and was mildly surprised that someone taking a bath in the predawn morning. Evidently his hasty ablution didn't count. He whistled a jaunty Highland melody and stuffed his soiled clothes into the plastic bag.

"Gus, is that you?"

"Jake?"

"You bastard!" The insult came loud and clear. "You rotten bastard! You can stick your Newfie Screech up your ass."

"Whit's eatin' ye?"

"Your blasted crabs are eating me!"

"Och, dinnae worry aboot them, their barks are no' as bad as their bites," his coarse laughter brought another stream of abuse from the other side of the bulkhead.

He took a quick look outside before turning in. The dark land had slid below the horizon and the liner's boiling wake churned up the black ocean. She was still working up to maximum revolutions. Homeward bound he reflected with a yawn and went back inside.

The Last Drop

Sunday, 7th January, 1962

On the second night out of Halifax, thick fog slumped over the liner like a wad of cotton wool. Angus and Jake had been in the wardroom for almost a couple of hours when the first reverberant blast came from one of the ship's whistles. Eyes swept around the room seeking that look of dismay. Archie MacAdam's drinking arm froze in midair as he glumly realized his name was next on the fog standby roster. He sighed and placed his tankard the bar.

The foghorn blew again.

MacAdam shook his head, stood up and headed towards the door where he stopped to look at his watch. There were only eight minutes left until the watch changed over. By the time he got to the engineroom his relief from the four-to-eight would be there. It wasn't worthwhile going below. He cackled with glee and ordered another beer.

The platform desk was being subjected to its usual burden, the weight of the current watchkeeper. This time it was Angus. Jake could be seen bobbing amongst the turbines and gearboxes on the eternal quest of reading bearing temperatures. Christie was mumbling something about the saltwater evaporators when he vanished behind the starboard condenser.

Everything was running smoothly although the engineroom telegraphs were still on standby reminding him that it was still foggy outside. The Mekon glanced up from his *Beano* at the clock. His sigh transformed into a yawn. "Two-an'-a-half hours yet," confirmed Angus.

"Piss off!" snarled The Mekon, his bleary eyes trying to focus on Beryl the Peril.

The bridge phone rasped.

"Engineroom."

A torrent of incomprehensible words drowned out by a horrendous blast from one of the liner's three foghorns was the response. Minutes later the caller hung up leaving him no wiser to the content of the message. He answered another call, this time through the vessel's main switchboard to the phone in the supposedly soundproofed dovecot mounted behind the port air ejectors. "Engineroom."

Again, the ship's foghorn drowned out the message. Shouting back that he couldn't understand what was being said it suddenly dawned on him that the racket was continuous instead of the intermittent cadence that normally sounded during periods of fog. "Whit whistle is it? Och, never mind. Ah'll be topside in a wee while."

After receiving permission to leave the engineroom he chose a handily sized wheelkey. He reached the working alleyway by way of the engineroom lift. Striding forward, he reached a wide companionway that led to R Deck Square. One of four elevators took him to Sun Deck where he could hear the continuous deafening drone from the ship's foghorn.

Still going forward he entered the bridge officers' quarters and up into the darkened wheelhouse. Up here the racket was much worse. A red light's glow silhouetted the quartermaster at the helm. The shadow of officer-of-the watch moved to reveal the green glow of a shrouded radar screen. He stood close to him and yelled in his ear. The engineer nodded and opened the wheelhouse door. He stepped over the high coaming and ambled across the starboard wing of the bridge.

The single whistle on the after funnel was gloriously sending out an uninterrupted blast in lower bass A. Steam ballooned into the atmosphere enhancing the fog. The bridge electrician tried plugging the solenoid to no avail. The whistle steam had to be closed manually but there was no local shutoff. The isolation valve was located down below in 3BR. Turning to retrace his steps he was confronted by an elderly gentleman in pyjamas and slippers. The doeskin jacket that he had donned as a cloak flaunted four bars of gold on each sleeve. The scrambled egg on his cap confirmed that he was indeed, Captain Cowell.

Authority had always made King feel nervous, and when nervous, he had an uncontrollable tendency to giggle. The fact that he couldn't understand any of the dialogue being shouted at him didn't help either. He just couldn't contain himself. This made the master even more upset. He appeared to do a soft-shoe shuffle or perhaps a little hornpipe right there on the misted deck. Jazz Johns' tap dance flashed into his mind. But what really broke him up were the captain's fluffy slippers, which emulated two cuddly puppies prancing under his feet. He beat a hasty retreat back through the wheelhouse.

He hurried along the starboard side of the passengers' suites on Sun Deck. He called for the elevator to carry him down to R Deck Square again. When the doors opened Hodgkin stepped out and tore into him about his state of dress in that area. The fourth mate threatened to report him to the captain. He just glared back at him, saying that the skipper already knew. This exchange of voices was loud enough to be heard over the whistle's sonorous blast. The heads of sleepy-eyed passengers popped out from their respective cabin doors. Disgusted, Angus entered the lift and jabbed the down button.

The doors opened on Main Deck allowing Davison and him to gape at each other in surprise. The murderer reacted first and slugged the engineer who managed to get to his feet by the time the elevator reached R Deck.

Angus was at a loss on what to do first. He wasn't hurt badly, and after all, his original objective was to isolate the after whistle. Upon his return to the engineroom he brought Christie up to date. The second told him that he would inform MacKay but in the meantime, he had to go into 3BR and shut off the steam supply to the foghorn. By time he got back Jake told him that an all-out search was going on topside.

When the elevator doors closed Davison went back to his stateroom. He stuffed a bottle of whisky and a blanket inside his holdall, donned a parka and went out onto Boat Deck.

Later that morning after some five hours sleep the young engineer was brooding at the ship's rail. Although the foggy was off, visibility was still bad. A heavy swell pushed the vessel both from aft and abeam so that she rolled, pitched, and yawed with disturbing frequency. The grey sea was spattered with white caps and the horizon had merged with low cloud.

A month and two days had sailed by since he'd signed on. He thought about his experiences so far - the good times and the bad. Some of the drinking binges had got out of hand though and he made up his mind so show more control. He took out a pack of cigarettes and placing one between his lips noticed that there was only three remaining. He'd opened that pack only last watch! Duty-free ciggies were encouraging him to smoke like a lum. They would have to be cut back too, he considered, replacing the cigarette in its tinfoil.

Betty came alongside him and slipped an arm around his waist. “A penny for your thoughts, Angus.”

“Hello Betty,” he said, a smile briefly lighting his face. “Och, Ah’m just thinkin’ that my first trip will be completed in a few days. An’ whit a voyage it’s been, an’ a’ the things that’s happened tae me durin’ that time,” he marvelled. “Have they nabbed Davison yet?”

She shook her head and held him tighter. “I must say it’s been quite different for me too. Now if we can capture him before we dock in Southampton it’ll be quite a feather in my cap. You’ve been a big help to me Angus and in more ways than one.”

“So Tilbury an’ his mob haven’t captured him yet eh? It makes ye wonder, does it no’? Ah mean, even though it’s a big ship, surely experienced personnel would ken every nook an’ cranny.”

“I’m sure they’ll get him Angus. Will I see after your watch?” she asked, giving him a peck on the cheek.

Before he could answer a slow handclap came from the landing above. It was Keyes. “I’d better be going Angus,” said Betty, and hurried away.

He plodded up the ladder to the leering Wheelkey. “Don’t ye ever sleep?”

He just grinned. “It’s all right for some.”

“Och, ye’re just jealous.”

“Damn right!”

The beckoning finger at the beginning of the noon to four watch gave the floater a feeling of foreboding. He crossed the platform to where the two seconds waited.

“Are you afraid of heights lad?” asked MacKay, waiting patiently for a reply that was slow in coming.

During the voyage the junior had been assigned more than a few tasks that one way or another got him into trouble. He'd climbed many a tree in his time and acrophobia had never affected him. So naively he shook his head.

"Good lad," beamed the walking second. "Have you got a heavy jacket? This was confirmed with a nod. "Well then laddie, I suggest you put another boilersuit on top of that one and get your jacket. Report to the deck engineer right away. You're going up in the world!"

A packing case confronted him when he entered the deckie's workshop, which was tucked away in a cross alley near midships on Boat Deck. The container was being split open by Lefty, a rating assigned to the Hotel Service engineers' gang. Standing end up, a round plate made of laminated spring-steel fitted snugly inside the narrow wooden crate. It was about two feet in diameter and perhaps an inch and quarter thick. It proved to be the spare diaphragm for the foghorn. It consisted of an alternating set of thin discs and rings all clamped together by a pre-tensioned bolt.

The deck engineer stepped away from a vise where he'd been filing a key. Mike Finney was a jovial fellow with blue eyes and cropped blonde hair. He was a bit taller and broader than Angus. His steady day job as deckie encompassed a host of equipment such as maintaining and repairing deck machinery; lifeboat engines, gym apparatus, valet service, washing machines; dryers, galley potato peelers, meat cutters, mincing machines, food mixers, egg timers, blenders, steam ovens, refrigerators, ice machines, and ship's whistles . . .

Three steering gear engineers, Alec Cameron, Jimmy Evans, and Teddy McBride came into the workshop. They only stood watch while the ship was leaving or entering port or in narrow waters. At sea they helped the deckie or air-conditioning engineers. Evans' arm was in a sling.

"Everybody know each other?" asked Finney, noting the affirming nods. "Well Angus, thanks for coming to help us. We've been pretty shorthanded lately and now it's even worse because Jimmy here tangled with the mechanical camel in the cabin class gym this morning. Now - he's not even able to fix our clockwork egg timers. You will remember to isolate the power before working on moving equipment next time, won't you Jimmy?"

Mike kicked the box containing the diaphragm. "This damned thing has to be changed this afternoon," he said. "Yes, I know, there are two working whistles on the forward funnel but our illustrious HSE blabbed to the skipper that we had another diaphragm in stock. So, no prizes for guessing what the skipper wanted him to do. I heard the Old Man is pissed at some engineer who was on his bridge last night so he's taking it out on the rest of us."

Angus wisely said nothing.

"Ok," said Finney kicking the box again. "This damn thing isn't going get up there by itself. Lefty, get a barrow or something and take it to the after funnel's base. Teddy and Gus grab that rope block and tackle and follow Lefty. I'll bring the handline and the rest of the tools. Alec, when you've finished that job down the cabin class galley, come and give us a hand."

The men were glad to unburden themselves of their load because it had been awkward transporting it all the way up to Sports Deck. There was about three hundred feet of rope reeved on the hickory pulleys. Lefty hand-rolled a cigarette and lit up. The four men gazed skywards. The top of the funnel swayed in slow motion against a grey background. According to a pamphlet on ship's trivia, a copy of which was supplied to passengers at the beginning of each trip, Number Two Funnel was sixty-seven feet six inches high. Angle-iron frames supported the foghorn and a section of catwalk just below the funnel rim.

It was cold on Sports Deck and a slight wind carried the flue gases off to port. A nearby Tannoy blared out *Morning* from Grieg's *Peer Gynt*. Finney checked his wristwatch. "Ok guys, it's lunchtime. What about you Gus?"

"No thanks Mike. Ah'd a big breakfast just a wee while ago."

"Well, do you want to sit in our workshop and read the Southern Echo? It's only about four weeks old."

"No thanks," he replied. "Ah'll ye whit. Ah'll take the hand line up an' take oot some o' the back cover bolts. Wi' a wee bitty luck Ah'll hae everythin' ready for ye when ye come back frae lunch."

Finney rubbed his chin dubiously. "I dunno Gus, will you be safe working by yourself? It moves around quite a bit up there, y'know."

"Och, Ah'll be a' right," he was assured. "As lang as Ah stay inside the rail, it'll be ok. Noo run awa' an' get some grub."

"Thanks Gus. I really appreciate your help. Let's go guys."

He watched them go. The hand line consisted of eighty feet of inch and three-quarter hemp. Ropes are measured by circumference. It was neatly coiled on the deck. Mike had brought a small grapnel too. He used one of his fishing knots to fasten the line to the grapnel's eye. The sheepskin parka and extra boilersuit that he was wearing was almost too bulky to get the coil of rope up his arm and over his head. Still, he managed after a bit of effort. He adjusted the rope so that the grapnel dangled over his back. Making sure that his trusty adjustable spanner was secure in his back pocket the floater put on his cotton cloves and started that long assent up the rusted steel ladder to the whistle platform.

The higher he rose the more the movement of the ship could be felt. At times he stopped to cling to the ladder, closing his eyes, and ponder that this might not be such a good idea after all. The strains of Franz von Suppé's *Poet and Peasant* eddied in the cold breeze. Not wanting to lose face he stoically kept ascending until his head was almost level with the catwalk.

The grapnel hooked onto a catwalk rung with a reassuring clunk. He unwound plenty of rope slack. The ship pitched and the momentum threatened to haul him off the ladder. It was a corkscrew motion that went into a ten-degree starboard roll. Uncomfortable at deck level it was much more alarming a hundred feet above the sea. He knew that looking downward would only make his predicament feel even worse but he couldn't help himself. Some force compelled to gaze down vertically into the sea. The ship appeared to be falling on its beam end before lifting and rolling the other way. He grasped the ladder tighter and stared at the funnel's amber paint in an effort to compose himself.

Sucking in a deep breath he moved up another rung where two massive hands seized the lapels of his parka and hoisted him swiftly to catwalk level. He hung nose-to-nose with a murderer, his legs dangling in space.

"Why do you keep hounding me?" Davison snarled through clenched teeth. His face was purplish with cold but his eyes blazed with anger.

"Ah-but, ah-but, ah-but," stuttered Angus, fear made his eyes pop out of his head while his body had gone limp.

The felon stood King on the catwalk and let him go. The engineer flopped over the whistle casing and clutched it like he did his mother on many occasions as a boy. The madness slowly left his antagonist's eyes. Now that there weren't any more hiding places for him on the ship. There was only one alternative because prison was not an option. And what about Oscar? He hadn't seen him since Nassau. Was he all right?

"Where's my kid?"

Angus stopped panting briefly. "Whit - whit kid sir?"

"My son," insisted Davison. "My son, Oscar."

"Are ye Oscar Davis' faither?" he squeaked, peering back over his shoulder at him.

"Yeah, where in the hell is he?"

The young man shivered, an action not entirely caused by the cold wind whipping at neither his clothing nor a starboard sea seemingly reaching up to claim him. "Eh - weel Ah mean - eh," he stammered. How does one go about telling a murderer that his son was burned alive when a deck made from the hardest wood in Britain lies sixty feet below? That thought was whisked from his mind when Davison grasped him firmly by the ankles and held him out over that particularly hard, oaken deck - still sixty far, far, far down feet below. The superstructure was a blur spinning wildly beneath him and the rope slapped his cheek. He whimpered hysterically, "Oh Mammy-Daddy! Mammy-Daddy!" And all the while Charles William's *The Devil's Galop* blared up.

The American hauled him back over the catwalk and flopped the trembling junior back onto the whistle casing before picking him up. "Well?"

'Between the devil and the deep blue sea' never seemed more apt, but the young man was too frightened to have the presence of mind to lie and say that Oscar was still safe and sound somewhere aboard the ship. Instead he babbled out the truth. His broad Scottish dialect gushing into the buffeting wind mangled the narrative and Davison, quite naturally, misunderstood. From the few words he could discern the fugitive assumed that somehow this guy was partly responsible. With tears of anguish coursing down his cheeks he placed a firm arm about the engineer's waist and stepped out into space.

From that point on everything happened so fast that it was just a blur to Angus. The hand line slid across the back of his neck, burning as the loops tightened. He jerked to a sudden stop. Davison kept on going, his grip popped buttons and ripped away half of the engineer's parka. He watched his assailant descend in what seemed to be a very slow spread-eagled spin.

Swinging like a case clock pendulum he gazed down in horror at the body far below. The rough coils constricted his chest, making it hard to breathe. He just dangled helplessly, too much in shock to consider how to get out of his predicament.

The bows of the vessel rose to meet the swells and made the grapnel hook slide along the catwalk's rung, smacking him against the funnel casing. The jolt was enough. On the next roll he seized a ladder rung. He was to relate afterwards that the bar had been gripped so hard that his fingerprints were probably embedded in the steel.

The rope was too tight to loosen and forced him to climb back up and free the grapnel, a task he was reluctant to do.

But it had to be done. It took him an age to descend and when he did, friendly hands were reaching up to help him down those last few feet.

Sports Deck had suddenly become a hive of activity. As well as Mike Finney and his crew, the ship's doctor and two nurses appeared, Hodgkin and some seamen with stretchers, a brace of MA's, the chief engineer and the HSE. Fortunately none of the passengers had witnessed the event because they were having lunch. Everybody wanted to know at once what had happened and the only one who was able to tell them sat on the deck speechless, too shocked to cry.

Some time afterwards Betty Stevenson tenderly coaxed him to relate frightening experience or as Wheelkey callously remarked while draining his first wardroom pint: "She shagged the shock right out of him."

A tipsy Angus glared back at his grinning countryman.

"I'll tell you boyo," Morgan averred. "If that had happened to me, I'd have shit myself, I can tell you, see."

"Shite mysel'? The fright made my sphincter freeze up solid. Ah might hae tae go doon tae Sick Bay tomorrow for some laxative."

"You don't have to do that mate," Maxie chimed in. "Just ask your Canuck buddy here for one of his Guinnesses. I guarantee that Right will fix you up!"

Jake roared with laughter and ordered a round of beer.

Docking Night

2225 Monday

Will Keyes peered over King's shoulder at the results of the arrival pool. "You lucky bastard!" he exclaimed. "Thirty-three! You had bloody thirty-three!"

The sighting of Nab Tower at 2133 officially denoted the end of the voyage. Fifty engineers and electricians had put a dollar apiece into the sweepstake to receive a number that corresponded with minutes in the hour. Thus 2132 was second prize and 2134 was third. If the kitty wasn't won because of the ten spare numbers it kept mounting. Angus was happy for he had won seventy-five dollars.

"Let's see who won second and third," said Wheelkey, leaning closer. "Jeez! Big John and the Chief! What a swindle! Oh well, next trip maybe." He hooked an arm round his friend's neck. "Come on. Let's celebrate."

"Ok."

They bumped into Jake White on the companionway.

"Come on Right," invited Wheelkey. "We're going to drink this lucky bugger's beer. He won the pool."

"Really? Some bastards have all the luck."

Inside the winner's cabin Wheelkey energetically tore open a case of beer and generously distributed a bottle to both engineers. "I'll have to rush this one," he said. "I'm on standby." He bugled away his bottle's contents in a jiffy and with a rude belch vacated the cabin.

Angus watched him leave and gazed at couple of suitcases on the cabin floor. "Are ye a' packed up, Jake?"

"No, still a few odds and ends yet," he said, reposing in a chair. "Well, this is the end of your first trip Gus. What did you think of it?"

"It could've been a wee bit less painful tae say the least," he replied. "The murders an' the murderers *that* Ah could've done withoot. Ither than that, Ah had a great time."

"So did I, except for that bastard Christie, which reminds me . . . I've still to get even with him - right, eh?"

"Whit evil plan dae ye hae in mind for him?"

"I'm not sure yet. The opportunity hasn't arisen. By the way, have you signed the customs manifest yet?"

"Aye. Ah signed it this afternoon."

"Did you declare anything?"

"No."

"Last trip, some idiot wrote 'one submachine gun' against Dirk Thompson's name. The customs guys went nuts. They went through our quarters with a fine-toothed comb. We never did find out who did it."

"Dae ye think standby will be finished by the time we go oan watch?"

"I doubt it," replied Jake. "But it won't be long. After we shut down I'll be finished for the trip."

Angus went over to the porthole and gazed out. Some meagre lights gleamed through the darkness. "Where dae ye reckon we are?"

"God knows. It's too dark to see anything. I should imagine we're well past Beaulieu."

"Ye ken, it's fascinatin' tae watch yon lights drift by."

This was a cue for Jake to start whistling that lovely haunting tune, *Fascination*. His shipmate pursed his lips and picked up the melody just as Keyes slammed the door ajar.

"How would one of you pair of fascinatin' bastards like to hand me a beer?" he pressed with a lewd grin. This choked the whistling and a bottle was sullenly shoved into his hand. It was soon emptied and he went back down below.

The standby dragged on and the new watch was called. Jazz paced up and down the platform behind the standby engineers. "Where are we Gus?"

"Oan the knuckle."

"Good. A couple more movements and we'll be alongside. Where's Jake?"

"He's in the changeroom," replied Angus. "He'll be doon in a minute."

"Thank God! What a bloody standby!" moaned Jazz? "I've been running around like a blue-arsed fly all watch while some bastards can fall asleep at the wheel."

He dug an elbow into Harris' back.

"Uh - what's up?" grunted Maxie who'd been dozing serenely, ably supported by the astern manoeuvring wheel.

"Wake up, you lazy git!" shot back Jazz. "You've been relieved."

Harris yawned, his larynx squeezing out; "Jolly good show. A fellow can get tired standing here."

"How in the hell can you get tired sleeping?" scorned Jazz.

"I don't know," was the yawning reply? "Goodnight."

He sauntered off the platform. Jake arrived to tell Angus to relieve The Mekon at the control valves for the turbine gland steam. He complied.

The telegraphs rang *Finished with Engines* at 0030. The eight-to-twelve dispersed with alacrity. And no wonder - Southampton at last - home for many of the officers and crew.

Within minutes they would be clumping down the gangways carrying hand luggage filled with gifts and dirty dhobi. Some would rush into the waiting arms of their sweethearts while others would plod home to their wives.

He left his station when Christie beckoned him to return to the platform. The second gave him a detailed explanation of the shutdown procedure while Jake hustled all over the place doing the actual work. King observed gauge needles waning to zero as his friend shut down each unit. Some pressures and temperatures would take hours to diminish completely.

Within forty-five minutes the engineroom was quiet again with the occasional belch of steam rudely flatulating from a steam trap. Jake's forehead was dripping sweat as clung to the desk. A mug of tepid cocoa was thirstily drained. If looks could kill, Black Bob would've been cremated on the spot by the fire in his eyes.

The second placed a fatherly arm around his pal's shoulders. "You'll have to help the Colonial to install the turning gear. As soon as the vacuum drops down to zero I would like you to open the harbour drains."

"Ok Bob."

The groan of the turning gear echoed through the engineroom a little while later.

"I've got the first port watch so I'm going topside for a few minutes to get some reading material," said Christie. He noticed White making his way to the changeroom access ladder. "So where in bloody hell do you think you're going?"

"Job's done, right?"

"You'll stay here until I return to the engineroom, *Mister*!"

He shrugged and stalked back to the desk. While the second had been reprimanding him Ronnie Livingstone, the greaser, came down that same ladder. He set down his oiling can and lit up a smoke. He had been busy topping up a few remaining oil cups before finishing for the night. Feeling pleased with him Christie slowly donned his snowy-white gloves before ambling over to that same ladder.

He gripped the handrails and began to climb when his face took on a peculiar expression. He stopped to frown in disgust at the oil stain on one of his gloves before trumpeting across the starboard gearbox at Ronnie. His finger pointed at the rating and redirected to a position at the bottom of the ladder. The miscreant scurried over. Black Bob gestured at the smear on the railing and the pool of oil on the floorplates. Livingston's excuse wilted under the ferocious stare and with bowed head awaited the verbal broadside.

"Look at that big bastard!" growled Jake. "He's still at it. What a sadist, right? He's shoved it up my ass for the whole trip. Do you know what? I'd just love to get even with him before I went on leave." While sympathizing with the berated Livingstone a cunning smirk split his face and he chuckled.

"Whit evil thoughts are lurkin' in that heid o' yours?"

"Listen Gus, I probably won't see you after I finish tonight," he said, ignoring the question. "I'm going straight ashore to stay with a girl friend. I'll be back in the morning to sign off."

Suspicion dwelled ominously. "Are ye gaun tae tell me whit ye're plannin' tae dae?"

"Don't ask. You'll find out soon enough," replied Jake, watching the rating being dismissed. The second ascended the engineroom ladder. "Look Gus, the vacuum's back to zero. You'd better go and open the harbour drains."

King grabbed a wheelkey and with a last questioning look disappeared into the bilge. His first discovery was that extreme care was needed when crawling around steam-heated pipes. Locating and opening the elusive valves was easier second time around.

He squirmed from under the 2nd IP turbine to a ladder and hauled his body up rung by rung to a standing position. His head was at floorplate level. On his right, and far above him, the platform second was beginning to descend the engineroom ladder. What happened next took less than the blink of an eye.

Still wearing that wicked grin Black Bob grasped the ladder's rails, and with his legs held out in front of him started to slide down, fully supported by his white-gloved hands. A disturbing "Oh no-oo!" welled from his lips to become a long drawn-out scream that preceded his accelerating body.

From his advantageous position King perceived a practical example of the Doppler affect as the second roller-coasted down towards the manoeuvring platform. An even shriller shriek signified a lateral change in direction when his posterior hit the floorplates. Momentum shot his body all the way to the boiler room telegraph where he halted with a solitary clang.

Jake beamed and waved goodbye to his friend. "Mister Christie has returned to the platform. I've been relieved. See you Gus - have a good trip!" He raced up the stairs and was soon out of sight.

The floater scurried up onto the platform and nearly landed on his rump. His feet slithered in opposite directions and he instinctively held onto a handrail for support. The floorplates were awash in lube-oil. A cursory glance at the ladder's handrails showed that they had been lubricated too. He shuffled and skidded towards Christie who lay winded on the plates. He crouched to help the second to his feet.

"Shit!" swore Black Bob, then laughed. "Well, well, well! I didn't think White had the guts to retaliate. I was right about one thing though," he groaned, rubbing his rear. "That guy is a pain in the arse!"

"Are ye gaun tae report him?"

"No Angus, you know that I'm not a vindictive man," he replied. "Do you mean to tell me you actually think that I'd wreak vengeance on White?"

Angus nodded.

Christie shook his head sadly and said, "Angus, I'm ashamed of you - such unkind thoughts about my nature. When White comes back from his leave, I'll just have a quiet talk with him. I'll probably even laugh and joke about it."

A Cheshire cat grin appeared.

"Then I'll boot him up the arse!"

The junior breathed a sigh of relief.

"Have you opened the harbour drains yet?"

"Aye Bob an' the turnin' gear's due for anither spin."

"Then you're finished. Turn to at eight tomorrow."

A knock on Jake's locked door brought no response. Sounds of music and merriment from Wheelkey's cabin beckoned him. He rapped the door and looked in. A docking night party was in full swing.

"Hi Gus! Grab a beer and find a pew."

"Thanks Wheelkey."

"I guess that you know everyone here," he yelled over the din. "Except maybe, these ladies over there. Hey Rona, Shirley, Anne - meet Gus. This was his first trip."

The purserettes waved cheerily. He reciprocated and helped himself to a beer. "Where's the opener?"

"Give me that," said Keyes, and with his usual flair popped the cap.

A lifejacket on a beer case became a seat. The music stopped. The Sphere hefted some long-playing records from the phonograph's turntable and perused the labels on a stack of others on the dresser.

"It's twelve o'clock in Britain and one o'clock in Germany," was the rotund announcement. "Time for Two-Way Family Favourites."

"Play an Elvis record," said Shirley.

"No - Connie Francis," insisted Anne.

"Any of you in the family way?"

The girls giggled emphatic noes.

"Well that case - request denied."

Treenie leered. "I'll oblige the ladies."

"Do any of you ladies have a friend in the Armed Forces?" The Sphere inquired.

"I'm their friend," said Larry. "I've got a weapon."

"You're not from Germany," protested The Sphere.

"My weapon got a German helmet. Does that count?"

"Very well, have it stand and be recognised!"

Short hysterical giggles erupted from the purserettes.

"Let's have a sing-song," bellowed Keyes.

Immediately Harry McAlistair, the eight-to-twelve a/c engineer, burst into song. It was the fellow's last trip Angus was informed. He was going to swallow the anchor and get married.

To the tune of *Bye-bye Blackbird*, he started to croon:

"Pack my bags and pack my grip,
I'm not coming back next trip!
Bye-bye - Pict Line.

Eff the Second, eff the Chief,
all they brought was tears and grief!
Bye-bye - Pict Line."

He stopped for a swig of beer.

"How's about 'Tiptoe across the tank tops?'"

"Pipe down Sphere!" yelled Keyes.

The racket inspired Jazz Johns to pop his head around the door's edge. He'd just showered and his apparel was not in vogue for such an occasion. In fact he was practically naked for only a towel encircled his waist.

"Hey guys, the customs are skulking about our accommodation. Make sure that you're under your limit," he nodded at the array of liquor bottles and lifted up an empty glass meaningfully. "If you need any help, I'll be glad to oblige."

The Mekon sloshed in a generous measure of gin.

"Cheers!" smiled Jazz.

"How's about Begin the Big End?"

"What are you Sphere? Some kind of an engineer?" scoffed Keyes. "Jazz, give us a tune on your spoons."

"I don't have 'em with me. There aren't any pockets in this." He patted the pseudo garment to prove his point. "And I can't tapdance in my flip-flops either."

The Sphere clapped on a Kingston Trio record and music filled the cabin while Jazz continued to mooch.

"Can someone lend me a cigarette? There aren't any pockets in this towel, y'see. Maybe I should get a bag to carry my stuff in."

Keyes zipped the towel away. "Use that bag there!"

Unperturbed Jazz made no attempt to cover himself. "It's got something in there already."

The girls didn't know whether to giggle or scream. They just gaped in awe at his endowment. Rona broke the silence. "It looks like God was kind to you."

"If you play your cards right it'll be kind to you," promised Jazz. "Besides, the long and short of it is that it's not the longest in this cabin."

The purserettes dragged their eyes away from Jazz and panned them back and forth across the cabin until they all focussed on King's beet-red face. Johns snatched the towel back from Keyes and carefully recovered his lower body. He casually sipped his gin as if nothing had happened.

"Hey!" said Harry. "I've just thought of something. I've got two bottles of hooch in my cabin. I'll have to hide one from the customs."

The Sphere burped. "It's kinda late to think of that now."

Jazz gave Harry a conspirative look. "Why don't you bring it in here? I'll fix you up."

"Not in here, you won't! I don't need any static from the customs."

"Don't worry Wheelkey," soothed Jazz. "I've done this a few times before and I've never been caught yet."

"Well, I don't know . . ."

"Oh come on - don't be chicken!" teased Jazz. "Go and get your bottle, Harry."

McAlistair jumped off the bunk and vacated the cabin. He was back in a trice with a bottle of Bell's Scotch Whisky tucked under his jacket.

"Hurry up and hide it, Jazz. The Cuzzies are just a couple of doors away."

Jazz drained his pint pot and rinsed it out at the sink. He edged his way past the women and was groped for his trouble.

He grinned momentarily at the culprit who smiled coyly, her pert brown eyes aflutter. He uncorked the whisky, poured about three-quarters of it into his glass before setting the bottle back down on the dresser. He cradled the tankard and then with a glint in his eye, squeezed in beside his improper assailant.

There was a knock on the door and it swung open. A peaked cap flaunting the dreaded portcullis crest came into view. "Who lives here?" asked the sombre face beneath the cap. Wheelkey's forefinger rose from his glass. "Is it convenient to search your cabin now sir?"

"Have you got a search warrant?"

"No sir, but if I do have to get one my investigation will be much more thorough." was the glib reply.

"Ok - go ahead. Sorry for the interruption, ladies."

The excise man scanned the cabin and lifted a couple of near-empty liquor bottles before moving towards the dresser. Curiously the newcomer was not groped. His eyes rested on the pint pot warming in Jazz's hands and received a dazzling smile in response. "That beer looks kind of flat," the customs officer remarked thoughtfully.

"Yes, it is. I poured it before I went for a shower," said Jazz, flicking his towel.

"It looks darker than the beer that the others are drinking."

"Eh - yes. Eh - Double Diamond, y'know."

"Mm - of course. Where's the empty bottle?"

"Back inside my cabin," Jazz lied. "I poured it there just before I went for a shower, and then brought with me when this gentleman invited me to his little gathering." He indicated vaguely with a waveing tankard of whisky towards the uneasy resident.

“Do you mind if I test this bottle of Bell’s whisky?” the offical asked.

“Afore ye go?” quipped Wheelkey.

“Naturally.”

It took a couple of seconds for the man to pick up on the Bell’s slogan. “Oh yes, quite.”

He removed a small leather case from his inside pocket and opened it to reveal a narrow brass goblet and hydrometer. He poured a sample and placed the instrument into the liquid. “Eighty proof - export stock. Well, there isn’t enough here to bother about.”

He returned the sample to the bottle and went through the motions of replacing his instruments back into their case. Quite inadvertently the official’s hydrometer plopped ‘accidentally’ into Jazz’s pint pot. The engineer, wise to the ways of officialdom, whipped out the hydrometer before it had a chance to bob on the surface.

“Oops! Sorry about that.”

Jazz sucked the instrument as if it was a lollipop. “That’s ok. It adds flavour to the beer.” To alleviate suspicion he nonchalantly took a long deep swig from the tankard and smacked his lips appreciatively.

“I won’t trouble you anymore,” said the exciseman. “Thank you for your cooperation. Goodbye.”

Every eye followed him out of the cabin and simultaneously, the returning serve focussed on Jazz’s countenance. His normal cheery face had the pallor of death. “Christ!” he gasped. “Somebody get me a drink of water!” A glass was filled at the sink and passed hand-to-hand to the victim who downed it gratefully. “That’s the first time I’ve drank whisky like that,” he groaned. “It’s not as easy as beer.”

"What are you moaning about?" objected Harry. "You got it for free."

Jazz rose, clasped his stomach, and leaned over the complainant's head. "Do you want it back?"

"Bugger off!" shouted Harry, and eased out of harm's way. The company laughed and The Sphere loaded a pile of LP's onto the record player and switched it on.

"I'll go and get dressed now," said Jazz. "Excuse me ladies." Edging by the women an exploratory hand drifted under his towel to pass between his legs and grasp his penis.

"Ding-dong," laughed Anne.

"Was that my death knell?"

"It could be. I can feel rigor mortis setting in!"

Jazz reached under the towel and gently disengaged the clutching digits. "Later sweetheart," he promised and left.

"So Jazz saved your bottle Harry," said Keyes."

"Yes, but he didn't have to drink as much."

"Shit!" scoffed The Sphere. "Some guys are never happy."

Anne laid her hand on Angus' arm. "Excuse me, but would you please escort me to the powder room?"

"Ah dinnae mind at a', Anne." He stuck his head out into the passageway and motioned all was clear.

"Where's Jazz's cabin?" the woman whispered.

They walked quickly and silently to Johns' cabin and knocked on his door. He stuck his head in and found him putting on his trousers.

"Hey Jazz, ye can take them aff again. Ye've got a visitor." Smirking, he ushered the girl inside and left.

Back at the party the other two purserettes were informed that their friend would be gone for the night. They speculated and giggled away to one another. This distraction allowed

Wheelkey the opportunity to ask King about the morrow's port watch.

"Ah'm no' oan watch. Ah'm oan days, courtesy o' Big John."

"Lucky bastard! I've got the eight-to-four tomorrow and the four-to-twelve the day after. What are you doing tomorrow night?"

"Ah really dinnae ken," replied Angus. "Ah'll maybe scout aroond toun Ah guess. Ye ken, Ah just had a wee glimpse o' the place when the taxi brought me through tae the ship."

"Come with me, I'm planning on a pub crawl."

"Hey Wheelkey, what do you mean - plannin'?" jeered The Sphere. "It's automatic with you."

"Cheeky bugger! How would you like to be a cube?"

"Do we have much work on for tomorrow?"

"Don't talk shop Sphere," censured Keyes. "There are ladies present. Anyway, there's still quite a lot left on the list - thanks to the bastard, Beery. Gus, nip down to his cabin and wake him up. Ask him if he wants to buy a battleship!"

The purserettes' laughter stopped abruptly when Betty Stevenson popped her head around the door. "Ah, there you are Angus. I've been looking all over for you."

"Are you going to be under arrest?" Treen asked.

Keyes scoffed at that. "Whatever he's going under - it won't give him a rest!"

The DS was ushered out before any more ribaldry took place. "Let's go tae my cabin." He relieved her of the little suitcase and portfolio and gestured up the passageway with his head. "Is this a' your luggage?"

"Yes, I wasn't given much time to pack when I got this assignment."

Inside his cabin he offered her a drink. Instead of replying she plucked at his patrol suit buttons. They disrobed each other, frantic fingers caressing and probing until all their clothing lay arrayed the deck. They flopped onto the bunk kissing and groping in heated passion until the act of sex was consummated and fell asleep in each other's arms.

The sound of running water awoke him. Betty was half dressed and dabbing a facecloth on her neck and cheeks. She reached for a towel and saw that he was awake. "Rise and shine Angus, your storeman will be rousing you shortly."

He eased down from his bunk and encircled her with his arms just as she was slipping on her suit jacket. "Ah'd raither be roused by you."

"Down big boy," she said, moving away from the embrace. "I've got to be in Southampton Central soon. I've got a train to catch at nine-thirty."

"Will they no' gie ye any leave after this big case?"

"Hah! If I know DI Cunningham he'll have been telling the brass that this case was just one big holiday. Anyway, I've got another case. The Yard has caught wind that an assassination is about to take place in a week or so. I've to be in Scotland Yard by noon today."

"Weel, guid luck. Ah hope ye catch the guy."

"You got that right, as your Canadian buddy would say," laughed Betty. She looked in the mirror and primped her hair a little. "How do I look?"

"Like a million dollars."

She smiled at the compliment then went serious. "You know, I couldn't have solved this case without your help. But there's still one thing that's bugging me."

"No' enough nooky?"

"No, you made sure of that," replied Betty. "For the life of me, I still can't figure out the meaning of that clue left by Katherine Davis."

"Whit clue was that then?"

She flipped open her portfolio, riffled through the folders, and showed him the close-up photograph of Brown's left shoulder. "What is the significance of that bloody en?"

He perused the picture and thought for a moment. "That Davis woman, didn't she hae an electrical business?"

"Yes," replied Betty. "She was into electronics big time."

He smiled. "That's no' a bluidy en. It's a bluidy omega!"

"Omega?" echoed Betty. "So what? I'm still lost."

"Omega is the electrical symbol for resistance - ohm." He laughed at the continued puzzlement on his paramour's face.

"Yon night oan the Boat Deck," he recalled. "It was right after the ship sailed when Ah spoke tae Homer Davidson - or Davison - or whitever his name is. He told me that he was nicknamed Om. O-h-m!" he spelled out. "Get it?"

Betty grabbed his head with both hands and kissed him. "Brilliant!" she laughed. "Boy! I just can't wait to see Cunningham's face when I casually mention that in front of the Superintendent."

She folded up her portfolio again just as the storekeeper popped his head in the door. He just gaped and closed the door again without saying anything.

"Gie me your address Betty, an' Ah'll write tae ye," he said, while all the time at the back of his mind, he knew that he probably wouldn't.

"I was between digs when I got the Davis-Brown case, Angus." Betty told him. "All my stuff is at my parents' house right now. After this case is over, I'll get set up in new digs and write to you then." And at the back of her mind she knew that too she probably wouldn't write either.

They kissed for one last time and she left with wolf whistles following her down the passageway.

Southampton

Tuesday afternoon

The engineroom elevator began its journey to Sun Deck. "Are ye haein' tea in the mess?"

"Am I hell!" retorted Keyes. "You've been here long enough to know what port meals are like, Gus." He leaned wearily against the wall and examined the black oil streak on the leg of his boilersuit. He ruefully shook his head. "First day back in Mushland and my clean overalls are dirty already."

"Yours are dirty?" echoed Angus. "Whit aboot me? He gestured at his own attire. "Up tae the eyes - Ah was - while the tools are handed doon tae me in the bilge by yoursel'."

"That's what floaters are for," he was told. "And you should've wiped that spanner clean before dragging it across my leg." The elevator doors crashed open. "I'm going ashore for a fish supper - coming?"

"Aye - ok. Ah'll see ye in a wee while."

He reflected on the day's work under the shower. It had been an easy morning performing routine chores: repacking valves and pump glands that had developed leaks during the voyage. It wasn't the job was difficult, just awkward - and dirty. Inevitably, as in most occupations, the junior got the short end of the stick. Accordingly he had been delegated bilge engineer for the duration of the job.

Keyes had enlightened him on lucky they were to be assigned dayshift although port watches had some good points too. His companion for the day had told him that port watches were better during the ship's annual lay-up in dry dock.

Instead of the regular eight hours on with twenty-four off the leisure period was extended to thirty-two hours off.Consequently if a colleague worked a watch for a friend, a seventy-two-hour leave might be managed - enough time to go home. It was hoped that the favour would be reciprocated.

It was just after five o'clock when the two Scotsmen strutted down the gangway. Ocean Terminal was quiet with only the occasional customs officer waiting to pounce on any individual toting dunnage. The taxi rank was empty. They began the long walk along the docks to the gate and Canute Road. They passed some well-known liners: *Mauretania*, *Oriana*, *Transvaal Castle*, and *Canberra*. Keyes noted that the *Franconia* would be sailing shortly.

"How dae ye ken that?"

"It's flying the Blue Peter."

"Whit's that?"

"Do you see that blue flag with the white square in the centre of it? It's just below the crosstree of the foremast."

"Aye."

"That's the international sign for a ship that will be sailing within the next twenty-four hours."

The air was cool and streetlights were flickering on. The engineers were breathing heavily and expelling great clouds of vapour by the time they reached the dock gates. A fish and chip shop, wafting a vinegary aroma of deep fried delight along Canute Road, enticed them to sate their appetites.

"We need something to wash that down," belched Keyes, placing his fork and knife onto his empty plate.

Angus read from a wall menu. "They've got tea or coffee."

"It was thinking of something stronger," said his guide, eying his wristwatch. "Well, whadyknow. It's opening time!"

They stopped in a High Street pub called *The Red Lion*. The familiar ruddy glow from a tiny keg displayed the brewer's product. Massive black oaken beams supported the high ceiling of the establishment. Whitewashed walls were decorated with Elizabethan style crosspieces of the same ebon timber. Banners, swords, pikestaffs, and ancient muskets adorned those same walls. The highly polished tables and chairs were heavy with intricately carved legs. They claimed a couple of plush stools at the bar. Angus had never tasted English draught beer so a pint had to be sampled.

"Two pints of Red Barrel please," requested Keyes.

The barmaid filled a couple of ornate pewter tankards and slid them over the counter.

"Hey sweetheart, this beer hasn't been ordained."

"I beg your pardon?"

"No dog collar."

The first sip of beer brought a grimace, which was all but spat out. The barmaid lifted the other pint and tasted it. "God, that barrel's off. I'll get you some beer from other barrel - on the house of course."

"Thanks darling," beamed Keyes at the prospects of getting a free beer. After downing a second he said, "Come on Gus and I'll show you the sights - Wheelkey style!"

"Ah suppose that means a pub crawl."

"*Mais naturellement*."

A short jaunt from *The Red Lion* lay *The Juniper Berry*, a queer little place with its bar located smack in the centre of a large room. It looked like it had last been decorated to celebrate the completion of Stonehenge. Many of the high wooden stools that surrounded the bar were occupied and it took a little while to catch the bartender's eye.

Angus ordered a pint for his friend and a half for himself, reasoning that the imminent pub-crawl might be too much for him. Slowly he became aware of the patrons' weird styles of apparel as he sipped his brew. Gaudy pantsuits, Danube bonnets, scented hair, and earrings were the order of the day.

"Hey Wheelkey," hissed out from the corner of his mouth. "There are twa queers in here."

"D'you mean to tell me that you've just noticed two?"

"Aye - you an' me!"

Keyes spluttered into his beer. Grinning, he wiped his lips with his handkerchief "That's a good one, Gus."

A youngish creature with pale-green hair, rouged lips and false eyelashes mounted above a powdered face tapped King on the back. "Hi sweetie!" it cooed. "Can I buy you a drink?"

His eyes bulged with distaste at the pink ruffled shirt and azure suit with skin tight pants with flared bottoms. High-heeled shoes completed his attire. "Piss aff!"

"Ooh - well I never!"

"An' Ah never either!" he shot at the apparition wiggling away. "Come oan Wheelkey, let's get tae hell oot o' here."

"Aye - ok."

At a table near the exit their steward Toni invited them to join him. The engineers glanced at one another and both shrugged. "Ok Toni, we can only stay for one."

Fifteen minutes later when they were halfway through their beers the first homosexual, jealous of Toni, broached Angus with, "What's she got that I haven't got?"

His face turned scarlet but whether from anger or embarrassment Keyes couldn't determine.

"If you played your cards right," the catamite hinted. "You could have me."

With a grin Keyes said, "He can't play cards with you honey - you don't have a full deck!"

"Ooh!" trilled the homosexual and wobbled away.

They downed their beers, thanked Toni, and departed in the direction of *The Spa* tavern, a little island of hospitality behind the premises of the *Southern Echo*, the local rag. "This is where a lot of the Cunard engineers usually hang out," Keyes informed him, squatting onto a barstool. "Hi Liz!"

"Don't you call me Liz, Will Keyes," scolded the well-endowed barmaid. "My name's Elizabeth. If you must abbreviate my name, call me Beth."

King's eyes were glued to the heaving white breasts that seemed eager to escape their confinement.

"Ok Liz," replied Wheelkey. "Liz, this is Angus - Angus, meet Liz."

Elizabeth's fire dampened noticeably when she smiled at her latest customer. She was in her early fifties and had a smooth round face. Her black hair was groomed straight back and kept in a bun with an ornate brown clasp. It was a daily struggle trying to maintain her figure when constantly surrounded by great pub grub. She bent over and reached for glasses below bar level. Down through the valley of Beth rode the fixed wond'red eyes.

"What would you like to drink Angus?"

Her sudden upward glance caught a guilty look.

"Twa - twa - " Caught off guard he stammered, "Twa pints o' tit, please!"

"Oh, these don't come in pints. They come in jugs!"

"More like churns!" roared Keyes, laughing uproariously at his friend's blush.

"Two pints o' Red Barrel - an' hae one for yourself."

Beth's eyes peered down her décolleté and said: "I don't think there's enough room for another one down there." As she giggled at her little joke, her bosom wobbled. Two smoothly poured pints found themselves foaming in front of the engineers. She laid a hand on King's and said, very seriously, "Now be a good boy and drink your milk!" Her shrill laughter added momentum as she cruised away to another customer.

Two more pints and two Mowbray pies later they were bound for the *Lord Louis* near the Civic Centre where yet another draught bitter was sampled. When Angus determined that Double Diamond was too sharp for his taste his shipmate told him that their next port of call would be more suitable since it was a free house.

"Whit's a free hoose?"

"It's a pub that sells beer made by different breweries. You see most of the pubs around here are owned by breweries who naturally just sell their own plonk."

"Ok, Ah'm game. Let's go."

The night air temperature had dropped noticeably during their sojourn in the *Lord Louis* and the cold beer in their stomachs didn't help either as they shivered outside. Snow was starting to fall when they flagged down a passing taxi. It tore along The Avenue and dropped them off at the *Albany Hotel*. Keyes paid the fare and they trudged up a gravel path to the entrance. It looked like the snow would be on for the night. They clumped and thumped their feet on the foyer's coconut mat and went into the bar.

The hotel was a relic from the Victorian era. Opposite the foyer desk an ebon banister raced a maroon carpeted stairway up to the next level. Chandeliers, ornate to the point of ugliness, dangled from the high ceiling. Plaques and dishes, cast in brass, adorned the dark panelled walls where every niche played host to its own alloyed oddity. The profusion of brass would've warmed the cockles of a scrap merchant's heart. King was led across a deep piled carpet to a doorway near the desk.

Two lounges were served by one bar. The first had a Spanish decor, with black wrought-iron chandeliers. Scrolled dividers supporting broad-leafed plants gave the illusion of privacy to the handful of tables within. A pair of wooden stools were commandeered in front of a manifold of five beer pump handles, each with its own logo urging patrons to buy their brand. Keyes nudged his companion, his eyes directed at the centre unit.

On a glowing opaque glass a little old man with a grey top hat, flowing white beard, red waistcoat, claw hammer jacket and yellow checked trousers advised them to get Younger every day.

Angus grinned at the barmaid. "Twa pints o' heavy please Miss."

"I beg your pardon?"

"Hello Jane," Wheelkey greeted her. "This is Angus King - he just joined the ship about a month ago." Then he translated for his friend. "Two pints of Younger's Tartan Bitter please."

"All right, Will."

The engineers patiently waited with anticipation as they watched their native beer was being poured. Angus ran an appreciative eye over the shapely frame of the attractive barmaid.

She was thirty-ish with short dark-blonde hair, blue eyes, a fair complexion, and a trim figure with long English legs. A clean frilly apron protected her print frock. Jane flashed him a winning smile with his beer and accepted his pound note.

Angus commented on her pleasant personality.

"Aye. She is nice," agreed Keyes. "But don't fall in love with her, that's her husband over there."

He nodded towards the far end of the bar, which served the other lounge where a glitzy jukebox sat.

"The stools ower there must be awfy high," observed Angus. "The bulk o' his body is above the bar."

"There aren't any stools over on that side,"Keyes informed him. "That's all him!"

"Oh!"

"Well Gus, that's you seen Southampton."

"Seen Southampton?" gibed his countryman. "By jings, that sure was some tour. Ah dinnae even ken whereaboots the post office is!"

"When you come out *The Spa* walk towards the High Street, it's right on the corner."

"Thanks very much," was the caustic reply. "Ah was plannin' tae see some o' the sights."

"What sights?"

"Ah dinnae ken. Whitever makes a town interestin'. Historical landmarks, art, architecture, parks, cinemas, an' such like. Ah cannae just go oot boozin' every time Ah hit port. It's too damnedexpensive for one thing."

"You don't have to go into a pub with the intention of drinking it dry. Besides, you've seen all the history, art, and architecture."

"Where?"

"The *Red Lion* is historical. It used to be King Henry the Eighth's courtroom. Art: *The Juniper Berry,* it's a bit abstract mind you but it's still art. And you liked the architecture in *The Spa*."

"Ah must've missed that!"

"Well, if Beth isn't built right I don't know what is."

Angus laughed.

"Besides," he continued. "Summer is the best time to see around the outlaying areas. We'll take a trip around Hampshire and I'll show you Winchester Cathedral, Stonehenge, Eastleigh, Pompey and plenty wee country pubs along the way."

When the traditional death knell 'Time gentlemen please', was called out by the manager, Keyes phoned for a taxi which took them back into town. He suggested going to a nightclub but Angus demurred saying that he'd had enough for one day. He went back to the ship alone after dropping his friend off at the *Silhouette Club*.

The next afternoon found Angus ashore shopping for small items that he needed for the next trip; extra razor blades, shaving soap, needles and thread, spare buttons, haircream, deodorant, tweezers, flip-flops for the shower and reading material. He got to know a bit more about the city while acquiring these essentials.

A film at the *Odeon* kept him amused for a time before he went for something to eat at *The Spa*. He spent an interesting hour with a trio of Cunard engineers discussing the merits and disadvantages of their respective companies before leaving in search of his shipmates.

He tried the haunts of the previous night without any luck. Other establishments such as *The Horse and Groom*, *The Park Lounge*, yielded similar results. Nearing a taxi rank he decided to go to the *Albany*. It was very busy and all the barstools were occupied. He found a niche between two businessmen.

"Hello Angus! What would you like to drink?"

It was Jane. Pleased that she recognised him by name he smiled and ordered a Scotch. Not long afterwards a cheery 'Hello, hello, hello!' at his back made him turn around. It was Jake. "Whit are ye daein' here?"

"My train leaves tomorrow - right? I live less than a block from here. My girl friend is in bed under the weather so I thought that I'd drop in for a quick one."

"Oh dear, whit's wrang with the lass?"

"She's come down with a bad case of ures," said Jake.

"Whit's ures?"

"A pint of Flowers!"

"Och, Ah walked right intae that one."

A couple of stools became vacant. Jake took one and promptly stood up again, his face grimacing in pain.

"Whit's the matter?" asked Angus.

"That bastard Christie!" blurted out White. "I went back to the ship this morning to sign off and get the rest of my luggage. Of all the bad luck, I was hoping to miss him. Anyway I'd just opened the engineroom elevator doors and bent down to pick up my cases when who should come around the corner and boot me up the ass. Jeez, his foot must've sunk in right up to his ankle!"

Rubbing his rear end he slowly eased back onto the stool. Angus sat beside him.

"Serves ye right. Ye nearly killed him."

"Really? Well, he never booted me for that. After extracting his boot from my rectum, he told me it was for wasting lubricating oil!"

That brought a laugh from Angus. In twos and threes *Dalriada* engineers drifted in and gradually the regulars were edged into a far corner of the bar.

It wasn't long before a party was going full swing and bawdy songs were desecrating the peaceful ambience of the hotel. The manager was reluctant to quieten them because trade was brisk. During a lull in the jovialities Jake asked him what job he'd been assigned on the next trip.

"Ah dinnae ken yet. My name's no' oan the watch list. There are twa blank spaces oan the four-tae-eight watch list. MacKay telt me that someone is supposed tae fill in the gap that ye left but the guy's no' showed up yet."

"Where's the other vacancy - eh?"

"Air conditioning."

"Grab that if you can - right? It's a real cushy number."

"That sounds guid," he agreed. "Especially next trip. Just imagine Lisbon, Las Palmas, an' Madeira."

"You're making me wish that I wasn't going on leave."

"Never mind Jake. Ah'm sure that ye've seen mair places than me." He drained his glass. "Get me a Younger's Tartan, will ye? Ah need tae go for a slash."

Inside the washroom a swarthy looking guy with greasy raven hair sidled up to him as he was washing his hands. "Heh, I overhear that you are going on cruise soon."

"Aye, the ship leaves on Thursday."

"So - this sheep - she is Queen of Dalradia?"

"*Dalriada*," corrected Angus. "Whit aboot it?"

Chips of anthracite eyes gazed around the washroom to make sure they were alone. "I make it worth your while to get me on board."

"Ah'm an engineer no' a bluidy travel agent!"

Just then Keyes ambled in. The man gave him a furtive look before leaving. From a urinal the Glaswegian called back, "Hey Gus, what was all that about?"

"Damned if Ah ken. The guy wanted a cheap cruise, Ah guess. Where were ye anyway?"

"In the *Park Lounge* trying my luck with a Mush broad."

"Ah was there aboot an hour ago. I didnae see ye then."

"I don't hang around the same pub too long Gus."

"Did ye get your nasties?"

He shook his head. "I'm here, aren't I? Like I told you when we first met - most Mush women are bitches."

When they got back to the bar there was a half-an-hour left before closing time. "What are you doing here Right - waiting for your arse to heal?"

"How did you know that - eh?"

"There are no secrets on board our ship," he was told. "Gus, we'll be on the same watch next trip."

"Aye, it's quite possible."

Jane warned her patrons that it was time for last call. Wheelkey slapped Angus on the back, and reminding him that he was the junior, badgered him buying the last round for the boys. He caught Jane's eye and swept a finger across his shipmates. "That'll be thirty-six shillings and sixpence, please Angus," she said, after serving up the drinks.

He looked into his wallet. There was only one ten-shilling note left. Keyes peered in too and said, "Oops!"

"Naw, it's all right. Ah'll just hae tae use my emergency fund." He fumbled at a small tear in the wallet lining.

"Watch out for man-eating moths!" joked Keyes.

"Ah!" He smiled in triumph and unravelled a tightly folded banknote and spread out flat on the counter.

Jane scrutinised the unusual bill carefully before taking it to the manager. He'd never seen a Scottish twenty-pound note either. "I'm afraid that I can't accept this sir," he said handing it back to him. It hung limply in his hand like a blue rectangular handkerchief.

"Why no'? It's legal tender."

"Not in England sir."

"Aye it is," argued Angus. "The Bank o' England backs a' five o' the Scottish banks."

"Even so sir, I cannot accept this note."

Angus looked at Jake who shrugged. His eyes caught Keyes' who shouted, "Drink up lads, it's on the house!"

Drinks suddenly began to vanish down the throats of about a dozen engineers so that the bewildered manager had no other option but to cash the banknote. The bar closed and the Dalriadians all piled into a single cab much to chagrin of the taxi driver. A substantial tip eased his feelings after they poured out at the dockside.

1545 Thursday

He reported to Bob Christie on the engineroom platform because sea watches were due to begin in fifteen minutes. On his arrival Angus met a small stout fellow, dwarfish in stature with greying hair. He was wandering about with a bewildered expression on his face. The second was propped against his desk watching every movement the wee fellow made.

"Hi Bob. How's it gaun?"

"Oh hello, Angus. I see by the watch list that you're going to be my engineroom junior this trip."

"That's whit Ah thought tae Bob, but Mister MacKay said that the list is bein' revised an' Ah might be assigned some ither job. Anyway Ah was telt tae stand this watch until everythin' was sorted oot." He nodded across the platform at the stranger. "Who's he?"

"The new floater!" Christie snarled. "God help us."

"He looks kinda auld tae be a junior."

"I can assure you that he's not old mentally!" he stood up straight and sighed. "Hold the fort Angus. I'm going topside for a crap. Keep an eye on him, will you?"

He spoke to the new junior before leaving the engineroom.

The little fellow approached Angus and hesitantly asked, "Excu-use me Sor, but could ye tell me -?" The Irish accent faded in mid sentence, interrupted by King's sudden laughter. "What's so funny?" he asked indignantly.

"Ah'm sorry," apologised Angus. "Whit was it that ye were gaun tae ask me?"

"Could ye tell me," lilted the little Irishman. "Whir t'e hirbor drains are?"

King laughed again.

"Oi fail to see what's so funny!"

"Ah'm awfy sorry," he replied, trying to keep his face solemn. "It's just that Ah had the distinct impression that ye were gaun tae ask me where Wimpy's was!"

"What kind of a ship is t'is, whir t'e junior is a gigglin' fool an' t'e Second Engineer is t'e Divil Incarnate?"

He apologized for the third time. "I'm sorry Paddy."

"Me name's not Paddy - 'tis Peter," the Irish gentleman informed his tormentor with feeling. He raised his eyes reverently to the engineroom hatch. "After t'e great Saint himself. He's t'e one who'll tirn ye away at t'e gate!" Aggressively, he continued. "Aye - Peter Deery. A great clan - t'e Deerys, y'know."

"If ye're finished wi' your family history, my name's Angus King." He offered a welcoming hand.

Deery took it like he was handling a snake. "Please t' meet ye - Oi t'ink!"

"So ye dinnae like Mister Christie?"

"A fearful man. A fearful man," judged Deery. "T'e sin just flows at ye from t'em black oiyes."

"Dae ye play chess?"

"No," replied the wee chap. "Oi'm afraid not Mister King. Moi priest said t'at chess was a game invented boi heat'ens."

"Too bad!"

"Oi beg your pardon?"

"Never mind."

Footsteps clunking up the platform ladder drew their attention. Slightly breathless, another engineer appeared clad in a white boilersuit.

"Angus King?"

"Aye."

"I'm Terry Baker, your relief. MacKay wants to see you right away. I just had a look at the updated watch list. You're on a/c this trip, you lucky bugger you!"

"Ok Terry - thanks," beamed Angus. "This is the new floater, Peter Deery. Hey Peter, come oan an' Ah'll show ye where the harbour drains are." He gently took the Irishman by the elbow and guided him to the bilge access ladder. "They're doon there," he whispered confidentially and handed him a wheelkey. "An' they're painted white. Dinnae come back until ye've closed four - white - valves."

"Excu-use me Mister King," said Deery. "Oi'm a stranger to t'is company an' Oi was wondering if ye could give a few pointers - sort o' help me t' learn t'e ropes, so to speak."

"Certainly," replied Angus. "In fact, Ah'll give ye the exact same advice that Ah was given oan my very first watch."

"An' what might t'at be, Sor?"

"Hang oan a Second!" replied Angus. He scurried down the platform ladder and headed for the engineroom elevator.

The little Irishman had misunderstood completely, as Angus knew he would. Deery waited patiently for his return. He hoped to receive a bounty of helpful hints when Christie returned to catch him lolling on a handrail.

The sound of Black Bob's bellowing rolled faintly up the elevator shaft to be drowned in peals of laughter.

Pict Line